PENGUIN C

THE PURPLE CLOUD

M. P. SHIEL (1865–1947) was born in Montserrat in the West Indies, his parents' ninth child and first son. Both his parents were of mixed race and Shiel's grandmothers had probably been slaves – something which, if true, he kept from public knowledge during his lifetime. At the age of fifteen he was 'crowned' by his father 'King Felipe of Redonda', Redonda being a rocky islet in the Caribbean. In 1885, Shiel came to England, where, he claimed, he briefly studied medicine at St Bartholomew's Hospital and tried his hand at schoolteaching. In 1895 he published his first novel, a detective story called *Prince Zaleski*, and from then on he earned his living through writing. As a novelist, he specialised in wildly imaginative science fiction, with a sideline in detective novels: *The Rajah's Sapphire* (1896) is the story of a gem which haunts its owners, while *The Yellow Danger* (1898) fantasises about Chinese world domination. However, *The Purple Cloud* (1901), which earned Shiel the status of an apocalyptic prophet, is the work for which he is most remembered today.

Shiel, who split his time between London and Paris, married his first wife in 1898, but abandoned her and their daughter after five years. During the same period, he fathered another daughter by a housemaid. He subsequently entered into simultaneous relationships with two different women, Elizabeth Price (with whom he had a son) and Lydia Furley. By the first decade of the twentieth century, his popularity had waned and, in 1914, he was sentenced to sixteen months in Wormwood Scrubs for 'indecently assaulting and carnally knowing' Elizabeth Price's twelve-year-old daughter. For many years it was believed that he had been imprisoned for fraud, whilst he himself described this period as 'work for the government'. In 1919 he married Lydia Furley; this marriage lasted until 1929. In his old age, he settled in a cottage in Sussex and became increasingly preoccupied with religious themes. Shiel died in 1947, having anointed the minor poet John Gawsworth as his successor to the kingship of Redonda.

JOHN SUTHERLAND is emeritus Lord Northcliffe Professor of Modern English Literature at University College London. He has edited many titles for Penguin Classics, including novels by William Thackeray, Wilkie Collins, Robert Louis Stevenson, Anthony Trollope, Anton Chekhov and H. G. Wells. In addition, he is the author of many works of literary criticism, biography and memoir, and is one of Britain's best-known literary reviewers.

M. P. SHIEL

The Purple Cloud

Edited and with an Introduction by
JOHN SUTHERLAND

PENGUIN BOOKS

PENGUIN CLASSICS

Published by the Penguin Group
Penguin Books Ltd, 80 Strand, London WC2R ORL, England
Penguin Group (USA) Inc., 375 Hudson Street, New York, New York 10014, USA
Penguin Group (Canada), 90 Eglinton Avenue East, Suite 700, Toronto, Ontario,
Canada M4P 2Y3 (a division of Pearson Penguin Canada Inc.)
Penguin Ireland, 25 St Stephen's Green, Dublin 2, Ireland (a division of Penguin Books Ltd)
Penguin Group (Australia), 707 Collins Street, Melbourne,
Victoria 3008, Australia (a division of Pearson Australia Group Pty Ltd)
Penguin Books India Pvt Ltd, 11 Community Centre, Panchsheel Park,
New Delhi – 110 017, India
Penguin Group (NZ), 67 Apollo Drive, Rosedale, Auckland 0632, New Zealand
(a division of Pearson New Zealand Ltd)
Penguin Books (South Africa) (Pty) Ltd, Block D, Rosebank Office Park, 181 Jan Smuts Avenue,
Parktown North, Gauteng 2193, South Africa

Penguin Books Ltd, Registered Offices: 80 Strand, London WC2R ORL, England

www.penguin.com

First published in serial form in *Royal Magazine* 1901
This text reprinted here is taken from the first book edition, published by Chatto & Windus 1901
Published in Penguin Classics 2012

017

Copyright by the Estate of M. P. Shiel, 1901
Editorial material © John Sutherland, 2012
All rights reserved

The moral right of the author and the editor has been asserted

Set in Postscript Adobe Sabon
Typeset by Firstsource Solutions Ltd

Printed and bound in Great Britain by Clays Ltd, Elcograf S.p.A.

ISBN: 978-0-141-19642-8

www.greenpenguin.co.uk

Contents

Chronology   vii
Introduction   xiii
Further Reading   xxxix
Note on the Text   xli

Foreword   3
THE PURPLE CLOUD   9

Notes   263

Chronology

In the chronology that follows, I draw on Harold Billings's two-volume biography and A. Reynolds Morse's *The Works of M. P. Shiel: A Study in Bibliography* (see Further Reading).

1865 21 July: Matthew Phipps Shiell is born in Plymouth, on the island of Montserrat. He is the ninth (probably) child and first son of Matthew Dowdy Shiell (1824–88), a then prosperous merchant, and Priscilla Ann Shiell (1830–1910). Both parents (certainly the mother) were of mixed racial descent.

1876 Offers first publication to the world, a 'penny periodical, seven copies a week for seven subscribers, written by hand'.

1877 autumn?: Sent to England to continue his school education in Devon. Returns to Montserrat in spring 1880.

1880 21 July: Crowned 'King of Redonda' on his fifteenth birthday.

1881 January: Goes to Harrison College, a boarding establishment in Barbados.

1883 December: Leaves Harrison College, having (after three attempts) passed the matriculation (i.e. qualifying) examination for the University of London.

1885 25 April: Leaves Montserrat for England, intending to find a teaching position and study in his own time for a degree. In November takes up a position at Bideford Grammar School, Devon, but is forced to resign after catching measles.

1886 summer: Obtains a teaching position at Hunt Bridge House, Matlock, Derbyshire, but returns to London after only a few months. On 10 October his favourite sister, Ada, dies, probably of cholera. Matthew Dowdy Shiell's business affairs deteriorate to the point of bankruptcy, causing the younger Shiell chronic financial embarrassment.

1887 May: Takes up a temporary post at Anglo-French High School in Hornsey, teaching 'for room and board' only. He reports himself as 'almost dying of starvation' and considers a return to the West Indies.

1888 7 January: Matthew Dowdy Shiell dies, leaving only debts. It is during this period that Shiell abbreviates his name to 'Shiel'. In later life he claimed to have enrolled in the spring of this year at King's College London to study English, but to have given it up for a medical career at Barts Hospital; however, there is no evidence for this.

1889 18 December: Shiel's first story, 'The Doctor's Bee', is published in *Rare Bits* and wins a £1 prize offered by the magazine. He is probably living off relatives in England during this period, in return for coaching their children.

1891 10–17 August: Acquires a temporary position as an interpreter to the International Congress of Hygiene and Demography in London. Two of his translations of French short stories are published in the *Strand Magazine*. Shiel then acquires an editorial position with the *Messenger*, a newspaper 'devoted to financial and racing news', where he works until 1892 for a weekly wage of £2.

1895 March: Publishes his esoteric detective stories, *Prince Zaleski*, under John Lane's imprint. The book is well received. Around May, Shiel's first known child is born, illegitimate, to 'Mary'. Around the same period he has a brief affair with another of Lane's authors, Ella d'Arcy (1857–1937).

1895–6 Publishes short stories in different genres and with various magazines. He makes the acquaintance of Arthur Machen, who will be a lifelong supporter.

1896 March: Publishes *The Rajah's Sapphire* (with Ward, Lock and Bowden) and *Shapes in the Fire* (in November, with John Lane). In Paris he sees the woman he will later marry, Carolina Garcia Gomez, skating at the *palais de glace*.

1898 spring: Having returned from a long stay in France, Shiel briefly shares a boarding house with the congenially decadent poet Ernest Dowson. He forms a professional relationship with Grant Richards, the publisher who will be most helpful in his later career. Richards publishes *The Yellow Danger* in July. On 3 November Shiel marries eighteen-year-old Carolina Gomez in a Catholic service at the Italian Church in Holborn, London. 'Lina' will live mainly with her mother in France over the next few years. A few weeks after the wedding, Shiel has a daughter (Ada), born to Nellie Seward, a chambermaid in Cheltenham. Despite his marriage, he keeps up the association with Seward for two years longer.

1899 March: Richards publishes *Contraband of War*. It sells poorly. In May Shiel is so indigent that he pawns his furniture. In July he first mentions 'The Second Adam' (i.e. *The Purple Cloud*) to Richards, who declines. Shiel turns to Chatto & Windus, who give him £70 for the copyright. In August a devastating storm strikes Montserrat, destroying what is left of the family property. Amy Machen dies (an event alluded to in *The Purple Cloud*). In November Richards publishes *Cold Steel*, giving Shiel £120 for the copyright.

1900 July: A daughter, Dolores, born to Shiel and Lina. The couple reside at temporary addresses when in London.

1901 January: First instalment of *The Purple Cloud* is published in *Royal Magazine*. It will run, in six monthly parts, until June. On 22 January Queen Victoria dies. In May *The Lord of the Sea* is published by Richards. Despite his frenetic literary output, Shiel, under huge financial pressure, pawns everything he can lay his hands on and bargains desperately with publishers. On 26 September Chatto & Windus publish *The Purple Cloud*.

1902 December: *The Weird o' It* is published by Richards.

1903 June: Marriage with Lina breaks up. She moves to Paris with their child and it is thought she died shortly after, probably in Spain. In September *Unto the Third Generation* is published by Chatto & Windus. A desperate Shiel sells the serial and book rights to three novels in progress for amounts between £50 and £160. He begins a tandem-writing arrangement with Louis Tracy, under the pseudonym 'Gordon Holmes'.

1904 Grant Richards, Shiel's most reliable publisher, declares bankruptcy. In September Shiel publishes *The Evil Men Do* with Ward, Lock & Co.

1905 *The Lost Viol* is published in America, under the Edward J. Clode imprint. The same firm publishes the first of the 'Gordon Holmes' titles, *A Mysterious Disappearance*. In June *The Yellow Wave* is published in Britain by Ward, Lock & Co. The novel, inspired by the current Russo-Japanese war, is, Shiel says, the book of his he 'likes best', although it is 'the worst seller'.

1907 January: *The Last Miracle* is published by T. Werner Laurie, having been on the stocks, unwanted by publishers, since 1898.

1908 January: *The White Wedding* is published by T. Werner Laurie. During this period Shiel becomes involved with Elizabeth Price Sircar, and later moves into her London flat. In summer 1908 he becomes sexually involved with his future wife, Lydia Furley (b. 1872). He proposes marriage to her on 3 November, but–living as she is with another partner – she turns him down. Their affair continues.

1909 January: T. Werner Laurie publishes *The Isle of Lies*. On 6 April the American explorer Robert Peary reaches the North Pole. In November Everett & Co. publish *This Knot of Life*.

1910 Shiel's mother dies.

1911 October: *The White Ape* is published by T. Werner Laurie and is mauled by the critics. The writing relationship with Tracy is suspended after the publication of *The House of Silence*.

1913 May: Grant Richards, having re-established himself, publishes the poorly received *The Dragon*. The novel is retitled as *The Yellow Peril* in 1929 by Chatto & Windus, to be published alongside the revised edition of *The Purple Cloud*. At this point the first phase of Shiel's fiction-writing career terminates.

1914 13 March: Caesar Kenneth Shiel, the illegitimate child of Shiel and Elizabeth Price Sircar, is born. On 26 April, Lydia Furley's common-law husband dies. In September Shiel applies to the Royal Literary Fund for financial assistance. They award a derisory £10. On 26 October Elizabeth Price Sircar files charges against Shiel on the grounds of his alleged 'carnal knowledge' of the twelve-and-a-half-year-old Dorothy Sircar. On 16 November he goes on trial at the Old Bailey. He is found guilty and sentenced to sixteen months' hard labour.

1915 January–June: Shiel serializes in *Red Magazine* the story 'The Two-gun Man', which is recognized as a flagrant plagiarism of another writer's work.

1916 February: Lives with Lydia following release from prison and contrives to keep real reason for incarceration generally unknown.

1919 31 January: Marries Lydia Furley. On 15 April Lydia and Shiel are ejected from the public gallery in the House of Commons for shouting pro-Soviet slogans.

1922 April: Shiel and Lydia embark on an eight-month vacation in Italy, returning in early 1923.

1923 January: *Children of the Wind*, an African adventure published by Richards, marks Shiel's return to writing full-length novels.

1926 9 May: Admiral Richard Byrd claims to have flown over the North Pole.

1927 May: Richards publishes *How the Old Woman Got Home*.

1928 September: Richards publishes a short story collection, *Here Comes the Lady*.

1929 March: Victor Gollancz publishes the revised text of *The Purple Cloud*, along with *Lord of the Sea* and *The Last Miracle*. In publicity material for Gollancz, Shiel, for the first time, makes public the fact that he is 'the King of Redonda'. In October *Dr Krasinski's Secret* is published in America by Vanguard Press. Shiel and Lydia separate amicably.

1930 March: Vanguard Press publishes the first American edition of *The Purple Cloud*. Shiel settles at L'Abri, a cottage near Horsham, Sussex. John Gawsworth, later the novelist's executor and 'King Juan I' of Redonda, makes his first contact with Shiel.

1931 February: Richards publishes *The Black Box*, a murder mystery.

1933 January: Ernest Benn publishes *Say Au R'voir but not Goodbye*. April: Vanguard Press publishes *This Above All*, a religious fantasy around the idea that Jesus still lives. The Gospels will be Shiel's main field of interest in his years of retirement in Horsham.

1934 Shiel allows John Gawsworth to complete a story he drafted in 1914, published as 'The Death-Dance'.

1935 October: Richards publishes the short story collection, *The Invisible Voices*. Shiel receives a Civil List Pension.

1936 November: Richards publishes *The Poems of M. P. Shiel*.

1937 December: Allen & Unwin publish Shiel's last novel, *The Young Men are Coming*.

1942 16 February: Lydia Furley Shiel dies.

1947 17 February: Shiel dies, and is cremated at Golders Green, London.

Introduction

*New readers are advised that this Introduction
makes details of the plot explicit.*

'*Do not be strange*' – the advice Shiel's father gave on his son's departing for England, fame and fortune.

The *Independent* newspaper, in 2009, ran a feature on M. P. Shiel under the headline 'unfairly forgotten authors'. It was not strictly true. Shiel was undeniably out of the literary spotlight for most of his long writing life, and posterity has been in no frantic rush to buy his books, but he has been preserved from utter oblivion by devotees[1] who recognize in his fiction something unique and – despite the paternal prohibition – extraordinarily strange.

If his work is strange, so too was his life. Matthew Phipps Shiell[2] was born in 1865 in Montserrat, one of a cluster of small islands in the British West Indies. His father was at different times a businessman-of-all-trades and lay Methodist minister in the principal town, grandly named 'Plymouth'. Both his parents were of mixed race and it is suspected that Shiel's grandparents (certainly on his mother's side) had been slaves – something he withheld from public knowledge during his lifetime. His swarthy pigmentation was universally noted. But when asked about his racial origins, Shiel would protest, jokingly, that he was a 'paddy'. He was, his biographer records, furious when he found a bookseller had shelved him among 'negro authors'.[3]

The surname 'Shiell' is certainly Irish – witnessing to the dominance of that nationality in the colonial elite of Montserrat. They had come to prosper. The Africans had been transported to cultivate sugar cane and suffer. Since emancipation (begun with Wilberforce's 1805 Act, and fully implemented in the 1830s), the wealth of the island had withered with global demand for its single cash crop. Nor was Montserrat, like neighbouring Antigua (another of the Leeward cluster), a useful base for the Royal Navy. When he travelled to the Caribbean in the 1850s, Anthony Trollope noted that 'Montserrat, I am told, is not prospering'. He did not think it worthy of a visit.

Shiel's biographer, Harold Billings, has valiantly traced the tangled strands of concubinage, rape, incest, blood-lines and common-law matrimony between the classes and races current on the island. Under the tropical sun, European standards of sexual conduct were not strictly upheld. Shiel fondly recorded losing his virginity, aged five, to a more experienced eight-year-old, Xena.[4] The pubescent or even prepubescent girl remained a preference throughout his life. It would cause him grief in places less tolerant about such things than Montserrat.

Shiel's place of birth has peculiar topographical relevance for *The Purple Cloud*. Montserrat is named after the volcano which dominates the island, quiescent throughout the nineteenth century, but ominously smouldering. 'Ships many a mile out at sea can smell the fume of Hell it sends', Shiel recalled.[5] Were it to erupt, the islanders would face instant extermination. The example of Krakatoa, which did explode in 1883, was a grim forecast of what lay – inevitably – in the future for Montserrat. Perhaps not that far in the future. In fact, it did not happen until 1997 – effectively wiping out human habitation on Montserrat. Is there, *The Purple Cloud* ponders, a supervolcano waiting to destroy the whole human race?

Shiel was the ninth (or, by some counts, tenth) child born to his indefatigably procreative mother, Priscilla. He was preceded by a host of sisters, who seem to have mattered less to their father, alongside the last-born prince of the family. Harold Billings plausibly diagnoses Shiel's 'vast megalomania' as originating in his glorious late arrival on the family scene. It encouraged a Messianic sense of self-worth, which found full expression in fictional heroes such as Adam Jefferson (i.e. Adam Jehova's-son), the 'second parent of the race' in *The Purple Cloud*. Shiel's inflated image of himself was confirmed when, aged fifteen, he was 'crowned' by his father 'King Felipe of Redonda'. Redonda is an uninhabitable 200-foot rocky islet, some twenty-five miles off Montserrat. It is used by gulls, principally, as a convenient place to drop guano – bird excrement. This, in the nineteenth century, was traded as a valuable commodity, as agricultural fertilizer. The Shiells had no known legal claim to Redonda – but then, they might have asked, what historical claim did the English have to Montserrat? In his late, more eccentric, years, Shiel may or may not have taken his 'kingship' seriously. It was a source of high merriment to that majority of the human race who happened not to be his subjects.

Shiel came to England in 1885, with hopes of finishing his education and, as he fondly expected, becoming an academic, a doctor or something similarly worthy of his abilities. He was precociously clever. He claimed to have mastered Greek by the age of eleven and to have been fluent in half a dozen languages in his maturity. He had received a good grounding at boarding schools and, having 'matriculated', could look forward to making his mark in England – assuming that he was subsidised financially for a few years while doing so.

It was not to be. Shiel's father had prospered during his son's growing-up years, but his business affairs would decline precipitously thereafter, effectively destroying any prospects of a professional career for his son. Nonetheless, things looked bright when the nineteen-year-old left Montserrat (for good, as it transpired) in April 1885. There was, however, a small cloud, which, probably, escaped the young man's attention. That same year, 1885, the 'Criminal Law Amendment Bill was passed into law by Parliament. Its 'sexual indecency' provisions would, years later, have as serious implications for Matthew Phipps Shiel as they did for Oscar Fingal O'Flahertie Wills Wilde. What would affect Shiel was not the new prohibition on 'gross indecency' between males, introduced by the Labouchere Amendment, but the raising of the age of sexual consent for young women to sixteen. Shiel devoutly believed that the previous threshold of thirteen years was quite sufficient – and acted accordingly when opportunity arose.

The conquest of English society proved more difficult than the young man expected, particularly after his father's financial support dried up. He resolved to keep body and soul together by school-teaching, while studying in his spare time for university entrance. He first thought he might read literature or languages at King's College London. But he found the subjects, as then taught, 'dull'. He switched to medicine, with the intention of enrolling at Barts Hospital, before discovering an aversion to blood (although he would spill it by the bucket in his later fiction). There is, as his biographer notes, no record of his actually having been a medical student.

Medicine failing, Shiel fell back on short-term teaching posts. Perhaps, in some cases, he was dismissed – not for incompetence, but moral turpitude. He mentions in one of his surviving letters of the period impregnating a girl known only as 'Mary'. He had other illegitimate children; more, one suspects, than we shall ever know about and possibly more than he himself knew about.

Without formal qualifications, money or powerful friends, no professional career opportunities were available to the young Shiel. He threw himself into Gissing's New Grub Street instead, where he might make his way by his wits, good looks and boundless energy. After 1892, he supported himself principally by his pen: first as a journalist and clerk, then as a prolific short story writer for the magazines, and finally as a writer of full-length serial novels. His literary god in these early years was Poe (who shared his interest in pubescent girls and married one). Also congenial were the *fin-de-siècle* decadents, who were much in vogue in the 1890s. Arthur Machen, another connoisseur of the supernatural, became a close, if wary, friend. By the late 1890s, as interest in his writing picked up, Shiel split his time between London and Paris. In the prelude to *The Purple Cloud*, he records himself as just back from two years there. What he was doing there has never been precisely recorded, but can be plausibly guessed at from his description of the French city as the '*fille de joie* of the cities of the earth'.[6] The whoring was stylish, we gather.

As a full-length novelist, Shiel tried his hand over the years at various genres. They include historical romances (e.g. *The Man-Stealers*), stories of the day (e.g. *The Yellow Wave*),

Bildungsromane drawing on elements of his own life (e.g. *The Weird o' It*), murder mysteries (e.g. *The Black Box*) and outright 'bloods' (e.g. *Contraband of War*). But his finest achievements are his wildly imaginative works of science fiction: 'berserk Poe', they have been aptly called. They are typically tinged with an occultism which can be traced back to his early immersion in chiliastic Christianity and the 'obeah', brought to Montserrat by its African slaves. He 'dreamed his plots', Shiel liked to say. Pipe dreams, one might be tempted to think. Opium and hashish figure prominently in *The Purple Cloud* (Adam Jeffson is royally high on opium as he watches London burn from his Hampstead eyrie). As hints in his correspondence confirm, Shiel himself was knowledgeable about narcotics more potent than *Cannabis indica*.

It took Shiel some time to find his niche, initially making his mark in the genre at that time popularized by Conan Doyle. The detective novel *Prince Zaleski* (1895), Shiel's first published book, appeared in John Lane's *Keynotes* series. The book takes the form of three crime mysteries, all solved by a marijuana-sodden sleuth with a curious expertise about syphilis, spectacularly more exotic than the tweedy residents of 221B Baker Street. This connection with John Lane placed Shiel alongside the *Yellow Book* set – decadents, esoterics and exquisites all of them. In addition to Aubrey Beardsley, there were Kenneth Grahame, Ella d'Arcy (the co-editor of the *Yellow Book*, with whom Shiel had a brief fling), Arthur Machen and, of course, Oscar Wilde, with whom, in later life and rather implausibly, Shiel claimed to be on dining terms. As Harold Billings reminds us, the young man from Montserrat was neither sufficiently well bred, nor sufficiently sophisticated, nor sufficiently rich, to mingle on equal terms with Wilde's set.

The Zaleski book was well received. Shiel followed up with *The Rajah's Sapphire* (1896), the story of a gem which haunts its owners. It too did well, and helped form influential friendships.[7] As with other writers associated, even marginally, with the *Yellow Book*, there was a hiccup in his authorial career after the Wilde scandals, when Lane cut his riskier 1890s writers loose. Shiel moved on to another publisher, Grant Richards, who would be a long-suffering patron over what would be the highpoint of Shiel's long literary career – roughly the decade extending to 1906.

This phase is marked by ferocious productivity and titanic imaginings. It crested with novels, all breathtakingly global in their vision. The first to hit the mark with the reading public was *The Yellow Danger* (1898), which fantasizes about future Chinese world domination. Somewhat improbably, the oriental potentate, Yen How, becomes infatuated with Ada Seward, a Fulham nursemaid, and starts a genocidal war to get her. His oriental hordes are foiled by the sturdily Anglo-Saxon John Hardy, in a sea battle which claims the lives of twenty million. The racism, here as elsewhere in Shiel's novels, grates. But the zest of the narrative carries the reader along irresistibly.

It is not accidental that Shiel, during this period, was himself in a relationship with a Cheltenham housemaid, Nellie Seward, by whom he would have the second of his children that we know about (she was christened 'Ada', in honour of the novel and of his dead sister, the most loved of his siblings). *The Purple Cloud* was conceived about the same time as *The Yellow Danger*, but was held back a year or two from completion. It too has a connection with the author's fraught love life. A couple of years earlier, Shiel's eye had been caught by a sixteen-year-old (possibly younger) Spanish girl, Carolina Gomez, ice-skating at the *palais de glace* in Paris. He laid siege to her and succeeded in winning her hand in 1898. 'Lina', as he lovingly called her, is pictured in the ingenuous and tawny 'Leda' (alias 'Eve'), with her imperfect lisping English, in *The Purple Cloud*. The couple – against the wishes of Lina's widowed mother, Lola, who disapproved of Shiel – married in a Catholic ceremony in London. This was also against the wishes of Shiel's staunchly Wesleyan family, none of whom attended. A couple of weeks after the ceremony, little Ada Seward was born in Cheltenham. Shiel, meanwhile, continued both his relationship with Nellie in England and with Lina, who largely lived with her mother, in Paris.

Shiel, never the most discreet of authors, had no qualms about introducing his friends and acquaintances into his fictions without their permission. The first half of the *The Purple*

Cloud is, for example, supposed to have been written by Adam Jeffson in the (imaginary) Cornwall cottage of Arthur Machen (see note to p. 116). The other writer can have been none too pleased by tactless allusion to his recent widowing. In 1899, Machen's beloved wife, Amy, who had (it is plausibly surmised) organized Shiel's wedding reception, died after a long struggle with cancer. Machen must have been even less pleased by *The Purple Cloud*'s fancifully wishing on him a consolingly lusty young 'Spanish' second wife (clearly based on 'Lina') before both Machens and their newborn baby are killed off by the deadly purple cloud. Jeffson subsequently appears on the scene to take up residence in their house and dispose of their mummified corpses, while writing up his own recent adventures. 'The man is an inveterate liar', Machen once said. His views on the lies about him in the novel are unrecorded.

The Purple Cloud exists, textually, in three different forms. A short version was serialized in *Royal Magazine* from January to June in 1901; a longer version (on which this edition is based) was published by Chatto & Windus in September 1901; and a revised edition was brought out by Victor Gollancz in 1929 (see 'Note on the Text'). The narrative of *The Purple Cloud* opens, almost simultaneously with the first serial instalment, at the turn of the century, 1900–1901. It's a little fuzzy, but the action is clearly cued to the first year of the twentieth century. The human race habitually fantasizes disasters at such moments, 'Y2K' being the most recent example (i.e. virtually every computer on the planet, it was then predicted, would malfunction. Cities would be plunged into darkness, aeroplanes would fall from the sky, electronic money would evaporate, chaos would come again. It didn't, but the fear, as the millennial clock ticked towards the fatal minute, was real and universal.).

Shiel was sensible enough to see that the centennial moment was not, as the unmathematical thought, January 1900 but January 1901. He held back *The Purple Cloud* (earlier called 'The Last Adam' and 'The Second Adam') for that ominous date. The story began serial publication in *Royal Magazine* in the first month of 1901. By extraordinary good luck (Shiel's that is, not the nation's), Queen Victoria chose to die in the same month. The event gave Shiel's story an eerie resonance – a royal purple glow. Unlike 'Y2K', something catastrophic had indeed happened. For most of the British population, who had lived their lives as 'Victorians', 22 January 1901 was the end of the world as they had known it. What lay ahead?

The Purple Cloud, in its first volume edition, has an intricate foreword, not printed in the serial version and substantially changed in the 1929 reprint. In May 1900, we are to understand, Shiel, *in propria persona*, received a mysterious package from a friend on his deathbed. Dr Alfred Lister Browne has only ever had one very wealthy and very strange patient, a 'seeress', Mary Wilson (now dead). Under Browne's hypnotic influence, Wilson is clairvoyant and can see into the future. Mesmerism (also known as 'animal magnetism', 'electrobiology' and, most popularly, 'hypnotism') was all the rage in the second half of the nineteenth century. Novelists – particularly 'sensation novelists' – seized on the pseudo-science as a plot device. Wilkie Collins, Charles Dickens, Edgar Allan Poe, Bram Stoker and, most magnificently, George Du Maurier (with Svengali), wrote fiction with hypnotism as its narrative mainspring, and Shiel has an honourable place in this hypno-fictional company.[8] In her trances Wilson is fluent in the primeval 'universal language' of those who have passed 'beyond the veil'. Her first intelligible communication is from what seems to be an astral reading group, located 811 miles above the earth, who are whiling away eternity by collectively reading aloud Gibbon's *Decline and Fall of the Roman Empire*. It is an ominous text.

Eavesdropping on his patient's astro-hypnotic transmissions, her hypnotist, Dr Browne, has transcribed four notebooks, which on his deathbed he now passes on to his friend, M. P. Shiel. Notebook I contains the text of what Shiel will later publish as *The Last Miracle*. The novel recounts an attempt by a Bohemian malefactor to overturn Christianity by engineering a series of contemporary Crucifixions and Miracles. He comes within an ace of succeeding. The world is mercifully saved by a message smuggled out of a dungeon on the leg of a wren.

Never let it be said that M. P. Shiel surrendered to the dictates of fictional plausibility.

The second Browne notebook contains the text of what Shiel will later publish as *The Lord of the Sea*. Briefly summarized, it foresees a mass immigration of Jews into England. They are not (as they historically were, at the turn of the century) wretched refugees, but predatory invaders. The newcomers, aided by their usuriously acquired wealth and banking skills, impose a Zionist dictatorship. Their malign tyranny is resisted and overthrown by a staunch English squire, Richard Hogarth. After escaping, Dumas-style, from the prison where he has been wrongly consigned, so that a wicked Jewish landlord can sexually debauch his sister, Hogarth becomes the possessor of a gigantic meteoric diamond. With his now greater than even Jewish wealth, he sets up a chain of massive forts on the ocean, from where he can rule the waves. In a surprise twist, Hogarth discovers that he himself is Jewish and, like George Eliot's Daniel Deronda, sets out to establish a new Israel in the Middle East. The mind-boggling mixture of anti-Semitism and philo-Semitism is pure Shiel.

The third Browne notebook contains what Shiel is currently offering us as *The Purple Cloud*. We are not to be informed what the fourth notebook contains. It will remain a kind of Joanna Southcott's box – containing, the reader apprehends, something terrible and mysterious. Or possibly a novel Shiel never quite got round to writing. We can assume, then, that what Shiel had in mind, at least notionally, was a trilogy, or perhaps a tetralogy, which would do something equivalent to Gibbon's *Decline and Fall*. This time it would be the British Empire that fell. The grand narrative design did not, unfortunately, come to fruition. The main reason was that Shiel was desperately pressed for money and could not negotiate the big deal that his complicated ensemble would require. Nor could he interest a publisher in taking on the whole set. The loyal Grant Richards published *The Lord of the Sea* in 1901, but baulked at two novels in a year. *The Purple Cloud* was sold outright, for a depressingly small sum (£70) to Chatto & Windus, a publisher that had no long-term interest in Shiel. *The*

Last Miracle could find no immediate takers, being deemed, as Richards tactfully pointed out, blasphemous. It was belatedly published in 1907.

Shiel was never a writer to devote much forward planning to his fiction. Manuscript pages, one observer said, fell from him like autumn leaves:

> Sheet after sheet used to drop from his desk. Sometimes when I called on him he would be in the middle of a chapter, and then he would ask me to sit down while his pen whirled imperturbably to the end. He could write in any noise, and he could throw off his work completely as soon as the pen was out of his hand.[9]

One can assume that he relied heavily on his redoubtable powers of improvisation. The irresistible flow in *The Purple Cloud* is enhanced by his decision to forgo chapters, sections or any of the other traditional punctuation of English fiction – the narrative surges out like water from a tap. Fanciful as it will seem, Matthew Phipps Shiel can be argued to have got to 'stream of consciousness' two decades before Virginia Woolf and James Joyce, planting a little flag of Montserrat on that admired literary form.

Among the surging narrative flow of *The Purple Cloud*, three large segments emerge. The first third of the novel chronicles the hero's expedition to the Arctic. The second section chronicles Jeffson's decades' long pyromaniac career, in which, under the influence of his dark self, he incinerates the great cities of the world. The third segment of the novel chronicles his turn to the light, during which he builds his temple on the Edenic island of Imbros and discovers his Eve. Things end with the possible regeneration of humanity. But who knows? Another purple cloud looms.

Preferences will vary, but most think that the first third of *The Purple Cloud* is the best of the many good things in the novel. The narrator-hero, Adam Jeffson, the 'second Parent of the world', as he is to be, is recruited for an expedition to the North Pole, as physician and botanist. At the time Shiel was writing, the icy surface of the North Pole had not yet felt the foot of man. But that frostbitten limb was not far off, and Shiel must have thought that his novel's publication would closely precede – perhaps even coincide – with latitude 90° North being finally conquered. In *The Purple Cloud* the endeavour is given a melodramatic twist by a Chicago millionaire's offering a $175-million prize for the individual (not the team) who achieves that feat. This sets up a version of the familiar 'tontine' plot, based on actual insurance schemes in which a syndicate would band together to contribute lifelong premiums. The last of the insured to survive would scoop the pot before the grim reaper took him off as well. The tontine set up a juicy scenario for the writer of fiction. What if someone, unwilling to let chance make the selection, decided to kill off his fellow *tontineurs* one by one? The best of the tontine novels, surely known to Shiel, is Robert Louis Stevenson's *The Wrong Box* (1889).

For his account of the *Boreal*'s assault on the Pole, Shiel drew on Fridtjof Nansen's recent account of his 'drift and dash' 1896 expedition, written up in two lively volumes as *Farthest North* (1897). There had been dozens of unsuccessful expeditions to the Pole in the last decades of the nineteenth century, and like every other explorer, the Norwegian had failed – though tantalizingly.[10] The necessity of man's achieving the Polar feat had been stoked to the pitch of mania by British and American popular newspapers and their magnate proprietors. Why was it proving so difficult? There were wild rumours of cannibalism, strange alien races and monsters where man had never been. Perhaps Mary Shelley's Frankenstein's monster – who takes up his last residence at the North Pole – was still striding those snowy wastes, killing all in his way.

Shiel thickened his Nansen-derived account of Jeffson's Arctic adventure with a rich concoction of ancient 'Arktos' myths.[11] These fantasized wildly what man – were man hubristic enough to try and lucky enough to succeed – would actually find at the Pole once he got there. One principal myth, still believed as late as Elisha Kent Kane's expedition in the mid-1850s, was that there was a warm ocean up there with geothermal 'gates', if only they could be located. Shiel hints, obliquely, at other long-standing myths. What was frustrating all those expeditions? Was it, perhaps, some energy force – a reverse magnetism? Was there, as the more devout feared, a divine prohibition against man's presumption? He cunningly lets such ideas dangle. In the early pages, central space is given to the rabid evangelical preacher, Mackay, who warns that for man to go to the Pole (the word 'pole' suggests a wooden upright, or tree) would be an offence to God, which He would surely punish. It would repeat Adam's sin in Genesis – the *culpa* which brought about the Fall of Man. All other trees in the Garden of Eden (a place some mystics argued was the pre-glacial North Pole) Adam was told he might touch. But one tree he must not touch. So too, Mackay warns in the early pages of *The Purple Cloud*, is Man forbidden from touching that other singular thing, the North Pole. Shiel – formidably versed in the occult – also alludes to pagan, but analogous, Norse myths. As recounted in the *Edda* the great Tree of Life, Yggdrasil, is rooted at the North Pole. It is 'the largest plant in the world', and man will approach Yggdrasil at his peril.

There are other 'Arktos' myths broadly hinted at in Shiel's novel. Most prominent among them is H. P. Blavatsky's 'Polarion' thesis, that the North Pole was the 'cap of the world'. It was, Blavatsky proclaimed, the 'imperishable sacred land' from which all the other continents had split off. The two poles, but particularly the northern, were central to her theosophical topography:

> The two poles are the right and left ends of our globe – the right being the North Pole – or the head and feet of the earth. Every beneficent (astral and cosmic) action comes from the North; every lethal influence from the South Pole. They are much connected with and influence 'right' and 'left' hand magic.[12]

It was at the North Pole, Blavatsky confided, that our ancestral 'Root-Race' originated. It was destined to be the 'cradle of the first man and the dwelling of the last divine mortal, chosen as a *Sishta* for the future seed of humanity'. That future seed would be planted in cataclysm. Shiel is too canny a writer to make his novel a mere vehicle for Blavatsky's lunacies. But he draws on her ideas as suggestive *décor*.

All these mythic fantasies resonate thrillingly in Shiel's novel for one reason only. No one had actually been to the North Pole in 1901, despite innumerable attempts. Like the Martian 'canals' which had inspired, three years before, H. G. Wells's *War of the Worlds* (1898), the North Pole was rich fodder for science fiction. There was, of course, the big difference that readers of Wells could never, in their wildest fantasy, plausibly imagine man travelling to Mars to verify that the canals were Martian-made. But man would, surely, reach the North Pole – perhaps even in a month or two. What would he find there?

Nothing, as it turned out. The myths Shiel draws on so artfully burst like bubbles when, nine years after the publication of *The Purple Cloud*, one of two Americans (either Robert Peary or Frederick Cook) planted the Stars and Stripes on the shifting ice of the North Pole. There has always been bitter dispute as to which of the two men got there first, but no dispute as to what they found and, more dispiritingly, what they did not find. There were no warm seas, no Yggdrasil, no *sishta*. Just snow, grinding pack ice and wind. And, henceforth, a US flag. The Americans' bleakly unexciting discovery lay in the future. Shiel could still fantasize, and did.

Having murdered his companions and made it to the 90th latitude, Jeffson discovers himself on the edge of a hot lake, surrounded by a carpet of meteoric diamonds. He dimly perceives a pillar at the lake's steamy centre, with illegible writing around its base. He swoons. Whether it is coincidental or not, at the precise moment Jeffson reaches the pole and collapses, humanity suffers its second and most drastic fall. Has Adam Jeffson, like his Edenic namesake, precipitated this universal disaster by his God-defying rashness? If so, why has he, the guiltiest of men, been spared the universal punishment? Or is Adam Jeffson merely fulfilling some as yet unrevealed prophecy? Is he cursed, or blessed?

There is a rational scientific explanation given us to balance these speculations. Adam (from a perusal of the last ever daily issue of *The Times* – the 'paper of record' to the end) will discover, many months later, that a super-volcano in Indonesia, in the same area as deadly Krakatoa twenty years earlier, erupted while he was in the northernmost Arctic. It released from the bowels of the earth vast quantities of cyanogen – gaseous cyanide – which has drifted, in a lethal purple cloud, across the face of the earth. Fortuitously (it being so cold where he was, the gas froze harmlessly and dropped as crystal), Jeffson alone has escaped the fate of all other air-breathing things.

Is it a natural or supernatural event? No one can predict, accurately, when volcanoes will erupt, as every inhabitant of Montserrat well knew. Nor can science predict the scale of destruction their explosions will visit on the planet. And they do spew out gas in lethal quantities: most of the inhabitants of Pompeii were asphyxiated, not cremated, by 'black and horrible clouds', as Pliny called them. Pompeii, as such things go, was small (only a six on the Volcanic Eruption Index). Vulcanologists today tell us that when the Yellowstone Park super-volcano erupts, with a full force ten on the VEI, and an accompanying 'superplume', it could mean an ELE (extinction level event) for the planet equivalent to the 'Devonian Extinction' which wiped out most species on earth 370 million years ago. There is geological plausibility in Shiel's science fiction for modern readers who may strain to swallow some of the novel's more far-fetched *bizarreries*.

Whatever the cause of the ELE in Shiel's novel, Adam Jeffson finds himself the last man on earth. Since the publication of *The Purple Cloud,* science fiction has thrown up a whole sub-genre of 'Last Man' novels. The genre's progenitor is Mary Shelley, whose *The Last Man* was published in 1826. The action is set futuristically in the last years of the twenty-first century, when England has become a republic. Following a world-wide plague, the anchorite philosopher-narrator Lionel Verney is left – a Robinson Crusoe of the future – the sole survivor of the 'merciless sickle'. In writing *The Purple Cloud*, Shiel drew heavily on another fine novel, Richard Jefferies's *After London* (1885). It foresees, at some unspecific future date, the end of urban civilization following a catastrophe enigmatically called 'the Event' (cause unknown) and the final revenge of nature over man's violations of her. England is dominated by a vast crystalline lake (London, the pride of man, has reverted to a stinking swamp) and most of the world has been inundated. The lonely hero, Felix Aquila, voyages by canoe in search of his dream partner, Aurora Thyma, paddling ever west towards the sunset.[13]

In the period just before embarking on *The Purple Cloud*, Shiel would surely have read Joshua Slocum's non-fiction account *Sailing Alone Around the World* (1899), which clearly gave him the basic idea for the middle section of the novel, as Nansen's *Farthest North* gave him the idea for the first section. Like the Ancient Mariner (another manifest influence on *The Purple Cloud*), Adam Jeffson travels back single-handed from the Arctic, all the crew he came with being dead. His voyage is made possible by the one plausible technical invention Shiel comes up with – maritime jet propulsion (see note to p. 25), which means a ship can be handled by a single man. On his grisly return voyage, Jeffson apprehends the full horror of his situation. Cyanide, with its perversely delicious fruity fragrance and dark-blue hue, kills instantaneously and mummifies the victim. The vessels Jeffson encounters resemble nothing so much as a world-wide waxwork chamber of horrors – 'Life in Death', as Coleridge called it. And after traversing the length and breadth of England by steam-train, he discovers it retains not a single surviving inhabitant. Even the mines beneath the ground's surface and carefully air-sealed houses are sarcophagi.

Most horrible is his reunion with his fiancée, the sinister Countess Clodagh, clutching a pillar on the balcony of the house of the man she and Jeffson have earlier murdered:

> Never did I see aught more horrid: there were the gracious curves of the woman's bust and hips still well preserved in a clinging dress of red cloth, very faded now; and her reddish hair floated loose in a large flimsy cloud about her; but her face, in that exposed position, had been quite eaten away by the winds to a noseless skeleton, which grinned from ear to ear, with slightly-dropped under-jaw – most horrid in contrast with the body, and frame of hair. I meditated upon her a long time that morning from

the opposite pavement. An oval locket at her throat contained, I
knew, my likeness: for eight years previously I had given it her. It
was Clodagh, the poisoner. [pp. 129–130]

Such experiences are too much for flesh and blood to bear.
Jeffson goes mad under the pressure of his cosmic solitude, sur-
rendering, as he believes, to what one would call the dark voice
within him. In his desperate search for sexual gratification, he
makes love, when his urges become overwhelming, to youthful-
looking female corpses before brutalizing their inert bodies.
The necrophile detail is handled with necessary (for 1901) cir-
cumlocutions and ellipses (see note to p. 133), but can still give
even hardened modern readers a *frisson*. Prudently the episode
was cut out in the 1929 revision of *The Purple Cloud*, as it had
been in the tamed-down magazine serialization.

The reason why God has spared him gradually takes form in
Adam's crazed mind: he has been appointed to carry out the
Almighty's threat to mankind, delivered after the primal deluge –
'the fire next time'. This is that next time. Jeffson, 'Jehova's-son',
has been appointed Jehova's arsonist, and it is his destiny to
purge the world of its sin by purifying flame. The dark voice in
his soul keeps him resolutely at the task over the twenty years
the world-wide conflagration requires. When he witnessed the
first atomic explosion, Robert Oppenheimer, the scientist principally responsible for 'the bomb', muttered to himself Vishnu's
boast from the *Bhagavad-Gita*: 'Now I am become Death, the
destroyer of worlds.' Shiel, who died in 1947, was alive to witness the dawn of the nuclear era and its terrible destruction of
Hiroshima and Nagasaki. He must have thought of his own
destroyer of worlds, Adam Jeffson (who, coincidentally, does
destroy Nagasaki; Hiroshima he spared).

London is the first metropolis Jeffson puts to the flame. A
modern Nero, he serenely contemplates the second great fire of
London from a house on Hampstead Hill:

There I had provided myself with a jar of pale tobacco mixed with
rose-leaves and opium, found in a foreign house in Seymour Street,
also a genuine Saloniki hookah, together with the best wines, nuts,

and so on, and a gold harp of the musician Krasinski, stamped
with his name, taken from his house in Portland Street. [p. 140]

Powered by his 'liquid air' engine, Jeffson then circumnavigates
the globe like a jet-propelled Flying Dutchman. Nemo's 20,000
leagues is a day-trip by comparison. During this pyromaniac
peregrination, he throws off such airy comments as:

> City-burning has now become a habit with me more enchaining –
> and infinitely more debased – than ever was opium to the smoker,
> or alcohol to the drunkard. I count it among the prime necessaries
> of my life: it is my brandy, my bacchanal, my secret sin. I have
> burned Calcutta, Pekin, and San Francisco. [p. 152]

Jeffson returns to the Bosphorus, in Sultan style, to enjoy its
Byzantine glories once more, before reducing Byzantium to
ashes. He contemplates the inscrutable Sphinx at midnight
(uninflammable, alas, but in such circumstances he uses dynamite). He loots art that takes his fancy from the world's finest
museums. The Mona Lisa, we may imagine, regards him enigmatically as he sips Chypre wine from a gold goblet he lifted
from Java's great Boro Budor temple.

Having razed every Sodom and Gomorrah of the world, cul-
minating with Constantinople, Jeffson's 'white voice' reasserts
itself. He must now, he apprehends, build. By this stage in the
novel he affects the silken dress, flowing hairstyle and sybaritic
habits of a turbaned Sultanic potentate. Like Kubla Khan, he
resolves to construct his Xanadu, on the Greek Island of Imbros.
It will be a fabulous gilt, jewelled and marbled pleasure dome
with perfumed lakes of wine to intoxicate the eye.

Why does Adam turn to the Orient so flamboyantly? Shiel,
one deduces, was clearly an admirer of Sir Richard Burton
(1821–90), an intrepid explorer (of the Nile, not the North
Pole) and even more intrepid sexual adventurer (translator of
the *Kama Sutra* and *The Perfumed Garden*). His much-
photographed 'Sultan' dress, turban and long forked beard are
faithfully reflected in Jeffson's appearance. Burton's translation
of *The Arabian Nights* haunts the last sections of the novel. If

Nansen inspired the first section of *The Purple Cloud*, and Slocum the second, Burton inspires the third.

Finally, Adam Jeffson finds his Eve cowering in a woody glen outside Constantinople. She was born to a dead mother, a Sultana, 'at the moment of the cloud'. Having taught this child of nature to dress, speak and read, Adam names her Leda (the name echoes that of Shiel's similarly young and tawny wife, 'Lina'). She herself proposes the name 'Eve', which he does not approve. This second Adam does not want any bone of his bone: he has come to relish his loneliness and does not want to share it. Indeed, his first inclination was to murder her and eat her flesh. The passage makes one curious about previous unmentioned cannibalisms.

Eventually, after an extended courtship, which involves guns and telephones, Leda becomes Adam's mate. More importantly, Leda is revealed to have been in direct communication, over the course of her short life, with a voice she knows only as 'He who spoke with me'. 'He' it was who instructed her in the arts of survival in the underground cellar in which her corpse mother left her as a newborn baby. It was done, it seems obvious, that she should be preserved for the arrival of Jeffson. The novel, having verged close to religious explanations, ends ambiguously. Another purple cloud is on the way. Will they, and the race, survive? God only knows.

One does know that Shiel's marriage to Lina, happy enough during the period that *The Purple Cloud* was flowing from his pen, broke down irreparably in 1903, after five years and one child, Dolores, born in 1900. His incorrigible philandering was one reason for the breakdown. Cash was another. Shiel, despite his frantic bouts of writing, could never afford a proper home in England or in France (which he might have preferred) for his family. A third reason, which Shiel himself stressed, was mother-in-law difficulties.

The Purple Cloud, incredibly, did not earn Shiel more than the measly £70 Chatto & Windus paid for it. Nor did it recruit the large readership its strikingly original conception and richly ornamented prose deserved (no American publisher would touch it, which hurt his reputation and his pocket). In the years following *The Purple Cloud*, he was driven into an ever more hectic round of journalism and hack writing. Indefatigably energetic and inexhaustibly imaginative as he was, the quality of his fiction deteriorated under the pressure of having to write so much of the stuff. It did not help that his most loyal publisher, Grant Richards, went bankrupt in 1904. Other publishers were less willing to put up with Shiel's pestering demands for money and niggling complaints about the production of his books.

In the first decade of the new century, Shiel entered into clandestine partnership with an inferior writer, Louis Tracy, producing conveyor-belt fiction for magazines and down-market publishers under the joint pseudonyms 'Gordon Holmes' and 'Robert Fraser'. According to Harold Billings, the collaborations with Tracy were lifesavers for Shiel. Not least because Tracy had associations with British and American publishers which, with Grant Richards out of play, Shiel lacked. None of the works the duo produced is anywhere near as good as *The Purple Cloud*, although they have generated fascinating puzzles for bibliographers.

On another hectic front, Shiel's love-life continued promiscuously and, eventually, disastrously. His appetite for casual affairs remained insatiable. Nellie, the mother of his love-child Ada, had apparently moved to South Africa by this point. Lina was probably dead. Shiel, who evidently liked a little anchorage in his love-life, now entered into two other long-lasting relationships. Being Shiel, he tried to keep them running at the same time, while philandering on the side. The first of these relationships was with Elizabeth Price and was begun, as well as can be dated, in 1908. Born in 1880, 'Lizzie' was rather old for Shiel's taste and his interest initially seems to have been directed towards a much younger sister, Mary Jane, still in her early teens. Three years earlier, around 1905, as Billings calculates, Shiel had been involved romantically with Elizabeth's elder sister, Kate. It is not impossible that he had sexual relations with all three Price women. As Harold Billings suggests, there is also the further possibility that, having been forbidden by her family from anything more to do with Shiel, Mary Jane, the youngest, attempted suicide or a self-administered abortion. At the time the Price family was living at Chepstow and Shiel was a frequent visitor. His welcome must have worn rather thin.

Lizzie Price's personal life was almost as complicated as Shiel's. In the early years of the century she had become involved with an Indian, Surja Kumar Sircar, a well-educated businessman. The couple probably did not marry, but she took Sircar's surname and bore two daughters by him, Dorothy (b. 1902) and Eileen (b. 1904). The Sircars separated in 1907 and Sircar went on to marry another woman. Lizzie was now in London, in the family house, which seems to have been left to her. At some point Shiel – chronically hard-up as ever – moved in with her and her daughters.

Lizzie Price was working class – like her predecessor, Nellie Seward, the Cheltenham chambermaid. In 1908, Shiel had become infatuated with a woman of a higher class, Lydia Furley.

Their sexual relationship began in summer 1908, after they met at a public lecture in London. As Billings observes, Lydia was the woman Shiel pursued more vigorously than any other in his life. She was, at thirty-six, older than his other women. But she was intellectual, politically radical – a 'new woman', and later a Fabian. Her family background was 'respectable' working class. When Lydia and Shiel formed their relationship in 1908, both were living with other partners. Shiel proposed marriage in November 1908, but Lydia, true to her feminist principles (and still attached to her common-law husband and their child) turned him down. Surviving correspondence confirms that the relationship was one of the mind, as well as the body. It may well have been an exciting novelty for Shiel to vary his usual form of sexual intimacy with discussions about Bernard Shaw, the Webbs, the Pankhursts and that interesting new writer H. G. Wells.

Although he was still churning out fiction – much of it with Tracy – Shiel's popularity, never high, was waning to the level of obscurity. He published not a single book under his own name in 1910. He was, however, drumming up money where he could with short stories, for which there was a healthy market, and which he could throw off effortlessly. Many are excellent of their kind.

All this pressure of work was bad, but much worse was to come. Lizzie Price, who had adopted the surname 'Shiel', became pregnant by him in the summer of 1913 and their child, Caesar Kenneth Shiel, was born in March 1914. Shiel, in his usual dire financial straits, applied to the Royal Literary Fund in 1914 for financial assistance, citing 'impecuniosity' and failing sight. He was earning, he said, only £150 a year and would soon be blind (a lie). Despite strong references, the fund awarded him a derisory £10. Probably the committee got wind of some ugly rumours about Shiel which would surface a few months later.

In April 1914, Lydia's common-law husband had died, leaving her reasonably well off, with a house to bring her child up in, and now free to make an open arrangement with Shiel. This possibility seems to have triggered a crisis with Lizzie. He is known to have left her house (and their newborn son) in mid-1914. She did not, one deduces, take the desertion well. On 26 October 1914, under the name 'Elizabeth Sircar', she filed charges against Shiel on grounds of 'carnal knowledge' with her twelve-and-a-half-year-old daughter, Dorothy Sircar. Shiel was arrested and went on trial at the Old Bailey. He chose to defend himself against an array of witnesses to his crime. He did not deny the accusation, but justified it on historical precedent (he cited Napoleon's mother, among other well-known sexually active juveniles). Furthermore, he argued, Dorothy was a 'Hindoo' – a race which reached puberty early in life. An unpersuaded jury found him guilty of 'indecently assaulting and carnally knowing' Dorothy. He was sentenced to sixteen months' hard labour in Wormwood Scrubs. For a man nearly in his fifties, it was not a pleasant prospect.[14]

In an extraordinary letter to his publisher, Grant Richards, a month before his release in February 1916, Shiel protested that he was as 'innocent as snow' – not that he didn't do it, but that what he did was no crime. 'I myself am wildly non-English,' he explained, 'I have copulated, *as a matter of course*, from the age of two or three with ladies of a similar age in lands where that is not considered at all extraordinary' [my italics].[15] As Arthur Machen once observed, 'I honestly think that "right" and "wrong" were words without meaning to him.'[16]

In one respect Shiel was lucky. There was a world war going on and no one paid much attention to a petty sexual criminal. When Prisoner 2225 was released from jail, he put it about that he had been briefly imprisoned for fraud of a minor kind. As late as 2004 the author of the entry on Shiel in the authoritative *Oxford Dictionary of National Biography* could only come up with: 'In December 1914 Shiel was briefly imprisoned in Wormwood Scrubs for reasons undetermined.' In fact, it was not until the critic Kirsten MacLeod examined court documents and published what they contained in 2008[17] that the full extent of Shiel's delinquency became known. The passing decades have lifted the aura of criminality from Oscar Wilde, but, if anything, they have darkened Shiel's image. Knowing what Dr MacLeod has told us, how do we, as twenty-first-century readers, react to the Adam and Eve plot in *The Purple Cloud*? As we can best calculate, Jefferson is close on fifty, while Leda has yet to reach twenty. But she strikes one as strangely younger than twenty – childlike, even, with her lisps and ingenuous questionings about things. He first discovers Leda in a wood, having heard a mysterious sob:

> Slow step by slow step, with daintiest noiselessness, I moved to a thread of moss that from the glade passed into the thicket, and along its winding way I stepped, in the direction of the sound. Now my ears caught the purling noise of a brooklet, and following the moss-path, I was led into a mass of bush only two or three feet higher than my head. Through this, prowling like a stealthy cat, I wheedled my painful way, emerged upon a strip of open long-grass, and now was faced, three yards before me, by a wall of acacia-trees, prickly-pear and pichulas, between which and a forest beyond I spied a gleam of running water.
>
> On hands and knees I crept toward the acacia-thicket, entered it a little, and leaning far forward, peered. And there – at once – ten yards to my right – I saw.
>
> [...] Her hair, somewhat lighter than auburn, and frizzy, was a real garment to her nakedness, covering her below the hips, some strings of it falling, too, into the water: her eyes, a dark blue, were wide in a most silly expression of bewilderment. [pp. 186–7]

There is something, knowing what one now does about Shiel, disturbing in this voyeuristic passage and the whole Adam–Leda relationship which ensues.

Whatever rumours were abroad about his private life, a peculiarly flagrant plagiarism of a cowboy story (one of the few genres in which he was less than expert) in 1915 had rendered Shiel damaged goods in the London book world. Nothing further of literary significance appeared under his name until 1923, when his writing career entered a minor second phase. Extraordinarily, Lydia had stood by her lover, although she must have known the whole sorry story. Although they did not immediately live together, she submitted to marrying him in January 1919. She was now forty-six; he was eight years older, but still, as photographs testify, a good-looking man. This second marriage lasted from 1919 to 1929 and sustained Shiel through some of the harder years of his life.

One assumes Lydia supported him financially in these authorially fallow years, from the income her first partner had left her. There is no gainful work recorded, by either of them, and they were able to enjoy lengthy holidays abroad. After the war Shiel tried his hand at film scenarios and plays, without success. He and Lydia then planned a school on radical pedagogic principles. It came to nothing. Both of them are recorded as being sympathetic to the Russian Revolution and were reported in *The Times* as shouting out pro-Soviet slogans in the public gallery of the House of Commons, from which they were then ejected. He even wrote a pamphlet in favour of Bolshevism, but Shiel then returned to full length fiction in 1923, with *Children of the Wind*, which has a South African setting and a Zulu adventure plot. Shiel had no more been to Africa than he had been to the North Pole, but he had read Rider Haggard (and, perhaps, Conrad). Given his own racial background, the novel has obvious interest, but it is feeble stuff compared to *The Purple Cloud*.

There were five more novels over the next ten years. In 1929, Gollancz, a firm which was beginning to take a serious interest in science fiction, brought out a 'revised' edition of *The Purple Cloud*. It was during this period, in an advertising flier for Gollancz, that Shiel informed the world that he was the 'King of

Redonda', and had been for forty years. It is unclear how mischievous he was in making known this title; Harold Billings suspects it was something of a jape. His disciples, nonetheless, took their king seriously. In 1930 he recruited the most devoted of those disciples, the (excessively) minor poet John Gawsworth (1912–70), who, while earning his bread as a publisher's clerk, wrote to Shiel, 'imbued with a fanatic literary enthusiasm'. His fanaticism had been fired by the Gollancz reissue of *The Purple Cloud*. Gawsworth appointed himself factotum and, after 1947, keeper of the Shiel flame, while inebriating himself nightly in the many poets' pubs in Fitzrovia. If there is ever a London monument to Shiel, it should be erected outside the Fitzroy Tavern, in Charlotte Street.

In 1929 the Shiels separated – without fuss, as Harold Billings records. They may just have been tired of each other. Neither can have been easy to live with and there were no children to hold them together. He left London for a cottage near Horsham called L'Abri, 'the shelter', where he passed the remainder of his days. He bought the cottage with money supplied by Lydia, one supposes, since he seems to have had no other substantial sources of income. In these last years it was his habit to sleep by day and roam the hills and write by night. Devotees came to pay him court.

Shiel's last published novel, *The Young Men are Coming*, was published in 1937 – at a period when the nation was more anxious that the Germans were coming. As A. Reynolds Morse blandly summarises it:

> A Dr Warwick is whisked away into space by a fantastic flying island whose inhabitants excrete sticks of carbon, so high is their body temperature. The Egg of one of these superbeings holds a learned discourse with the Doctor.[18]

A version of the traditional 'elixir of life' fable ensues.

Shiel, though not immortal, lived to a great age, and became preoccupied with racist fantasies of the Nietzschean 'Overman' in his later years. In the context of World War Two, it did not add to his general appeal. His last work, *Jesus*, remains unpublished in its entirety. There were a mere thirteen mourners at his funeral (Shiel would have liked the symbolism – a Messiah and twelve disciples). The poet Edward Shanks (1892–1953), who gave the eulogy, stressed *The Purple Cloud* as the distinctive achievement of this remarkable man:

> [This book] was a legend, an apocalypse, out of space, out of time … the first and last thing to be said about him is that he had the character of a poet and a prophet – a prophet, I mean, in the Old Testament sense.[19]

Jeremiah comes inevitably to mind, predicting the destruction of Jerusalem.

Shiel anointed the faithful Gawsworth as his successor to the kingship of Redonda on his death. 'King Juan I' reverently kept Shiel's royal ashes in a biscuit tin on his mantelpiece, dropping a pinch as condiment into the food of any particularly honoured guest. The comedian and scholar of nineteenth-century decadent literature, Barry Humphries, was, as he has told me, one such diner – unwillingly and 'out of mere politeness'.

John Sutherland, 2012

NOTES

1   See 'Further Reading' section. As will be evident, I am particu-
     larly indebted in this introduction to Shiel's principal biographer,
     Harold Billings, the critic Dr Kirsten MacLeod and the Shiel web-
     site, http://alangullette.com/lit/shiel/, maintained by Alan Gullette.
2   Shiell renamed himself 'Shiel' on launching into literary life in
     1890. I use that spelling throughout.
3   See Harold Billings, *M. P. Shiel: A Biography of his Early Years*
     (2005), p. 42.
4   Ibid., p. 43.
5   Ibid., p. 45.
6   Harold Billings, *M. P. Shiel: The Middle Years 1897–1923* (2010),
     p. 55.

7   One of the most influential patrons was the journalist and
    editor W. T. Stead, who is acknowledged on the title page of
    The Rajah's Sapphire as having given Shiel the plot 'viva voce'.
    Immensely helpful as Stead was to Shiel, he was also, curiously,
    largely responsible for his later downfall. In 1885 Stead resolved
    to demonstrate the scandal of under-age prostitution by 'buying'
    a thirteen-year-old girl, Eliza Armstrong, in order (ostensibly) to
    sexually abuse her. He wrote it up as the protest article 'The
    Maiden Tribute of Babylon'. Although he was imprisoned for
    the act (he did nothing untoward with Armstrong – the sentence
    was outrageous), Stead's campaign was instrumental in raising
    the age of consent to sixteen from thirteen in the Criminal Law
    Amendment Act. Stead went down in the *Titanic* in 1912 and
    did not live to see his friend Shiel go to prison for sexual rela-
    tions with a twelve-and-a-half-year-old girl in 1914.

8   For the mania, and for the exploitation of it by novelists, see
    Alison Winter, *Mesmerized: Powers of Mind in Victorian Britain*
    (1998).

9   Billings, 2,135.

10 The authoritative account of the Arctic Mania is chronicled in
    Michael F. Robinson, *The Coldest Crucible* (2006).

11 For a comprehensive account, see Joscelyn Godwin, *Arktos: The
    Polar Myth* (1996).

12 H. P. Blavatsky, *The Secret Doctrine* (1888), II, 400.

13 Both Shiel and Jefferies are clear influences on J. G. Ballard's fine
    'Last Man' novel, *The Drowned World* (1962).

14 Billings, 2,208.

15 Ibid., 2,286–7.

16 Ibid., 2,49.

17 See Kirsten MacLeod, 'M. P. Shiel and the Love of Pubescent
    Girls', *English Literature in Transition 1880–1920* (2008), pp.
    335–380.

18 A. Reynolds Morse, *The Works of M. P. Shiel: A Study in Bibli-
    ography* (1948), p. 110.

19 Ibid., pp. 161–2.

Further Reading

A useful starting place is the website run by Alan Gullette, http://alangullette.com/lit/shiel/index.html. Among a wealth of other relevant Shieliana (updates on recent publications, 'news', other 'webography', online texts), Gullette's site offers a convenient gateway to the extensive body of scholarship built up on the author by John D. Squires.

The authoritative biography is:

Harold Billings, *M. P. Shiel: A Biography of his Early Years* (Austin, Texas: Beacham, 2005)

Harold Billings, *M. P. Shiel: The Middle Years, 1897 – 1923* (Austin, Texas: Beacham, 2010).

A completing third volume is keenly awaited.

Essential for any understanding of Shiel's complex interactions of life and work are:

Kirsten MacLeod, *Fictions of British Decadence* (London: Palgrave, 2006)

Kirsten MacLeod, 'M. P. Shiel and the Love of Pubescent Girls', *ELT* (2008), pp. 335–80.

The most convenient guide to the Shiel *oeuvre* (and the fullest account of the publication history of *The Purple Cloud*) is:

A. Reynolds Morse, *The Works of M. P. Shiel: A Study in Bibliography* (Los Angeles: Fantasy Publishing, 1948).

The volume, originally for limited publication, has been reissued accessibly by Kessinger Legacy Reprints.

Note on the Text

Shiel wrote *The Purple Cloud*, under pressure, in 1899, although it was in his mind for some time before then. The first reference Harold Billings cites, from surviving correspondence, is in 1898, when he started circulating among publishers ideas for a batch of future fiction, of which 'The Second Adam' was one.[1] At this primal stage Shiel's first idea was a trilogy of apocalyptic romances comprising *The Purple Cloud*, *The Lord of the Sea* and *The Last Miracle*. When this fell through, he opportunistically sold *The Purple Cloud* outright, for a measly £70, to Chatto & Windus, a publisher with whom he had no close or lasting relationship but who were evidently in the market for a catalogue-filler.

Chatto bought cheap and published shoddily. The first September 1901, six-shilling, volume edition of *The Purple Cloud* is disfigured by loose typography, misprints and a dull green binding. Its first appearance was not, however, in volume form, but as a six-part serial (January–June 1901) in the monthly *Royal Magazine*, illustrated (very ably) by J. J. Cameron. A Pearson production, *Royal Magazine* had been set up in opposition to Newnes's fabulously successful *Strand Magazine* (for which Shiel also occasionally wrote). Each of the six instalments is headed by a corpulent vignette of 'Sultan' Jeffson, a transformation which figures late in the narrative. Cameron obviously had a whole text to work from, as did the magazine editors – most likely the galley proofs, run off by Chatto's printers, Spottiswoode. These proofs would have been marked by Shiel for minor corrections and were, one deduces, hacked down to required size by the less loving hands of the magazine's editorial staff. 'Synopses' were offered at the head of instalments for readers coming late into the story. The magazine layout was double column, royal-octavo, on good quality paper and finely illustrated:

It is not clear whether Shiel received the subsidiary payment from the magazine or whether it went to Chatto, to whom he had signed over the property.

At midnight there was a sudden and visible increase of the conflagration.

Shiel was ill-served by the serialization, whose truncation was done insensitively. If one matches the serial parts (eight to eleven pages of the magazine) with the number of pages of the 1901 Chatto first edition, it is clear how severely Shiel's narrative was shrivelled down to size. The first two instalments (January–February 1901) contained virtually everything Shiel put into his full-length book edition. Abbreviation kicked in with the third number in the *Royal Magazine* and became drastic – not to say brutal – with the fourth. The page counts are as follows:

January: 11 pages of the magazine / 28 pages of 1901 text
February: 8/31
March: 9/58
April: 8/121
May: 9/110
June: 11/102

The cutting down represents narrative vandalism. Jefferson's long meditations, the arresting tableaux of a dead world, the macabre vignettes, the intoxicated verbosity were all ruthlessly stripped away in the serialization, leaving a skeletal 'what happens next' story.

Since they had invested in a first-rate illustrator, one has to ask why *Royal Magazine* mistreated *The Purple Cloud* in this way. The most plausible deduction is that reader feedback suggested that Shiel was not going down well with subscribers. A nine-month serialization was, I suspect, scheduled and then compressed to six in the face of what readers were telling the magazine. They were either baffled or did not like *The Purple Cloud*. For whatever reason, the serialization ended on 1 June. The novel, in Chatto's volume form, did not appear until 26 September 1901. The long hiatus must have chilled sales.

Chatto & Windus, whose main title in autumn 1901 was Hall Caine's *The Deemster*, gave no prominence to Shiel's novel in their advertisements. The 'Boomster', as Caine was nicknamed, pulled in as much as £10,000 per title. A seventy-quid merchant like Shiel could not stand up against that kind of money. The reviews of *The Purple Cloud* were, on the whole, favourable, but they were none of them in prominent places and most of them were perfunctory. The *Athenaeum* declared the book a 'considerable success', but devoted only a couple of hundred words to what made it a success. The *Morning Leader* thought it a 'large book', whatever 'large' meant. The *Speaker* applauded it as 'original in concept'. The *Standard* commended it chattily as a 'fine bit of work'. The *Weekend* concluded that it 'towers high over the ordinary novel'. According to the *Leeds Mercury* 'lovers of sensational fiction will read *The Purple Cloud* with breathless haste' (as, clearly, had the reviewer). *The Sunday Times*, the only heavyweight to take on the novel, offered a mild health warning:

> It is an unconventional and horribly fascinating romance – one which I would not recommend for perusal just before going to bed.

Hearth and Home was similarly overwhelmed:

> The idea at the root of it is tremendous, appalling, cosmic … the story is a profound psychology [sic] study as well as a thrilling narrative of marvellous events.

It was all to the good, but they were small reviews and most of them in small places. They put no wind behind the novel. Chatto did not succeed in getting an American taker for the novel, and possibly didn't try very hard. There was a 3/6d second edition in 1902, which may have been unsold copies of the first 6/- edition, after which *The Purple Cloud* went out of print for the best part of thirty years.[2]

The Purple Cloud was given a second lease of life when the copyright was purchased (with a handful of other Shiel titles) in the late 1920s by Victor Gollancz, who was pioneering a line of science fiction. Shiel revised the text for its new owner, tempering some of the blasphemies (see note to p. 82) and making a few judicious updatings (see note to p. 78). He prudently excised the 'necrophile' episode (see note to p. 133) and laid less stress on such things as Leda's naked body (see note to

pp. 186–7). But most of the many changes he made were mar-
ginal and incidental. They mainly comprise synonym changes
and random alterations of dates and numbers (see, e.g., note to
p. 12). The host of trivial changes suggest that Shiel primarily
wanted to convey to Chatto that he was taking the task of revision very seriously.

For the reader of 1929, *The Purple Cloud* must have looked
dated. The technology is anachronistic (no aeroplanes, primitive telephony, horse-drawn carts). The automobiles in which
Jeffson hurtles round England would have recalled, in 1929,
the London to Brighton rally. Most significantly, the North Pole
was no longer, as it had been in 1901, a terra incognita. When
it first came out, *The Purple Cloud* was as topical as newspaper
headlines. In 1929 central elements of its narrative were musty
history. For the contemporary reader, however, the turn-of-the-
century antiquity adds to the gothic charm of the book.

A case has been made that the 1929 text is 'tightened' and is
to be preferred over that of 1901. My sense is that the 1901
version has more vitality, as did the thirty-five-year-old author
at the peak of his creative career. Readers can judge for themselves by consulting the 'Bison Frontiers of Science Fiction'
edition, based on the 1929 edition, published by the University
of Nebraska Press in 2000, with an introduction by John Clute.
Those interested in J. J. Cameron's illustrations are directed to
the Tartarus Press *edition de luxe*, with an introduction by
Brian Stableford, published in 2004.

Shiel had hopes towards the end of his life that Paramount
Pictures would film *The Purple Cloud*, but the project came to
nothing. It is fortunate that he did not live to see the film which
was made, in 1959, under the title *The World, the Flesh and the
Devil*, starring Harry Belafonte.

NOTES

1   Billings, 1.164.
2   A comprehensive account of the publication history of the novel
    is given in Morse, pp. 58–61.

ἔσται καὶ Σάμος ἄμμος, ἐσεῖται Δῆλος ἄδηλος
Sibylline Prophecy

Foreword

About three months ago – that is to say, toward the end of May of this year of 1900* – the writer whose name appears on the title-page received as noteworthy a letter, and packet of papers, as it has been his lot to examine. They came from a very good friend of mine, whose name there is no reason that I should now conceal – Dr Arthur Lister Browne, M.A. (Oxon.), F.R.C.P. It happened that for two years I had been spending most of my time in France,* and as Browne had a Norfolk practice, I had not seen him during my visits to London. Moreover, though our friendship was of the most intimate kind, we were both atrocious correspondents: so that only two notes passed between us during those years.

Till, last May, there reached me the letter – and the packet – to which I refer. The packet consisted of four note-books, quite crowded throughout with those giddy shapes of Pitman's short-hand,* whose *ensemble* so resembles startled swarms hovering in flighty poses on the wing. They were scribbled in pencil, with little distinction between thick and thin strokes, few vowels: so that their slow deciphering, I can assure the reader, has been no holiday. The letter also was pencilled in shorthand; and this letter, together with the second of the note-books which I have deciphered (it was marked 'III.'), I now publish.

[I must say, however, that in some five instances there will occur sentences rather crutched by my own guess-work;* and in two instances the characters were so impossibly mystical, that I had to abandon the passage with a head-ache. But all this will be found immaterial to the general narrative.]

The following is Browne's letter:

'Dear Old Shiel, – I have just been lying thinking of you, and wishing that you were here to give one a last squeeze of the hand before I— "*go*": for, by all appearance, "going" I am. Four days ago, I began to feel a soreness in the throat, and passing by old Johnson's surgery at Selbridge, went in and asked him to have a look at me. He muttered something about membranous laryngitis which made me smile, but by the time I reached home I was hoarse, and not smiling: before night I had dyspnœa and laryngeal stridor.* I at once telegraphed to London for Morgan, and, between him and Johnson, they have been opening my trachea, and burning my inside with chromic acid and the galvanic cautery. The difficulty as to breathing has subsided, and it is wonderful how little I suffer: but I am much too old a hand not to know what's what: the bronchi are involved – *too far* involved – and as a matter of absolute fact, there isn't any hope. Morgan is still, I believe, fondly dwelling upon the possibility of adding me to his successful-tracheotomy statistics, but prognosis was always my strong point, and I say No. The very small consolation of my death will be the beating of a specialist in his own line. So we shall see.

'I have been arranging some of my affairs this morning, and remembered these notebooks. I intended letting you have them months ago, but my habit of putting things off, and the fact that the lady was alive from whom I took down the words, prevented me. Now she is dead, and as a literary man, and a student of life, you should be interested, if you can manage to read them. You may even find them valuable.

'I am under a little morphia at present, propped up in a nice little state of languor, and as I am able to write without much effort, I will tell you in the old Pitman's something about her. Her name was Miss Mary Wilson; she was about thirty when I met her, forty-five when she died, and I knew her intimately all those fifteen years. Do you know anything about the philosophy of the hypnotic trance? Well, that was the relation between us – hypnotist and subject. She had been under another man before my time, but no one was ever so successful with her as I. She suffered from *tic douloureux* of the fifth nerve.* She had had most of her teeth drawn before I saw her, and an attempt had been made to wrench out the nerve on the left side by the external scission. But it made no difference: all the clocks in hell tick-tacked in that poor woman's jaw, and it was the mercy of Providence that ever she came across *me*. My organisation was found to have almost complete, and quite easy, control over hers, and with a few passes I could expel her Legion.

'Well, you never saw anyone so singular in personal appearance as my friend, Miss Wilson. Medicine-man as I am, I could never behold her suddenly without a sensation of shock: she suggested so inevitably what we call "the *other* world", one detecting about her some odour of the worm, with the feeling that here was rather ghost than woman. And yet I can hardly convey to you the why of this, except by dry details as to the contours of her lofty brow, meagre lips, pointed chin, and ashen cheeks. She was tall and deplorably emaciated, her whole skeleton, except the thigh-bones, being quite visible. Her eyes were of the bluish hue of cigarette smoke, and had in them the strangest, feeble, unearthly gaze; while at thirty-five her paltry wisp of hair was quite white.

'She was well-to-do, and lived alone in old Wooding Manorhouse, five miles from Ash Thomas. As you know, I was "beginning" in these parts at the time, and soon took up my residence at the manor. She insisted that I should devote myself to her alone; and that one patient constituted the most lucrative practice which I ever had.

'Well, I quickly found that, in the state of trance, Miss Wilson possessed very remarkable powers: remarkable, I mean, not, of course, because peculiar to herself in *kind*, but because they were so constant, reliable, exact, and far-reaching, in degree. The veriest fledgling in psychical science will now sit and discourse finically to you about the reporting powers of the mind in its trance state – just as though it was something quite new! This simple fact, I assure you, which the Psychical Research Society,* only after endless investigation, admits to be scientific, has been perfectly well known to every old crone since the Middle Ages, and, I assume, long previously. What an unnecessary air of discovery! The certainty that someone in trance in Manchester can tell you what is going on in London, or in

Pekin, was not, of course, left to the acumen of an office in Fleet
Street; and the society, in establishing the fact beyond doubt for
the general public, has not gone one step toward explaining it.
They have, in fact, revealed nothing that many of us did not,
with absolute assurance, know before.

'But talking of poor Miss Wilson, I say that her powers
were *remarkable*, because, though not exceptional in *genre*,
they were so special in quantity, – so "constant", and "far-
reaching". I believe it to be a fact that, *in general*, the powers
of trance manifest themselves more particularly with regard
to space, as distinct from time: the spirit roams in the present – it
travels over a plain – it does not *usually* attract the interest of
observers by great ascents, or by great descents. I fancy that is
so. But Miss Wilson's gift was special to this extent, that she
travelled in every direction, and easily in all but one, north
and south, up and down, in the past, the present, and the
future.

'This I discovered, not at once, but gradually. She would emit
a stream of sounds in the trance state* – I can hardly call it
speech, so murmurous, yet guttural, was the utterance, mixed
with puffy breath-sounds at the languid lips. This state was
accompanied by an intense contraction of the pupils, absence
of the knee-jerk, considerable rigor, and a rapt and arrant
expression. I got into the habit of sitting long hours at her bed-
side, quite fascinated by her, trying to catch the import of that
opiate and visionary language which came puffing and fluttering in deliberate monotone from her lips. Gradually, in the
course of months, my ear learned to detect the words; "the veil
was rent"* for me also; and I was able to follow somewhat the
course of her musing and wandering spirit.

'At the end of six months I heard her one day repeat some
words which were familiar to me. They were these: "Such were
the arts by which the Romans extended their conquests, and
attained the palm of victory; and the concurring testimony of
different authors enables us to describe them with precision ..."
I was startled: they are part of Gibbon's "Decline and Fall",*
which I easily guessed that she had never read.

'I said in a stern voice: "Where are you?"

'She replied, "Us are in a room, eight hundred and eleven miles above.* A man is writing. Us are reading."

'I may tell you two things: first, that in trance she never spoke of herself as "I", nor even as "we", but, for some unknown reason, in the *objective* way, as "*us*": "us are", she would say – "us will", "us went"; though, of course, she was an educated lady, and I don't think ever lived in the West of England, where they say "us" in that way; secondly, when wandering in the past, she always represented herself as being "*above*" (the earth?), and higher the further back in time she went; in describing present events she appears to have felt herself *on* (the earth); while, as regards the future, she invariably declared that "*us*" were so many miles "within" (the earth).

'To her excursions in this last direction, however, there seemed to exist certain fixed limits: I say seemed, for I cannot be sure, and only mean that, in spite of my efforts, she never, in fact, went far in this direction. Three, four thousand "miles" were common figures on her lips in describing her distance "above"; but her distance "within" never got beyond sixty-three. Usually, she would say twenty, twenty-five. She appeared, in relation to the future, to resemble a diver in the deep sea, who, the deeper he strives, finds a more resistant pressure, till, at no great depth, resistance becomes prohibition, and he can no further strive.

'I am afraid I can't go on: though I had a good deal to tell you about this lady. During fifteen years, off and on, I sat listening by her dim bed-side to her murmuring trances! At last my expert ear could detect the sense of her faintest sigh. I heard the "Decline and Fall" from beginning to end. Some of her reports were the most frivolous nonsense: over others I have hung in a horror of interest. Certainly, my friend, I have heard some amazing words proceed from those wan lips of Mary Wilson. Sometimes I could hitch her repeatedly to any scene or subject that I chose by the mere exercise of my will; at others, the flighty waywardness of her spirit eluded and baffled me: she resisted – she disobeyed: otherwise I might have sent you, not four note-books, but twenty, or forty. About the fifth year it struck me that it would be well to jot down her more connected utterances, since I knew shorthand. The note-book marked "I.",[1] which seems to me the most curious, belongs to the seventh year. Its history, like those of the other three, is this: I heard her one afternoon murmuring in the intonation used when *reading*; the matter interested me; I asked her where she was. She replied: "Us are forty-five miles within: us read, and another writes"; from which I concluded that she was some fifteen to thirty years in the future, perusing an as yet unpublished work. After that, during some weeks, I managed to keep her to the same subject, and finally, I fancy, won pretty well the whole work. I believe you would find it striking, and hope you will be able to read my notes.

'But no more of Mary Wilson now. Rather let us think a little of A. L. Browne, F.R.C.P.! – with a breathing-tube in his trachea, and Eternity under his pillow...' [Dr Browne's letter then continues on a subject of no interest here.]

[The present writer may add that Dr Browne's prognosis of his own case proved correct, for he passed away two days after writing the above. My transcription of the shorthand book marked 'III.' I now proceed to give without comment, merely reminding the reader that the words form the substance of a book or document to be written, or to be motived (according to Miss Wilson) in that Future, which, no less than the Past, substantively exists in the Present – though, like the Past, we see it not. I need only add that the title, division into paragraphs, &c., have been arbitrarily contrived by myself for the sake of form and convenience.]

---

[1] This I intend to publish under the title of 'The Last Miracle'; 'II.' will bear that of 'The Lord of the Sea'; the present book is marked 'III.' The perusal of 'IV.' I have not yet finished, but so far do not consider it suitable for publication.'

The Purple Cloud

(Here begins the note-book marked 'III.')

Well, the memory seems to be getting rather impaired now,*
rather weak. What, for instance, was the name of that parson
who preached, just before the *Boreal** set out, about the wickedness of any further attempt to reach the North Pole? I have
forgotten! Yet four years ago it was familiar to me as my own
name.

Things which took place before the voyage seem to be getting
a little cloudy in the memory now. I have sat here, in the loggia of
this Cornish villa,* to write down some sort of account of what
has happened – God knows why, since no eye can ever read it –
and at the very beginning I cannot remember the parson's name.

He was a strange sort of man surely, a Scotchman from Ayr-
shire, big and gaunt, with tawny hair. He used to go about London
streets in shough and rough-spun clothes, a plaid flung from one
shoulder. Once I saw him in Holborn with his rather wild stalk,
frowning and muttering to himself. He had no sooner come to
London, and opened chapel (I think in Fetter Lane), than the little
room began to be crowded; and when, some years afterwards, he
moved to a big establishment in Kensington, all sorts of men,
even from America and Australia, flocked to hear the thunder-
storms that he talked, though certainly it was not an age apt to fly
into enthusiasms over that species of pulpit prophets and prophe-
cies. But this particular man undoubtedly did wake the strong
dark feelings that sleep in the heart; his eyes were very singular
and powerful; his voice from a whisper ran gathering, like snow-
balls, and crashed, as I have heard the pack-ice in commotion far
yonder in the North; while his gestures were as uncouth and
gawky as some wild man's of the primitive ages.

Well, this man – what *was* his name? – Macintosh? Mackay? I think – yes, that was it! *Mackay*. Mackay saw fit to take offence at the new attempt to reach the Pole in the *Boreal*; and for three Sundays, when the preparations were nearing completion, stormed against it at Kensington.

The excitement of the world with regard to the North Pole had at this date reached a pitch which can only be described as *fevered*,* though that word hardly expresses the strange ecstasy and unrest which prevailed: for the abstract interest which mankind, in mere desire for Knowledge, had always felt in this unknown region, was now, suddenly, a thousand and a thousand times intensified by a new, concrete interest – a tremendous *money* interest.

And the new zeal had ceased to be healthy in its tone as the old zeal was: for now the fierce demon Mammon was making his voice heard in this matter.

Within the ten years preceding the *Boreal* expedition, no less than twenty-seven expeditions had set out, and failed.

The secret of this new rage lay in the last will and testament of Mr Charles P. Stickney of Chicago,* that king of faddists, supposed to be the richest individual who ever lived: he, just ten years before the *Boreal* undertaking, had died, bequeathing 175 million dollars to the man, of whatever nationality, who first reached the Pole.

Such was the actual wording of the will – '*the man who first reached*': and from this loose method of designating the person intended had immediately burst forth a prolonged heat of controversy in Europe and America as to whether or no the testator meant *the Chief* of the first expedition which reached: but it was finally decided, on the highest legal authority, that, in any case, the actual wording of the document held good; and that it was the individual, whatever his station in the expedition, whose foot first reached the 90th degree of north latitude, who would have title to the fortune.*

At all events, the public ferment had risen, as I say, to a pitch of positive fever; and as to the *Boreal* in particular, the daily progress of her preparations was minutely discussed in the newspapers, everyone was an authority on her fitting, and she was in every mouth a bet, a hope, a jest, or a sneer: for now, at last, it was felt that success was probable. So this Mackay had an acutely interested audience, if a somewhat startled, and a somewhat cynical, one.

A truly lion-hearted man this must have been, after all, to dare proclaim a point-of-view so at variance with the spirit of his age! One against four hundred millions,* they bent one way, he the opposite, saying that they were wrong, all wrong! People used to call him 'John the Baptist Redivivus': and without doubt he did suggest something of that sort. I suppose that at the time when he had the face to denounce the *Boreal* there was not a sovereign on any throne in Europe who, but for shame, would [not] have been glad of a subordinate post on board.

On the third Sunday night of his denunciation I was there in that Kensington chapel, and I heard him. And the wild talk he talked! He seemed like a man delirious with inspiration.

The people sat quite spell-bound, while Mackay's prophesying voice ranged up and down through all the modulations of thunder, from the hurrying mutter to the reverberant shock and climax: and those who came to scoff remained to wonder.*

Put simply, what he said was this: That there was undoubtedly some sort of Fate, or Doom, connected with the Poles of the earth in reference to the human race: that man's continued failure, in spite of continual efforts, to reach them, abundantly and super-abundantly proved this; and that this failure constituted a lesson – *and a warning* – which the race disregarded at its peril.

The North Pole, he said, was not so very far away, and the difficulties in the way of reaching it were not, on the face of them, so very great: human ingenuity had achieved a thousand things a thousand times more difficult; yet in spite of over half-a-dozen well-planned efforts in the nineteenth century, and thirty-one in the twentieth, man had never reached [it]: always he had been baulked, baulked, by some seeming chance – some restraining Hand: and herein lay the lesson – *herein the warning*. Wonderfully – really *wonderfully* – like the Tree of Knowledge in Eden, he said, was that Pole: all the rest of earth lying open and offered to man – but *That* persistently veiled and 'forbidden'. It was as when a father lays a hand upon his son, with: 'Not here, my child; wheresoever you will – but not here.'

But human beings, he said, were free agents, with power to stop their ears, and turn a callous consciousness to the whispers and warning indications of Heaven; and he believed, he said, that the time was now come when man would find it absolutely in his power to stand on that 90th of latitude, and plant an impious right foot on the head of the earth – just as it had been given into the absolute power of Adam to stretch an impious right hand, and pluck of the Fruit of Knowledge; but, said he – his voice pealing now into one long proclamation of awful augury – just as the abuse of that power had been followed in the one case by catastrophe swift and universal, so, in the other, he warned the entire race to look out thenceforth for nothing from God but a lowering sky, and thundery weather.

The man's frantic earnestness, authoritative voice, and savage gestures, could not but have their effect upon all; as for me, I declare, I sat as though a messenger from Heaven addressed me. But I believe that I had not yet reached home, when the whole impression of the discourse had passed from me like water from a duck's back. The Prophet in the twentieth century was not a success. John [the] Baptist himself, camel-skin and all,* would have met with only tolerant shrugs. I dismissed Mackay from my mind with the thought: 'He is behind his age, I suppose.'

But haven't I thought differently of Mackay since, my God...?

Three weeks – it was about that – before that Sunday night discourse, I was visited by Clark, the chief of the coming expedition – a mere visit of friendship. I had then been established about a year at No. 11, Harley Street, and, though under twenty-five,* had, I suppose, as *élite* a practice as any doctor in Europe.

Élite – but small. I was able to maintain my state, and move among the great: but now and again I would feel the secret pinch of moneylessness. Just about that time, in fact, I was only saved from considerable embarrassment by the success of my book, *Applications of Science to the Arts*.

In the course of conversation that afternoon, Clark said to me in his light hap-hazard way:

'Do you know what I dreamed about you last night, Adam Jeffson? I dreamed that you were with us on the expedition.'

I think he must have seen my start: on the same night I had myself dreamed the same thing; but not a word said I about it now. There was a stammer in my tongue when I answered:

'Who? I? – on the expedition? – I would not go, if I were asked.'

'Oh, you would.'

'I wouldn't. You forget that I am about to be married.'

'Well, we need not discuss the point, as Peters is not going to die,' said he. 'Still, if anything did happen to him, you know, it is you I should come straight to, Adam Jeffson.'

'Clark, you jest,' I said: 'I know really very little of astronomy, or magnetic phenomena. Besides, I am about to be married…'

'But what about your botany, my friend? *There's* what we should be wanting from you: and as for nautical astronomy, poh, a man with your scientific habit would pick all that up in no time.'

'You discuss the matter as gravely as though it were a possibility, Clark,' I said, smiling. 'Such a thought would never enter my head: there is, first of all, my *fiancée*—'

'Ah, the all-important Countess, eh? – Well, but she, as far as I know the lady, would be the first to force you to go. The chance of stamping one's foot on the North Pole does not occur to a man every day, my son.'

'Do talk of something else!' I said. 'There is Peters…'

'Well, of course, there is Peters. But believe me, the dream I had was so clear—'

'Let me alone with your dreams, and your Poles!' I laughed.

Yes, I remember: I pretended to laugh loud! But my secret heart knew, even *then*, that one of those crises was occurring in my life which, from my youth, has made it the most extraordinary which any creature of earth ever lived. And I knew that this was so, firstly, because of the two dreams, and secondly, because, when Clark was gone, and I was drawing on my gloves to go to see my *fiancée*, I heard distinctly the old two Voices talk within me: and One said: 'Go not to see her now!' and the Other: 'Yes, go, go!'

The two Voices of my life! An ordinary person reading my words would undoubtedly imagine that I mean only two ordinary contradictory impulses – or else that I rave: for what modern man could comprehend how real-seeming were those voices, how loud, and how, ever and again, I heard them contend within me, with a nearness 'nearer than breathing', as it says in the poem,* and 'closer than hands and feet'.

About the age of seven it happened first to me. I was playing one summer evening in a pine-wood of my father's; half a mile away was a quarry-cliff; and as I played, it suddenly seemed as if someone said to me, inside of me: 'Just take a walk toward the cliff'; and as if someone else said: 'Don't go that way at all!' – mere whispers then, which gradually, as I grew up, seemed to swell into cries of wrathful contention! I did go toward the cliff: it was steep, thirty feet high, and I fell. Some weeks later, on recovering speech, I told my astonished mother that 'someone had pushed me' over the edge, and that someone else 'had caught me' at the bottom!

One night, soon after my eleventh birthday,* lying in bed, the thought struck me that my life must be of great importance to some thing or things which I could not see; that two Powers, which hated each other, must be continually after me, one wishing for some reason to kill me, and the other for some reason to keep me alive, one wishing me to do so and so, and the other to do the opposite; that I was not a boy like other boys, but a creature separate, special, marked for – something. Already I had notions, touches of mood, passing instincts, as occult and primitive, I verily believe, as those of the first man that stepped; so that such Biblical expressions as 'The Lord spake to So-and-so, saying' have hardly ever suggested any question in my mind as to how the Voice was *heard*: I did not find it so very difficult to comprehend that originally man had more ears than two; nor should have been surprised to know that I, in these latter days, more or less resembled those primeval ones.

But not a creature, except perhaps my mother, has ever dreamed me what I here state that I was. I seemed the ordinary youth of my time, bow in my Varsity eight, cramming for exams, dawdling in clubs. When I had to decide as to a profession, who could have suspected the conflict that transacted itself in my soul, while my brain was indifferent to the matter – that agony of strife with which the brawling voices shouted, the one: 'Be a scientist – a doctor,' and the other: 'Be a lawyer, an engineer, an artist – be *anything* but a doctor!'

A doctor I became, and went to what had grown into the greatest of medical schools – Cambridge; and there it was that I came across a man, named Scotland, who had a rather odd view of the world. He had rooms, I remember, in the New Court at Trinity, and a set of us were generally there. He was always talking about certain 'Black' and 'White' Powers, till it became absurd, and the men used to call him 'black-and-white-mystery-man', because, one day, when someone said something about 'the black mystery of the universe', Scotland interrupted him with the words: 'the black-and-white mystery'.

Quite well I remember Scotland now – the sweetest, gentle soul he was, with a passion for cats, and Sappho, and the Anthology,* very short in stature, with a Roman nose, continually making the effort to keep his neck straight, and draw his paunch in. He used to say that the universe was being frantically contended for by two Powers: a White and a Black; that the White was the stronger, but did not find the conditions on our particular planet very favourable to his success; that he had got the best of it up to the Middle Ages in Europe, but since then had been slowly and stubbornly giving way before the Black; and that finally the Black would win – not everywhere perhaps, but *here* – and would carry off, if no other earth, at least *this* one, for his prize.

This was Scotland's doctrine, which he never tired of repeating; and while others heard him with mere toleration, little could they divine with what agony of inward interest, I, cynically smiling there, drank in his words. Most profound, most profound, was the impression they made upon me.

But I was saying that when Clark left me, I was drawing on my gloves to go to see my *fiancée*, the Countess Clodagh, when I heard the two voices most clearly.

Sometimes the urgency of one or other impulse is so over-powering, that there is no resisting it: and it was so then with the one that bid me go.

I had to traverse the distance between Harley Street and Hanover Square, and all the time it was as though something shouted at my physical ear: 'Since you go, breathe no word of the *Boreal*, and Clark's visit'; and another shout: 'Tell, tell, hide nothing!'

It seemed to last a month: yet it was only some minutes before I was in Hanover Square, and Clodagh in my arms.

She was, in my opinion, the most superb of creatures, Clodagh – that haughty neck which seemed always scorning something just behind her left shoulder. Superb! but ah – I know it now – a godless woman, Clodagh, a bitter heart.

Clodagh once confessed to me that her favourite character in history was Lucrezia Borgia,* and when she saw my horror, immediately added: 'Well, no, I am only joking!' Such was her duplicity: for I see now that she lived in the constant effort to hide her heinous heart from me. Yet, now I think of it, how completely did Clodagh enthral me!

Our proposed marriage was opposed by both my family and hers: by mine, because her father and grandfather had died in lunatic asylums; and by hers, because, forsooth, I was neither a rich nor a noble match. A sister of hers, much older than herself, had married a common country doctor, Peters of Taunton, and this so-called *mésalliance* made the so-called *mésalliance* with me doubly detestable in the eyes of her relatives. But Clodagh's extraordinary passion for me was to be stemmed neither by their threats nor prayers. What a flame, after all, was Clodagh! Sometimes she frightened me.

She was at this date no longer young, being by five years my senior, as also, by five years, the senior of her nephew, born from the marriage of her sister with Peters of Taunton. This nephew was Peter Peters, who was to accompany the *Boreal* expedition as doctor, botanist, and meteorological assistant.

On that day of Clark's visit to me I had not been seated five minutes with Clodagh, when I said:

'Dr Clark – ha! ha! ha! – has been talking to me about the Expedition. He says that if anything happened to Peters, I should be the first man he would run to. He has had an absurd dream...'

The consciousness that filled me as I uttered these words was the *wickedness* of me – the crooked wickedness. But I could no more help it than I could fly.

Clodagh was standing at a window holding a rose at her face. For quite a minute she made no reply. I saw her sharp-cut, florid face in profile, steadily bent and smelling. She said presently in her cold, rapid way:

'The man who first plants his foot on the North Pole will certainly be ennobled. I say nothing of the many millions ... I only wish that I was a man!'

'I don't know that I have any special ambition that way,' I rejoined. 'I am very happy in my warm Eden with my Clodagh. I don't like the outer Cold.'

'Don't let me think little of you!' she answered pettishly.

'Why should you, Clodagh? I am not bound to desire to go to the North Pole, am I?'

'But you *would* go, I suppose, if you could?'

'I might – I – doubt it. There is our marriage...'

'Marriage indeed! It is the one thing to transform our marriage from a sneaking difficulty to a ten times triumphant event.'

'You mean if *I* personally were the first to stand at the Pole. But there are many in an expedition. It is very unlikely that *I*, personally—'

'For *me* you will, Adam—' she began.

'"*Will*," Clodagh?' I cried. 'You say "*will*"? there is not even the slightest shadow of a probability—!'

'But why? There are still three weeks before the start. They say...'

She stopped, she stopped.

'They say what?'

Her voice dropped:

'That Peter takes atropine.'*

Ah, I started then. She moved from the window, sat in a rocking-chair, and turned the leaves of a book, without reading. We were silent, she and I; I standing, looking at her, she drawing the thumb across the leaf-edges, and beginning again, contemplatively. Then she laughed dryly a little – a dry, mad laugh.

'Why did you start when I said that?' she asked, reading now at random.

'*I!* I did not start, Clodagh! What made you think that I started? I did not start! Who told you, Clodagh, that Peters takes atropine?'

'He is my nephew: I should know. But don't look dumb-foundered in that absurd fashion: I have no intention of poisoning him in order to see you a multimillionaire, and a Peer of the Realm...'

'My dearest Clodagh!'

'I easily might, however. He will be here presently. He is bringing Mr Wilson for the evening.' (Wilson was going as electrician of the expedition.)

'Clodagh,' I said, 'believe me, you jest in a manner which does not please me.'

'Do I really?' she answered with that haughty, stiff half-turn of her throat: 'then I must be more exquisite. But, thank Heaven, it is only a jest. Women are no longer admired for doing such things.'

'Ha! ha! ha! – no – no longer admired, Clodagh! Oh, my good Lord! let us change this talk...'

But now she could talk of nothing else. She got from me that afternoon the history of all the Polar expeditions of late years, how far they reached, by what aids, and why they failed. Her eyes shone; she listened eagerly. Before this time, indeed, she had been interested in the *Boreal*, knew the details of her outfit-ting, and was acquainted with several members of the expedition. But now, suddenly, her mind seemed wholly possessed, my mention of Clark's visit apparently setting her well a-burn with the Pole-fever.

The passion of her kiss as I tore myself from her embrace that day I shall not forget. I went home with a pretty heavy heart.

The house of Dr Peter Peters was three doors from mine, on the opposite side of the street. Toward one that night, his footman ran to knock me up with the news that Peters was very ill. I hurried to his bed-side, and knew by the first glance at his deliriums and his staring pupils that he was poisoned with atropine.

Wilson, the electrician, who had passed the evening with him at Clodagh's in Hanover Square, was there.

'What on earth is the matter?' he said to me.

'Poisoned,' I answered.

'Good God! what with?'

'Atropine.'

'Good Heavens!'

'Don't be frightened: I think he will recover.'

'Is that certain?'

'Yes, I think – that is, if he leaves off taking the drug, Wilson.'

'What! it is he who has poisoned himself?'

I hesitated, I hesitated. But I said:

'He is in the habit of taking atropine, Wilson.'

Three hours I remained there, and, God knows, toiled hard for his life: and when I left him in the dark of the fore-day, my mind was at rest: he would recover.

I slept till 11 A.M., and then hurried over again to Peters. In the room were my two nurses, and Clodagh.

My beloved put her forefinger to her lips, whispering:

'Sh-h-h! he is asleep...'

She came closer to my ear, saying:

'I heard the news early. I am come to stay with him, till – the last...'

We looked at each other some time – eye to eye, steadily, she and I: but mine dropped before Clodagh's. A word was on my mouth to say, but I said nothing.

The recovery of Peters was not so steady as I had expected. At the end of the first week he was still prostrate. It was then that I said to Clodagh:

'Clodagh, your presence at the bed-side here somehow does not please me. It is so unnecessary.'

'Unnecessary certainly,' she replied: 'but I always had a genius for nursing, and a passion for watching the battles of the body. Since no one objects, why should you?'

'Ah! ... I don't know. This is a case that I dislike. I have half a mind to throw it to the devil.'

'Then do so.'

'And you, too – go home, go home, Clodagh!'

'But *why*? – if one does no harm. In these days of "the corruption of the upper classes", and Roman decadence of everything, shouldn't every innocent whim be encouraged by you upright ones who strive against the tide? Whims are the brakes of crimes: and this is mine. I find a sensuous pleasure, almost a sensual, in dabbling in delicate drugs – like Helen, for that matter, and Medea, and Calypso, and the great antique women, who were all excellent chymists.* To study the human ship in a gale, and the slow drama of its foundering – isn't that a quite thrilling distraction? And I want you to get into the habit at once of letting me have my little way—'

Now she touched my hair with a lofty playfulness that soothed me: but even then I looked upon the rumpled bed, and saw that the man there was really very sick.

I have still a nausea to write about it! Lucrezia Borgia in her own age may have been heroic: but Lucrezia in this late century! One could retch up the heart...

The man grew sick on that bed, I say. The second week passed, and only ten days remained before the start of the expedition.

At the end of that second week, Wilson, the electrician, was one evening sitting by Peters' bedside when I entered.

At the moment, Clodagh was about to administer a dose to Peters; but seeing me, she put down the medicine-glass on the night table, and came toward me; and as she came, I saw a sight which stabbed me: for Wilson took up the deposited medicine-glass, elevated it, looked at it, smelled into it: and he did it with a kind of hurried, light-fingered stealth; and he did it with an under-look, and a meaningness of expression which, I thought, proved mistrust...

Meantime, Clark came each day. He had himself a medical degree, and about this time I called him in professionally, together with Alleyne of Cavendish Square, to consultation over Peters. The patient lay in a semi-coma broken by passionate vomitings, and his condition puzzled us all. I formally stated that he took atropine – had been originally poisoned by atropine: but we saw that his present symptoms were not atropine symptoms, but, it almost seemed, of some other vegetable poison, which we could not precisely name.

'Mysterious thing,' said Clark to me, when we were alone.

'*I* don't understand it,' I said.

'Who are the two nurses?'

'Oh, highly recommended people of my own.'

'At any rate, my dream about you comes true, Jeffson. It is clear that Peters is out of the running now.'

I shrugged.

'I now formally invite you to join the expedition,' said Clark: 'do you consent?'

I shrugged again.

'Well, if that means consent,' he said, 'let me remind you that you have only eight days, and all the world to do in them.'

This conversation occurred in the dining-room of Peters' house: and as we passed through the door, I saw Clodagh gliding down the passage outside – rapidly – away from us.

Not a word I said to her that day about Clark's invitation. Yet I asked myself repeatedly: Did she not know of it? Had she not *listened*, and heard?

However that was, about midnight, to my great surprise, Peters opened his eyes, and smiled. By noon the next day, his fine vitality, which so fitted him for an Arctic expedition, had re-asserted itself. He was then leaning on an elbow, talking to Wilson, and except his pallor, and strong stomach-pains, there was now hardly a trace of his late approach to death. For the pains I prescribed some quarter-grain tablets of sulphate of morphia, and went away.

Now, David Wilson and I never greatly loved each other, and that very day he brought about a painful situation as between Peters and me, by telling Peters that I had taken his place in the expedition.

Peters, a touchy fellow, at once dictated a letter of protest to Clark; and Clark sent Peters' letter to me, marked with a big note of interrogation in blue pencil.

Now, all Peters' preparations were made, mine not; and he had six days in which to recover himself. I therefore wrote to

Clark, saying that the changed circumstances of course annulled my acceptance of his offer, though I had already incurred the inconvenience of negotiating with a *locum tenens*.

This decided it: Peters was to go, I stay. The fifth day before the departure dawned. It was a Friday, the 15th June. Peters was now in an arm-chair. He was cheerful, but with a fevered pulse, and still the stomach-pains. I was giving him three quarter-grains of morphia a day. That Friday night, at 11 P.M., I visited him, and found Clodagh there, talking to him. Peters was smoking a cigar.

'Ah,' Clodagh said, 'I was waiting for you, Adam. I didn't know whether I was to inject anything to-night. Is it Yes or No?'

'What do you think, Peters?' I said: 'any more pains?'

'Well, perhaps you had better give us another quarter,' he answered: 'there's still some trouble in the tummy off and on.'

'A quarter-grain, then, Clodagh,' I said.

As she opened the syringe-box, she remarked with a pout:

'Our patient has been naughty! He has taken some more atropine.'

I became angry at once.

'Peters,' I cried, 'you know you have no right to be doing things like that without consulting me! Do that once more, and I swear I have nothing further to do with you!'

'Rubbish,' said Peters: 'why all this unnecessary heat? It was a mere flea-bite. I felt that I needed it.'

'He injected it with his own hand...' remarked Clodagh.

She was now standing at the mantel-piece, having lifted the syringe-box from the night-table, taken from its velvet lining both the syringe and the vial containing the morphia tablets, and gone to the mantel-piece to melt one of the tablets in a little of the distilled water there. Her back was turned upon us, and she was a long time. I was standing; Peters in his arm-chair, smoking. Clodagh then began to talk about a Charity Bazaar which she had visited that afternoon.

She was long, she was long. The crazy thought passed through some dim region of my soul: 'Why is she so *long*?'

'Ah, that was a pain!' went Peters: 'never mind the bazaar, aunt – think of the morphia.'

Suddenly an irresistible impulse seized me – to rush upon her, to dash syringe, tabloids, glass, and all, from her hands. I *must* have obeyed it – I was on the tip-top point of obeying – my body already leant prone: but at that instant a voice at the opened door behind me said:

'Well, how is everything?'

It was Wilson, the electrician, who stood there. With lightning swiftness I remembered an under-look of mistrust which I had once seen on his face. Oh, well, I would not, and could not! – she was my love – I stood like marble…

Clodagh went to meet Wilson with frank right hand, in the left being the fragile glass containing the injection. My eyes were fastened on her face: it was full of reassurance, of free innocence. I said to myself: 'I must surely be mad!'

An ordinary chat began, while Clodagh turned up Peters' sleeve, and, kneeling there, injected his fore-arm. As she rose, laughing at something said by Wilson, the drug-glass dropped from her hand, and her heel, by an apparent accident, trod on it. She put the syringe among a number of others on the mantel-piece.

'Your friend has been naughty, Mr Wilson,' she said again with that same pout: 'he has been taking more atropine.'

'Not really?' said Wilson.

'Let me alone, the whole of you,' answered Peters: 'I ain't a child.'

These were the last intelligible words he ever spoke. He died shortly before 1 A.M. He had been poisoned by a powerful dose of atropine.*

From that moment to the moment when the *Boreal* bore me down the Thames, all the world was a mere tumbling nightmare to me, of which hardly any detail remains in my memory. Only I remember the inquest, and how I was called upon to prove that Peters had himself injected himself with atropine. This was corroborated by Wilson, and by Clodagh: and the verdict was in accordance.

And in all that chaotic hurry of preparation, three other things only, but those with clear distinctness now, I remember.

The first – and chief – is that tempest of words which I heard at Kensington from that big-mouthed Mackay on the Sunday night. What was it that led me, busy as I was, to that chapel that night? Well, perhaps I know.

There I sat, and heard him: and most strangely have those words of his peroration planted themselves in my brain, when, rising to a passion of prophecy, he shouted: 'And as in the one case, transgression was followed by catastrophe swift and universal, so, in the other, I warn the entire race to look out thenceforth for nothing from God but a low lowering sky, and thundery weather.'

And this second thing I remember:* that on reaching home, I walked into my disordered library (for I had had to hunt out some books), where I met my housekeeper in the act of rearranging things. She had apparently lifted an old Bible by the front cover to fling it on the table, for as I threw myself into a chair my eye fell upon the open print near the beginning. The print was very large, and a shaded lamp cast a light upon it. I had been hearing Mackay's wild comparison of the Pole with the tree of Eden, and that no doubt was the reason why such a start convulsed me: for my listless eyes had chanced to rest upon some words.

'The woman gave me of the tree, and I did eat...'*

And a third thing I remember in all that turmoil of doubt and flurry: that as the ship moved down with the afternoon tide a telegram was put into my hand; it was a last word from Clodagh; and she said only this:

'Be first – for Me.'*

The *Boreal* left St Katherine's Docks in beautiful weather on the afternoon of the 19th June,* full of good hope, bound for the Pole.

All about the docks was one region of heads stretched far in innumerable vagueness, and down the river to Woolwich a continuous dull roar and murmur of bees droned from both banks to cheer our departure.

The expedition was partly a national affair, subvented by Government; and if ever ship was well-found it was the *Boreal*. She had a frame tougher far than any battle-ship's, capable of ramming some ten yards of drift-ice; and she was stuffed with sufficient pemmican, cod-roe, fish-meal, and so on, to last us not less than six years.

We were seventeen, all told, the five Heads (so to speak) of the undertaking being Clark (our Chief), John Mew (commander), Aubrey Maitland (meteorologist), Wilson (electrician), and myself (doctor, botanist and assistant meteorologist).

The idea was to get as far east as the 100°, or the 120°, of longitude; to catch there the northern current; to push and drift our way northward; and when the ship could no further penetrate, to leave her (either three, or else four, of us, on ski), and with sledges drawn by dogs and reindeer make a dash for the Pole.

This had also been the plan of the last expedition – that of the *Nix** – and of several others. The *Boreal* only differed from the *Nix*, and others, in that she was a thing of nicer design, and of more exquisite forethought.

Our voyage was without incident up to the end of July, when we encountered a drift of ice-floes. On the 1st August we were at Kabarova, where we met our coal-ship, and took in a little coal for emergency, liquid air being our proper motor;* also forty-three dogs, four reindeer, and a quantity of reindeer-moss; and two days later we turned our bows finally northward and eastward, passing through heavy 'slack' ice under sail and liquid air in crisp weather, till, on the 27th August, we lay moored to a floe off the desolate island of Taimur.

The first thing which we saw here was a bear on the shore, watching for young whitefish: and promptly Clark, Mew, and Lamburn (engineer) went on shore in the launch, I and Maitland following in the pram, each party with three dogs.

It was while climbing away inland that Maitland said to me:

'When Clark leaves the ship for the dash to the Pole, it is three, not two, of us, after all, that he is going to take with him, making a party of four.'

I: 'Is that so? Who knows?'

Maitland: 'Wilson does. Clark has let it out in conversation with Wilson.'

I: 'Well, the more the merrier. Who will be the three?'

Maitland: 'Wilson is sure to be in it, and there may be Mew, making the third. As to the fourth, I suppose *I* shall get left out in the cold.'

I: 'More likely I.'

Maitland: 'Well, the race is between us four: Wilson, Mew, you and I. It is a question of physical fitness combined with special knowledge. You are too lucky a dog to get left out, Jeffson.'

I: 'Well, what does it matter, so long as the expedition as a whole is successful? That is the main thing.'

Maitland: 'Oh yes, that's all very fine talk, Jeffson! But is it quite sincere? Isn't it rather a pose to affect to despise $175,000,000? *I* want to be in at the death, and I mean to be, if I can. We are all more or less self-interested.'

'*Look*,' I whispered – 'a bear.'

It was a mother and cub: and with determined trudge she came wagging her low head, having no doubt smelled the dogs. We separated on the instant, doubling different ways behind ice-boulders, wanting her to go on nearer the shore, before killing; but, passing close, she spied, and bore down at a trot upon me. I fired into her neck, and at once, with a roar, she turned tail, making now straight in Maitland's direction. I saw him run out from cover some hundred yards away, aiming his long-gun: but no report followed: and in half a minute he was under her fore-paws, she striking out slaps at the barking, shrinking dogs. Maitland roared for my help: and at that moment, I, poor wretch, in far worse plight than he, stood shivering in ague: for suddenly one of those wrangles of the voices of my destiny was filling my bosom with loud commotion, one urging me to fly to Maitland's aid, one passionately commanding me be still. But it lasted, I believe, some seconds only: I ran and got a shot into the bear's brain, and Maitland leapt up with a rent down his face.

But singular destiny! Whatever I did – if I did evil, if I did good – the result was the same: tragedy dark and sinister! Poor Maitland was doomed that voyage, and my rescue of his life was the means employed to make his death the more certain.

I think that I have already written, some pages back, about a man called Scotland, whom I met at Cambridge. He was always talking about certain 'Black' and 'White' beings, and their contention for the earth. We others used to call him the black-and-white mystery-man, because, one day – but that is no matter now. Well, with regard to all that, I have a fancy, a whim of the mind – quite wide of the truth, no doubt – but I have it here in my brain, and I will write it down now. It is this: that there may have been some sort of arrangement, or understanding, between Black and White, as in the case of Adam and the fruit, that, should mankind force his way to the Pole and the old forbidden secret biding there, then some mishap should not fail to overtake the race of man; that the White, being kindly disposed to mankind, did not wish this to occur, and intended, for the sake of the race, to destroy our entire expedition before it reached; and that the Black, knowing that the White meant to do this, and by what means, used *me* – *me!* – to outwit this design, first of all working that I should be one of the party of four to leave the ship on ski.

But the childish attempt, my God, to read the immense riddle of the world! I could laugh loud at myself, and at poor Black-and-White Scotland, too. The thing can't be so simple.*

Well, we left Taimur the same day, and good-bye now to both land and open sea. Till we passed the latitude of Cape Chelyuskin (which we did not sight), it was one succession of ice-belts, with Mew in the crow's-nest tormenting the electric bell to the engine-room, the anchor hanging ready to drop, and Clark taking soundings. Progress was slow, and the Polar night gathered round us apace, as we stole still onward and onward into that blue and glimmering land of eternal frore. We now left off bed-coverings of reindeer-skin and took to sleeping-bags. Eight of the dogs had died by the 25th September, when we were experiencing 19° of frost. In the darkest part of our night, the Northern Light spread its silent solemn banner over us, quivering round the heavens in a million fickle gauds.

The relations between the members of our little crew were excellent – with one exception: David Wilson and I were not good friends.

There was a something – a tone – in the evidence which he had given at the inquest on Peters, which made me mad every time I thought of it. He had heard Peters admit just before death that he, Peters, had administered atropine to himself: and he had had to give evidence of that fact. But he had given it in a most half-hearted way, so much so, that the coroner had asked him: 'What, sir, are you hiding from me?' Wilson had replied: 'Nothing. I have nothing to tell.'

And from that day he and I had hardly exchanged ten words, in spite of our constant companionship in the vessel; and one day, standing alone on a floe, I found myself hissing with clenched fist: 'If he dared suspect Clodagh of poisoning Peters, I could *kill* him!'

Up to 78° of latitude the weather had been superb, but on the night of the 7th October – well I remember it – we experienced a great storm. Our tub of a ship rolled like a swing, drenching the whimpering dogs at every lurch, and hurling everything on board into confusion. The petroleum-launch was washed from the davits; down at one time to 40° below zero sank the thermometer; while a high aurora was whiffed into a dishevelled chaos of hues, resembling the smeared palette of some turbulent painter of the skies,* or mixed battle of long-robed seraphim, and looking the very symbol of tribulation, tempest, wreck and distraction. I, for the first time, was sick.

It was with a dizzy brain, therefore, that I went off watch to my bunk. Soon, indeed, I fell asleep: but the rolls and shocks of the ship, combined with the heavy Greenland anorak which I had on, and the state of my body, together produced a fearful nightmare, in which I was conscious of a vain struggle to move, a vain fight for breath, for the sleeping-bag turned to an iceberg on my bosom. Of Clodagh was my gasping dream. I dreamed that she let fall, drop by drop, a liquid, coloured like pomegranate-seeds,* into a glass of water; and she presented the glass to Peters. The draught, I knew, was poisonous as death: and in a last effort to break the bands of that dark slumber, I was conscious, as I jerked myself upright, of screaming aloud:

'Clodagh! Clodagh! *Spare the man...!*'

My eyes, starting with horror, opened to waking; the electric light was shining in the cabin; and there stood David Wilson looking at me.

Wilson was a big man, with a massively-built, long face, made longer by a beard, and he had little nervous contractions of the flesh at the cheek-bones, and plenty of big freckles. His clinging pose, his smile of disgust, his whole air, as he stood crouching and lurching there, I can shut my eyes, and see now.

What he was doing in my cabin I did not know. To think, my good God, that he should have been led there just then! This was one of the four-men starboard berths: *his* was a-port: yet there he was! But he explained at once.

'Sorry to interrupt your innocent dreams,' says he: 'the mercury in Maitland's thermometer is frozen, and he asked me to hand him his spirits-of-wine* one from his bunk…'

I did not answer. A hatred was in my heart against this man.

The next day the storm died away, and either three or four days later the slush-ice between the floes froze definitely. The *Boreal*'s way was thus blocked. We warped her with ice-anchors and the capstan into the position in which she should lay up for her winter's drift. This was at about 79° 20′ N. The sun had now totally vanished from our bleak sky, not to reappear till the following year.

Well, there was sledging with the dogs, and bear-hunting among the hummocks, as the months, one by one, went by. One day Wilson, by far our best shot, got a walrus-bull; Clark followed the traditional pursuit of a Chief, examining crustacea; Maitland and I were in a relation of close friendship, and I assisted his meteorological observations in a snow-hut built near the ship. Often, through the twenty-four hours, a clear blue moon, very spectral, very fair, suffused all our dim and livid clime.

It was five days before Christmas* that Clark made the great announcement: he had determined, he said, if our splendid northward drift continued, to leave the ship about the middle of next March for the dash to the Pole. He would take with him the four reindeer, all the dogs, four sledges, four kayaks, and three companions. The companions whom he had decided to invite were: Wilson, Mew and Maitland.

He said it at dinner; and as he said it, David Wilson glanced at my wan face with a smile of pleased malice: for *I* was left out.

I remember well: the aurora that night was in the sky, and at its edge floated a moon surrounded by a ring, with two mock-moons.* But all shone very vaguely and far, and a fog, which had already lasted some days, made the ship's bows indistinct to me, as I paced the bridge on my watch, two hours after Clark's announcement.

For a long time all was very still, save for the occasional whine of a dog. I was alone, and it grew toward the end of my watch, when Maitland would succeed me. My slow tread tolled like a passing-bell, and the mountainous ice lay vague and white around me, its sheeted ghastliness not less dreadfully silent than eternity itself.

Presently, several of the dogs began barking together, left off, and began again. I said to myself: 'There is a bear about some-where.'

And after some five minutes I saw – I thought that I saw – it. The fog had, if anything thickened; and it was now very near the end of my watch.

It had entered the ship, I concluded, by the boards which slanted from an opening in the port bulwarks down to the ice. Once before, in November, a bear, having smelled the dogs, had ventured on board at midnight: but *then* there had resulted a perfect hubbub among the dogs. *Now*, even in the midst of my excitement, I wondered at their quietness, though some whim-pered – with fear, I thought. I saw the creature steal forward from the hatchway toward the kennels a-port; and I ran noise-lessly, and seized the watch-gun* which stood always loaded by the companion-way.

By this time, the form had passed the kennels, reached the bows, and now was making toward me on the starboard side. I took aim. Never, I thought, had I seen so huge a bear – though I made allowance for the magnifying effect of the fog.

My finger was on the trigger: and at that moment a deathly shivering sickness took me, the wrangling voices shouted at me, with 'Shoot!' 'Shoot not!' 'Shoot!' Ah well, that latter shout was irresistible. I drew the trigger. The report hooted through the Polar night.

The creature dropped; both Wilson and Clark were up at once: and we three hurried to the spot.

But the very first near glance showed a singular kind of bear. Wilson put his hand to the head, and a lax skin came away at his touch ... It was Aubrey Maitland who was underneath it, and I had shot him dead.

For the past few days he had been cleaning skins, among them the skin of the bear from which I had saved him at Taimur. Now, Maitland was a born pantomimist, continually inventing practical jokes; and perhaps to startle me with a false alarm in the very skin of the old Bruin which had so nearly done for him, he had thrown it round him on finishing its cleaning, and so, in mere wanton fun, had crept on deck at the hour of his watch. The head of the bear-skin, and the fog, must have prevented him from seeing me taking aim.

This tragedy made me ill for weeks. I saw that the hand of Fate was upon me. When I rose from bed, poor Maitland was lying in the ice behind the great camel-shaped hummock near us.

By the end of January we had drifted to 80° 55′; and it was then that Clark, in the presence of Wilson, asked me if I would make the fourth man, in the place of poor Maitland, for the dash in the spring. As I said 'Yes, I am willing,' David Wilson spat with a disgusted emphasis. A minute later he sighed, with 'Ah, poor Maitland...' and drew in his breath with a *tut! tut!*

God knows, I had an impulse to spring then and there at his throat, and strangle him: but I curbed myself.

There remained now hardly a month before the dash, and all hands set to work with a will, measuring the dogs, making harness and seal-skin shoes for them, overhauling sledges and kayaks, and cutting every possible ounce of weight. But we were not destined, after all, to set out that year. About the 20th February, the ice began to pack, and the ship was subjected to an appalling pressure. We found it necessary to make trumpets of our hands to shout into one another's ears, for the whole ice-continent was crashing, popping, thundering everywhere in terrific upheaval. Expecting every moment to see the *Boreal* crushed to splinters, we had to set about unpacking provisions, and placing sledges, kayaks, dogs and everything in a position for instant flight. It lasted five days, and was accompanied by a tempest from the north, which, by the end of February, had driven us back south into latitude 79° 40'. Clark, of course, then abandoned the thought of the Pole for that summer.

And immediately afterwards we made a startling discovery: our stock of reindeer-moss was found to be somehow ridiculously small. Egan, our second mate, was blamed; but that did not help matters: the sad fact remained. Clark was advised to kill one or two of the deer, but he pig-headedly refused: and by the beginning of summer they were all dead.

Well, our northward drift recommenced. Toward the middle of February we saw a mirage of the coming sun above the horizon; there were flights of Arctic petrels and snow-buntings;* and spring was with us. In an ice-pack of big hummocks and narrow lanes we made good progress all the summer.

When the last of the deer died, my heart sank; and when the dogs killed two of their number, and a bear crushed a third, I was fully expecting what actually came; it was this: Clark announced that he could now take only two companions with him in the spring: and they were Wilson and Mew. So once more I saw David Wilson's pleased smile of malice.

We settled into our second winter-quarters. Again came December, and all our drear sunless gloom, made worse by the fact that the wind-mill would not work, leaving us without the electric light.

Ah me, none but those who have felt it could dream of one half the mental depression of that long Arctic night; how the soul takes on the hue of the world; and without and within is nothing but gloom, gloom, and the reign of the Power of Darkness.

Not one of us but was in a melancholic, dismal and dire mood; and on the 13th December Lamburn, the engineer, stabbed Cartwright, the old harpooner, in the arm.

Three days before Christmas a bear came close to the ship, and then turned tail. Mew, Wilson, I and Meredith (a general hand) set out in pursuit. After a pretty long chase we lost him, and then scattered different ways. It was very dim, and after yet an hour's search, I was returning weary and disgusted to the ship, when I saw some shadow like a bear sailing away on my left, and at the same time sighted a man – I did not know whom – running like a handicapped ghost some little distance to the right. So I shouted out:

'There he is – come on! This way!'

The man quickly joined me, but as soon as ever he recognised me, stopped dead. The devil must have suddenly got into him, for he said:

'No, thanks, Jeffson: alone with you I am in danger of my life...'

It was Wilson. And I, too, forgetting at once all about the bear, stopped and faced him.

'I see,' said I. 'But, Wilson, you are going to explain to me *now* what you mean, you hear? What *do* you mean, Wilson?'

'What I say,' he answered deliberately, eyeing me up and down: 'alone with you I am in danger of my life. Just as poor Maitland was, and just as poor Peters was. Certainly, you are a deadly beast.'

Fury leapt, my God, in my heart. Black as the tenebrous Arctic night was my soul.

'Do you mean,' said I, 'that I want to put you out of the way in order to go in your place to the Pole? Is that your meaning, man?'

'That's about my meaning, Jeffson,' says he: 'you are a deadly beast, you know.'

'Stop!' I said, with blazing eye. 'I am going to kill *you*, Wilson – as sure as God lives: but I want to hear first. Who *told* you that I killed Peters?'

'Your lover killed him – with *your* collusion. Why, I heard you, man, in your beastly sleep, calling the whole thing out. And I was pretty sure of it before, only I had no proofs. By God, I should enjoy putting a bullet into you, Jeffson!'

'You wrong me – you, you wrong me!' I shrieked, my eyes staring with ravenous lust for his blood; 'and now I am going to pay you well for it. *Look out, you!*'

I aimed my gun for his heart, and I touched the trigger. He held up his left hand.

'Stop,' he said, 'stop.' (He was one of the coolest of men ordinarily.) 'There is no gallows on the *Boreal*, but Clark could easily rig one for you. I want to kill you, too, because there are no criminal courts up here, and it would be doing a good action for my country. But not here – not now. Listen to me – don't shoot. Later we can meet, when all is ready, so that no one may be the wiser, and fight it all out.'

As he spoke I let the gun drop. It was better so. I knew that he was much the best shot on the ship, and I an indifferent one: but I did not care, I did not care, if I was killed.

It is a dim, inclement land, God knows: and the spirit of darkness and distraction is there.

Twenty hours later we met behind the great saddle-shaped hummock, some six miles to the S.E. of the ship. We had set out at different times, so that no one might suspect. And each brought a ship's-lantern.

Wilson had dug an ice-grave near the hummock, leaving at its edge a heap of brash-ice and snow to fill it. We stood separated by an interval of perhaps seventy yards, the grave between us, each with a lantern at his feet.

Even so we were mere shadowy apparitions one to the other. The air glowered very drearily, and present in my inmost soul were the frills of cold. A chill moon, a mere abstraction of light, seemed to hang far outside the universe. The temperature was at 55° below zero, so that we had on wind-clothes over our anoraks, and heavy foot-bandages under our Lap boots. Nothing but a weird morgue seemed the world, haunted with despondent madness; and exactly like that world about us were the minds of us two poor men, full of macabre, bleak and funereal feelings.

Between us yawned an early grave for one or other of our bodies.

I heard Wilson cry out:

'Are you ready, Jeffson?'

'Aye, Wilson!' cried I.

'*Then here goes!*' cries he.

Even as he spoke, he fired. Surely, the man was in deadly earnest to kill me.

But his shot passed harmlessly by me: as indeed was only likely: we were mere shadows one to the other.

I fired perhaps ten seconds later than he:* but in those ten seconds he stood perfectly revealed to me in clear, lavender light.

An Arctic fire-ball had traversed the sky,* showering abroad a sulphurous glamour over the snow-landscape. Before the intenser blue of its momentary shine had passed away, I saw Wilson stagger forward, and drop. And him and his lantern I buried deep there under the rubble ice.

On the 13th March,* nearly three months later, Clark, Mew and I left the *Boreal* in latitude 85° 15′.

We had with us thirty-two dogs, three sledges, three kayaks, human provisions for 112 days, and dog provisions for 40. Being now about 340 miles from the Pole, we hoped to reach it in 43 days, then, turning south, and feeding living dogs with dead, make either Franz Josef Land or Spitzbergen, at which latter place we should very likely come up with a whaler.

Well, during the first days, progress was very slow, the ice being rough and laney, and the dogs behaving most badly, stopping dead at every difficulty, and leaping over the traces. Clark had had the excellent idea of attaching a gold-beater's-skin balloon, with a lifting power of 35 pounds, to each sledge, and we had with us a supply of zinc and sulphuric-acid to repair the hydrogen-waste from the bags; but on the third day Mew overfilled and burst his balloon, and I and Clark had to cut ours loose in order to equalise weights, for we could neither leave him behind, turn back to the ship, nor mend the bag. So it happened that at the end of the fourth day out, we had made only nineteen miles, and could still from a hummock discern afar the leaning masts of the old *Boreal*. Clark led on ski, captaining a sledge with 400 lbs. of instruments, ammunition, pemmican, aleuronate bread;* Mew followed, his sledge containing provisions only; and last came I, with a mixed freight. But on the third day Clark had an attack of snow-blindness, and Mew took his place.

Pretty soon our sufferings commenced, and they were bitter enough. The sun, though constantly visible day and night, gave no heat. Our sleeping-bags (Clark and Mew slept together in one, I in another) were soaking wet all the night, being thawed by our warmth; and our fingers, under wrappings of senne-grass and wolf-skin, were always bleeding. Sometimes our frail bamboo-cane kayaks, lying across the sledges, would crash perilously against an ice-ridge – and they were our one hope of reaching land. But the dogs were the great difficulty: we lost six mortal hours a day in harnessing and tending them. On the twelfth day Clark took a single-altitude observation, and found that we were only in latitude 86° 45′; but the next day we passed beyond the furthest point yet reached by man, viz. 86° 53′, attained by the *Nix* explorers four years previously.*

Our one secret thought now was food, food – our day-long lust for the eating-time. Mew suffered from 'Arctic thirst'.*

Under these conditions, man becomes in a few days, not a savage only, but a mere beast, hardly a grade above the bear and walrus. Ah, the ice! A long and sordid nightmare was that, God knows.

On we pressed, crawling our little way across the Vast, upon whose hoar silence, from Eternity until then, Böotes only, and that Great Bear,* had watched.

After the eleventh day our rate of march improved: all lanes disappeared, and ridges became much less frequent. By the fif-teenth day I was leaving behind the ice-grave of David Wilson at the rate of ten to thirteen miles a day.

Yet, as it were, his arm reached out and touched me, even there.

His disappearance had been explained by a hundred differ-ent guesses on the ship – all plausible enough. I had no idea that anyone connected me in any way with his death.

But on our twenty-second day of march, 140 miles from our goal, he caused a conflagration of rage and hate to break out among us three.

It was at the end of a march, when our stomachs were hollow, our frames ready to drop, and our mood ravenous and inflamed. One of Mew's dogs was sick: it was necessary to kill it: he asked me to do it.

'Oh,' said I, 'you kill your own dog, of course.'

'Well, I don't know,' he replied, catching fire at once, 'you ought to be used to killing, Jeffson.'

'How do you mean, Mew?' said I with a mad start, for madness and the flames of Hell were instant and uppermost in us all: 'you mean because my profession—'

'Profession! damn it, no,' he snarled like a dog: 'go and dig up David Wilson – I dare say you know where to find him – and *he* will tell you my meaning, right enough.'

I rushed at once to Clark, who was stooping among the dogs, unharnessing: and savagely pushing his shoulder, I exclaimed:

'That beast accuses me of murdering David Wilson!'

'Well?' said Clark.

'I'd split his skull as clean—!'

'Go away, Adam Jeffson, and let me be!' snarled Clark.

'Is that all you've got to say about it, then – you?'

'To the devil with you, man, say I, and let me be!' cried he: '*you know your own conscience best*, I suppose.'

Before this insult I stood with grinding teeth, but impotent. However, from that moment a deeper mood of brooding malice occupied my spirit. Indeed the humour of us all was one of dangerous, even murderous, fierceness. In that pursuit of riches into that region of cold, we had become almost like the beasts that perish.

On the 10th April we passed the 89th parallel of latitude, and though sick to death, both in spirit and body, pressed still on. Like the lower animals, we were stricken now with dumbness, and hardly once in a week spoke a word one to the other, but in selfish brutishness on through a real hell of cold we moved. It is a cursed region – beyond doubt cursed – not meant to be penetrated by man: and rapid and awful was the degeneration of our souls. As for me, never could I have conceived that savagery so heinous could brood in a human bosom as now I felt it brood in mine. If men could enter into a country specially set apart for the habitation of devils, and there become possessed of evil, as we were so would they be.

As we advanced, the ice every day became smoother; so that, from four miles a day, our rate increased to fifteen, and finally (as the sledges lightened) to twenty.

It was now that we began to encounter a succession of strange-looking objects lying scattered over the ice, whose number continually increased as we proceeded. They had the appearance of rocks, or pieces of iron, incrusted with glass-fragments of various colours, and they were of every size. Their incrustations we soon determined to be diamonds, and other precious stones. On our first twenty-mile day Mew picked up a diamond-crystal as large as a child's foot,* and such objects soon became common. We thus found the riches which we sought, beyond all dream; but as the bear and the walrus find them: for ourselves we had lost; and it was a loss of riches barren as ashes, for for all those millions we would not have given an ounce of fish-meal. Clark grumbled something about their being meteor-stones, whose ferruginous substance had been lured by the magnetic Pole, and kept from frictional burning in their fall by the frigidity of the air:* and they quickly ceased to interest our sluggish minds, except in so far as they obstructed our way.

We had all along had good weather: till, suddenly, on the morning of the 13th April, we were overtaken by a tempest from the S.W., of such mighty and solemn volume that the heart quailed beneath it. It lasted in its full power only an hour, but during that time snatched two of our sledges long distances, and compelled us to lie face-downward. We had travelled all the sun-lit night, and were gasping with fatigue; so as soon as the wind allowed us to huddle together our scattered things, we crawled into the sleeping-bags, and instantly slept.

We knew that the ice was in awful upheaval around us; we heard, as our eyelids sweetly closed, the slow booming of distant guns, and brittle cracklings of artillery. This may have been a result of the tempest stirring up the ocean beneath the ice. Whatever it was, we did not care: we slept deep.

We were within ten miles of the Pole.*

In my sleep it was as though someone suddenly shook my shoulder with urgent '*Up! up!*' It was neither Clark nor Mew, but a dream merely: for Clark and Mew, when I started up, I saw lying still in their sleeping-bag.

I suppose it must have been about noon. I sat staring a minute, and my first numb thought was somehow this: that the Countess Clodagh had prayed me 'Be first' – for her. Wondrous little now cared I for the Countess Clodagh in her far unreal world of warmth – precious little for the fortune which she coveted: millions on millions of fortunes lay unregarded around me. But that thought, *Be first!* was deeply suggested in my brain, as if whispered there. Instinctively, brutishly, as the Gadarean swine* rushed down a steep place, I, rubbing my daft eyes,* arose.

The first thing which my mind opened to perceive was that, while the tempest was less strong, the ice was now in extraordinary agitation. I looked abroad upon a vast plain, stretched out to a circular, but waving horizon, and varied by many hillocks, boulders, and sparkling meteor-stones that everywhere tinselled the blinding white, some big as houses, most small as limbs. And this great plain was now rearranging itself in a widespread drama of havoc, withdrawing in ravines like mutual backing curtsies, then surging to clap together in passionate mountain-peaks, else jostling like the Symplegades,* fluent and inconstant as billows of the sea, grinding itself, piling itself, pouring itself in cataracts of powdered ice, while here and there I saw the meteor-stones leap spasmodically, in dusts and heaps, like geysers or spurting froths in a steamer's wake, a tremendous uproar, meantime, filling all the air. As I stood, I plunged and staggered, and I found the dogs sprawling, with whimperings, on the heaving floor.

I did not care. Instinctively, daftly, brutishly, I harnessed ten of them to my sledge; put on Canadian snow-shoes: and was away northward – alone.

The sun shone with a clear, benign, but heatless shining: a ghostly, remote, yet quite limpid light, which seemed designed for the lighting of other planets and systems, and to strike here by happy chance. A great wind from the S.W., meantime, sent thin snow-sweepings flying northward past me.

The odometer which I had with me had not yet measured four miles, when I began to notice two things: first that the jewelled meteor-stones were now accumulating beyond all limit, filling my range of vision to the northern horizon with a dazzling glister: in mounds, and parterres, and scattered disconnection they lay, like largesse of autumn leaves, spread out over those Elysian fields and fairy uplands of wealth, trillions of billions, so that I had need to steer my twining way among them. Now, too, I noticed that, but for these stones, all roughness had disappeared, not a trace of the upheaval going on a little further south being here, for the ice lay positively as smooth as a table before me. It is my belief that this stretch of smooth ice has never, never felt one shock, or stir, or throe, and reaches right down to the bottom of the deep.

And now with a wild hilarity I flew. Gradually, a dizziness, a lunacy, had seized upon me, till finally, up-buoyed on air, and dancing mad, I sped, I spun, with grinning teeth that chattered and gibbered, and eyeballs of distraction: for a Fear, too – most cold and dreadful – had its hand of ice upon my heart, I being so alone in that place, face to face with the Ineffable: but still, with a giddy levity, and a fatal joy, and a blind hilarity, on I sped, I spun.

The odometer measured nine miles from my start. I was in the immediate neighbourhood of the Pole.

I cannot say when it began, but now I was conscious of a sound in my ears, distinct and near, a steady sound of splashing, or fluttering, resembling the noising of a cascade or brook: and it grew. Forty more steps I took (slide I could not now for the meteorites) – perhaps sixty – perhaps eighty: and now, to my sudden horror, I stood by a circular clean-cut lake.*

One minute only, swaying and nodding there, I stood: and then I dropped down flat in swoon.

*

In a hundred years, I suppose, I should never succeed in analysing *why* I swooned: but my consciousness still retains the
impression of that horrid thrill. I saw nothing distinctly, for my
whole being reeled and toppled drunken, like a spinning-top in
desperate death-struggle at the moment when it flags, and wob-
bles dissolutely to fall; but the very instant that my eyes met
what was before me, I knew, I knew, that here was the Sanctity
of Sanctities, the old eternal inner secret of the Life of this
Earth, which it was a most burning shame for a man to see.*
The lake, I fancy, must be a mile across, and in its middle is a
pillar of ice, very low and broad; and I had the clear impression, or dream, or notion, that there was a name, or word,
graven all round in the ice of the pillar in characters which I
could never read; and under the name a long date; and the fluid
of the lake seemed to me to be wheeling with a shivering ecstasy,
splashing and fluttering, round the pillar, always from west to
east, in the direction of the spinning of the earth; and it was
borne in upon me – I can't at all say how – that this fluid was
the substance of a living creature; and I had the distinct fancy,
as my senses failed, that it was a creature with many dull and
anguished eyes, and that, as it wheeled for ever round in fluttering lust, it kept its eyes always turned upon the name and the
date graven in the pillar. But this must be my madness...

It must have been not less than an hour before a sense of life
returned to me; and when the thought stabbed my brain that a
long, long time I had lain there in the presence of those gloomy
orbs, my spirit seemed to groan and die within me.

In some minutes, however, I had scrambled to my feet,
clutched at a dog's harness, and without one backward glance,
was flying from that place.

Half-way to the halting-place, I waited Clark and Mew,
being very sick and doddering, and unable to advance. But they
did not come.

Later on, when I gathered force to go further, I found that
they had perished in the upheaval of the ice. One only of the
sledges, half buried, I saw near the spot of our bivouac.

*

Alone that same day I began my way southward, and for five days made good progress. On the eighth day I noticed, stretched right across the south-eastern horizon, a region of purple vapour which luridly obscured the face of the sun: and day after day I saw it steadily brooding there. But what it could be I did not understand.*

Well, onward through the desert ice* I continued my lonely way, with a baleful shrinking terror in my heart; for very stupendous, alas! is the burden of that Arctic solitude upon one poor human soul.

Sometimes on a halt I have lain and listened long to the hollow silence, recoiling, crushed by it, hoping that at least one of the dogs might whine. I have even crept shivering from the thawed sleeping-bag to flog a dog, so that I might hear a sound.

I had started from the Pole with a well-filled sledge, and the sixteen dogs left alive from the ice-packing which buried my comrades. This was on the evening of the 13th April. I had saved from the wreck of our things most of the whey-powder, pemmican, &c., as well as the theodolite, compass, chronometer, train-oil lamp for cooking, and other implements: I was therefore in no doubt as to my course, and I had provisions for ninety days. But ten days from the start my supply of dog-food failed, and I had to begin to slaughter my only companions, one by one.

Well, in the third week the ice became horribly rough, and with moil and toil enough to wear a bear to death, I did only five miles a day. After the day's work I would crawl with a dying sigh into the sleeping-bag, clad still in the load of skins which stuck to me a mere filth of grease, to sleep the sleep of a swine, indifferent if I never woke.

Always – day after day – on the southeastern horizon, brooded sullenly that curious stretched-out region of purple vapour, like the smoke of the conflagration of the world. And I noticed that its length constantly reached out and out, and silently grew.

Once I had a very pleasant dream. I dreamed that I was in a

garden – an Arabian paradise – so sweet was the perfume. All the time, however, I had a sub-consciousness of the gale which was actually blowing from the S.E. over the ice, and, at the moment when I awoke, was half-wittedly droning to myself: 'It is a Garden of Peaches; but I am not really in the garden: I am really on the ice; only, the S.E. storm is wafting to me the aroma of this Garden of Peaches.'

I opened my eyes – I started – I sprang to my feet! For, of all the miracles! – I could not doubt – an actual aroma like peach-blossom *was* in the algid air about me!*

Before I could collect my astonished senses, I began to vomit pretty violently, and at the same time saw some of the dogs, mere skeletons as they were, vomiting, too. For a long time I lay very sick in a kind of daze, and, on rising, found two of the dogs dead, and all very queer. The wind had now changed to the north.

Well, on I staggered, fighting every inch of my deplorably weary way. This odour of peach-blossom, my sickness, and the death of the two dogs, remained a wonder to me.

Two days later, to my extreme mystification (and joy), I came across a bear and its cub lying dead at the foot of a hummock. I could not believe my eyes. There she lay on her right side, a spot of dirty-white in a disordered patch of snow, with one little eye open, and her fierce-looking mouth also; and the cub lay across her haunch, biting into her rough fur. I set to work upon her, and allowed the dogs a glorious feed on the blubber, while I myself had a great banquet on the fresh meat. I had to leave the greater part of the two carcasses, and I can feel again now the hankering reluctance – quite unnecessary, as it turned out – with which I trudged onwards. Again and again I found myself asking: 'Now, what could have killed those two bears?'

With brutish stolidness I plodded ever on, almost like a walking machine, sometimes nodding in sleep while I helped the dogs, or manoeuvred the sledge over an ice-ridge, pushing or pulling. On the 3rd June, a month and a half from my start, I took an observation with the theodolite, and found that I was not yet 400 miles from the Pole, in latitude 84° 50'. It was just as though some Will, some Will, was obstructing and retarding me.

However, the intolerable cold was over, and soon my clothes no longer hung stark on me like armour. Pools began to appear in the ice, and presently, what was worse, my God, long lanes, across which, somehow, I had to get the sledge. But about the same time all fear of starvation passed away: for on the 6th June I came across another dead bear, on the 7th three, and thenceforth, in rapidly growing numbers, I met not bears only, but fulmars, guillemots, snipes, Ross's gulls, little awks – all, all, lying dead on the ice. And never anywhere a living thing, save me, and the two remaining dogs.

If ever a poor man stood shocked before a mystery, it was I now. I had a big fear on my heart.

On the 2nd July the ice began packing dangerously, and soon another storm broke loose upon me from the S.W. I left off my trek, and put up the silk tent on a five-acre square of ice surrounded by lanes: and *again* – for the second time – as I lay down, I smelled that delightful strange odour of peach-blossom, a mere whiff of it, and presently afterwards was taken sick. However, it passed off this time in a couple of hours.

Now it was all lanes, lanes, alas! yet no open water, and such was the difficulty and woe of my life, that sometimes I would drop flat on the ice, and sob: 'Oh, no more, no more, my God: here let me die.' The crossing of a lane might occupy ten or twelve entire hours, and then, on the other side I might find another one opening right before me. Moreover, on the 8th July, one of the dogs, after a feed on blubber, suddenly died; and there was left me only 'Reinhardt', a white-haired Siberian dog, with little pert up-sticking ears,* like a cat's. Him, too, I had to kill on coming to open water.

This did not happen till the 3rd August, nearly four months from the Pole.

I can't think, my God, that any heart of man ever tholed the appalling nightmare and black abysm of sensations in which, during those four long desert months, I weltered: for though I was as a brute, I had a man's heart to feel. What I had seen, or dreamed, at the Pole followed and followed me; and if I shut my poor weary eyes to sleep, those others yonder seemed to watch me still with their distraught and gloomy gaze, and in my spinning dark dreams spun that eternal ecstasy of the lake.

However, by the 28th July I knew from the look of the sky, and the absence of fresh-water ice, that the sea could not be far; so I set to work, and spent two days in putting to rights the now battered kayak. This done, I had no sooner resumed my way than I sighted far off a streaky haze, which I knew to be the basalt cliffs of Franz Josef Land; and in a craziness of joy I stood there, waving my ski-staff about my head, with the senile cheers of a very old man.

In four days this land was visibly nearer, sheer basaltic cliffs mixed with glacier, forming apparently a great bay, with two small islands in the mid-distance; and at fore-day of the 3rd August I arrived at the definite edge of the pack-ice in moderate weather at about the freezing-point.

I at once, but with great reluctance, shot Reinhardt, and set to work to get the last of the provisions, and the most necessary of the implements, into the kayak, making haste to put out to the toilless luxury of being borne on the water, after all the weary trudge. Within fourteen hours I was coasting, with my little lug-sail spread, along the shore-ice of that land. It was midnight of a calm Sabbath, and low on the horizon smoked the drowsing red sun-ball, as my canvas skiff lightly chopped her little way through this silent sea. Silent, silent: for neither snort of walrus, nor yelp of fox, nor cry of startled kittiwake, did I hear: but all was still as the jet-black shadow of the cliffs and glacier on the tranquil sea: and many bodies of dead things strewed the surface of the water.

When I found a little fjord, I went up it to the end where stood a stretch of basalt columns, looking like a shattered temple of Antediluvians;* and when my foot at last touched land, I sat down there a long, long time in the rubbly snow, and silently wept. My eyes that night were like a fountain of tears. For the firm land is health and sanity, and dear to the life of man; but I say that the great ungenial ice is a nightmare, and a blasphemy, and madness, and the realm of the Power of Darkness.

*

I knew that I was at Franz Josef Land, somewhere or other in the neighbourhood of C. Fligely (about 82° N.) and though it was so late, and getting cold, I still had the hope of reaching Spitzbergen that year, by alternately sailing all open water, and dragging the kayak over the slack drift-ice. All the ice which I saw was good flat fjord-ice, and the plan seemed feasible enough; so after coasting about a little and then three days' good rest in the tent at the bottom of a ravine of columnar basalt opening upon the shore, I packed some bear and walrus flesh, with what artificial food was left, into the kayak, and I set out early in the morning, coasting the shore-ice with sail and paddle. In the afternoon I managed to climb a little way up an iceberg, and made out that I was in a bay whose terminating headlands were invisible. I accordingly decided to make S.W. by W. to cross it, but in doing so, I was hardly out of sight of land, when a northern storm overtook me toward midnight; before I could think, the little sail was all but whiffed away, and the kayak upset. I only saved it by the happy chance of being near a floe with an ice-foot, which, projecting under the water, gave me foot-hold; and I lay on the floe in a mooning state the whole night under the storm, for I was half drowned.

And at once, on recovering myself, I abandoned all thought of whalers and of Europe for that year. Happily, my instruments, &c., had been saved by the kayak-deck when she capsized.

A hundred yards inland from the shore-rim, in a circular place where there was some moss and soil, I built myself a semi-subterranean Eskimo den for the long Polar night.* The spot was quite surrounded by high sloping walls of basalt, except to the west, where they opened in a three-foot cleft to the shore, and the ground was strewn with slabs and boulders of granite and basalt. I found there a dead she-bear, two well-grown cubs, and a fox, the latter having evidently fallen from the cliffs; in three places the snow was quite red, overgrown with a red lichen, which at first I took for blood. I did not even yet feel secure from possible bears, and took care to make my den fairly tight, a work which occupied me nearly four weeks, for I had no tools, save a hatchet, knife and metal-shod ski-staff. I dug a passage in the ground two feet wide, two deep, and ten long, with perpendicular sides, and at its north end a circular space, twelve feet across, also with perpendicular sides, which I lined with stones; the whole excavation I covered with inch-thick walrus-hide, skinned during a whole bitter week from four of a number that lay about the shore-ice; for ridge-pole I used a thin pointed rock which I found near, though, even so, the roof remained nearly flat. This, when it was finished, I stocked well, putting in everything, except the kayak, blubber to serve both for fuel and occasional light, and foods of several sorts, which I procured by merely stretching out the hand. The roof of both circular part and passage was soon buried under snow and ice, and hardly distinguishable from the general level of the white-clad ground. Through the passage, if I passed in or out, I crawled flat, on hands and knees: but that was rare: and in the little round interior, mostly sitting in a cowering attitude, I win-tered, harkening to the large and windy ravings of darkling December storms above me.

All those months the burden of a thought bowed me; and an unanswered question, like the slow turning of a mechanism, revolved in my gloomy spirit: for everywhere around me lay bears, walruses, foxes, thousands upon thousands of little awks, kittiwakes, snow-owls, eider-ducks, gulls – dead, dead. Almost the only living things which I saw were some walruses on the drift-floes: but very few compared with the number which I expected. It was clear to me that some inconceivable catas-trophe had overtaken the island during the summer, destroying all life about it, except some few of the amphibia, cetacea and crustacea.

On the 5th December, having crept out from the den during a southern storm, I had, for the third time, a distant whiff of that self-same odour of peach-blossom: but now without any after-effects.

Well, again came Christmas, the New Year – Spring: and on the 22nd May I set out with a well-stocked kayak. The water was fairly open, and the ice so good, that at one place I could sail the kayak over it, the wind sending me sliding at a fine pace. Being on the west coast of Franz Josef Land, I was in as favourable a situation as possible, and I turned my bow southward with much hope, keeping a good many days just in sight of land. Toward the evening of my third day out I noticed a large flat floe, presenting far-off a singular and lovely sight, for it seemed freighted thick with a profusion of pink and white roses, showing in its clear crystal the empurpled reflection. On getting near I saw that it was covered with millions of Ross's gulls, all dead, whose pretty rosy bosoms had given it that appearance.

Up to the 29th June I made good progress southward and westward (the weather being mostly excellent), sometimes meeting dead bears, floating away on floes, sometimes dead or living walrus-herds, with troop after troop of dead kittiwakes, glaucus and ivory gulls, skuas, and every kind of Arctic fowl. On that last day – the 29th June – I was about to encamp on a floe soon after midnight, when, happening to look toward the sun, my eye fell, far away south across the ocean of floes, upon something – *the masts of a ship.**

A phantom ship, or a real ship: it was all one; real, I must have instantly felt, it could not be: but at a sight so incredible my heart set to beating in my bosom as though I must surely die, and feebly waving the cane oar about my head, I staggered to my knees, and thence with wry mouth toppled flat.

So overpoweringly sweet was the thought of springing once more, like the beasts of Circe, from a walrus into a man. At this time I was tearing my bear's-meat just like a bear; I was washing my hands in walrus-blood to produce a glairy sort of pink cleanliness, in place of the black grease which chronically coated them.

Worn as I was, I made little delay to set out for that ship; and I had not travelled over water and ice four hours when, to my indescribable joy, I made out from the top of a steep floe that she was the *Boreal*. It seemed most strange that she should be anywhere hereabouts: I could only conclude that she must have forced and drifted her way thus far westward out of the ice-block in which our party had left her, and perhaps now was loitering here in the hope of picking us up on our way to Spitzbergen.

In any case, wild was the haste with which I fought my way to be at her, my gasping mouth all the time drawn back in a *rictus* of laughter at the anticipation of their gladness to see me, their excitement to hear the grand tidings of the Pole attained. Anon I waved the paddle, though I knew that they could not yet see me, and then I dug deep at the whitish water. What astonished me was her main-sail and fore-mast square-sail – set that calm morning; and her screws were still, for she moved not at all. The sun was abroad like a cold spirit of light, touching the great ocean-room of floes with dazzling spots, and a tint almost of rose was on the world, as it were of a just-dead bride in her spangles and white array. The *Boreal* was the one little distant jet-black spot in all this purity: and upon her, as though she were Heaven, I paddled, I panted. But she was in a queerish state: by 9 A.M. I could see that. Two of the windmill arms were not there, and half lowered down her starboard beam a boat hung askew; moreover, soon after 10 I could clearly see that her main-sail had a long rent down the middle.

I could not at all make her out. She was not anchored, though a sheet-anchor hung over at the starboard cathead; she was not moored; and two small ice-floes, one on each side, were sluggishly bombarding her bows.

I began now to wave the paddle, battling for my breath, ecstatic, crazy with excitement, each second like a year to me. Very soon I could make out someone at the bows, leaning well over, looking my way. Something put it into my head that it was Sallitt,* and I began impassioned shouting. 'Hi! Sallitt! Hallo! Hi!' I called.

I did not see him move: I was still a good way off: but there he stood, leaning steadily over, looking my way. Between me and the ship now was all navigable water among the floes, and the sight of him so visibly near put into me such a shivering eagerness, that I was nothing else but a madman for the time, sending the kayak flying with venomous digs in quick-repeated spurts, and mixing with the diggings my crazy wavings, and with both the daft shoutings of 'Hallo! Hi! Bravo! *I have been to the Pole!'*

Well, vanity, vanity. Nearer still I drew: it was broad morning, going on toward noon: I was half a mile away, I was fifty yards. But on board the *Boreal*, though now they *must* have heard me, seen me, I observed no movement of welcome, but all, all was still as death that still Arctic morning, my God. Only, the ragged sail flapped a little, and – one on each side – two ice-floes sluggishly bombarded the bows, with hollow sounds.

I was certain now that Sallitt it was who looked across the ice: but when the ship swung a little round, I noticed that the direction of his gaze was carried with her movement, he no longer looking my way.

'Why, Sallitt!' I shouted reproachfully: 'why, Sallitt, man...!' I whined.

But even as I shouted and whined, a perfect wild certainty was in my heart: for an aroma like peach, my God, had been suddenly wafted from the ship upon me, and I must have very well known then that that watchful outlook of Sallitt saw nothing, and on the *Boreal* were dead men all; indeed, very soon I saw one of his eyes looking like a glass eye which has slid askew, and glares distraught. And now again my wretched body failed, and my head dropped forward, where I sat, upon the kayak-deck.

Well, after a long time, I lifted myself to look again at that forlorn and wandering craft. There she lay, quiet, tragic, as it were culpable of the dark secret she bore; and Sallitt, who had been such good friends with me, would not cease his stare. I knew quite well why he was there: he had leant over to vomit, and had leant ever since, his forearms pressed on the bulwark-beam, his left knee against the boards, and his left shoulder propped on the cathead. When I came quite near, I saw that with every bump of the two floes against the bows, his face shook in response, and nodded a little; strange to say, he had no covering on his head, and I noted the play of the faint breezes in his uncut hair. After a time I would approach no more, for I was

afraid; I did not dare, the silence of the ship seemed so sacred
and awful: and till late afternoon I sat there, watching the black
and massive hull. Above her water-line emerged all round a
half-floating fringe of fresh-green sea-weed, proving old neglect;
an abortive attempt had apparently been made to lower, or
take in, the larch-wood pram,* for there she hung by a jammed
davit-rope, stern up, bow in the water; the only two arms of the
windmill moved this way and that, through some three degrees,
with an *andante* creaking sing-song; some washed clothes, tied
on the bow-sprit rigging to dry, were still there; the iron casing
all round the bluff bows was red and rough with rust; at several
points the rigging was in considerable tangle; occasionally the
boom moved a little with a tortured skirling cadence; and the
sail, rotten, I presume, from exposure – for she had certainly
encountered no bad weather – gave out anon a heavy languid
flap at a rent down the middle. Besides Sallitt, looking out there
where he had jammed himself, I saw no one.

By a paddle-stroke now, and another presently, I had closely
approached her about four in the afternoon, though my awe of
the ship was complicated by that perfume of hers, whose fearful
effects I knew. My tentative approach, however, proved to me,
when I remained unaffected, that, here and now, whatever danger
there had been was past; and finally, by a hanging rope, with a
thumping desperation of heart, I clambered up her beam.

They had died, it seemed, very suddenly, for nearly all the twelve
were in poses of activity. Egan was in the very act of ascending the
companion-way; Lamburn was sitting against the chart-room
door, apparently cleaning two carbines; Odling at the bottom of
the engine-room stair seemed to be drawing on a pair of reindeer
komagar; and Cartwright, who was often in liquor, had his arms
frozen tight round the neck of Martin, whom he seemed to be
kissing, they two lying stark at the foot of the mizzen-mast.

Over all – over men, decks, rope-coils – in the cabin, in the
engine-room – between sky-light leaves – on every shelf, in
every cranny – lay a purplish ash or dust, very impalpably fine.
And steadily reigning throughout the ship, like the very spirit of
death, was that aroma of peach-blossom.

*

Here it had reigned, as I could see from the log-dates, from the rust on the machinery, from the look of the bodies, from a hundred indications, during something over a year. It was, therefore, mainly by the random workings of winds and currents that this fragrant ship of death had been brought hither to me.

And this was the first direct intimation which I had that the Unseen Powers (whoever and whatever they may be), who through the history of the world had been so very, very careful to conceal their Hand from the eyes of men, hardly any longer intended to be at the pains to conceal their Hand from *me*. It was just as though the *Boreal* had been openly presented to me by a spiritual agency, which, though I could not see it, I could readily apprehend.

The dust, though very thin and flighty above-decks, lay thickly deposited below, and after having made a tour of investigation throughout the ship, the first thing which I did was to examine that – though I had tasted nothing all day, and was exhausted to death. I found my own microscope where I had left it in the box in my berth to starboard, though I had to lift up Egan to get at it, and to step over Lamburn to enter the chart-room; but there, toward evening, I sat at the table and bent to see if I could make anything of the dust, while it seemed to me as if all the myriad spirits of men that have sojourned on the earth, and angel and devil, and all Time and all Eternity, hung silent round for my decision; and such an ague had me, that for a long time my wandering finger-tips, all ataxic with agitation, eluded every delicate effort which I made, and I could nothing do.

Of course, I know that an odour of peach-blossom in the air, resulting in death, could only be associated with some vaporous effluvium of cyanogen, or of hydrocyanic ('prussic') acid, or of both; and when I at last managed to examine some of the dust under the microscope, I was not therefore surprised to find, among the general mass of purplish ash, a number of bright-yellow particles, which could only be minute crystals of potassic ferrocyanide. What potassic ferrocyanide was doing on board the *Boreal* I did not know, and I had neither the means, nor the force of mind, alas! to dive then further into the mystery; I understood only that by some extraordinary means the air of the region just south of the Polar environ had been impregnated with a vapour which was either cyanogen, or some product of cyanogen; also, that this deadly vapour, which is very soluble, had by now either been dissolved by the sea, or else dispersed into space (probably the latter), leaving only its faint after-perfume; and seeing this, I let my poor abandoned head drop again on the table, and long hours I sat there staring mad, for I had a suspicion, my God, and a fear, in my breast.

The *Boreal*, I found, contained sufficient provisions, untouched by the dust, in cases, casks, &c., to last me, probably, fifty years. After two days, when I had partially scrubbed and boiled the filth of fifteen months from my skin, and solaced myself with better food, I overhauled her thoroughly, and spent three more days in oiling and cleaning the engine. Then, all being ready, I dragged my twelve dead and laid them together in two rows on the chart-room floor; and I hoisted for love the poor little kayak which had served me through so many tribulations. At nine in the morning of the 6th July, a week from my first sighting of the *Boreal*, I descended to the engine-room to set out.

The screws, like those of most quite modern ships, were driven by the simple contrivance of a constant stream of liquid air, contained in very powerful tanks, exploding through capillary tubes into non-expansion slide-valve chests, much as in the ordinary way with steam: a motor which gave her, in spite of her bluff hulk, a speed of sixteen knots. It is, therefore, the simplest thing for one man to take these ships round the world, since their movement, or stopping, depend upon nothing but the depressing or raising of a steel handle, provided that one does not get blown to the sky meantime, as liquid air, in spite of its thousand advantages, occasionally blows people. At any rate, I had tanks of air sufficient to last me through twelve years' voyaging; and there was the ordinary machine on board for making it, with forty tons of coal, in case of need, in the bunkers, and two excellent Belleville boilers:* so I was well supplied with motors at least.

The ice here was quite slack, and I do not think I ever saw Arctic weather so bright and gay, the temperature at 41°. I found that I was midway between Franz Josef and Spitzbergen, in latitude 79° 23′ N. and longitude 39° E.; my way was perfectly clear; and something almost like a mournful hopefulness was in me as the engines slid into their clanking turmoil, and those long-silent screws began to churn the Arctic sea. I ran up with alacrity and took my stand at the wheel; and the bows of my eventful Argo* turned southward and westward.

When I needed food or sleep, the ship slept, too: when I awoke, she continued her way.

Sixteen hours a day sometimes I stood sentinel at that wheel, overlooking the varied monotony of the ice-sea, till my knees would give, and I wondered why a wheel at which one might sit was not contrived, rather delicate steering being often required among the floes and bergs. By now, however, I was less weighted with my ball of Polar clothes, and stood almost slim in a Lap great-coat, a round Siberian fur cap on my head.

At midnight when I threw myself into my old berth, it was just as though the engines, subsided now into silence, were a dead thing, and had a ghost which haunted me; for I heard them still, and yet not them, but the silence of their ghost.

Sometimes I would startle from sleep, horrified to the heart at some sound of exploding iceberg, or bumping floe, noising far through that white mystery of quietude, where the floes and bergs were as floating tombs, and the world a liquid cemetery. Never could I describe the strange Doom's-day shock with which such a sound would recall me from far depths of chaos to recollection of myself: for often-times, both waking and in nightmare, I did not know on which planet I was, nor in which Age, but felt myself adrift in the great gulf of time and space and circumstance, without bottom for my consciousness to stand upon; and the world was all mirage and a new show to me; and the boundaries of dream and waking lost.

Well, the weather was most fair all the time, and the sea like a pond. During the morning of the fifth day, the 11th July, I entered, and went moving down, an extraordinary long avenue of snow-bergs and floes, most regularly placed, half a mile across and miles long, like a Titanic double-procession of statues, or the Ming Tombs,* but rising and sinking on the cadenced swell; many towering high, throwing placid shadows on the aisle between; some being of a lucid emerald tint; and three or four pouring down cascades that gave a far and chaunting sound. The sea between was of a strange thick bluishness, almost like raw egg-white; while, as always here, some snow-clouds, white and woolly, floated in the pale sky. Down this avenue, which produced a mysterious impression of Cyclopean cathedrals and odd sequesteredness, I had not passed a mile, when I sighted a black object at the end.

I rushed to the shrouds, and very soon made out a whaler.

Again the same panting agitations, mad rage to be at her, at once possessed me; I flew to the indicator, turned the lever to full, then back to give the wheel a spin, then up the main-mast ratlins, waving a long foot-bandage of vadmel tweed picked up at random, and by the time I was within five hundred yards of her, had worked myself to such a pitch, that I was again shouting that futile madness: 'Hullo! Hi! Bravo! *I have been to the Pole!*'

And those twelve dead that I had in the chart-room there must have heard me, and the men on the whaler must have heard me, and smiled their smile.

For, as to that whaler, I should have known better at once, if I had not been crazy, since she *looked* like a ship of death, her boom slamming to port and starboard on the gentle heave of the sea, and her fore-sail reefed that serene morning. Only when I was quite near her, and hurrying down to stop the engines, did the real truth, with perfect suddenness, drench my heated brain; and I almost ran into her, I was so stunned.

However, I stopped the *Boreal* in time, and later on lowered the kayak, and boarded the other.

This ship had evidently been stricken silent in the midst of a perfect drama of activity, for I saw not one of her crew of sixty-two who was not busy, except one boy. I found her a good-sized thing of 500 odd tons, ship-rigged, with auxiliary engine of seventy horse-power, and pretty heavily armour-plated round the bows. There was no part of her which I did not overhaul, and I could see that they had had a great time with whales, for a mighty carcass, attached to the outside of the ship by the powerful cant-purchase tackle, had been in process of flensing and cutting-in, and on the deck two great blankets of blubber, looking each a ton-weight, surrounded by twenty-seven men in many attitudes, some terrifying to see, some disgusting, several grotesque, all so unhuman, the whale dead, and the men dead, too, and death was there, and the rank-flourishing germs of Inanity, and a mesmerism, and a silence, whose dominion was established, and its reign was growing old. Four of them, who had been removing the gums from a mass of stratified whalebone at the mizzen-mast foot, were quite imbedded in whale-flesh; also, in a barrel lashed to the top of the main topgallant masthead was visible the head of a man with a long pointed beard, looking steadily out over the sea to the S.W., which made me notice that five only of the probable eight or nine boats were on board; and after visiting the 'tween-decks, where I saw considerable quantities of stowed whalebone plates, and about fifty or sixty iron oil-tanks, and cut-up blubber; and after visiting cabin, engine-room, fo'cas'le, where I saw a lonely boy of fourteen with his hand grasping a bottle of rum under all the turned-up clothes in a chest, he, at the moment of death, being evidently intent upon hiding it; and after two hours' search of the ship, I got back to my own, and half an hour later came upon all the three missing whale-boats about a mile apart, and steered zig-zag near to each. They contained five men each and a steerer, and one had the harpoon-gun fired, with the loose line coiled round and round the head and upper part of the stroke line-manager; and in the others hundreds of fathoms of coiled rope, with toggle-irons, whale-lances, hand-harpoons, and dropped heads, and grins, and lazy *abandon*, and eyes that stared, and eyes that dozed, and eyes that winked.

After this I began to sight ships not infrequently, and used regularly to have the three lights burning all night. On the 12th July I met one, on the 15th two, on the 16th one, on the 17th three, on the 18th two – all Greenlanders, I think: but, of the nine, I boarded only three, the glass quite clearly showing me, when yet far off, that on the others was no life; and on the three which I boarded were dead men; so that that suspicion which I had, and that fear, grew very heavy upon me.

I went on southward, day after day southward, sentinel there at my wheel; clear sunshine by day, when the calm pale sea sometimes seemed mixed with regions of milk, and at night the immense desolation of a world lit by a sun that was long dead, and by a light that was gloom. It was like Night blanched in death then; and wan as the very kingdom of death and Hades I have seen it, most terrifying, that neuter state and limbo of nothingness, when unreal sea and spectral sky, all boundaries lost, mingled in a vast shadowy void of ghastly phantasmagoria, pale to utter huelessness, at whose centre I, as if annihilated, seemed to swoon in immensity of space. Into this disembodied world would come anon waftures of that peachy scent which I knew: and their frequency rapidly grew. But still the *Boreal* moved, traversing, as it were, bottomless Eternity: and I reached latitude 72°, not far now from Northern Europe.

And now, as to that blossomy peach-scent – even while some floes were yet around me – I was just like some fantastic mariner, who, having set out to search for Eden and the Blessed Islands, finds them, and balmy gales from their gardens come out, while he is yet afar, to meet him with their perfumes of almond and champac, cornel and jasmin and lotus. For I had now reached a zone where the peach-aroma was constant; all the world seemed embalmed in its spicy fragrance; and I could easily imagine myself voyaging beyond the world toward some clime of perpetual and enchanting Spring.

Well, I saw at last what whalers used to call 'the blink of the ice';* that is to say, its bright apparition or reflection in the sky when it is left behind, or not yet come-to. By this time I was in a region where a good many craft of various sorts were to be seen; I was continually meeting them; and not one did I omit to investigate, while many I boarded in the kayak or the larch-wood pram. Just below latitude 70° I came upon a good large fleet of what I sup-

posed to be Lafoden cod and herring fishers,* which must have
drifted somewhat on a northward current. They had had a great
season, for the boats were well laden with curing fish. I went from
one to the other on a zig-zag course, they being widely scattered,
some mere dots to the glass on the horizon. The evening was still
and clear with that astral Arctic clearness, the sun just beginning
his low-couched nightly drowse. These sturdy-looking brown
boats stood rocking gently there with slow-creaking noises, as of
things whining in slumber, without the least damage, awaiting the
appalling storms of the winter months on that tenebrous sea,
when a dark doom, and a deep grave, would not fail them. The
fishers were braw carles, wearing, many of them, fringes of beard
well back from the chin-point, with hanging woollen caps. In
every case I found below-decks a number of cruses of corn-
brandy, marked *aquavit*, two of which I took into the pram. In
one of the smacks an elderly fisher was kneeling in a forward
sprawling pose, clasping the lug-mast with his arms, the two
knees wide apart, head thrown back, and the yellow eye-balls
with their islands of grey iris staring straight up the mast-pole. At
another of them, instead of boarding in the pram, I shut off the
Boreal's liquid air at such a point that, by delicate steering, she
slackened down to a stoppage just a-beam of the smack, upon
whose deck I was thus able to jump down. After looking around
I descended the three steps aft into the dark and garrety below-
decks, and with stooping back went calling in an awful whisper:
'*Anyone? Anyone?*' Nothing answered me: and when I went up
again, the *Boreal* had drifted three yards beyond my reach. There
being a dead calm, I had to plunge into the water, and in that half-
minute there a sudden cold throng of unaccountable terrors beset
me, and I can feel again now that abysmal desolation of loneliness, and sense of a hostile and malign universe bent upon eating
me up: for the ocean seemed to me nothing but a great ghost.

Two mornings later I came upon another school, rather
larger boats these, which I found to be Brittany cod-fishers.
Most of these, too, I boarded. In every below-decks was a
wooden or earthenware image of the Virgin, painted in gaudy
faded colours; and in one case I found a boy who had been
kneeling before the statue, but was toppled sideways now, his

knees still bent, and the cross of Christ in his hand. These stalwart blue woollen blouses and tarpaulin sou'-westers lay in
every pose of death, every detail of feature and expression still
perfectly preserved. The sloops were all the same, all, all: with
sing-song creaks they rocked a little, nonchalantly: each, as it
were, with a certain sub-consciousness of its own personality,
and callous unconsciousness of all the others round it: yet each
a copy of the others: the same hooks and lines, disembowelling-
knives, barrels of salt and pickle, piles and casks of opened cod,
kegs of biscuit, and low-creaking rockings, and a bilgy smell,
and dead men. The next day, about eighty miles south of the
latitude of Mount Hekla,* I sighted a big ship, which turned
out to be the French cruiser Lazare Tréport. I boarded and
overhauled her during three hours, her upper, main, and
armoured deck, deck by deck, to her lowest black depths, even
childishly spying up the tubes of her two big, rusted turret-
guns. Three men in the engine-room had been much mangled,
after death, I presume, by a burst boiler; floating about 800
yards to the northeast lay a long-boat of hers, low in the water,
crammed with marines, one oar still there, jammed between the
row-lock and the rower's forced-back chin; on the ship's starboard deck, in the long stretch of space between the two masts,
the blue-jackets had evidently been piped up, for they lay there
in a sort of serried disorder, to the number of two hundred and
seventy-five. Nothing could be of suggestion more tragic than
the wasted and helpless power of this poor wandering vessel,
around whose stolid mass myriads of wavelets, busy as aspen-
leaves, bickered with a continual weltering splash that was
quite loud to hear. I sat a good time that afternoon in one of her
steely port main-deck casemates on a gun-carriage, my head
sunken on my breast, furtively eyeing the bluish turned-up feet,
all shrunk, ex-sanguined, of a sailor who lay on his back before
me; his soles were all that I could see, the rest of him lying
head-downwards beyond the steel door-sill.

Drenched in seas of lugubrious reverie I sat, till, with a shud-
dering start, I awoke, paddled back to the Boreal, and, till sleep
conquered me, went on my way. At ten the next morning,
coming on deck, I spied to the west a group of craft, and turned

my course upon them. They turned out to be eight Shetland sixerns,* which must have drifted north-eastward hither. I examined them well, but they were as the long list of the others: for all the men, and all the boys, and all the dogs on them were dead.

I could have come to land a long time before I did: but I would not: I was so afraid. For I was used to the silence of the ice: and I was used to the silence of the sea: but, God knows it, I was afraid of the silence of the land.

Once, on the 15th July, I had seen a whale, or thought I did, spouting very remotely afar on the S.E. horizon; and on the 19th I distinctly saw a shoal of porpoises vaulting the sea-surface, in their swift-successive manner, northward: and seeing them, I had said pitifully to myself: 'Well, I am not quite alone in the world, then, my good God – not quite alone.'

Moreover, some days later, the *Boreal* had found herself in a bank of cod making away northward, millions of fish, for I saw them, and one afternoon caught three, hand-running, with the hook.

So the sea, at least, had its tribes to be my mates.

But if I should find the land as still as the sea, without even the spouting whale, or school of tumbling sea-hogs – *if Paris were dumber than the eternal ice* – what then, I asked myself, should I do?

I could have made short work, and landed at Shetland, for I found myself as far westward as longitude 11° 23' W.: but I would not: I was so afraid. The shrinking within me to face that vague suspicion which I had, turned me first to a foreign land.

I made for Norway, and on the first night of this definite intention, at about nine o'clock, the weather being gusty, the sky lowering, the air sombrous, and the sea hard-looking, dark, and ridged, I was steaming along at a good rate, holding the wheel, my poor port and starboard lights still burning there, when, without the least notice, I received the roughest physical shock of my life, being shot bodily right over the wheel, thence, as from a cannon, twenty feet to the cabin-door, through it head-foremost down the companion-way, and still beyond some six yards along the passage. I had crashed into some dark and dead ship, probably of large size, though I never saw her, nor any sign of her; and all that night, and the next day till four in the afternoon, the *Boreal* went driving alone over the sea, whither she would: for I lay unconscious. When I woke, I found that I had received really very small injuries, considering: but I sat there on the floor a long time in a sulky, morose, disgusted, and bitter mood; and when I rose, pettishly stopped the ship's engines, seeing my twelve dead all huddled and disfigured. Now I was afraid to steam by night, and even in the daytime I would not go on for three days: for I was childishly angry with I know not what, and inclined to quarrel with Those whom I could not see.

However, on the fourth day, a rough swell which knocked the ship about, and made me very uncomfortable, coaxed me into moving; and I did so with bows turned eastward and southward.

I sighted the Norway coast four days later, in latitude 63° 19′, at noon of the 11th August, and pricked off my course to follow it; but it was with a slow and dawdling reluctance that I went, at much less than half-speed. In some eight hours, as I knew from the chart, I ought to sight the lighthouse light on Smoelen Island;* and when quiet night came, the black water being branded with trails of still moonlight, I passed quite close to it, between ten and twelve, almost under the shadow of the mighty hills: but, oh my God, no light was there. And all the way down I marked the rugged sea-board slumber darkling, afar or near, with never, alas! one friendly light.

Well, on the 15th August I had another of those maniac raptures, whose passing away would have left an elephant racked and prostrate. During four days I had seen not one sign of present life on the Norway coast, only hills, hills, dead and dark, and floating craft, all dead and dark; and my eyes now, I found, had acquired a crazy fixity of stare into the very bottom of the vacant abyss of nothingness, while I remained unconscious of being, save of one point, rainbow-blue, far down in the infinite, which passed slowly from left to right before my consciousness a little way, then vanished, came back, and passed slowly again, from left to right continually; till some prick, or voice, in my brain would startle me into the consciousness that I was staring, whispering the profound confidential warning: '*You must not stare so, or it is over with you!*' Well, lost in a blank trance of this sort, I was leaning over the wheel during the afternoon of the 15th, when it was as if some instinct or premonition in my soul leapt up, and said aloud: 'If you look just yonder, *you will see...!*' I started, and in one instant had surged up from all that depth of reverie to reality: I glanced to the right: and there, at last, my God, I saw something human which moved, rapidly moved: at last! – and it came to me.

That sense of recovery, of waking, of new solidity, of the comfortable usual, a million-fold too intense for words – how sweetly consoling it was! Again now, as I write, I can fancy and feel it – the rocky solidity, the adamant ordinary, on which to base the feet, and live. From the day when I stood at the Pole, and saw there the dizzy thing that made me swoon, there had come into my way not one sign or trace that other beings like myself were alive on the earth with me: till now, suddenly, I had the sweet indubitable proof: for on the south-western sea, not four knots away, I saw a large, swift ship: and her bows, which were sharp as a hatchet, were steadily chipping through the smooth sea at a pretty high pace, throwing out profuse ribbony foams that went wide-vawering, with outward undulations, far behind her length, as she ran the sea in haste, straight northward.

At the moment, I was steering about S.E. by S., fifteen miles out from a shadowy-blue series of Norway mountains; and just giving the wheel one frantic spin to starboard to bring me down upon her, I flew to the bridge, leant my back on the main-mast, which passed through it, put a foot on the white iron rail before me, and there at once felt all the mocking devils of distracted revelry possess me, as I caught the cap from my long hairs, and commenced to wave and wave and wave, red-faced maniac that I was: for at the second nearer glance, I saw that she was

flying an ensign at the main, and a long pennant at the main-
top, and I did not know what she was flying those flags there
for: and I was embittered and driven mad.

With distinct minuteness did she print herself upon my
consciousness in that five minutes' interval: she was painted a
dull and cholera yellow, like many Russian ships, and there
was a faded pink space at her bows under the line where the
yellow ceased: the ensign at her main I made out to be the
blue-and-white saltire, and she was clearly a Russian passen-
ger-liner, two-masted, two-funnelled, though from her funnels
came no trace of smoke, and the position of her steam-cones
was anywhere. All about her course the sea was spotted with
wobbling splendours of the low sun, large coarse blots of
glory near the eye, but lessening to a smaller pattern in the
distance, and at the horizon refined to a homogeneous band
of livid silver.

The double speed of the *Boreal* and the other, hastening
opposite ways, must have been thirty-eight or forty knots, and
the meeting was accomplished in certainly less than five minutes: yet into that time I crowded years of life. I was shouting
passionately at her, my eyes starting from my head, my face all
inflamed with rage the most prone, loud and urgent. For she
did not stop, nor signal, nor make sign of seeing me, but came
furrowing down upon me like Juggernaut, with steadfast run. I
lost reason, thought, memory, purpose, sense of relation, in that
access of delirium which transported me, and can only remember now that in the midst of my shouting, a word, uttered by
the fiends who used my throat to express their frenzy, set me
laughing high and madly: for I was crying: 'Hi! Bravo! Why
don't you stop? *Madmen! I have been to the Pole!*'

That instant an odour arose, and came, and struck upon my
brain, most detestable, most execrable; and while one might
count ten, I was aware of her near-sounding engines, and that
cursed charnel went tearing past me on her mænad way,* not
fifteen yards from my eyes and nostrils. She was a thing, my
God, from which the vulture and the jackal, prowling for offal,
would fly with shrieks of loathing. I had a glimpse of decks
piled thick with her festered dead.

In big black letters on the round retreating yellow stern my eye-corner caught the word *Yaroslav*, as I bent over the rail to retch and cough and vomit at her. She was a horrid thing.

This ship had certainly been pretty far south in tropical or sub-tropical latitudes with her great crowd of dead: for all the bodies which I had seen till then, so far from smelling ill, seemed to give out a certain perfume of the peach. She was evidently one of those many ships of late years which have substituted liquid air for steam, yet retained their old steam-funnels, &c., in case of emergency: for air, I believe, was still looked at askance by several builders, on account of the terrible accidents which it sometimes caused. The *Boreal* herself is a similar instance of both motors. This vessel, the *Yaroslav*, must have been left with working engines when her crew were overtaken by death, and, her air-tanks being still unexhausted, must have been ranging the ocean with impunity ever since, during I knew not how many months, or, it might be, years.

Well, I coasted Norway for nearly a hundred and sixty miles without once going nearer land than two or three miles: for something held me back. But passing the fjord-mouth where I knew that Aadheim was,* I suddenly turned the helm to port, almost before I knew that I was doing it, and made for land.

In half an hour I was moving up an opening in the land with mountains on either hand, streaky crags at their summit, umbrageous boscage below; and the whole softened, as it were, by veils woven of the rainbow.

This arm of water lies curved about like a thread which one drops, only the curves are much more pointed, so that every few minutes the scene was changed, though the vessel just crawled her way up, and I could see behind me nothing of what was passed, or only a land-locked gleam like a lake.

I never saw water so polished and glassy, like clarid polished marble, reflecting everything quite clean-cut in its lucid abysm, over which hardly the faintest zephyr breathed that still sun-down; it wimpled about the bluff *Boreal*, which seemed to move as if careful not to bruise it, in rich wrinkles and creases, like glycerine, or dewy-trickling lotus-oil; yet it was only the sea: and the spectacle yonder was only crags, and autumn-foliage and mountain-slope: yet all seemed caught-up and chaste, rapt in a trance of rose and purple, and made of the stuff of dreams and bubbles, of pollen-of-flowers, and rinds of the peach.

I saw it not only with delight, but with complete astonishment: having forgotten, as was too natural in all that long barrenness of ice and sea, that anything could be so ethereally fair: yet homely, too, human, familiar, and consoling. The air here was richly spiced with that peachy scent, and there was a Sabbath and a nepenthe and a charm in that place at that hour, as it were of those gardens of Hesperus, and fields of asphodel, reserved for the spirits of the just.

Alas! but I had the glass at my side, and for me nepenthe was mixed with a despair immense as the vault of heaven, my good God: for anon I would take it up to spy some perched hut of the peasant, or burg of the 'bonder', on the peaks: and I saw no one there; and to the left, at the third marked bend of the fjord, where there is one of those watch-towers that these people used for watching in-coming fish, I spied, lying on a craggy slope just before the tower, a body which looked as if it must surely tumble head-long, but did not. And when I saw that, I felt definitely, for the first time, that shoreless despair which I alone of men have felt, high beyond the stars, and deep as hell; and I fell to staring again that blank stare of Nirvana and the lunacy of Nothingness, wherein Time merges in Eternity, and all being, like one drop of water, flies scattered to fill the bottomless void of space, and is lost.

The *Boreal*'s bow walking over a little empty fishing-boat roused me, and a minute later, just before I came to a new promontory and bend, I saw two people. The shore there is some three feet above the water, and edged with boulders of rock, about which grows a fringe of shrubs and small trees: behind this fringe is a path, curving upward through a sombre wooded little gorge; and on the path, near the water, I saw a driver of one of those Norwegian sulkies that were called kar-jolers:* he, on the high front seat, was dead, lying sideways and backwards, with low head resting on the wheel; and on a trunk strapped to a frame on the axle behind was a boy, his head, too, resting sideways on the wheel, near the other's; and the little pony was dead, pitched forward on its head and fore-knees, tilting the shafts downward; and some distance from them on the water floated an empty skiff.

When I turned the next fore-land, I all at once began to see a number of craft, which increased as I advanced, most of them small boats, with some schooners, sloops, and larger craft, the majority a-ground: and suddenly now I was conscious that, mingling with that delicious odour of spring-blossoms – profoundly modifying, yet not destroying it – was another odour, wafted to me on the wings of the very faint land-breeze: and 'Man,' I said, 'is decomposing': for I knew it well: it was the odour of human corruption.

The fjord opened finally in a somewhat wider basin, shut-in by quite steep, high-towering mountains, which reflected themselves in the water to their last cloudy crag: and, at the end of this I saw ships, a quay, and a modest, homely old town.

Not a sound, not one: only the languidly-working engines of the *Boreal*. Here, it was clear, the Angel of Silence had passed, and his scythe mown.

I ran and stopped the engines, and, without anchoring, got down into an empty boat that lay at the ship's side when she stopped; and I paddled twenty yards toward the little quay. There was a brigantine with all her courses set, three jibs, staysails, square-sails, main and fore-sails, and gaff-top-sail, looking hanging and listless in that calm place, and wedded to a still copy of herself, mast-downward, in the water; there were three lumber-schooners, a forty-ton steam-boat, a tiny barque, five Norway herring-fishers, and ten or twelve shallops:* and the sailing-craft had all fore-and-aft sails set, and about each, as I passed among them, brooded an odour that was both sweet and abhorrent, an odour more suggestive of the very genius of mortality – the inner mind and meaning of Azrael – than aught that I could have conceived: for all, as I soon saw, were crowded with dead.

Well, I went up the old mossed steps, in that strange dazed state in which one notices frivolous things: I remember, for instance, feeling the lightness of my new clothes: for the weather was quite mild, and the day before I had changed to Summer things, having on now only a common undyed woollen shirt, the sleeves rolled up, and cord trousers, with a belt, and a cloth cap over my long hair, and an old pair of yellow shoes, without laces, and without socks. And I stood on the unhewn stones of the edge of the quay, and looked abroad over a largish piece of unpaved ground, which lay between the first house-row and the quay.

What I saw was not only most woeful, but wildly startling: woeful, because a great crowd of people had assembled, and lay dead, there; and wildly startling, because something in their *tout ensemble* told me in one minute why they were there in such number.

They were there in the hope, and with the thought, to fly westward by boat.

And the something which told me this was a certain *foreign* air about that field of the dead as the eye rested on it, something un-northern, southern, and Oriental.

Two yards from my feet, as I stepped to the top, lay a group of three: one a Norway peasant-girl in skirt of olive-green, scarlet stomacher, embroidered bodice, Scotch bonnet trimmed with silver lace, and big silver shoe-buckles; the second was an old Norway man in knee-breeches, and eighteenth-century small-clothes, and red worsted cap; and the third was, I decided, an old Jew of the Polish Pale, in gaberdine and skull-cap, with ear-locks.

I went nearer to where they lay thick as reaped stubble between the quay and a little stone fountain in the middle of the space, and I saw among those northern dead two dark-skinned women in costly dress, either Spanish or Italian, and the yellower mortality of a Mongolian, probably a Magyar, and a big negro in zouave dress, and some twenty-five obvious French, and two Morocco fezes, and the green turban of a shereef, and the white of an Ulema.

And I asked myself this question: 'How came these foreign stragglers here in this obscure northern town?'

And my wild heart answered: 'There has been an impassioned stampede, northward and westward, of all the tribes of Man. And this that I, Adam Jeffson, here see is but the far-tossed spray of that monstrous, infuriate flood.'*

Well, I passed up a street before me, careful, careful where I trod. It was not utterly silent, nor was the quay-square, but haunted by a pretty dense cloud of mosquitoes, and dreamy twinges of music, like the drawing of the violin-bow in elf-land. The street was narrow, pavered, steep and dark; and the sensations with which I, poor bent man, passed through that dead town, only Atlas, fabled to bear the burden of this Earth, could divine.

I thought to myself: If now a wave from the Deep has washed over this planetary ship of earth, and I, who alone happened to be in the extreme bows, am the sole survivor of that crew? ... What then, my God, shall I do?

I felt, I felt, that in this townlet, save the water-gnats of Norway, was no living thing; that the hum and the savour of Eternity filled, and wrapped, and embalmed it.

The houses are mostly of wood, some of them fairly large, with a *porte-cochère* leading into a semi-circular yard, around which the building stands, very steep-roofed, and shingled, in view of the heavy snow-masses of winter. Glancing into one open casement near the ground, I saw an aged woman, stout and capped, lie on her face before a very large porcelain stove; but I paced on without stoppage, traversed several streets, and came out, as it became dark, upon a piece of grass-land leading downward to a mountain-gorge. It was some distance along this gorge that I found myself sitting the next morning: and how, and in what trance, I passed that whole blank night is obliterated from my consciousness. When I looked about with the return of light I saw majestic fir-grown mountains on either hand, almost meeting overhead at some points, deeply shading the mossy gorge. I rose, and careless of direction, went still onward, and walked and walked for hours, unconscious of hunger; there was a profusion of wild mountain-strawberries, very tiny, which must grow almost into winter, a few of which I ate; there were blue gentianellas, and lilies-of-the-valley, and luxuriance of verdure, and a noise of waters. Occasionally, I saw little cataracts on high, fluttering like white wild rags, for they broke in the mid-fall, and were caught away, and scattered; patches also of reaped hay and barley, hung up, in a singular way, on stakes six feet high, I suppose to dry; there were perched huts, and a seemingly inaccessible small castle or burg, but none of these did I enter: and five bodies only I saw in the gorge, a woman with a babe, and a man with two small oxen.

About three in the afternoon I was startled to find myself there, and turned back. It was dark when I again passed through those gloomy streets of Aadheim, making for the quay, and now I felt both my hunger and a dropping weariness. I had no thought of entering any house, but as I passed by one open *porte-cochère*, something, I know not what, made me turn sharply in, for my mind had become as fluff on the winds, not working of its own action, but the sport of impulses that seemed external. I went across the yard, and ascended a wooden spiral stair by a twilight which just enabled me to pick my way among five or six vague forms fallen there. In that confined place fantastic qualms beset me; I mounted to the first landing, and tried the door, but it was locked; I mounted to the second: the door was open, and with a chill reluctance I took a step inward where all was pitch darkness, the window-stores being drawn. I hesitated: it was very dark. I tried to utter that word of mine, but it came in a whisper inaudible to my ears: I tried again, and this time heard myself say: '*Anyone?*' At the same time I had made another step forward, and trodden upon a soft abdomen; and at that contact terrors the most cold and ghastly thrilled me through and through, for it was as though I saw in that darkness the sudden eyeballs of Hell and frenzy glare upon me, and with a low gurgle of affright I was gone, helter-skelter down the stairs, treading upon flesh, across the yard, and down the street, with pelting feet, and open arms, and sobbing bosom, for I thought that all Aadheim was after me; nor was my horrid haste appeased till I was on board the *Boreal*, and moving down the fjord.

Out to sea, then, I went again; and within the next few days I visited Bergen, and put in at Stavanger. And I saw that Bergen and Stavanger were dead.

It was then, on the 19th August, that I turned my bow toward my native land.*

From Stavanger I steered a straight course for the Humber.

I had no sooner left behind me the Norway coast than I began to meet the ships, the ships – ship after ship; and by the time I entered the zone of the ordinary alternation of sunny day and sunless night, I was moving through the midst of an incredible number of craft, a mighty and wide-spread fleet.

Over all that great expanse of the North Sea, where, in its most populous days of trade, the sailor might perhaps sight a sail or two, I had now at every moment at least ten or twelve within scope of the glass, oftentimes as many as forty, forty-five.

And very still they lay on a still sea, itself a dead thing, livid as the lips of death; and there was an intensity in the calm that was appalling: for the ocean seemed weighted, and the air drugged.

Extremely slow was my advance, for at first I would not leave any ship, however remotely small, without approaching sufficiently to investigate her, at least with the spy-glass: and a strange multitudinous mixture of species they were, trawlers in hosts, war-ships of every nation, used, it seemed, as passenger-boats, smacks, feluccas, liners, steam-barges, great four-masters with sails, Channel boats, luggers, a Venetian *burchiello*, colliers, yachts, *remorqueurs*, training ships, dredgers, two *dahabeeahs* with curving gaffs, Marseilles fishers, a Maltese *speronare*, American off-shore sail, Mississippi steam-boats, Sorrento lug-schooners, Rhine punts, yawls, old frigates and three-deckers, called to novel use, Stromboli caiques, Yarmouth tubs, xebecs, Rotterdam flat-bottoms, floats, mere gunwaled rafts – anything from anywhere that could bear a human freight on water had come, and was here: and all, I knew, had been making westward, or northward, or both; and all, I knew, were crowded; and all were tombs, listlessly wandering, my God, on the wandering sea with their dead.

And so fair was the world about them, too: the brightest suavest autumn weather; all the still air aromatic with that vernal perfume of peach: yet not so utterly still, but if I passed close to the lee of any floating thing, the spicy stirrings of morning or evening wafted me faint puffs of the odour of mortality over-ripe for the grave.

So abominable and accursed did this become to me, such a plague and a hissing, vague as was the offence, that I began to shun rather than seek the ships, and also I now dropped my twelve, whom I had kept to be my companions all the way from the Far North, one by one, into the sea: for now I had definitely passed into a zone of settled warmth.

I was convinced, however, that the poison, whatever it might be, had some embalming, or antiseptic, effect upon the bodies: at Aadheim, Bergen and Stavanger, for instance, where the temperature permitted me to go without a jacket, only the merest hints and whiffs of the processes of dissolution had troubled me.

Very benign, I say, and pleasant to see, was sky and sea during all that voyage: but it was at sun-set that my sense of the wondrously beautiful was roused and excited, in spite of that great burden which I carried. Certainly, I never saw sun-sets resembling those, nor could have conceived of aught so flamboyant, extravagant, and bewitched: for the whole heaven seemed turned into an arena for warring Hierarchies, warring for the universe, or it was like the wild countenance of God defeated, and flying marred and bloody from His enemies. But many evenings I watched with unintelligent awe, believing it but a portent of the un-sheathed sword of the Almighty; till, one morning, a thought pricked me like a sword, for I suddenly remembered the great sun-sets of the later nineteenth century, witnessed in Europe, America, and, I believe, over the world, after the eruption of the volcano of Krakatoa.*

And whereas I had before said to myself: 'If now a wave from the Deep has washed over this planetary ship of earth...'

I said now: 'A wave – but not from the Deep: a wave rather which she had reserved, and has spouted, from her own un-motherly entrails...'

I had some knowledge of Morse telegraphy*, and of the manipu-lation of tape-machines, telegraphic typing-machines, and the ordinary wireless transmitter and coherer, as of most little things of that sort which came within the outskirts of the inter-est of a man of science; I had collaborated with Professor Stanistreet in the production of a text-book called *Applications of Science to the Arts*, which had brought us some notoriety; and, on the whole, the *minutiæ* of modern things were still pretty fresh in my memory. I could therefore have wired from Bergen or Stavanger, supposing the batteries not run down, to somewhere: but I would not: I was so afraid; afraid lest for ever from nowhere should come one answering click, or flash, or stirring...

I could have made short work, and landed at Hull: but I would not: I was so afraid. For I was used to the silence of the ice: and I was used to the silence of the sea: but I was afraid of the silence of England.

I came in sight of the coast on the morning of the 26th August, somewhere about Hornsea, but did not see any town, for I put the helm to port, and went on further south, no longer bothering with the instruments, but coasting at hap-hazard, now in sight of land, and now in the centre of a circle of sea; not admitting to myself the motive of this loitering slowness, nor thinking at all, but ignoring the deep-buried fear of the to-morrow which I shirked, and instinctively hiding myself in to-day. I passed the Wash, I passed Yarmouth, Felixstowe. By now the things that floated motionless on the sea were beyond numbering, for I could hardly lower my eyes ten minutes and lift them, without seeing yet another there: so that soon after dusk I, too, had to lie still among them all, till morning: for they lay dark, and to move at any pace would have been to drown the already dead.

Well, I came to the Thames-mouth, and lay pretty well in among the Flats and Pan Sands towards eight one evening, not seven miles from Sheppey and the North Kent coast: and I did not see any Nore Light, nor Girdler Light:* and all along the coast I had seen no light: but as to that I said not one word to myself, not admitting it, nor letting my heart know what my brain thought, nor my brain know what my heart surmised; but with a daft and mock-mistrustful under-look I would regard the darkling land, holding it a sentient thing that would be playing a prank upon a poor man like me.

And the next morning, when I moved again, my furtive eye-corners were very well aware of the Prince's Channel light-ship, and also the Tongue ship, for there they were: but I would not look at them at all, nor go near them: for I did not wish to have anything to do with whatever might have happened beyond my own ken, and it was better to look straight before, seeing nothing, and concerning one's-self with one's-self.

The next evening, after having gone out to sea again, I was in a little to the E. by S. of the North Foreland: and I saw no light there, nor any Sandhead light; but over the sea vast signs of wreckage, and the coasts were strewn with old wrecked fleets. I turned about S.E., very slowly moving – for anywhere hereabouts hundreds upon hundreds of craft lay dead within a ten-mile circle of sea – and by two in the fore-day had wandered up well in sight of the French cliffs: for I had said: 'I will go and see the light-beam of the great revolving-drum on Calais pier* that nightly beams half-way over-sea to England.' And the moon shone clear in the southern heaven that morning, like a great old dying queen whose Court swarms distantly from around her, diffident, pale, and tremulous, the paler the nearer; and I could see the mountain-shadows on her spotty full-face, and her misty aureole, and her lights on the sea, as it were kisses stolen in the kingdom of sleep; and all among the quiet ships mysterious white trails and powderings of light, like palace-corridors in some fairy-land forlorn, full of breathless wan whispers, scandals, and runnings-to-and-fro, with leers, and agitated last embraces, and flight of the princess, and death-bed of the king; and on the N.E. horizon a bank of brown cloud that seemed to have no relation with the world; and yonder, not far, the white coast-cliffs, not so low as at Calais near, but arranged in masses separated by vales of sward, each with its wreck: but no light of any revolving-drum I saw.

I could not sleep that night: for all the operations of my mind and body seemed in abeyance. Mechanically I turned the ship westward again; and when the sun came up, there, hardly two miles from me, were the cliffs of Dover; and on the crenulated summit of the Castle I spied the Union Jack hang motionless.

I heard eight, nine o'clock strike in the cabin, and I was still at sea. But some mad, audacious whisper was at my brain: and at 10.30, the 2nd September, immediately opposite the Cross Wall Custom House, the *Boreal*'s anchor-chain, after a voyage of three years, two months, and fourteen days, ran thundering, thundering, through the starboard hawse-hole.

Ah heaven! but I must have been stark mad to let the anchor go! for the effect upon me of that shocking obstreperous hubbub, breaking in upon all that cemetery repose that blessed morning, and lasting it seemed a year, was most appalling; and at the sudden racket I stood excruciated, with shivering knees and flinching heart, God knows: for not less terrifically uproarious than the clatter of the last Trump it raged and raged, and I thought that all the billion dead could not fail to start, and rise, at alarum so excessive, and question me with their eyes ...

On the top of the Cross Wall near I saw a grey crab fearlessly crawl; at the end where the street begins, I saw a single gas-light palely burn that broad day, and at its foot a black man lay on his face, clad only in a shirt and one boot; the harbour was almost packed with every sort of craft, and on a Calais-Dover boat, eight yards from my stern, which must have left Calais crowded to suffocation, I saw the rotted dead lie heaped, she being unmoored, and continually grinding against an anchored green brig.

And when I saw that, I dropped down upon my knees at the capstan, and my poor heart sobbed out the frail cry: 'Well, Lord God, Thou hast destroyed the work of Thy hand...'*

*

After a time I got up,* went below in a state of somnambulism, took a packet of pemmican cakes, leapt to land, and went following the railway that runs from the Admiralty Pier. In an enclosed passage ten yards long, with railway masonry on one side, I saw five dead lie, and could not believe that I was in England, for all were dark-skinned people, three gaudily dressed, and two in flowing white robes. It was the same when I turned into a long street, leading northward, for here were a hundred, or more, and never saw I, except in Constantinople, where I once lived eighteen months, so variegated a mixture of races, black, brunette, brown, yellow, white, in all the shades, some emaciated like people dead from hunger, and, over-looking them all, one English boy with a clean Eton collar sitting on a bicycle, supported by a lamp-post which his arms clasped, he proving clearly the extraordinary suddenness of the death which had overtaken them all.

I did not know whither, nor why, I went, nor had I the least idea whether all this was visually seen by me in the world which I had known, or in some other, or was all phantasy of my disembodied spirit* – for I had the thought that I, too, might be dead since old ages, and my spirit wandering now through the universe of space, in which there is neither north nor south, nor up nor down, nor measure nor relation, nor aught whatever, save an uneasy consciousness of a dream about bottomlessness. Of grief or pain, I think, I felt nothing; though I have a sort of memory now that some sound, resembling a sob or groan, though it was neither, came at regular clock-work intervals from my bosom during three or four days. Meantime, my brain registered like a tape-machine details the most frivolous, the most ludicrous – the name of a street, Strond Street, Snargate Street; the round fur cap – black fur for the side, white ermine for the top – of a portly Karaite priest* on his back, whose robes had been blown to his spread knees, as if lifted and neatly folded there; a violin-bow gripped between the thick, irregular teeth of a little Spaniard with brushed-back hair and mad-looking eyes; odd shoes on the foot of a French girl, one black, one brown. They lay in the street about as numerous as gunners who fall round their carriage, at intervals of five to ten feet, the majority – as was the case also in Norway, and on the ships – in poses of distraction, with spread arms, or wildly distorted limbs, like men who, the instant before death, called upon the rocks and hills to cover them.

On the left I came to an opening in the land, called, I believe, 'The Shaft',* and into this I turned, climbing a very great number of steps, almost covered at one point with dead: the steps I began to count, but left off, then the dead, and left off. Finally, at the top, which must be even higher than the Castle, I came to a great open space laid out with gravel-walks, and saw fortifications, barracks, a citadel. I did not know the town, except by passings-through, and was surprised at the breadth of view. Between me and the Castle to the east lay the district of crowding houses, brick and ragstone, mixed in the distance with vague azure haze; and to the right the harbour, the sea, with their ships; and visible around me on the heights seven or eight dead, biting the dust; the sun now high and warm, with hardly a cloud in the sky; and yonder a mist, which was the coast of France.

It seemed too big for one poor man.

My head nodded. I sat on a bench, black-painted and hard, the seat and back of horizontal boards, with intervals; and as I looked, I nodded, heavy-headed and weary: for it was too big for me. And as I nodded, with forehead propped on my left hand, and the packet of pemmican cakes in my right, there was in my head, somehow, an old street-song of my childhood: and I groaned it sleepily, like coronachs and drear funereal nenias,* dirging; and the packet beat time in my right hand, falling and raising, falling heavily and rising, in time.

> I'll buy the ring,
> You'll rear the kids:
> Servants to wait on our ting, ting, ting.
>
> Ting, ting,
> Won't we be happy?
> Ting, ting,
> That shall be it:
> I'll buy the ring,

> You'll rear the kids:
> Servants to wait on our ting, ting, ting.

So maundering, I fell forward upon my face, and for twenty-three hours, the living undistinguished from the dead, I slept there.

I was awakened by drizzle, leapt up, looked at a silver chronometer which, attached by a leather to my belt, I carried in my breeches-pocket, and saw that it was 10 A.M. The sky was dark, and a moaning wind – almost a new thing now to me – had arisen.

I ate some pemmican, for I had a reluctance – needless as it turned out – to touch any of the thousand luxuries here, sufficient no doubt, in a town like Dover alone, to last me five or six hundred years, if I could live so long; and, having eaten, I descended The Shaft, and spent the whole day, though it rained and blustered continually, in wandering about. Reasoning, in my numb way, from the number of ships on the sea, I expected to find the town overcrowded with dead: but this was not so; and I should say, at a venture, that not a thousand English, nor fifteen thousand foreigners, were in it: for that westward rage and stampede must have operated here also, leaving the town empty but for the ever new-coming hosts.

The first thing which I did was to go into an open grocer's shop, which was also a post and telegraph office, with the notion, I suppose, to get a message through to London. In the shop a single gas-light was burning its last, and this, with that near the pier, were the only two that I saw: and ghastly enough they looked, transparently wannish, and as it were ashamed, like blinking night-things overtaken by the glare of day. I conjectured that they had so burned and watched during months, or years: for they were now blazing diminished, with streaks and rays in the flame, as if by effort, and if these were the only two, they must have needed time to all but exhaust the works. Before the counter lay a fashionably-dressed negro with a number of tied parcels scattered about him, and on the counter an empty till, and behind it a tall thin woman with her face resting sideways in the till, fingers clutching the outer counter-rim, and such an expression of frantic terror as I never saw. I got over the counter to a table behind a wire-gauze, and, like a numb fool, went over the Morse alphabet in my mind before touching the transmitting key, though I knew no code-words, and there, big enough to be seen, was the ABC dial,* and who was to answer my message I did not ask myself: for habit was still strong upon me, and my mind refused to reason from what I saw to what I did not see; but the moment I touched the key, and peered greedily at the galvanometer-needle at my right, I saw that it did not move, for no current was passing; and with a kind of fright, I was up, leapt, and got away from the place, though there was a great number of telegrams about the receiver which, if I had been in my senses, I would have stopped and read.

Turning the corner of the next street, I saw wide-open the door of a substantial large house, and went in. From bottom to top there was no one there, except one English girl, sitting back in an easy-chair in the drawing-room, which was richly furnished with Valenciennes curtains and azure-satin things. She was a girl of the lowest class, hardly clad in black rags, and there she lay with hanging jaw, in a very crooked and awkward pose, a jemmy at her feet, in her left hand a roll of bank-notes, and in her lap three watches. In fact, the bodies which I saw here were, in general, either those of new-come foreigners, or else of the very poor, the very old, or the very young.

But what made me remember this house was that I found here on one of the sofas a newspaper: *The Kent Express*; and sitting unconscious of my dead neighbour, I pored a long while over what was written there.

It said in a passage which I tore out and kept:

'Telegraphic communication with Tilsit, Insterburg, Warsaw, Cracow, Przemysl, Gross Wardein, Karlsburg and many smaller towns lying immediately eastward of the 21st parallel of longitude has ceased during the night. In some at least of them there must have been operators still at their duty, undrawn into the great westward-rushing torrent: but as all messages from Western Europe have been answered only by that dread mysterious silence which, just three months and two days since, astounded the world in the case of Eastern New Zealand, we can only assume that these towns, too, have been added to the long and mournful list; indeed, after last evening's Paris telegrams we might have prophesied with some certainty, not merely their overthrow, but even the hour of it: for the rate-uniformity of the slow-riding vapour which is touring our globe is no longer doubtful, and has even been definitely fixed by Professor Craven at 100½ miles per day, or 4 miles 330 yards per hour. Its nature, its origin, remains, of course, nothing but matter of conjecture: for it leaves no living thing behind it: nor, God knows, is that of any moment now to us who remain. The rumour that it is associated with an odour of almonds is declared, on high authority, to be improbable; but the morose purple of its impending gloom has been attested by tardy fugitives from the face of its rolling and smoky march.

'Is this the end? We do not, and cannot, believe it. Will the pure sky which we to-day see above us be invaded in nine days, or less, by this smoke of the Pit of Darkness? In spite of the assurances of the scientists, we still doubt. For, if so, to what purpose that long drama of History, in which we seem to see the Hand of the Dramaturgist? Surely, the end of a Fifth Act should be obvious, satisfying to one's sense of the complete: but History, so far, long as it has been, resembles rather a Prologue than a Fifth Act. Can it be that the Manager, utterly dissatisfied, would sweep all off, and "hang up" the piece for ever? Certainly, the sins of mankind have been as scarlet: and if the fair earth which he has turned into Hell, send forth now upon him the smoke of Hell, little the wonder. But we cannot yet believe. There is a sparing strain in nature, and through the world, as a thread, is spun a silence which smiles, and on the end of events we find placarded large the words: "Why were ye afraid?" A dignified Hope, therefore – even now, when we cower beneath this world-wide shadow of the wings of the Condor of Death – becomes us: and, indeed, we see such an attitude among some of the humblest of our people, from whose heart ascends the cry: "Though He slay me, yet will I trust in Him." Here, therefore, O Lord! O Lord, look down, and save!*

'But even as we thus write of hope, Reason, if we would hear her, whispers us "fool": and inclement is the sky of earth. No more ships can New York Harbour contain, and whereas among us men die weekly of privations by the hundred thousand, yonder across the sea they perish by the million: for where the rich are pinched, how can the poor live? Already 700 out of the 1000 millions of our race* have perished, and the empires of civilisation have crumbled like sand-castles in a horror of anarchy. Thousands upon thousands of unburied dead, anticipating the more deliberate doom that comes and smokes, and rides and comes and comes, and does not fail, encumber the streets of London, Manchester, Liverpool. The guides of the nation have fled; the father stabs his child, and the wife her husband, for a morsel of food; the fields lie waste; wanton crowds carouse in our churches, universities, palaces, banks and hospitals; we understand that late last night three territorial regiments, the Munster Fusiliers, and the Lotian and East Lancashire Regiments, riotously disbanded themselves, shooting two officers; infectious diseases, as we all know, have spread beyond limit; in several towns the police seem to have disappeared, and, in nearly all, every vestige of decency; the results following upon the sudden release of the convicts appear to be monstrous in the respective districts; and within three short months Hell seems to have acquired this entire planet, sending forth Horror, like a rabid wolf, and Despair, like a disastrous sky, to devour and confound her. Hear, therefore, O Lord, and forgive our iniquities! O Lord, we beseech Thee! Look down, O Lord, and spare!'

When I had read this, and the rest of the paper, which had one whole sheet-side blank, I sat a long hour there, eyeing a little patch of the purple ash on a waxed board near the corner where the girl sat with her time-pieces, so useless in her Eternity; and there was not a feeling in me, except a pricking of curiosity, which afterwards became morbid and ravenous, to know something more of that cloud, or smoke, of which this man spoke, of its dates, its origin, its nature, its minute details. Afterwards, I went down, and entered several houses, searching for more papers, but did not find any; then I found a paper-shop which was open, with boards outside, but either it had been deserted, or printing must have stopped about the date of the paper which I had read, for the only three news-papers there were dated long prior, and I did not read them.

Now it was raining, and a blustering autumn day it was, distributing the odours of the world, and bringing me continual mixed whiffs of flowers and the hateful stench of decay. But I would not mind it much.

I wandered and wandered, till I was tired of spahi and bashi-bazouk, of Greek and Catalan, of Russian 'pope' and Coptic abuna, of dragoman and Calmuck, of Egyptian maulawi and Afghan mullah, Neapolitan and sheik, and the nightmare of wild poses, colours, stuffs and garbs, the yellow-green kefie of the Bedouin, shawl-turbans of Baghdad, the voluminous rose-silk tob of women, and face-veils, and stark distorted nakedness, and sashes of figured muslin, and the workman's cords, and the red tarboosh. About four, for very weariness, I was sitting on a door-step, bent beneath the rain; but soon was up again, fascinated no doubt by this changing bazaar of sameness, its chance combin-ations and permutations, and novelty in monotony. About five I was at a station, marked Harbour Station, in and about which lay a considerable crowd, but not one train. I sat again, and rested, rose and roamed again; soon after six I found myself at another station, called 'Priory'; and here I saw two long trains, both crowded, one on a siding, and one at the up-platform.

I examined both engines, and found them of the old boiler steam-type with manholes, heaters, autoclaves, feed-pump, &c., now rare in western countries, except England. In one there was no water, but in that at the platform, the float-lever, barely tilted toward the float, showed that there was some in the boiler. Of this one I overhauled all the machinery, and found it good, though rusted. There was plenty of fuel, and oil, which I supplemented from a near shop: and during ninety minutes my brain and hands worked with an intelligence as it were auto-matic, of their own motion. After three journeys across the station and street, I saw the fire blaze well, and the manometer move;* when the lever of the safety-valve, whose load I lightened

by half an atmosphere, lifted, I jumped down, and tried to dis-
connect the long string of carriages from the engine: but failed,
the coupling being an automatic arrangement new to me; nor
did I care. It was now very dark; but there was still oil for
bull's-eye and lantern, and I lit them. I forgot nothing. I rolled
driver and stoker – the guard was absent – one to the platform,
one upon the rails: and I took their place there. At about 8.30
I ran out from Dover, my throttle-valve pealing high a long
falsetto through the bleak and desolate night.

My aim was London. But even as I set out, my heart smote me:
I knew nothing of the metals, their junctions, facing-points,
sidings, shuntings, and complexities. Even as to whether I was
going toward, or away from, London, I was not sure. But just
in proportion as my first timorousness of the engine hardened
into familiarity and self-sureness, I quickened speed, wilfully,
with an obstinacy deaf and blind.

Finally, from a mere crawl at first, I was flying at a shocking
velocity, while something, tongue in cheek, seemed to whisper
me: 'There must be other trains blocking the lines, at stations,
in yards, and everywhere – it is a maniac's ride, a ride of death,
and Flying Dutchman's frenzy: remember your dark five-deep
brigade of passengers, who rock and bump together, and will
suffer in a collision.' But with mulish stubbornness I thought:
'They wished to go to London'; and on I raged, not wildly
exhilarated, so far as I can remember, nor lunatic, but feeling
the dull glow of a wicked and morose Unreason urge in my
bosom, while I stoked all blackened at the fire, or saw the vague
mass of dead horse or cow, running trees and fields, and dark
homestead and deep-slumbering farm, flit ghostly athwart the
murky air, as the half-blind saw 'men like trees walking'.*

Long, however, it did not last: I could not have been twenty
miles from Dover when, on a long reach of straight lines, I
made out before me a tarpaulined mass opposite a signal-point:
and at once callousness changed to terror within me. But even
as I plied the brake, I felt that it was too late: I rushed to the
gangway to make a wild leap down an embankment to the
right, but was thrown backward by a quick series of rough

bumps, caused by eight or ten cattle which lay there across the
lines: and when I picked myself up, and leapt, some seconds
before the impact, the speed must have considerably slackened,
for I received no fracture, but lay in semi-coma in a patch of
yellow-flowered whin on level ground, and was even conscious
of a fire on the lines forty yards away, and, all the night, of
vague thunder sounding from somewhere.

About five, or half-past, in the morning I was sitting up, rubbing my eyes, in a dim light mixed with drizzle. I could see that
the train of my last night's debauch was a huddled-up chaos of
fallen carriages and disfigured bodies. A five-barred gate on my
left opened into a hedge, and swung with creaks: two yards
from my feet lay a little shaggy pony with swollen wan abdomen, the very picture of death, and also about me a number of
dead wet birds.

I picked myself up, passed through the gate, and walked up
a row of trees to a house at their end. I found it to be a little
country-tavern with a barn, forming one house, the barn part
much larger than the tavern part. I went into the tavern by a
small side-door – behind the bar – into a parlour – up a little
stair – into two rooms: but no one was there. I then went round
into the barn, which was paved with cobble-stones, and there
lay a dead mare and foal, some fowls, with two cows. A ladder-
stair led to a closed trap-door in the floor above. I went up, and
in the middle of a wilderness of hay saw nine people – labour-
ers, no doubt – five men and four women, huddled together,
and with them a tin-pail containing the last of some spirit; so
that these had died merry.

I slept three hours among them, and afterwards went back to
the tavern, and had some biscuits of which I opened a new tin,
with some ham, jam and apples, of which I made a good meal,
for my pemmican was gone.

Afterwards I went following the rail-track on foot, for the
engines of both the collided trains were smashed. I knew
northward from southward by the position of the sun: and after
a good many stoppages at houses, and by railway-banks, I came,
at about eleven in the night, to a great and populous town.

By the Dane John and the Cathedral,* I immediately recognised it as Canterbury, which I knew quite well. And I walked
up Castle Street to the High Street, conscious for the first time
of that regularly-repeated sound, like a sob or groan, which
was proceeding from my throat. As there was no visible moon,
and these old streets very dim, I had to pick my way, lest I
should desecrate the dead with my foot, and they all should rise
with hue and cry to hunt me. However, the bodies here were
not numerous, most, as before, being foreigners: and these,
scattered about this strict old English burg that mourning dark
night, presented such a scene of the baneful wrath of God, and
all abomination of desolation, as broke me quite down at one
place, where I stood in travail with jeremiads and sore sobbings
and lamentations, crying out upon it all, God knows.

Only when I stood at the west entrance of the Cathedral I
could discern, spreading up the dark nave, to the lantern, to the
choir, a phantasmagorical mass of forms: I went a little inward,
and striking three matches, peered nearer: the two transepts,
too, seemed crowded – the cloister-doorway was blocked – the
south-west porch thronged, so that a great congregation must
have flocked hither shortly before their fate overtook them.

Here it was that I became definitely certain that the after-
odour of the poison was not simply lingering in the air, but was
being more or less given off by the bodies: for the blossomy
odour of this church actually overcame that other odour, the
whole rather giving the scent of old mouldy linens long
embalmed in cedars.

Well, away with stealthy trot I ran from the abysmal silence
of that place, and in Palace Street near made one of those
sudden immoderate rackets that seemed to outrage the universe, and left me so woefully faint, decrepit, and gasping for
life (the noise of the train was different, for there I was flying,
but here a captive, and which way I ran was capture). Passing
in Palace Street, I saw a little lamp-shop, and wanting a lantern,
tried to get in, but the door was locked; so, after going a few
steps, and kicking against a policeman's truncheon, I returned
to break the window-glass. I knew that it would make a fearful
noise, and for some fifteen or twenty minutes stood hesitating:

but never could I have dreamed, my good God, of *such* a noise, so passionate, so dominant, so divulgent, and, O Heaven, so long-lasting: for I seemed to have struck upon the weak spot of some planet, which came suddenly tumbling, with protracted bellowing and *débâcle*, about my ears. It was a good hour before I would climb in; but then quickly found what I wanted, and some big oil-cans; and till one or two in the morning, the innovating flicker of my lantern went peering at random into the gloomy nooks of the town.

Under a deep old Gothic arch that spanned a pavered alley,* I saw the little window of a little house of rubble, and between the two diamond-paned sashes rags tightly beaten in, the idea evidently being to make the place air-tight against the poison. When I went in I found the door of that room open, though it, too, apparently, had been stuffed at the edges; and on the threshold an old man and woman lay low. I conjectured that, thus protected, they had remained shut in, till either hunger, or the lack of oxygen in the used-up air, drove them forth, where-upon the poison, still active, must have instantly ended them. I found afterwards that this expedient of making air-tight had been widely resorted to; and it might well have proved success-ful, if both the supply of inclosed air, and of food, had been anywhere commensurate with the durability of the poisonous state.

Weary, weary as I grew, some morbid persistence sustained me, and I would not rest. About four in the morning I was at a station again, industriously bending, poor wretch, at the sooty task of getting another engine ready for travel. This time, when steam was up, I succeeded in uncoupling the carriages from the engine, and by the time morning broke, I was lightly gliding away over the country, whither I did not know, but making for London.

Now I went with more intelligence and caution, and got on very well, travelling seven days, never at night, except it was very clear, never at more than twenty or twenty-five miles, and crawling through tunnels. I do not know the maze into which the train took me, for very soon after leaving Canterbury it

must have gone down some branch-line, and though the names
were marked at stations, that hardly helped me, for of their
situation relatively to London I was seldom sure. Moreover,
again and again was my progress impeded by trains on the
metals, when I would have to run back to a shunting-point or
a siding, and, in two instances, these being far behind, changed
from my own to the impeding engine. On the first day I travelled unhindered till noon, when I stopped in open country that
seemed uninhabited for ages, only that half a mile to the left, on
a shaded sward, was a large stone house of artistic design,
coated with tinted harling, the roof of red Ruabon tiles,* and
timbered gables. I walked to it after another row with putting
out the fire and arranging for a new one, the day being bright
and mild, with great masses of white cloud in the sky. The house
had an outer and an inner hall, three reception-rooms, fine oil-
paintings, a kind of museum, and a large kitchen. In a bed-room
above-stairs I found three women with servants' caps, and a
footman, arranged in a strange symmetrical way, head to head,
like rays of a star. As I stood looking at them, I could have
sworn, my good God, that I heard someone coming up the
stairs. But it was some slight creaking of the breeze in the house,
augmented a hundred-fold to my inflamed and fevered hearing:
for, used for years now to this silence of Eternity, it is as though
I hear all sounds through an ear-trumpet. I went down, and
after eating, and drinking some clary-water,* made of brandy,
sugar, cinnamon, and rose-water, which I found in plenty, I lay
down on a sofa in the inner hall, and slept a quiet sleep until
near midnight.

I went out then, still possessed with the foolish greed to reach
London, and after getting the engine to rights, went off under a
clear black sky thronged with worlds and far-sown spawn,
some of them, I thought, perhaps like this of mine, whelmed
and drowned in oceans of silence, with one only inhabitant to
see it, and hear its silence. And all the long night I travelled,
stopping twice only, once to get the coal from an engine which
had impeded me, and once to drink some water, which I took
care, as always, should be running water. When I felt my head
nod, and my eyes close about 5 A.M., I threw myself, just out-

side the arch of a tunnel upon a grassy bank, pretty thick with stalks and flowers, the workings of early dawn being then in the east: and there, till near eleven, slept.

On waking, I noticed that the country now seemed more like Surrey than Kent: there was that regular swell and sinking of the land; but, in fact, though it must have been either, it looked like neither, for already all had an aspect of return to a state of wild nature, and I could see that for a year at the least no hand had tended the soil. Near before me was a stretch of lucerne of such extraordinary growth, that I was led during that day and the succeeding one to examine the condition of vegetation with some minuteness, and nearly everywhere I detected a certain hypertrophic tendency in stamens, calycles, pericarps, and pistils, in every sort of bulbiferous growth that I looked at, in the rushes, above all, the fronds, mosses, lichens, and all cryptogamia, and in the trefoils, clover especially, and some creepers.* Many crop-fields, it was clear, had been prepared, but not sown; some had not been reaped: and in both cases I was struck with their appearance of rankness, as I was also when in Norway, and was all the more surprised that this should be the case at a time when a poison, whose action is the arrest of oxidation, had traversed the earth; I could only conclude that its presence in large volumes in the lower strata of the atmosphere had been more or less temporary, and that the tendency to exuberance which I observed was due to some principle by which Nature acts with freer energy and larger scope in the absence of man.

Two yards from the rails I saw, when I got up, a little rill beside a rotten piece of fence, barely oozing itself onward under masses of foul and stagnant fungoids: and here there was a sudden splash, and life: and I caught sight of the hind legs of a diving young frog. I went and lay on my belly, poring over the clear dulcet little water, and presently saw two tiny bleaks, or ablets,* go gliding low among the swaying moss-hair of the bottom-rocks, and thought how gladly would I be one of them, with my home so thatched and shady, and my life drowned in their wide-eyed reverie. At any rate, these little creatures are alive, the batrachians also,* and, as I found the next day, pupæ and chrysales of one sort or another, for, to my deep emotion, I saw a little white butterfly staggering in the air over the flower-garden of a rustic station named Butley.

It was while I was lying there, poring upon that streamlet, that a thought came into my head: for I said to myself: 'If now I be here alone, alone, alone ... alone, alone ... one on the earth ... and my girth have a spread of 25,000 miles ... what will happen to my mind? Into what kind of creature shall I writhe and change? I may live two years so! What will have happened then? I may live five years – ten! What will have happened after the five? the ten? I may live twenty, thirty, forty...'

Already, already, there are things that peep and sprout within me...!

I wanted food and fresh running water, and walked from the engine half a mile through fields of lucerne* whose luxuriance quite hid the foot-paths, and reached my shoulder. After turning the brow of a hill, I came to a park, passing through which I saw some dead deer and three persons, and emerged upon a terraced lawn, at the end of which stood an Early English house of pale brick with copings, plinths, stringcourses of limestone, and spandrels of carved marble; and some distance from the porch a long table, or series of tables, in the open air, still spread with cloths that were like shrouds after a month of burial; and the table had old foods on it, and some lamps; and all around it, and all on the lawn, were dead peasants. I seemed to know the house, probably from some print which I may have seen, but I could not make out the escutcheon, though I saw from its simplicity that it must be very ancient. Right across the façade spread still some of the letters in evergreens of the motto: 'Many happy returns of the day', so that someone must have come of age, or something, for inside all was gala, and it was clear that these people had defied a fate which they, of course, foreknew. I went nearly throughout the whole spacious place of thick-carpeted halls, marbles, and famous oils, antlers and arras, and gilt saloons, and placid large bed-chambers: and it took me an hour. There were here not less than a hundred and eighty people. In the first of a vista of three large reception-rooms lay what could only have been a number of quadrille parties, for to the *coup d'œil* they presented a two-and-two appearance, made very repulsive by their jewels and evening-dress. I had to steel my heart to go through this house, for I did not know if these people were looking at me as soon as my back was turned. Once I was on the very point of flying, for I was going up the great central stairway, and there came a pelt of dead leaves against a window-pane in a corridor just above on the first floor, which thrilled me to the inmost soul. But I thought that if I once fled, they would all be at me from behind, and I should be gibbering mad long, long before I reached the outer hall, and so stood my ground, even defiantly advancing. In a small dark bedroom in the north wing on the second floor – that is to say, at the top of the house – I saw a tall young lady and a groom, or wood-man, to judge by his clothes, horribly riveted in an embrace on a settee, she with a light coronet on her head in low-necked dress,* and their lipless teeth still fiercely pressed together. I collected in a bag a few delicacies from the under-regions of this house, Lyons sausages, salami, mortadel, apples, roes, raisins, artichokes, biscuits, a few wines, a ham, bottled fruit, pickles, coffee, and so on, with a gold plate, tin-opener, cork-screw, fork, &c., and dragged them all the long way back to the engine before I could eat.

My brain was in such a way, that it was several days before the perfectly obvious means of finding my way to London, since I wished to go there, at all occurred to me; and the engine went wandering the intricate railway-system of the south country, I having twice to water her with a coal-bucket from a pool, for the injector was giving no water from the tank under the coals, and I did not know where to find any near tank-sheds. On the fifth evening, instead of into London, I ran into Guildford.

That night, from eleven till the next day, there was a great storm over England: let me note it down. And ten days later, on the 17th of the month came another; and on the 23rd another; and I should be put to it to count the great number since. And they do not resemble English storms, but rather Arctic ones, in a

certain very suggestive something of personalness, and a carous-
ing malice, and a Tartarus gloom, which I cannot quite describe.
That night at Guildford, after wandering about, and becoming
very weary, I threw myself upon a cushioned pew in an old
Norman church with two east apses, called St Mary's, using a
Bible-cushion for pillow, and placing some distance away a
little tin lamp turned low, whose ray served me for *veilleuse**
through the night. Happily I had taken care to close up everything, or, I feel sure, the roof must have gone. Only one dead,
an old lady in a chapel on the north side of the chancel, whom
I rather mistrusted, was there with me: and there I lay listening:
for, after all, I could not sleep a wink, while outside vogued the
immense tempest. And I communed with myself, thinking: 'I,
poor man, lost in this conflux of infinitudes and vortex of the
world, what can become of me, my God? For dark, ah dark, is
the waste void into which from solid ground I am now plunged
a million fathoms deep,* the sport of all the whirlwinds: and it
were better for me to have died with the dead, and never to
have seen the wrath and turbulence of the Ineffable, nor to
have heard the thrilling bleakness of the winds of Eternity,
when they pine, and long, and whimper, and when they vocifer-
ate and blaspheme, and when they expostulate and intrigue
and implore, and when they despair and die, which ear of man
should never hear. For they mean to eat me up, I know, these
Titanic darknesses: and soon like a whiff I shall pass away, and
leave the world to them.' So till next morning I lay mumping,
with shivers and cowerings: for the shocks of the storm per-
vaded the locked church to my very heart; and there were
thunders that night, my God, like callings and laughs and
banterings, exchanged between distant hill-tops in Hell.

Well, the next morning I went down the steep High Street, and
found a young nun at the bottom whom I had left the previous
evening with a number of girls in uniform opposite the Guildhall – half-way up the street. She must have been spun down,
arm over arm, for the wind was westerly, and whereas I had left
her completely dressed to her wimple and beads, she was now
nearly stripped, and her little flock scattered. And branches of

trees, and wrecked houses, and reeling clouds of dead leaves were everywhere that wild morning.

This town of Guildford appeared to be the junction of an extraordinary number of railway-lines, and before again setting out in the afternoon, when the wind had lulled, having got an ABC guide,* and a railway-map, I decided upon my line, and upon a new engine, feeling pretty sure now of making London, only thirty miles away. I then set out, and about five o'clock was at Surbiton, near my aim; I kept on, expecting every few minutes to see the great city, till darkness fell, and still, at considerable risk, I went, as I thought, forward: but no London was there. I had, in fact, been on a loop-line, and at Surbiton gone wrong again; for the next evening I found myself at Wokingham, farther away than ever.

I slept on a rug in the passage of an inn called The Rose, for there was a wild, Russian-looking man, with projecting topteeth, on a bed in the house, whose appearance I did not like, and it was late, and I too tired to walk further; and the next morning pretty early I set out again, and at 10 A.M. was at Reading.

The notion of navigating the land by precisely the same means as the sea, simple and natural as it was, had not at all occurred to me: but at the first accidental sight of a compass in a little shop-window near the river at Reading, my difficulties as to getting to any desired place in the world vanished once and for all: for a good chart or map, the compass, a pair of compasses, and, in the case of longer distances, a quadrant, sextant or theodolite, with a piece of paper and pencil, were all that were necessary to turn an engine into a land-ship, one choosing the lines that ran nearest the direction of one's course, whenever they did not run precisely.

Thus provided, I ran out from Reading about seven in the evening, while there was still some light, having spent there some nine hours. This was the town where I first observed that shocking crush of humanity, which I afterwards met in every large town west of London. Here, I should say, the English were quite equal in number to the foreigners: and there were enough of both, God knows: for London must have poured many here.

There were houses, in every room of which, and on the stairs, the dead actually overlay each other, and in the streets before them were points where only on flesh, or under carriages, was it possible to walk. I went into the great County Gaol, from which, as I had read, the prisoners had been released two weeks before-hand, and there I found the same pressed condition, cells occupied by ten or twelve, the galleries continuously rough-paved with faces, heads, and old-clothes-shops of robes; and in the parade-ground, against one wall, a mass of human stuff, like tough grey clay mixed with rags and trickling black gore, where a crush as of hydraulic power must have acted. At a corner between a gate and a wall near the biscuit-factory of this town I saw a boy, whom I believe to have been blind, standing jammed, at his wrist a chain-ring, and, at the end of the chain, a dog; from his hap-hazard posture I conjectured that he, and chain, and dog had been lifted from the street, and placed so, by the storm of the 7th of the month; and what made it very curious was that his right arm pointed a little outward just over the dog, so that, at the moment when I first sighted him, he seemed a drunken fellow setting his dog at me. In fact, all the dead I found much mauled and stripped and huddled: and the earth seemed to be making an abortive effort to sweep her streets.

Well, some little distance from Reading I saw a big flower-seed farm, looking dead in some plots, and in others quite rank: and here again, fluttering quite near the engine, two little winged aurelians in the quiet evening air. I went on, passing a great number of crowded trains on the down-line, two of them in collision, and very broken up, and one exploded engine; even the fields and cuttings on either hand of the line had a rather populous look, as if people, when trains and vehicles failed, had set to trudging westward in caravans and streams. When I came to a long tunnel near Slough, I saw round the foot of the arch an extraordinary quantity of wooden *débris*, and as I went very slowly through, was alarmed by the continuous bumping of the train, which, I knew, was passing over bodies; at the other end were more *débris*; and I easily guessed that a company of desperate people had made the tunnel air-tight at the two arches, and provisioned themselves, with the hope to live there till the day of destiny was passed; whereupon their barricades must have been crashed through by some up-train and themselves crushed, or else, other crowds, mad to share their cave of refuge, had stormed the boardings. This latter, as I afterwards found, was a very usual event.

I should very soon have got to London now, but, as my bad luck would have it, I met a long up-train on the metals, with not one creature in any part of it. There was nothing to do but to tranship, with all my things, to its engine, which I found in good condition with plenty of coal and water, and to set it going, a hateful labour: I being already jet-black from hair to toes. However, by half-past ten I found myself stopped by another train only a quarter of a mile from Paddington, and walked the rest of the way among trains in which the standing dead still stood, propped by their neighbours, and over metals where bodies were as ordinary and cheap as waves on the sea, or twigs in a forest. I believe that wild crowds had given chase on foot to moving trains, or fore-run them in the frenzied hope of inducing them to stop.

I came to the great shed of glass and girders which is the station, the night being perfectly soundless, moonless, starless, and the hour about eleven.

I found later that all the electric generating-stations, or all that I visited, were intact; that is to say, must have been shut down before the arrival of the doom; also that the gas-works had almost certainly been abandoned some time previously: so that this city of dreadful night, in which, at the moment when Silence choked it, not less than forty to sixty millions swarmed* and droned, must have more resembled Tartarus and the foul shades of Hell than aught to which my fancy can liken it.

For, coming nearer the platforms, I saw that trains, in order to move at all, must have moved through a slough of bodies pushed from behind, and forming a packed homogeneous mass on the metals: and I knew that they *had* moved. Nor could *I* now move, unless I decided to wade: for flesh was everywhere, on the roofs of trains, cramming the interval between them, on the platforms, splashing the pillars like spray, piled on trucks and lorries, a carnal quagmire; and outside, it filled the space between a great host of vehicles, carpeting all that region of London. And all here that odour of blossoms, which nowhere yet, save on one vile ship, had failed, was now wholly overcome by another: and the thought was in my head, my God, that if the soul of man had sent up to Heaven the odour which his body gave to me, then it was not so strange that things were as they were.

I got out from the station, with ears, God knows, that still awaited the accustomed noising of this accursed town, habituated as I now was to all the dumb and absent void of Soundlessness; and I was overwhelmed in a new awe, and lost in a wilder woesomeness, when, instead of lights and business, I saw the long street which I knew brood darker than Babylons long desolate, and in place of its ancient noising, heard, my God, a shocking silence, rising higher than I had ever heard it, and blending with the silence of the inane, eternal stars in heaven.

I could not get into any vehicle for some time, for all thereabouts was practically a mere block; but near the Park, which I attained by stooping among wheels, and selecting my foul steps, I overhauled a Daimler car, found in it two cylinders of petrol, lit the ignition-lamp, removed with averted abhorrence three bodies, mounted, and broke that populous stillness. And through streets nowhere empty of bodies I went urging eastward my jolting, and spattered, and humming way.

That I should have persisted, with so much pains, to come to this unbounded catacomb, seems now singular to me: for by that time I could not have been sufficiently daft to expect to find another being like myself on the earth, though I cherished, I remember, the irrational hope of yet somewhere finding dog, or cat, or horse, to be with me, and would anon think bitterly of Reinhardt, my Arctic dog, which my own hand had shot. But, in reality, a morbid curiosity must have been within me all the time to read the real truth of what had happened, so far as it was known, or guessed, and to gloat upon all that drama, and cup of trembling, and pouring out of the vials of the wrath of God,* which must have preceded the actual advent of the end of Time. This inquisitiveness had, at every town which I reached, made the search for newspapers uppermost in my mind; but, by bad luck, I had found only four, all of them ante-dated to the one which I had read at Dover, though their dates gave me some idea of the period when printing must have ceased, viz. soon after the 17th July – about three months sub-sequent to my arrival at the Pole – for none I found later than this date; and these contained nothing scientific, but only ori-sons and despairings. On arriving, therefore, at London, I made straight for the office of *The Times*, only stopping at a chemist's in Oxford Street for a bottle of antiseptic to hold near my nose, though, having once left the neighbourhood of Paddington, I had hardly much need of this.

I made my way to the square where the paper was printed, to find that, even there, the ground was closely strewn with calpac and pugaree, black abayeh and fringed praying-shawl, hob-nail and sandal, figured lungi and striped silk, all very muddled and mauled. Through the dark square to the twice-dark building I passed, and found open the door of an advertisement-office; but on striking a match, saw that it had been lighted by electricity, and had therefore to retrace my stumbling steps, till I came to a shop of lamps in a near alley, walking meantime with timid cares that I might hurt no one – for in this enclosed neighbourhood I began to feel strange tremors and kept striking matches, which, so still was the black air, hardly flickered.

When I returned to the building with a little lighted lamp, I at once saw a file on a table, and since there were a number of dead there, and I wished to be alone, I took the heavy mass of paper between my left arm and side, and the lamp in my right hand; passed then behind a counter; and then, to the right, up a stair which led me into a very great building and complexity of wooden steps and corridors, where I went peering, the lamp visibly trembling in my hand, for here also were the dead. Finally, I entered a good-sized carpeted room with a baize-covered table in the middle, and large smooth chairs, and on the table many manuscripts impregnated with purple dust, and around were books in shelves. This room had been locked upon a single man, a tall man in a frock-coat, with a pointed grey beard, who at the last moment had decided to fly from it, for he lay at the threshold, apparently fallen dead the moment he opened the door. Him, by drawing his feet aside, I removed, locked the door upon myself, sat at the table before the dusty file, and, with the little lamp near, began to search.

I searched and read till far into the morning. But God knows, He alone…

I had not properly filled the little reservoir with oil, and at about three in the fore-day, it began to burn sullenly lower, letting sparks, and turning the glass grey: and in my deepest chilly heart was the question: 'Suppose the lamp goes out before the daylight…'

I knew the Pole, and cold, I knew them well: but to be frozen by panic, my God! I read, I say, I searched, I would not stop: but I read that night racked by terrors such as have never yet entered into the heart of man to conceive. My flesh moved and crawled like a lake which, here and there, the breeze ruffles. Sometimes for two, three, four minutes, the profound interest of what I read would fix my mind, and then I would peruse an entire column, or two, without consciousness of the meaning of one single word, my brain all drawn away to the innumerable host of the wan dead that camped about me, pierced with horror lest they should start, and stand, and accuse me: for the grave and the worm was the world; and in the air a sickening stirring of cerements and shrouds; and the taste of the pale and insubstantial grey of ghosts seemed to infect my throat, and faint odours of the loathsome tomb my nostrils, and the toll of deep-toned passing-bells my ears; finally the lamp smouldered very low, and my charnel fancy teemed with the screwing-down of coffins, lych-gates and sextons, and the grating of ropes that lower down the dead, and the first sound of the earth upon the lid of that strait and gloomy home of the mortal; that lethal look of cold dead fingers I seemed to see before me, the insipidness of dead tongues, the pout of the drowned, and the vapid froths that ridge their lips, till my flesh was moist as with the stale washing-waters of morgues and mortuaries, and with such sweats as corpses sweat, and the mawkish tear that lies on dead men's cheeks; for what is one poor insignificant man in his flesh against a whole world of the disembodied, he alone with them, and nowhere, nowhere another of his kind, to whom to appeal against them? I read, and I searched: but God, God knows... If a leaf of the paper, which I slowly, warily, stealingly turned, made but one faintest rustle, how did that *reveille* boom in echoes through the vacant and haunted chambers of my poor aching heart, my God! and there was a cough in my throat which for a cruelly long time I would not cough, till it burst in horrid clamour from my lips, sending crinkles of cold through my inmost blood. For with the words which I read were all mixed up visions of crawling hearses, wails, and lugubrious crapes, and piercing shrieks of madness in strange earthy vaults, and all the mournfulness of the black Vale of Death, and the tragedy of corruption. Twice during the ghostly hours of that night the absolute and undeniable certainty that some presence – some most gashly silent being – stood at my right elbow, so thrilled me, that I leapt to my feet to confront it with clenched fists, and hairs that bristled stiff in horror and frenzy. After that second time I must have fainted; for when it was broad day, I found my dropped head over the file of papers, supported on my arms. And I resolved then never again after sunset to remain in any house: for that night was enough to kill a horse, my good God; and that this is a haunted planet I know.

What I read in *The Times* was not very definite,* for how could it be? but in the main it confirmed inferences which I had myself drawn, and fairly satisfied my mind.

There had been a battle royal in the paper between my old collaborator Professor Stanistreet and Dr Martin Rogers, and never could I have conceived such an indecorous piece of business, men like them calling one another 'tyro', 'dreamer', and in one place 'block-head'. Stanistreet denied that the perfumed odour of almonds attributed to the advancing cloud could be due to anything but the excited fancy of the reporting fugitives, because, said he, it was unknown that either Cn, HCn, or

K_4FeCn_6 had been given out by volcanoes, and the destructiveness to life of the travelling cloud could only be owing to CO and CO_2. To this Rogers, in an article characterised by extraordinary heat, replied that he could not understand how even a 'tyro' (!) in chemical and geological phenomena would venture to rush into print with the statement that HCn had not commonly been given out by volcanoes; that it *had* been, he said, was perfectly certain; though whether it had been or not could not affect the decision of a reasoning mind as to whether it was being: for that cyanogen, as a matter of fact, was not rare in nature, though not directly occurring, being one of the products of the common distillation of pit-coal, and found in roots, peaches, almonds, and many tropical flora; also that it had been actually pointed out as probable by more than one thinker that some salt or salts of Cn, the potassic, or the potassic ferrocyanide, or both, must exist in considerable stores in the earth at volcanic depths. In reply to this, Stanistreet in a two-column article used the word 'dreamer', and Rogers, when Berlin had been already silenced, finally replied with his amazing 'block-head'. But, in my opinion, by far the most learned and lucid of the scientific dicta was from the rather unexpected source of Sloggett, of the Dublin Science and Art Department: he, without fuss, accepted the statements of the fugitive eye-witnesses, down to the assertion that the cloud, as it rolled travelling, seemed mixed from its base to the clouds with languid tongues of purple flame, rose-coloured at their edges. This, Sloggett explained, was the characteristic flame of both cyanogen and hydrocyanic acid vapour, which, being inflammable, may have become locally ignited in the passage over cities, and only burned in that limited and languid way on account of the ponderous volumes of carbonic anhydride with which they must, of course, be mixed: the dark empurpled colour was due to the presence of large quantities of the scoriæ of the trappean rocks: basalts, green-stone, trachytes, and the various porphyries. This article was most remarkable for its clear divination, because written so early – not long, in fact, after the cessation of telegraphic communication with Australia and China; and at a date so early Sloggett stated that the character of the devastation not only proved an eruption – another, but far greater Krakatoa – probably in some South Sea region, but indicated that its most active product must be, not CO, but potassic ferrocyanide (K_4FeCn_6), which, undergoing distillation with the products of sulphur in the heat of eruption, produced hydrocyanic acid (HCn); and this volatile acid, he said, remaining in a vaporous state in all climates above a temperature of 26.5°C, might involve the entire earth, if the eruption proved sufficiently powerful, travelling chiefly in a direction contrary to the earth's west-to-east motion, the only regions which would certainly be exempt being the colder regions of the Arctic circles, where the vapour of the acid would assume the liquid state, and fall as rain. He did not anticipate that vegetation would be permanently affected, unless the eruption were of inconceivable duration and activity, for though the poisonous quality of hydrocyanic acid consisted in its sudden and complete arrest of oxidation, vegetation had two sources of life – the soil as well as the air; with this exception, all life, down to the lowest evolutionary forms, would disappear (here was the one point in which he was somewhat at fault), until the earth reproduced them. For the rest, he fixed the rate of the on-coming cloud at from 100 to 105 miles a day; and the date of eruption, either the 14th, 15th, or 16th of April – which was either one, two, or three days after the arrival of the *Boreal* party at the Pole; and he concluded by saying that, if the facts were as he had stated them, then he could suggest no hiding-place for the race of man, unless such places as mines and tunnels could be made air-tight; nor could even they be of use to any considerable number, except in the event of the poisonous state of the air being of very short duration.

I had thought of mines before: but in a very languid way, till this article, and other things that I read, as it were struck my brain a slap with the notion. For 'there', I said, 'if anywhere, shall I find a man...'

I went out from that building that morning feeling like a man bowed down with age, for the depths of unutterable horror into which I had had glimpses during that one night made me very feeble, and my steps tottered, and my brain reeled.

I got out into Farringdon Street, and at the near Circus, where four streets meet, had under my furthest range of vision nothing but four fields of bodies, bodies, clad in a rag-shop of every faded colour, or half-clad, or not clad at all, actually, in many cases, over-lying one another, as I had seen at Reading, but here with a markedly more skeleton appearance: for I saw the swollen-looking shoulders, sharp hips, hollow abdomens, and stiff bony limbs of people dead from famine, the whole having the grotesque air of some *macabre* battle-field of fallen marionettes. Mixed with these was an extraordinary number of vehicles of all sorts, so that I saw that driving among them would be impracticable, whereas the street which I had taken during the night was fairly clear. I thought a minute what I should do: then went by a parallel back-street, and came out to a shop in the Strand, where I hoped to find all the information which I needed about the excavations of the country. The shutters were up, and I did not wish to make any noise among these people, though the morning was bright, it being about ten o'clock, and it was easy to effect entrance, for I saw a crowbar in a big covered furniture-van near. I, therefore, went northward, till I came to the British Museum, the cataloguing-system of which I knew well, and passed in. There was no one at the library-door to bid me stop, and in the great round reading-room not a soul, except one old man with a bag of goître hung at his neck, and spectacles, he lying up a book-ladder near the shelves, a 'reader' to the last.* I got to the printed catalogues, and for an hour was upstairs among the dim sacred galleries of this still place, and at the sight of certain Greek and Coptic papyri, charters, seals, had such a dream of this ancient earth, my good God, as even an angel's pen could not half express on paper. Afterwards, I went away loaded with a good hundred-weight of Ordnance-maps, which I had stuffed into a bag found in the cloak-room, with three topographical books; I then, at an instrument-maker's in Holborn, got a sextant and theodolite, and at a grocer's near the river put into a sack-bag provisions to last me a week or two; at Blackfriars Bridge wharf-station I found a little sharp white steamer of a few tons, which happily was driven by liquid air, so that I had no troublesome fire to light: and by noon I was cutting my solitary way up the Thames, which flowed as before the ancient Britons were born, and saw it, and built mud-huts there amid the primæval forest; and afterwards the Romans came, and saw it, and called it Tamesis, or Thamesis.

That night, as I lay asleep on the cabin-cushions of my little boat under the lee of an island at Richmond, I had a clear dream, in which something, or someone, came to me, and asked me a question: for it said: 'Why do you go seeking another man? – that you may fall upon him, and kiss him? or that you may fall upon him, and murder him?' And I answered sullenly in my dream: 'I would not murder him. I do not wish to murder anyone.'

What was essential to me was to know, with certainty, whether I was really alone; for some instinct began to whisper me: 'Find that out: be sure, be sure: for without the assurance you can never be – yourself.'

I passed into the great Midland Canal, and went northward, leisurely advancing, for I was in no hurry. The weather remained very warm, and great part of the country was still dressed in autumn leaves. I have written, I think, of the terrific character of the tempests witnessed in England since my return: well, the calms were just as intense and novel. This observation was forced upon me: and I could not but be surprised. There seemed no middle course now: if there was a wind, it was a storm: if there was not a storm, no leaf stirred, not a roughening zephyr ran the water. I was reminded of maniacs that laugh now, and rave now – but never smile, and never sigh.

On the fourth afternoon I passed by Leicester, and the next morning left my pleasant boat, carrying maps and compass, and at a small station took engine, bound for Yorkshire, where I loitered and idled away two foolish months, sometimes travelling by steam-engine, sometimes by automobile, sometimes by bicycle, and sometimes on foot, till the autumn was quite over.

*

There were two houses in London to which especially I had thought to go: one in Harley Street, and one in Hanover Square: but when it came to the point, I would not; and there was a little embowered home in Yorkshire, where I was born, to which I thought to go: but I would not, confining myself for many days to the eastern half of the county.

One morning, while passing on foot along the coast-wall from Bridlington to Flambro', on turning my eyes from the sea, I was confronted by a thing which for a moment or two struck me with the most profound astonishment. I had come to a mansion, surrounded by trees, three hundred yards from the cliffs: and there, on a path at the bottom of the domain, right before me, was a board marked: 'Trespassers will be Prosecuted'. At once a mad desire – the first which I had had – to laugh, to roar with laughter, to send wild echoes of merriment clapping among the chalk gullies, and abroad on the morning air, seized upon me: but I kept it under, though I could not help smiling at this poor man, with his little delusion that a part of the earth was his.

Here the cliffs are, I should say, seventy feet high, broken by frequent slips in the upper stratum of clay, and, as I proceeded, climbing always, I encountered some rather formidable gullies in the chalk, down and then up which I had to scramble, till I came to a great mound or barrier, stretching right across the great promontory, and backed by a natural ravine, this, no doubt, having been raised as a rampart by some of those old invading pirate-peoples, who had their hot life-scuffle, and are done now, like the rest. Going on, I came to a bay in the cliff, with a great number of boats lodged on the slopes, some quite high, though the declivities are steep; toward the inner slopes is a lime-kiln which I explored, but found no one there. When I came out on the other side, I saw the village, with an old tower at one end, on a bare stretch of land; and thence, after an hour's rest in the kitchen of a little inn, went out to the coast-guard station, and the lighthouse.

Looking across the sea eastward, the light-keepers here must have seen that thick cloud of convolving browns and purples, perhaps mixed with small tongues of fire, slowly walking the water, its roof in the clouds, upon them: for this headland is in precisely the same longitude as London; and, reckoning from the hour when, as recorded in *The Times*, the cloud was seen from Dover over Calais, London and Flambro' must have been overtaken soon after three o'clock on the Sunday afternoon, the 25th July. At sight in open daylight of a doom so gloomy – prophesied, but perhaps hoped against to the last, and now come – the light-keepers must have fled howling, supposing them to have so long remained faithful to duty: for here was no one, and in the village very few. In this lighthouse, which is a circular white tower, eighty feet high, on the edge of the cliff, is a book for visitors to sign their names: and I will write something down here in black and white: for the secret is between God only, and me: After reading a few of the names, I took my pencil, and I wrote my name there.

The reef before the Head stretches out a quarter of a mile, looking bold in the dead low-water that then was, and showing to what extent the sea has pushed back this coast, three wrecks impaled on them, and a big steamer quite near, waiting for the first movements of the already strewn sea to perish. All along the cliff-wall to the bluff crowned by Scarborough Castle northward, and to the low vanishing coast of Holderness southward, appeared those cracks and caves which had brought me here, though there seemed no attempts at barricades; however, I got down a rough slope on the south side to a rude wild beach, strewn with wave-worn masses of chalk: and never did I feel so paltry and short a thing as there, with far-outstretched bays of crags about me, their bluffs encrusted at the base with stale old leprosies of shells and barnacles, and crass algæ-beards, and, higher up, the white cliff all stained and weather-spoiled, the rock in some parts looking quite chalky, and elsewhere gleaming hard and dull like dirty marbles, while in the huge withdrawals of the coast yawn darksome gullies and caverns. Here, in that morning's walk, I saw three little hermit-crabs, a limpet, and two ninnycocks in a pool of weeds under a bearded rock. What astonished me here, and, indeed, above, and everywhere, in London even, and other towns, was the incredible number of birds that strewed the ground, at some points resembling a real rain, birds of nearly every sort, including tropic specimens: so that I had to conclude that they, too, had fled before the cloud from country to country, till conquered by weariness and grief, and then by death.*

By climbing over rocks thick with periwinkles, and splashing through great sloppy stretches of crinkled sea-weed, which give a raw stench of brine, I entered the first of the gullies: a narrow, long, winding one, with sides polished by the sea-wash, and the floor rising inwards. In the dark interior I struck matches, able still to hear from outside the ponderous spasmodic rush and jostle of the sea between the crags of the reef, but now quite faintly. Here, I knew, I could meet only dead men, but urged by some curiosity, I searched to the end, wading in the middle through a three-feet depth of sea-weed twine: but there was no one; and only belemnites* and fossils in the chalk. I searched several to the south of the headland, and then went northward past it toward another opening and place of perched boats, called in the map North Landing: where, even now, a distinct smell of fish, left by the old crabbers and herring-fishers, was perceptible. A number of coves and bays opened as I proceeded; a faded green turf comes down in curves at some parts on the cliff-brows, like wings of a young soldier's hair, parted in the middle, and plastered on his brow; isolated chalk-masses are numerous, obelisks, top-heavy columns, bastions; at one point no less than eight headlands stretched to the end of the world before me, each pierced by its arch, Norman or Gothic, in whole or in half; and here again caves, in one of which I found a carpet-bag stuffed with a wet pulp like bread, and, stuck to the rock, a Turkish tarboosh; also, under a limestone quarry, five dead asses: but no man. The east coast had evidently been shunned. Finally, in the afternoon I reached Filey, very tired, and there slept.

I went onward by train-engine all along the coast to a region of iron-ore, alum, and jet-excavations round Whitby and Middlesborough. By by-ways near the small place of Goldsborough I got down to the shore at Kettleness, and reached the middle of a bay in which is a cave called the Hob-Hole,* with excavations all around, none of great depth, made by jet-diggers and quarrymen. In the cave lay a small herd of cattle, though for what purpose put there I cannot guess; and in the jet-excavations I found nothing. A little further south is the chief alum-region, as at Sandsend, but as soon as I saw a works, and the great gap in the ground like a crater, where the lias is quarried, containing only heaps of alum-shale, brushwood-stacks, and piles of cement-nodules extracted from the lias, I concluded that here could have been found no hiding; nor did I purposely visit the others, though I saw two later. From round Whitby, and those rough moors, I went on to Darlington, not far now from my home: but I would not continue that way, and after two days' indecisive lounging, started for Richmond and the lead mines about Arkengarth Dale, near Reeth. Here begins a region of mountain, various with glens, fells, screes, scars, swards, becks, passes, villages, river-heads and dales. Some of the faces which I saw in it almost seemed to speak to me in a broad dialect which I knew. But they were not numerous in proportion: for all this countryside must have had its population multiplied by at least some hundreds; and the villages had rather the air of Danube, Levant, or Spanish villages. In one, named Marrick, I saw that the street had become the scene either of a great battle or a great massacre; and soon I was everywhere coming upon men and women, English and foreign, dead from violence: cracked heads, wounds, unhung jaws, broken limbs, and so on. Instead of going direct to the mines from Reeth, that waywardness which now rules my mind, as squalls an abandoned boat, took me somewhat further southwest to the village of Thwaite, which I actually could not enter, so occupied with dead was every spot on which the eye rested a hundred yards about it. Not far from here I turned up, on foot now, a very steep, stony road to the right, which leads over the Buttertubs Pass into Wensleydale, the day being very warm and bright, with large clouds that looked like lakes of molten silver giving off grey fumes in their centre, casting moody shadows over the swardy dale, which below Thwaite expands, showing Muker two miles off, the largest village of Upper Swaledale. Soon, climbing, I could look down upon miles of

Swaledale and the hills beyond, a rustic panorama of glens and grass, river and cloud-shadow, and there was something of lightness in my step that fair day, for I had left all my maps and things, except one, at Reeth, to which I meant to return, and the earth, which is very good, was – mine. The ascent was rough, and also long: but if I paused and looked behind – I saw, I saw. Man's notion of a Heaven, a Paradise, reserved for the spirits of the good, clearly arose from impressions which the earth made upon his mind: for no Paradise can be fairer than this; just as his notion of a Hell arose from the squalid mess into which his own foolish habits of thought and action turned this Paradise. At least, so it struck me then: and, thinking it, there was a hiss in my breath, as I went up into what more and more acquired the character of a mountain-pass, with points of almost Alpine savagery: for after I had skirted the edge of a deep glen on the left, the slopes changed in character, heather was on the mountain-sides, a fretting beck sent up its noise, then screes, and scars, and a considerable waterfall, and a landscape of crags; and lastly a broad and rather desolate summit, palpably nearer the clouds.

Two days later I was at the mines: and here I first saw that wide-spread scene of horror with which I have since become familiar. The story of six out of ten of them all is the same, and short: selfish 'owners', an ousted world, an easy bombardment, and the destruction of all concerned, before the arrival of the cloud in many cases. About some of the Durham pit-mouths I have been given the impression that the human race lay collected there; and that the notion of hiding himself in a mine must have occurred to every man alive, and sent him thither.

In these lead mines, as in most vein-mining, there are more shafts than in collieries, and hardly any attempt at artificial ventilation, except at rises, winzes* and cul-de-sacs. I found accordingly that, though their depth does not exceed three hundred feet, suffocation must often have anticipated the other dreaded death. In nearly every shaft, both up-take and down-take, was a ladder, either of the mine, or of the fugitives, and I was able to descend without difficulty, having dressed myself in a house at the village in a check flannel shirt, a pair of two-buttoned trousers with circles of leather at the knees, thick boots and a miner's hat, having a leather socket attached to it, into which fitted a straight handle from a cylindrical candle-stick; with this light, and also a Davy-lamp,* which I carried about with me for a good many months, I lived for the most part in the deeps of the earth, searching for the treasure of a life, to find everywhere, in English duckies and guggs,* Pomer-anian women in gaudy stiff cloaks, the Walachian, the Mameluk, the Khirgiz, the Bonze, the Imaum, and almost every type of man.

One most brilliant Autumn day I walked by the village market-cross at Barnard, come at last, but with a tenderness in my heart, and a reluctance, to where I was born; for I said I would go and see my sister Ada,* and – the other old one. I leaned and loitered a long time on the bridge, gazing up to the craggy height, which is heavy with waving wood, and crowned by the Castle-tower, the Tees sweeping round the mountain-base, smooth here and sunlit, but a mile down, where I wished to go, but would not, brawling bedraggled and lacerated, like a sweet strumpet, all shallow among rocks under reaches of shadow – the shadow of Rokeby Woods. I climbed very leisurely up the hill-side, having in my hand a bag with a meal, and up the stair in the wall to the top I went, where there is no parapet, but a massiveness of wall that precludes danger; and here in my miner's attire I sat three hours, brooding sleepily upon the scene of lush umbrageous old wood that marks the long way the river takes, from Marwood Chase up above, and where the rapid Balder bickers in, down to bowery Rokeby, touched now with autumn; the thickness of trees lessening away toward the uplands, where there are far etherealized stretches of fields within hedgerows, and in the sunny mirage of the farthest azure remoteness hints of lonesome moorland. It was not till near three that I went down along the river, then, near Rokeby, tra-versing the old meadow, and ascending the old hill: and there, as of old, was the little black square with yellow letters on the gate-wall:

Hunt Hill House.

No part, no house, I believe, of this country-side was empty of strange corpses: and they were in Hunt Hill, too. I saw three in the weedy plot to the right of the garden-path, where once the hawthorn and lilac tree had grown from well-rollered grass, and in the little bush-wilderness to the left, which was always a wilderness, one more: and in the breakfast-room, to the right of the hall, three; and in the new wooden clinker-built attachment opening upon the breakfast-room, two, half under the billiard-table; and in her room overlooking the porch on the first floor, the long thin form of my mother on her bed, with crushed-in left temple, and at the foot of the bed, face-downward on the floor, black-haired Ada in a night-dress.

Of all the men and women who died, they two alone had burying. For I digged a hole with the stable-spade under the front lilac; and I wound them in the sheets, foot and form and head; and, not without throes and qualms, I bore and buried them there.

Some time passed after this before the long, multitudinous, and perplexing task of visiting the mine-regions again claimed me. I found myself at a place called Ingleborough, which is a big table-mountain, with a top of fifteen to twenty acres, from which the sea is visible across Lancashire to the west; and in the sides of this strange hill are a number of caves which I searched during three days, sleeping in a garden-shed at a very rural and flower-embowered village, for every room in it was thronged, a place marked Clapham in the chart, in Clapdale, which latter is a dale penetrating the slopes of the mountain: and there I found by far the greatest of the caves which I saw, having ascended a path from the village to a hollow between two grass slopes, where there is a beck, and so entering an arch to the left, screened by trees, into the limestone cliff. The passage narrows pretty rapidly inwards, and I had not proceeded two yards before I saw the clear traces of a great battle here. All this region had, in fact, been invaded, for the cave must have been famous, though I did not remember it myself, and for some miles round

the dead were pretty frequent, making the immediate approach
to the cave a matter for care, if the foot was to be saved from
pollution. It is clear that there had been an iron gate across the
entrance, that within this a wall had been built across, shutting
in I do not know how many, perhaps one or two, perhaps hundreds: and both gate and wall had been stormed and broken
down, for there still were the sledges and rocks which, without
doubt, had done it. I had a lamp, and at my forehead the lighted
candle, and I went on quickly, seeing it useless now to choose
my steps where there was no choice, through a passage
incrusted, roof and sides, with a scabrous petrified lichen, the
roof low for some ninety yards, covered with down-looking
cones, like an inverted forest of children's toy-trees. I then came
to a round hole, apparently artificial, opening through a curtain of stalagmitic formation into a great cavern beyond, which
was quite animated and festal with flashes, sparkles, and
diamond-lustres, hung in their myriads upon a movement of
the eye, these being produced by large numbers of snowy wet
stalagmites, very large and high, down the centre of which ran
a continuous long lane of clothes and hats and faces; with hasty
reluctant feet I somehow passed over them, the cave all the time
widening, thousands of stalactites appearing on the roof of
every size, from virgin's breast to giant's club, and now everywhere the wet drip, drip, as it were a populous busy bazaar of
perspiring brows and hurrying feet, in which the only business
is to drip. Where stalactite meets stalagmite there are pillars:
where stalactite meets stalactite in fissures long or short there
are elegances, flimsy draperies, delicate fantasies; there were
also pools of water in which hung heads and feet, and there
were vacant spots at outlying spaces, where the arched roof,
which continually heightened itself, was reflected in the chill
gleam of the floor. Suddenly, the roof came down, the floor
went up, and they seemed to meet before me; but looking, I
found a low opening, through which, drawing myself on the
belly over slime for some yards in repulsive proximity to dead
personalities, I came out upon a floor of sand and pebbles under
a long dry tunnel, arched and narrow, grim and dull, without
stalactites, suggestive of monks, and catacomb-vaults, and the

route to the grave; and here the dead were much fewer, proving either that the general mob had not had time to penetrate so far inward, or else that those within, if they were numerous, had gone out to defend, or to harken to, the storm of their citadel. This passage led me into an open space, the grandest of all, loftily vaulted, full of genie riches and buried treasures of light, the million-fold *ensemble* of lustres dancing schottishe with the eye, as it moved or was still: this place, I should guess, being quite half a mile from the entrance. My prying lantern showed me here only nineteen dead, men of various nations, and at the far end two holes in the floor, large enough to admit the body, through which from below came up a sound of falling water. Both of these holes, I could see, had been filled with cement concrete – wisely, I fancy, for a current of air from somewhere seemed to be now passing through them: and this would have resulted in the death of the hiders. Both, however, of the fillings had been broken through, one partially, the other wholly, by the ignorant, I presume, who thought to hide in a secret place yet beyond, where they may have believed, on seeing the artificial work, that others were. I had my ear a long time at one of these openings, listening to that mysterious chant down below in a darkness most murky and dismal; and afterwards, spurred by the stubborn will which I had to be thorough, I went back, took a number of outer robes from the bodies, tied them well together, then one end round the nearest pillar, and having put my mouth to the hole, calling: '*Anyone? Anyone?*' let myself down by the rope of garments, the candle at my head: I had not, however, descended far into those mournful shades, when my right foot plunged into water: and instantly the feeling of terror pierced me that all the evil things in the universe were at my leg to drag me down to Hell: and I was up quicker than I went down: nor did my flight cease till, with a sigh of deliverance, I found myself in open air.

After this, seeing that the autumn warmth was passing away, I set myself with more system to my task, and within the next six months worked with steadfast will, and strenuous assiduity, seeking, not indeed for a man in a mine, but for some evidence

of the possibility that a man might be alive, visiting in that time
Northumberland and Durham, Fife and Kinross, South Wales
and Monmouthshire, Cornwall and the Midlands, the lead
mines of Derbyshire, of Allandale and other parts of Northumberland, of Alston Moor and other parts of Cumberland, of
Arkendale and other parts of Yorkshire, of the western part of
Durham, of Salop, of Cornwall, of the Mendip Hills of Somersetshire, of Flint, Cardigan, and Montgomery, of Lanark and
Argyll, of the Isle of Man, of Waterford and Down; I have gone
down the 360-ft, Grand Pipe iron ladder of the abandoned
graphite-mine at Barrowdale in Cumberland,* half-way up a
mountain 2,000 feet high; and visited where cobalt and manganese ore is mined in pockets at the Foel Hiraeddog mine near
Rhyl in Flintshire, and the lead and copper Newton Stewart
workings in Galloway; the Bristol coal-fields, and mines of
South Staffordshire, where, as in Somerset, Gloucester, and
Shropshire, the veins are thin, and the mining-system is the
'long-wall', whereas in the North, and Wales, the system is the
'pillar-and stall'; I have visited the open workings for iron ores
of Northamptonshire, and the underground stone-quarries,
and the underground slate-quarries, with their alternate pillars
and chambers, in the Festiniog district of North Wales; also the
rock-salt workings; the tin, copper and cobalt workings of
Cornwall; and where the minerals were brought to the surface
on the backs of men, and where they were brought by adit-
levels* provided with rail-roads, and where, as in old Cornish
mines, there are two ladders in the shaft, moved up and down
alternately, see-saw, and by skipping from one to the other at
right moments you ascended or descended, and where the
drawing-up is by a gin or horse-whinn,* with vertical drum;
the Tisbury and Chilmark quarries in Wiltshire, the Spinkwell
and Cliffwood quarries in Yorkshire; and every tunnel, and
every recorded hole: for something urged within me, saying:
'You must be *sure* first, or you can never be – yourself.'

At the Farnbrook Coal-field, in the Red Colt Pit, my inexperience
nearly ended my life: for though I had a minute theoretical
knowledge of all British workings, I was, in my practical relation

to them, like a man who has learnt seamanship on shore. At this place the dead were accumulated, I think beyond precedent, the dark plain around for at least three miles being as strewn as a reaped field with stacks, and, near the bank, much more strewn than stack-fields, filling the only house within sight of the pit-mouth – the small place provided for the company's officials – and even lying over the great mountain-heap of wark, composed of the shale and *débris* of the working. Here I arrived on the morning of the 15th December, to find that, unlike the others, there was here no rope-ladder or other contrivance fixed by the fugitives in the ventilating-shaft, which, usually, is not very deep, being also the pumping-shaft, containing a plug-rod at one end of the beam-engine which works the pumps; but looking down the shaft, I discerned a vague mass of clothes, and afterwards a thing that could only be a rope-ladder, which a batch of the fugitives, by hanging to it their united weight, must have dragged down upon themselves, to prevent the descent of yet others. My only way of going down, therefore, was by the pit-mouth, and as this was an important place, after some hesitation I decided, very rashly. First I provided for my coming up again by getting a great coil of half-inch rope, which I found in the bailiff's office, probably 130 fathoms long, rope at most mines being so plentiful, that it almost seemed as if each fugitive had provided himself in that way. This length of rope I threw over the beam of the beam-engine in the bite where it sustains the rod, and paid one end down the shaft, till both were at the bottom: in this way I could come up, by tying one rope-end to the rope-ladder, hoisting it, fastening the other end below, and climbing the ladder; and I then set to work to light the pit-mouth engine-fire to effect my descent. This done, I started the engine, and brought up the cage from the bottom, the 300 yards of wire-rope winding with a quaint deliberateness round the drum, reminding me of a camel's nonchalant leisurely obedience. When I saw the four meeting chains of the cage-roof emerge, the pointed roof, and two-sided frame, I stopped the ascent, and next attached to the knock-off gear a long piece of twine which I had provided; carried the other end to the cage, in which I had five companions; lit my hat-candle, which was my test for choke-damp, and the Davy; and without the least reflection, pulled the string. That hole was 900 feet deep. First the cage gave a little up-leap, and then began to descend – quite normally, I thought, though the candle at once went out – nor had I the least fear; a strong current of air, indeed, blew up the shaft: but that happens in shafts. *This* current, however, soon became too vehemently boisterous for anything: I saw the lamp-light struggle, the dead cheeks quiver, I heard the cage-shoes* go singing down the wire-rope guides, and quicker we went, and quicker, that facile descent of Avernus, slipping lightly, then raging, with sparks at the shoes and guides, and a hurricane in my ears and eyes and mouth. When we bumped upon the 'dogs'* at the bottom, I was tossed a foot upwards with the stern-faced others, and then lay among them in the eight-foot space without consciousness.

It was only when I sat, an hour later, disgustedly reflecting on this incident, that I remembered that there was always some 'hand-working' of the engine during the cage-descents, an engineman reversing the action by a handle at every stroke of the piston, to prevent bumping. However, the only permanent injury was to the lamp: and I found many others inside.

I got out into the coal-hole, a large black hall 70 feet square by 15 high, the floor paved with iron sheets; there were some little holes round the wall, dug for some purpose which I never could discover, some waggons full of coal and shale standing about, and all among the waggons, and on them, and under them, bodies, clothes. I got a new lamp, pouring in my own oil, and went down a long steep ducky-road, very rough, with numerous rollers, over which ran a rope to the pit-mouth for drawing up the waggons; and in the sides here, at regular intervals, man-holes, within which to rescue one's self from down-tearing waggons; and within these man-holes, here and there, a dead, and in others every sort of food, and at one place on the right a high dead heap, and the air here hot at 64 or 65 degrees, and getting hotter with the descent.

The ducky led me down into a standing – a space with a turn-table – of unusual size, which I made my base of operations for exploring. Here was a very considerable number of

punt-shaped putts* on carriages, and also waggons, such as
took the new-mined coal from putt to pit-mouth; and raying
out from this open standing, several avenues, some ascending
as guggs, some descending as dipples, and the dead here all
arranged in groups, the heads of this group pointing up this
gugg, of that group toward that twin-way,* of that other down
that dipple, and the central space, where weighing was done,
almost empty: and the darksome silence of this deep place, with
all these multitudes, I found extremely gravitating and hypnotic, drawing me, too, into their great Passion of Silence in
which they lay, all, all, so fixed and veteran; and at one time I
fell a-staring, nearer perhaps to death and the empty Gulf than
I knew; but I said I would be strong, and not sink into their
habit of stillness, but let them keep to their own way, and follow
their own fashion, and I would keep to my own way, and follow
my own fashion, nor yield to them, though I was but one
against many; and I roused myself with a shudder; and setting
to work, caught hold of the drum-chain of a long gugg, and
planting my feet in the chogg-holes* in which rested the wheels
of the putt-carriages that used to come roaring down the gugg,
I got up, stooping under a roof only three feet high, till I came,
near the end of the ascent, upon the scene of another battle: for
in this gugg about fifteen of the mine-hands had clubbed to
wall themselves in, and had done it, and I saw them lie there all
by themselves through the broken cement, with their bare feet,
trousers, naked bodies all black, visage all fierce and wild, the
grime still streaked with sweat-furrows, the candle in their
rimless hats, and, outside, their own 'getting' mattocks and
boring-irons to besiege them. From the bottom of this gugg I
went along a very undulating twin-way, into which, every thirty
yards or so, opened one of those steep putt-ways which they
called topples, the twin-ways having plates of about 2½ ft
gauge for the putts from the headings, or workings, above to
come down upon, full of coal and shale: and all about here, in
twin-way and topples, were ends and corners, and not one had
been left without its walling-in, and only one was then intact,
some, I fancied, having been broken open by their own builders
at the spur of suffocation, or hunger; and the one intact I broke

into with a mattock – it was only a thin cake of plaster, but air-
tight – and in a space not seven feet long behind it I found the
very ill-smelling corpse of a carting-boy, with guss and tugger
at his feet,* and the pad which protected his head in pushing
the putts, and a great heap of loaves, sardines, and bottled beer
against the walls, and five or six mice that suddenly pitched
screaming through the opening which I made, greatly startling
me, there being of dead mice an extraordinary number in all
this mine-region. I went back to the standing, and at one point
in the ground, where there was a windlass and chain, lowered
myself down a 'cut' – a small pit sunk perpendicularly to a
lower coal-stratum, and here, almost thinking I could hear the
perpetual rat-tat of notice once exchanged between the putt-
boys below and the windlass-boys above, I proceeded down a
dipple to another place like a standing, for in this mine there
were six, or perhaps seven, veins: and there immediately I came
upon the acme of the horrible drama of this Tartarus, for all
here was not merely crowded, but, at some points, a packed
congestion of flesh, giving out a strong smell of the peach, curi-
ously mixed with the stale coal-odour of the pit, for here
ventilation must have been very limited; and a large number of
these masses had been shot down by only three hands, as I
found: for through three hermetical holes in a plaster-wall,
built across a large gugg, projected a little the muzzles of three
rifles, which must have glutted themselves with slaughter; and
when, after a horror of disgust, having swum as it were through
a dead sea, I got to the wall, I peeped from a small clear space
before it through a hole, and made out a man, two youths in
their teens, two women, three girls, and piles of cartridges and
provisions; the hole had no doubt been broken from within at
the spur of suffocation, when the poison must have entered;
and I conjectured that here must be the mine-owner, director,
manager, or something of that sort, with his family. In another
dipple-region, when I had re-ascended to a higher level, I
nearly fainted before I could retire from the commencement of
a region of after-damp, where there had been an explosion, the
bodies lying all hairless, devastated, and grotesque. But I did
not desist from searching every other quarter, no momentary

work, for not till near six did I go up by the pumping-shaft
rope-ladder.

One day, standing in that wild region of bare rock and sea,
called Cornwall Point, whence one can see the crags and postil-
lion wild rocks where Land's End dashes out into the sea, and
all the wild blue sea between, and not a house in sight, save the
chimney of some little mill-like place peeping between the rocks
inland – on that day I finished what I may call my official
search.

In going away from that place, walking northward, I came
upon a lonely house by the sea, a very beautiful house, made, it
was clear, by an artist, of the bungalow type, with an exquisitely sea-side expression. I went to it, and found its special
feature a spacious loggia or verandah, sheltered by the overhanging upper story. Up to the first floor, the exterior is of stone
in rough-hewn blocks with a distinct batter, while extra protec-
tion from weather is afforded by green slating above. The roofs,
of low pitch, are also covered with green slates, and a feeling of
strength and repose is heightened by the very long horizontal
lines. At one end of the loggia is a hexagonal turret, opening
upon the loggia, containing a study or nook. In front, the garden
slopes down to the sea, surrounded by an architectural sea-
wall; and in this place I lived three weeks. It was the house of
the poet Machen, whose name, when I saw it, I remembered
very well, and he had married a very beautiful young girl of
eighteen, obviously Spanish, who lay on the bed in the large
bright bedroom to the right of the loggia, on her left exposed
breast being a baby* with an India-rubber comforter in its
mouth, both mother and child wonderfully preserved, she still
quite lovely, white brow under low curves of black hair. The
poet, strange to say, had not died with them, but sat in the sit-
ting-room behind the bedroom in a long loose silky-grey jacket,
at his desk – actually writing a poem! Writing, I could see, furi-
ously fast, the place all littered with the written leaves – at three
o'clock in the morning, when, as I knew, the cloud overtook this
end of Cornwall, and stopped him, and put his head to rest on
the desk; and the poor little wife must have got sleepy, waiting

for it to come, perhaps sleepless for many long nights before, and gone to bed, he perhaps promising to follow in a minute to die with her, but bent upon finishing that poem, and writing feverishly on, running a race with the cloud, thinking, no doubt, 'just two couplets more', till the thing came, and put his head to rest on the desk, poor carle: and I do not know that I ever encountered aught so complimentary to my race as this dead poet Machen, and his race with the cloud: for it is clear now that the better kind of those poet men did not write to please the vague inferior tribes who might read them, but to deliver themselves of the divine warmth that thronged in their bosom; and if all the readers were dead, still they would have written; and for God to read they wrote. At any rate, I was so pleased with these poor people, that I stayed with them three weeks, sleeping under blankets on a couch in the drawing-room, a place full of lovely pictures and faded flowers, like all the house: for I would not touch the young mother to remove her. And finding on Machen's desk a big note-book with soft covers, dappled red and yellow, not yet written in, I took it, and a pencil, and in the little turret-nook wrote day after day for hours this account of what has happened, nearly as far as it has now gone. And I think that I may continue to write it, for I find in it a strange consolation, and companionship.

In the Severn Valley, somewhere in the plain between Gloucester and Cheltenham, in a rather lonely spot, I at that time travelling on a tricycle-motor,* I spied a curious erection, and went to it. I found it of considerable size, perhaps fifty feet square, and thirty high, made of pressed bricks, the perfectly flat roof, too, of brick, and not one window, and only one door: this door, which I found open, was rimmed all round its slanting rims with india-rubber, and when closed must have been perfectly air-tight. Just inside I came upon fifteen English people of the dressed class, except two, who were evidently bricklayers: six ladies, and nine men: and at the further end, two more, men, who had their throats cut; along one wall, from end to end were provisions; and I saw a chest full of mixed potassic chlorate and black oxide of manganese, with an apparatus for heating it, and producing oxygen – a foolish thing, for additional oxygen could not alter the quantity of breathed carbonic anhydride,* which is a direct narcotic poison. Whether the two with cut throats had sacrificed themselves for the others when breathing difficulties commenced, or been killed by the others, was not clear. When they could bear it no longer, they must have finally opened the door, hoping that by then, after the passage of many days perhaps, the outer air would be harmless, and so met their death. I believe that this erection must have been run up by their own hands under the direction of the two bricklayers, for they could not, I suppose, have got workmen, except on the condition of the workmen's admission: on which condition they would naturally employ as few as possible.

In general, I remarked that the rich must have been more urgent and earnest in seeking escape than the others: for the poor realised only the near and visible, lived in to-day, and cherished the always-false notion that to-morrow would be just like to-day. In an out-patients' waiting-room, for instance, in the Gloucester infirmary, I chanced to see an astonishing thing: five bodies of poor old women in shawls, come to have their ailments seen-to on the day of doom; and these, I concluded, had been unable to realise that anything would really happen to the daily old earth which they knew, and had walked with assurance on: for if everybody was to die, they must have thought, who would preach in the Cathedral on Sunday evenings? – so they could not have believed. In an adjoining room sat an old doctor at a table, the stethoscope-tips still clinging in his ears: a woman with bared chest before him; and I thought to myself: 'Well, this old man, too, died doing his work...'

In this same infirmary there was one surgical ward – for in a listless mood I went over it – where the patients had died, not of the poison, nor of suffocation, but of hunger: for the doctors, or someone, had made the long room air-tight, double-boarding the windows, felting the doors, and then locking them outside; they themselves may have perished before their precautions for the imprisoned patients were complete: for I found a heap of maimed shapes, mere skeletons, crowded round the door within. I knew very well that they had not died of the cloud-poison, for the pestilence of the ward was unmixed with that odour of peach which did not fail to have more or less embalming effects upon the bodies which it saturated. I rushed stifling from that place; and thinking it a pity, and a danger, that such a horror should be, I at once set to work to gather combustibles to burn the building to the ground.

It was while I sat in an arm-chair in the street the next afternoon, smoking, and watching the flames of this structure, that something was suddenly born in me, something from the lowest Hell: and I smiled a smile that never yet man smiled. And I said: 'I will burn, I will burn: I will return to London...'

While I was on this Eastward journey, stopping for the night at the town of Swindon, I had a dream: for I dreamed that a little brown bald old man, with a bent back, whose beard ran in one thin streamlet of silver from his chin to trail along the ground, said to me: 'You think that you are alone on the earth, its sole Despot: well, have your fling: but as sure as God lives, as God lives, as God lives' – he repeated it six times – 'sooner or later, later or sooner, you will meet another...'

And I started from that frightful sleep with the brow of a corpse, wet with sweat...

I returned to London on the 29th of March, arriving within a hundred yards of the Northern Station one windy dark evening about eight, where I alighted, and walked to Euston Road, then eastward along it, till I came to a shop which I knew to be a jeweller's, though it was too dark to see any painted words. The door, to my annoyance, was locked, like nearly all the shop-doors in London: I therefore went looking near the ground, and into a cart, for something heavy, very soon saw a labourer's ponderous boots, cut one from the shrivelled foot, and set to beat at the glass till it came raining; then knocked away the bottom splinters, and entered.

No horrors now at that clatter of broken glass; no sick qualms; my pulse steady; my head high; my step royal; my eye cold and calm.

*

Eight months previously, I had left London a poor burdened, cowering wight. I could scream with laughter now at that folly! But it did not last long. I returned to it – the Sultan.*

No private palace being near, I was going to that great hotel in Bloomsbury:* but though I knew that numbers of candlesticks would be there, I was not sure that I should find sufficient: for I had acquired the habit within the past few months of sleeping with at least sixty lighted about me, and their form, pattern, style, age, and material was of no small importance. I selected ten from the broken shop, eight gold and silver, and two of old ecclesiastical brass, and having made a bundle, went out, found a bicycle at the Metropolitan Station, pumped it, tied my bundle to the handle-bar, and set off riding. But since I was too lazy to walk, I should certainly have procured some other means of travelling, for I had not gone ten jolted and creaking yards, when something went snap – it was a front fork – and I found myself half on the ground, and half across the bare knees of a Highland soldier. I flew with a shower of kicks upon the foolish thing: but that booted nothing; and this was my last attempt in that way in London, the streets being in an unsuitable condition.

All that dismal night it blew great guns: and during nearly three weeks, till London was no more, there was a storm, with hardly a lull, that seemed to behowl her destruction.

I slept in a room on the second-floor of a Bloomsbury hotel that night; and waking the next day at ten, ate with accursed shiverings in the cold banqueting-room; went out then, and under drear low skies walked a long way to the West district, accompanied all the time by a sound of flapping flags – fluttering robes and rags – and grotesquely grim glimpses of decay. It was pretty cold, and though I was warmly clad, the base *bizarrerie* of the European clothes which I wore had become a perpetual offence and mockery in my eyes: at the first moment, therefore, I set out whither I knew that I should find such clothes as a man might wear: to the Turkish Embassy in Bryanston Square.*

I found it open, and all the house, like most other houses, almost carpeted with dead forms. I had been acquainted with

Redouza Pasha,* and cast an eye about for him amid that invasion of veiled hanums, fierce-looking Caucasians in skins of
beasts, a Sheik-ul-Islam in green cloak, a khalifa, three emirs in
cashmere turbans, two tziganes, their gaudy brown mortality
more glaringly abominable than even the Western's. I could rec-
ognise no Redouza here: but the stair was fairly clear, and I
soon came to one of those boudoirs which sweetly recall the
deep-buried inner seclusion and dim sanctity of the Eastern
home: a door encrusted with mother-of-pearl, sculptured ceiling, candles clustered in tulips and roses of opal, a brazen
brasero, and, all in disarray, the silken chemise, the long winter-
cafetan doubled with furs, costly cabinets, sachets of aromas,
babooshes, stuffs of silk. When, after two hours, I went from
the house, I was bathed, anointed, combed, scented, and
robed.

I have said to myself: 'I will ravage and riot in my Kingdoms. I
will rage like the Cæsars, and be a withering blight where I pass
like Sennacherib, and wallow in soft delights like Sardanapalus.* I will build me a palace, vast as a city, in which to strut
and parade my Monarchy before the Heavens, with stones of
pure molten gold, and rough frontispiece of diamond, and
cupola of amethyst, and pillars of pearl. For there were many
men to the eye: but there was One only, really: and I was he.
And always I knew it – some faintest secret whisper which
whispered me: "*You* are the Arch-one,* the *motif* of the world,
Adam, and the rest of men not much." And they are gone – all!
all! – as no doubt they deserved: and I, as was meet, remain.
And there are wines, and opiums, and haschish; and there are
oils, and spices, fruits and bivalves, and soft-breathing Cyclades, and scarlet luxurious Orients.* I will be restless and
turbulent in my territories: and again, I will be languishing and
fond. I will say to my soul: "Be Full."'

I watch my mind, as in the old days I would watch a new pre-
cipitate in a test-tube, to see into what sediment it would settle.

I am very averse to trouble of any sort, so that the necessity
for the simplest manual operations will rouse me to indignation:

but if a thing will contribute largely to my ever-growing volup-tuousness, I will undergo a considerable amount of labour to accomplish it, though without steady effort, being liable to side-winds and whims, and purposeless relaxations.

In the country I became very irritable at the need which con-fronted me of occasionally cooking some green vegetable – the only item of food which it was necessary to take some trouble over: for all meats, and many fish, some quite delicious, I find already prepared in forms which will remain good probably a century after my death, should I ever die. In Gloucester, how-ever, I found peas, asparagus, olives, and other greens, already prepared to be eaten without base cares: and these, I now see, exist everywhere in stores so vast comparatively to the needs of a single man, that they may be called infinite. Everything, in fact, is infinite compared with my needs. I take my meals, there-fore, without more trouble than a man who had to carve his joint, or chicken: though even that little I sometimes find most irksome. There remains the detestable degradation of lighting fires for warmth, which I have occasionally to do: for the fire at the hotel invariably goes out while I sleep. But that is an incon-venience of this vile northern island only, to which I shall soon bid eternal glad farewells.

During the afternoon of my second day in London, I sought out a strong petrol motor in Holborn, overhauled and oiled it a little, and set off over Blackfriars Bridge, making for Wool-wich through that other more putrid London on the south river-side. One after the other, I connected, as I came upon them, two drays, a cab, and a private carriage, to my motor in line behind, having cut away the withered horses, and using the reins, chain-harness, &c., as impromptu couplings. And with this novel train, I rumbled eastward.

Half-way I happened to look at my old silver chronometer of *Boreal*-days, which I have kept carefully wound – and how I can be still thrown into these sudden frantic agitations by a nothing, a *nothing*, my good God! I do not know. This time it was only the simple fact that the hands chanced to point to 3.10 P.M., the precise moment at which all the clocks of London had stopped – for each town has its thousand weird fore-fingers, pointing, pointing still, to the moment of doom. In London it was 3.10 on a Sunday afternoon. I first noticed it going up the river on the face of the 'Big Ben' of the Parliament-house, and I now find that they all, all, have this 3.10 mania, time-keepers still, but keepers of the end of Time, fixedly noting for ever and ever that one moment. The cloud-mass of fine penetrating scoriæ* must have instantly stopped their works, and they had fallen silent with man. But in their insistence upon this particular minute I had found something so hideously solemn, yet mock-solemn, personal, and as it were addressed to *me*, that when my own watch dared to point to the same moment, I was thrown into one of those sudden, paroxysmal, panting turmoils of mind, half rage, half horror, which have hardly once visited me since I left the *Boreal*. On the morrow, alas, another awaited me; and again on the second morrow after.

My train was execrably slow, and not until after five did I arrive at the entrance-gates of the Woolwich Royal Arsenal; and seeing that it was too late to work, I uncoupled the motor, and leaving the others there, turned back; but overtaken by lassitude, I procured candles, stopped at the Greenwich Observatory, and in that old dark pile, remained for the night, listening to a furious storm. But, a-stir by eight the next morning, I got back by ten to the Arsenal, and proceeded to analyse that vast and multiple entity. Many parts of it seemed to have been abandoned in undisciplined haste, and in the Cap Factory, which I first entered, I found tools by which to effect entry into any desired part. My first search was for time-fuses of good type, of which I needed two or three thousand, and after a wearily long time found a great number symmetrically arranged in rows in a range of buildings called the Ordnance Store Department. I then descended, walked back to the wharf, brought up my train, and began to lower the fuses in bag-fulls by ropes through a shoot, letting go each rope as the fuses reached the cart. However, on winding one fuse, I found that the mechanism would not go, choked with scoriæ; and I had to resign myself to the task of opening and dusting every one: a wretched labour in which I spent that day, like a workman. But about four I threw them to the devil, having done two hundred odd, and then hummed back in the motor to London.

That same evening at six I paid, for the first time, a visit to my old self in Harley Street. It was getting dark, and a bleak storm that hooted like whooping-cough swept the world. At once I saw that even *I* had been invaded: for my door swung open, banging, a lowered catch preventing it from slamming; in the passage the car-lamp shewed me a young man who seemed a Jew, sitting as if in sleep with dropped head, a back-tilted silk-hat pressed down upon his head to the ears; and lying on face, or back, or side, six more, one a girl with Arlesienne head-dress, one a negress, one a Deal lifeboat's-man, and three of uncertain race; the first room – the waiting-room – is much more numer-ously occupied, though there still, on the table, lies the volume of *Punch*, the *Gentlewoman*, and the book of London views in heliograph.* Behind this, descending two steps, is the study and consulting-room, and there, as ever, the revolving-cover oak writing-desk: but on my little shabby-red sofa, a large lady much too big for it, in shimmering brown silk, round her left wrist a *trousseau* of massive gold trinkets, her head dropped right back, almost severed by an infernal gash from the throat. Here were two old silver candle-sticks, which I lit, and went up-stairs: in the drawing-room sat my old house-keeper, pla-cidly dead in a rocking-chair, her left hand pressing down a batch of the open piano-keys, among many strangers. But she was very good: she had locked my bedroom against intrusion; and as the door stands across a corner behind a green-baize curtain, it had not been seen, or, at least, not forced. I did not know where the key might be, but a few thumps with my back drove it open: and there lay my bed intact, and everything tidy. This was a strange coming-back to it, Adam.

But what intensely interested me in that room was a big thing standing at the maroon-and-gold wall between wardrobe and dressing-table – that gilt frame – and that man painted within it there. It was myself in oils, done by – I forget his name now: a towering celebrity he was, and rather a close friend of mine at one time. In a studio in St John's Wood,* I remember, he did it; and many people said that it was quite a great work of art. I suppose I was standing before it quite thirty minutes that night, holding up the bits of candle, lost in wonder, in amused contempt at that thing there. It is I, certainly: that I must admit. There is the high-curving brow – really a King's brow, after all, it strikes me now – and that vacillating look about the eyes and mouth which used to make my sister Ada say: 'Adam is weak and luxurious.' Yes, that is wonderfully done, the eyes, that dear, vacillating look of mine; for although it is rather a staring look, yet one can almost see the dark pupils stir from side to side: very well done. And there is the longish face; and the rather thin, stuck-out moustache, shewing both lips which pout a bit; and there is the nearly black hair; and there is the rather visible paunch; and there is, oh good Heaven, the neat pink cravat – ah, it must have been *that* – *the cravat* – that made me burst out into laughter so loud, mocking and uncontrollable the moment my eye rested there! 'Adam Jeffson,' I muttered reproachfully when it was over, 'could that poor thing in the frame have been *you*?'

I cannot quite state why the tendency toward Orientalism – Oriental dress – all the manner of an Oriental monarch – has taken full possession of me: but so it is: for surely I am hardly any longer a Western, 'modern' mind, but a primitive and Eastern one. Certainly, that cravat in the frame has receded a million, million leagues, ten thousand forgotten æons, from me! Whether this is a result due to my own personality, of old acquainted with Eastern notions, or whether, perhaps, it is the natural accident to any mind wholly freed from trammels, I do not know. But I seem to have gone right back to the very beginnings, and resemblance with man in his first, simple, gaudy conditions. My hair, as I sit here writing, already hangs a black, oiled string down my back; my scented beard sweeps in two opening whisks to my ribs; I have on the *izar*, a pair of drawers of yomani cloth like cotton, but with yellow stripes; over this a soft shirt, or *quamis*, of white silk, reaching to my calves; over this a short vest of gold-embroidered crimson, the *sudeyree*; over this a khaftan of green-striped silk, reaching to the ankles, with wide, long sleeves divided at the wrist, and bound at the waist with a voluminous gaudy shawl of Cashmere for girdle; over this a warm wide-flowing torrent of white drapery, lined with ermine. On my head is the skull-cap, covered by a high crimson cap with deep-blue tassel; and on my feet is a pair of thin yellow-morocco shoes, covered over with thick red-morocco babooshes. My ankles – my ten fingers – my wrists – are heavy with gold and silver ornaments; and in my ears, which, with considerable pain, I bored three days since, are two needle-splinters, to prepare the holes for rings.

O Liberty! I am free ...

While I was going to visit my old home in Harley Street that night, at the very moment when I turned from Oxford Street into Cavendish Square, this thought, fiercely hissed into my ears, was all of a sudden seething in me: 'If now I should lift my eyes, and see a man walking yonder – just yonder – *at the corner there* – turning from Harewood Place into Oxford Street – what, my good God, should I do? – I without even a knife to run and plunge into his heart?'*

And I turned my eyes – ogling, suspicious eyes of furtive horror – reluctantly, lingeringly turned – and I peered deeply with lowered brows across the murky winds at that same spot: but no man was there.

Hideously frequent is this nonsense now become with me – in streets of towns – in deep nooks of the country: the invincible assurance that, if I but turn the head, and glance *there* – at a certain fixed spot – I shall surely see – I *must* see – a man. And glance I must, glance I must, though I perish: and when I glance, though my hairs creep and stiffen like stirring amœbæ, yet in my eyes, I know, is monarch indignation against the intruder, and my neck stands stiff as sovereignty itself, and on my brow sits more than all the lordship of Persepolis and Iraz.

To what point of wantonness this arrogance of royalty may lead me, I do not know: I will watch, and see. It is written: 'It is not good for man to be alone!' But good or no, the arrange-ment of One planet, One inhabitant, already seems to me, not merely a natural and proper, but the *only* natural and proper, condition; so much so, that any other arrangement has now, to my mind, a certain improbable, wild, and far-fetched unreality, like the utopian schemes of dreamers and faddists. That the whole world should have been made for *me* alone – that London should have been built only in order that *I* might enjoy the vast heroic spectacle of its burning – that all history, and all civilisation should have existed only in order to accumulate for *my* pleasures its inventions and facilities, its stores of purple and wine, of spices and gold – no more extraordinary does it all seem to me than to some little unreflecting Duke of my former days seemed the possessing of lands which his remote forefathers seized, and slew the occupiers: nor, in reality, is it even so extraordinary, I being alone. But what sometimes strikes me with some surprise is, not that the present condition of the world, with one sole master, should seem the common-place and natural condition, but that it should have come to seem *so* common-place and natural – in nine months. The mind of Adam Jefferson is adaptable.

I sat a long time thinking such things by my bed that night, till finally I was disposed to sleep there. But I had no considerable number of candle-sticks, nor was even sure of candles. I remembered, however, that Peter Peters, three doors away on the other side of the street, had had four handsome silver candelabra in his drawing-room, each containing six stems; and I said to myself: 'I will search for candles in the kitchen, and if I find any, I will go and get Peter Peters' candelabra, and sleep here.'

I took then the two lights which I had, my good God; went down to the passage; then down to the basement; and there had no difficulty in finding three packets of large candles, the fact being, I suppose, that the cessation of gas-lighting had compelled everyone to provide themselves in this way, for there were a great many wherever I looked. With these I re-ascended, went into a little alcove on the second-floor where I had kept some drugs, got a bottle of carbolic oil, and for ten minutes went dashing all the corpses in the house. I then left the two lighted bits of candle on the waiting-room table, and, with the car-lamp, passed along the passage to the front-door, which was very violently banging. I stepped out to find that the storm had increased to a mighty turbulence (though it was dry), which at once caught my clothes, and whirled them into a flapping cloud about and above me; also, I had not crossed the street when my lamp was out. I persisted, however, half blinded, to Peters' door. It was locked: but immediately near the pavement was a window, the lower sash up, into which, with little trouble, I lifted myself and passed. My foot, as I lowered it, stood on a body: and this made me angry and restless. I hissed a curse, and passed on, scraping the carpet with my soles, that I might hurt no one: for I did not wish to hurt any one. Even in the almost darkness of the room I recognised Peters' furniture, as I expected: for the house was his on a long lease, and I knew that his mother had had the intention to occupy it after his death. But as I passed into the passage, all was mere blank darkness, and I, depending upon the lamp, had left the matches in the other house. I groped my way to the stairs, and had my foot on the first step, when I was stopped by a vicious shaking of the front-door, which someone seemed to be at with hustlings and the most urgent poundings: I stood with peering stern brows two or three minutes, for I knew that if I once yielded to the flinching at my heart, no mercy would be shown me in this house of tragedy, and thrilling shrieks would of themselves arise and ring through its haunted chambers. The rattling continued an inordinate time, and so instant and imperative, that it seemed as if it could not fail to force the door. But, though horrified, I whispered to my heart that it could only be the storm which was struggling at it like the grasp of a man, and after a time went on, feeling my way by the broad rail, in my brain somehow the thought of a dream which I had had in the *Boreal* of the woman Clodagh, how she let drop a fluid like pomegranate-seeds into water, and tendered it to Peter Peters: and it was a mortal purging-draught; but I would not stop, but step by step went up, though I suffered very much, my brows peering at the utter darkness, and my heart shocked at its own rashness. I got to the first landing, and as I turned to ascend the second part of the stair, my left hand touched something icily cold: I made some quick instinctive movement of terror, and, doing so, my foot struck against something, and I stumbled, half falling over what seemed a small table there. Immediately a horrible row followed, for something fell to the ground; and at that instant, ah, I heard something – a voice – a human voice, which uttered words close to my ear – the voice of Clodagh, for I knew it: yet not the voice of Clodagh in the flesh, but her voice clogged with clay and worms, and full of effort, and thick-tongued: and in that ghastly speech of the grave I distinctly heard the words:

'*Things being as they are in the matter of the death of Peter…*'

And there it stopped dead, leaving me so sick, my God, so sick, that I could hardly snatch my robes about me to fly, fly, fly, soft-footed, murmuring in pain, down the steps, down like a sneaking thief, but quick, snatching myself away, then wrestling with the cruel catch of the door which she would not let me open, feeling her all the time behind me, watching me. And when I did get out, I was away up the length of the street, trailing my long *jubbah*, glancing backward, panting, for I thought that she might dare to follow, with her daring evil will. And all that night I lay on a common bench in the wind-tossed and dismal Park.

The first thing which I did when the sun was up was to return to that place: and I returned with hard and masterful brow.

Approaching Peters' house I saw now, what the darkness had hidden from me, that on his balcony was someone – quite alone there. The balcony is a slight open-work wrought-iron structure, connected to a small roof by three slender voluted pillars, two at the ends, one in the middle: and at the middle one I saw someone, a woman – kneeling – her arms clasped tight about the pillar, and her face rather upward-looking. Never did I see aught more horrid: there were the gracious curves of the woman's bust and hips still well preserved in a clinging dress of red cloth, very faded now; and her reddish hair floated loose in a large flimsy cloud about her; but her face, in that exposed position, had been quite eaten away by the winds to a noseless skeleton, which grinned from ear to ear, with slightly-dropped under-jaw – most horrid in contrast with the body, and frame of hair. I meditated upon her a long time that morning from the opposite pavement. An oval locket at her throat contained, I knew, my likeness: for eight years previously I had given it her. It was Clodagh, the poisoner.

I thought that I would go into that house, and walk through it from top to bottom, and sit in it, and spit in it, and stamp in it, in spite of any one: for the sun was now high. I accordingly went in again, and up the stairs to the spot where I had been frightened, and had heard the words. And here a great rage took me, for I at once saw that I had been made the dupe of the malign wills that beset me, and the laughing-stock of Those for whom I care not a fig. From a little mahogany table there I had knocked sideways to the ground, in my stumble, a small phonograph with a great 25-inch japanned-tin horn, which, the moment that I now noticed it, I took and flung with a great racket down the stairs: for that this it was which had addressed me I did not doubt; it being indeed evident that its clock-work mechanism had been stopped by the volcanic scoriæ in the midst of the delivery of a record, but had been started into a few fresh oscillations by the shock of the fall, making it utter those thirteen words, and stop. I was sufficiently indignant at the moment, but have since been glad, for I was thereby put upon the notion of collecting a number of cylinders with records,* and have been touched with indescribable sensations, sometimes thrilled, at hearing the silence of this Eternity broken by those singing and speaking voices, so life-like, yet most ghostly, of the old dead.

Well, the most of that same day I spent in a high chamber at Woolwich, dusting out, and sometimes oiling, time-fuses: a work in which I acquired such facility in some hours, that each finally occupied me no more than ninety to a hundred seconds, so that by evening I had, with the previous day's work, close on 600. The construction of these little things is very simple, and, I believe, effective, so that I should have no difficulty in making them myself in large numbers, if it were necessary. Most contain a tiny dry battery, which sends a current along a bell or copper wire at the running-down moment, the clocks being contrived to be set for so many days, hours, and minutes, while others ignite by striking. I arranged in rows in the covered van those which I had prepared, and passed the night in an inn near the Barracks. I had brought candle-sticks from London in the morning, and arranged the furniture – a settee, chest-of-drawers, basin-stand, table, and a number of chairs – in three-quarter-circle round the bed, so getting a triple-row altar of lights, mixed with vases of the house containing small palms and evergreens; with this I mingled a smell of ambergris from the scattered contents of some Turkish sachets which I had; in the bed a bottle of sweet Chypre-wine,* with *bon-bons*, nuts, and Havannas. As I lay me down, I could not but reflect, with a smile which I knew to be evil, upon that steady, strong, smouldering lust within me which was urging me through all those pains at the Arsenal, I who shirked every labour as unkingly. So, however, it was: and the next morning I was at it again after an early breakfast, my fingers at first quite stiff with cold, for it blew a keen and January gale. By nine I had 820 fuses; and judging those sufficient to commence with, got into the motor, and took it round to a place called the East Laboratory, a series of detached buildings, where I knew that I should find whatever I wanted: and I prepared my mind for a day's labour. In this place I found incredible stores: mountains of percussion-caps, more chambers of fuses, small-arm cartridges, shells, and all those murderous explosive mixtures, a-making and made, with which modern savagery occupied its leisure in exterminating itself: or, at least, savagery civilised in its top-story only: for civilisation was apparently from the head downwards, and never once grew below the neck in all those centuries, those people being certainly much more mental than cordial, though I doubt if they were genuinely mental either – reminding one rather of that composite image of Nebuchadnezzar, head of gold, breast brazen, feet of clay – head man-like, heart cannibal, feet bestial – like ægipeds, and mermaids, and puzzling undeveloped births.* However, it is of no importance: and perhaps I am not much better than the rest, for I, too, after all, am of them. At any rate, their lyddites, melanites, cordites, dynamites, powders,

jellies, oils, marls and civilised barbarisms and obiahs, came in
very well for their own destruction:* for by two o'clock I had
so worked, that I had on the first cart the phalanx of fuses; on
the second a goodly number of kegs, cartridge-cases and car-
tridge-boxes, full of powder, explosive cottons and gelatines,
and liquid nitro-glycerine, and earthy dynamite, with some
bombs, two reels of cordite, two pieces of tarred cloth, a small
iron ladle, a shovel, and a crow-bar; the cab came next, containing a considerable quantity of loose coal; and lastly, in the
private carriage lay four big cans of common oil. And first, in
the Laboratory, I connected a fuse-conductor with a huge tun
of blasting-gelatine, and I set the fuse on the ground, timed for
the midnight of the twelfth day thence; and after that I visited
the Main Factory, the Carriage Department, the Ordnance
Store Department, the Royal Artillery Barracks, and the Powder
Magazines in the Marshes, traversing, as it seemed to me, miles
of building; and in some I laid heaps of oil-saturated coal with
an explosive in suitable spots on the ground-floor near wood-
work, and in some an explosive alone: and all I timed for
ignition at midnight of the twelfth day.

Hot now, and black as ink, I proceeded through the town,
stopping with perfect system at every hundredth door: and I
laid the faggots of a great burning; and timed them all for ignition at midnight of the twelfth day.*

Whatever door I found closed against me I drove at it with a
maniac malice.

Shall I commit the whole dark fact to paper? – that deep, deep
secret of the human organism?

As I wrought, I waxed wicked as a demon! And with lowered neck, and forward curve of the lower spine, and the
blasphemous strut of tragic play-actors, I went. For here was
no harmless burning which I did – but the crime of arson; and
a most fiendish, though vague, malevolence, and the rage to
burn and raven and riot, was upon me like a dog-madness, and
all the mood of Nero, and Nebuchadnezzar:* and from my
mouth proceeded all the obscenities of the slum and of the

gutter, and I sent up such hisses and giggles of challenge to Heaven that day as never yet has man let out. But this way lies a spinning frenzy...

I have taken a dead girl with wild huggings to my bosom; and I have touched the corrupted lip, and spat upon her face, and tossed her down, and crushed her teeth with my heel, and jumped and jumped upon her breast, like the snake-stamping zebra, mad, mad...!

I was desolated, however, that first day of the faggot-laying, even in the midst of my sense of omnipotence, by one thing, which made me give some kicks to the motor: for it was only crawling, so that a good part of the way I was stalking by its side; and when I came to that hill near the Old Dover Road, the whole thing stopped, and refused to move, the weight of the train being too great for my horse-power traction. I did not know what to do, and stood there in angry impotence a full half-hour, for the notion of setting up an electric station, with or without automatic stoking-gear, presented so hideous a picture of labour to me, that I would not entertain it. After a time, however, I thought that I remembered that there was a comparatively new power-station in St Pancras* driven by turbines: and at once, I uncoupled the motor, covered the drays with the tarpaulins, and went driving at singing speed, choosing the emptier by-streets, and not caring whom I crushed. After some trouble I found, in fact, the station in an obscure by-street made of two long walls, and went in by a window, a rage upon me to have my will quickly accomplished. I ran up some stairs, across two rooms, into a gallery containing a switch-board, and in the room below saw the works, all very neat-looking, but, as I soon found, very dusty. I went down, and fixed upon a generating set – there were three – that would give a decent load, and then saw that the switch-gear belonging to this particular generator was in order. I then got some cloths and thoroughly cleaned the dust off the commutators; ran next – for I was in a strange fierce haste – and turned the water into the turbines, and away went the engine; I hurried to set the lubricators running on the bearings, and in a couple of minutes had adjusted the speed, and the brushes of the generators, and switched the current on to the line. By this time, however, I saw that it was getting dark, and feared that little could be done that day; still, I hurried out, the station still running, got into the car, and was off to look for a good electric one, of which there are hosts in the streets, in order at least to clean up and adjust the motor that night. I drove down three by-streets, till I turned into Euston Road: but I had no sooner reached it than I pulled up – with sudden jerk – with a shout of astonishment.

That cursed street was all lighted up and gay! and three shimmering electric globes, not far apart, illuminated every feature of a ghastly battle-field of dead.

And there was a thing there, the grinning impression of which I shall carry to my grave: a thing which spelled and spelled at me, and ceased, and began again, and ceased, and spelled at me. For, above a shop which faced me was a flag, a red flag with white letters, fluttering on the gale the words: 'Metcalfe's Stores'; and beneath the flag, stretched right across the house, was the thing which spelled, letter by letter, in letters of light: and it spelled two words, deliberately, coming to the end, and going back to recommence:

Drink
ROBORAL.

And that was the last word of civilised Man to me, Adam Jeffson – its final counsel – its ultimate gospel and message – to *me*, my good God! *Drink Roboral!**

I was put into such a passion of rage by this blatant ribaldry, which affected me like the laughter of a skeleton, that I rushed from the car, with the intention, I believe, of seeking stones to stone it: but no stones were there: and I had to stand impotently enduring that rape of my eyes, its victoriously-dogged iteration, its taunting leer, its Drink Roboral – D, R, I, N, K R, O, B, O, R, A, L.

It was one of those electrical spelling-advertisements, worked by a small motor commutator driven by a works-motor, and I had now set it going: for on some night before that Sabbath of doom the chemist must have set it to work, but finding the works abandoned, had not troubled to shut it down again. At any rate, this thing stopped my work for that day, for when I went to shut down the works it was night; and I drove to the place which I had made my home in sullen and weary mood: for I knew that Roboral would not cure the least of all my sores.

The next morning I awoke in quite another frame of mind, disposed to idle, and let things go. After rising, dressing, washing in cold diluted rose-water, and descending to the *salle-à-manger*, where I had laid my morning-meal the previous evening, I promenaded an hour the only one of these long sombrous tufted corridors in which there were not more than two dead, though behind the doors on either hand, all of which I had locked, I knew that they lay in plenty. When I was warmed, I again went down, looked into my motor, got three cylinders from one of a number of motors standing near, lit up, and drove away – to Woolwich, as I thought at first: but instead of crossing the river by Blackfriars, I went more eastward; and having passed from Holborn into Cheapside, which was impassable, unless I crawled, was about to turn, when I noticed a phonograph-shop: into this I got by a side-door, suddenly seized by quite a curiosity to hear what I might hear. I took a good one with microphone diaphragm, and a number of record-cylinders in a brass-handled box, and I put them into the car, for there was still a very strong peach-odour in this closed shop, which displeased me. I then proceeded southward and westward through by-streets, seeking some probable house into which to go from the rough cold winds, when I saw the Parliament-house, and thither, turning river-ward by Westminster Hall to Palace Yard, I went, and with my two parcels, one weighting each arm, walked into this old place along a line of purple-dusted busts; I deposited my boxes on a table beside a massive brass thing lying there, which, I suppose, must be what they called the Mace; and I sat to hear.

Unfortunately, the phonograph was a clockwork one, and when I wound it, it would not go: so that I got very angry at my absurdity in not bringing an electric mechanism, as I could with much less trouble have put in a chemical than cleaned the clock-work; and this thing put me into such a rage, that I nearly tore it to pieces, and was half for kicking it: but there was a man sitting in an old straight-backed chair quite near me, which they called the Speaker's Chair, who was in such a pose, that he had, every time I glanced suddenly at him, precisely the air of bending forward with interest to watch what I was doing, a Mohrgrabim kind of man, almost black, with Jewish nose, crinkled hair, keffie, and flowing robe, probably, I should say, an Abyssinian Galla;* with him were only five or six people about the benches, mostly leaning forward with rested head, so that this place had quite a void sequestered mood. At all events, this Galla, or Bedouin, with his grotesque interest in my doings, restrained my hands: and, finally, by dint of peering, poking, dusting, and adjusting, in an hour's time I got the phonograph to go very well.

And all that morning, and far into late afternoon, forgetful of food, and of the cold which gradually possessed me, I sat there listening, musing – cylinder after cylinder: frivolous songs, orchestras, voices of famous men whom I had spoken with, and shaken their solid hands, speaking again to me, but thick-tongued, with hoarse effort and gurgles, from out the vague void beyond the grave: most strange, most strange. And the third cylinder that I put on, ah, I knew, with a fearful start, that voice of thunder, I knew it well: it was the preacher, Mackay's; and many, many times over I heard those words of his that day, originally spoken, it seems, when the cloud had just passed the longitude of Vienna; and in all that torrent of speech not one single word of 'I told you so': but he cries:

'...praise Him, O Earth, for He is He: and if He slay me, I will laugh raillery at His Sword, and banter Him to His face: for His Sword is sharp Mercy, and His poisons kill my death. Fear not, therefore, little flock of Man! but take my comfort to your heart to-night, and my sweets to your tongue: for though ye have sinned, and hardened yourselves as brass, and gone far, far astray in these latter wildernesses, yet He is infinitely greater than your sin, and will lead you back. Break not, break not,

poor broken heart of Earth: for from Him I run herald to thee
this night with the sweet and secret message, that of old He
chose thee, and once mixed conjugally with thee in an ancient
sleep, O Afflicted: and He is thou, and thou art He, flesh of His
flesh, and bone of His bone; and if thou perish utterly, it is that
He has perished utterly, too: for thou art He. Hope, therefore,
most, and cheeriest smile, at the very apsis and black nadir of
Despair: for He is nimble as a weasel, and He twists like
Proteus, and His solstices and equinoxes, His tropics and turn-
ing-points and recurrences are innate in Being, and when He
falls He falls like harlequin and shuttle-cocks, shivering plumb
to His feet, and each third day, lo, He is risen again, and His
defeats are but the stepping-stones and rough scaffolding from
which He builds His Parthenons, and from the densest basalt
gush His rills, and the last end of this Earth shall be no poison-
cloud, I say to you, but Carnival and Harvest-home ...though
ye have sinned, poor hearts...'

So Mackay, with thick-tongued metallic effort. I found this brown
room of the Commons-house, with its green benches, and grilled
galleries, so agreeable to my mood, that I went again the next
morning, and listened to more records, till they tired me: for what
I had was a prurient itch to hear secret scandals, and revelations
of the festering heart, but these cylinders, gathered from a shop,
divulged nothing. I then went out to make for Woolwich, but in
the car saw the poet's note-book in which I had written: and I
took it, went back, and was writing an hour, till I was tired of
that, too; and judging it too late for Woolwich that day, wandered
about the dusty committee-rooms and recesses of this considerable place. In one room another foolishness suddenly seized upon
me, shewing how my slightest whim has become more imperious
within me than all the laws of the Medes and Persians: for in that
room, Committee Room No. 15, I found an apparently young
policeman lying flat on his back, who pleased me: his helmet tilted
under his head, and near one white-gloved hand a blue official
envelope; the air of that stagnant quiet room was still perceptibly
peach-scented, and he gave not the slightest odour that I could
detect, though he had been corporal and stalwart, his face now

the colour of dark ashes, in each hollow cheek a ragged hole about the size of a sixpence, the flimsy vaulted eye-lids well embedded in their caverns, from under whose fringe of eye-lash seemed whispered the word: '*Eternity*.' His hair seemed very long for a policeman, or perhaps it had grown since death; but what interested me about him, was the envelope at his hand: for 'what,' I asked myself, 'was this fellow doing here with an envelope at three o'clock on a Sunday afternoon?' This made me look closer, and then I saw by a mark at the left temple that he had been shot, or felled; whereupon I was thrown into quite a great rage, for I thought that this poor man was killed in the execution of his duty, when many of his kind perhaps, and many higher than he, had fled their post to pray or riot. So, after looking at him a long time, I said to him: 'Well, D. 47, you sleep very well: and you did well, dying so: I am pleased with you, and to mark my favour, I decree that you shall neither rot in the common air, nor burn in the common flames: for by my own hand shall you be distinguished with burial.' And this wind so possessed me, that I at once went out: with the crow-bar from the car I broke the window of a near iron-monger's in Parliament Street, got a spade, and went into Westminster Abbey. I soon prised up a grave-slab of some famous man in the north transept, and commenced to shovel: but, I do not know how, by the time I had digged a foot the whole impulse passed from me; I left off the work, promising to resume it: but nothing was ever done, for the next day I was at Woolwich, and busy enough about other matters.

During the next nine days I worked with a fever on me, and a map of London before me.

There were places in that city! – secrets, vastnesses, horrors! In the wine-vaults at London Docks was a vat which must certainly have contained between twenty and thirty thousand gallons: and with dancing heart I laid a train there; the tobacco-warehouse must have covered eighty acres: and there I laid a fuse. In a house near Regent's Park, standing in a garden, and shut from the street by a high wall, I saw a thing...! and what shapes a great city hid I now first know.

*

I left no quarter unremembered, taking a train, no longer of four, but of eight, vehicles, drawn by an electric motor which I re-charged every morning, mostly from the turbine station in St Pancras, once from a steam-station with very small engine and dynamo, found in the Palace Theatre, which gave little trouble, and once from a similar little station in a Strand hotel. With these I visited West Ham and Kew, Finchley and Clapham, Dalston and Marylebone; I exhausted London; I deposited piles in the Guildhall, in Holloway Gaol, in the new pillared Justicehall of Newgate, in the Tower, in the Parliament-house, in St Giles' Workhouse, in the Crypt and under the organ of St Paul's, in the South Kensington Museum, in the Royal Agricultural Society, in Whiteley's place, in the Trinity House, in Liverpool Street, in the Office of Works, in the secret recesses of the British Museum; in a hundred inflammable warehouses, in five hundred shops, in a thousand private dwellings. And I timed them all for ignition at midnight of the 23rd April.

By five in the afternoon of the 22nd, when I left my train in Maida Vale, and drove alone to the solitary house on high ground near Hampstead Heath which I had chosen, the work was well finished.

The great morning dawned, and I was early astir: for I had much to do that day.

I intended to make for the sea-shore the next morning, and had therefore to choose a good petrol motor, store it, and have it in a place of safety; I had also to drag another vehicle after me, stored with trunks of time-fuses, books, clothes, and other little things.

My first journey was to Woolwich, whence I took all that I might ever require in the way of mechanism; thence to the National Gallery, where I cut from their frames the 'Vision of St Helena', Murillo's 'Boy Drinking', and 'Christ at the Column';* and thence to the Embassy to bathe, anoint myself, and dress.

As I had anticipated, and hoped, a blustering spring gale was blowing from the north.

Even as I set out from Hampstead, about 9 A.M., I had been able to guess that some of my fuses had somehow anticipated the appointed hour: for I saw three red hazes at various points in the air, and heard the far vague booming of an occasional explosion; and by 11 A.M. I felt sure that a large region of north-eastern London must be in flames. With the solemn feelings of bridegrooms and marriage-mornings – with a flinching, a flinching heart, God knows, yet a heart up-buoyed on thrilling joys – I went about making preparations for the Gargantuan orgy of the night.

The house at Hampstead, which no doubt still stands, is of rather pleasing design in quite a stone and rural style, with good breadths of wall-surface, two plain coped gables, mullioned windows, and oversailing slate verge roofs, but, rather spoiling it, a high square three-storied tower at the south-east angle,* on the topmost floor of which I had slept the previous night. There I had provided myself with a jar of pale tobacco mixed with rose-leaves and opium, found in a foreign house in Seymour Street, also a genuine Saloniki hookah, together with the best wines, nuts, and so on, and a gold harp of the musician Krasinski,* stamped with his name, taken from his house in Portland Street.

But so much did I find to do that day, and so many odd things turned up which I thought that I would take with me, that it was not till near six that I drove finally northward through Camden Town. And now an ineffable awe possessed my soul at the solemn noise which everywhere encompassed me, an ineffable awe, a blissful terror. Never, never could I have dreamed of aught so great and potent. All above my head there rushed southward with wide-spread wing of haste a sparkling smoke; and mixed with the immense roaring I heard mysterious hubbubs of tumblings and rumblings, which I could not at all comprehend, like the moving-about of furniture in the houses of Titans; while pervading all the air was a most weird and tearful sound, as it were threnody, and a wild wail of pain, and dying swan-songs, and all lamentations and tribulations of the world. Yet I was aware that, at an hour so early, the flames must be far from general; in fact, they had not well commenced.

*

As I had left a good semicircular region of houses, with a radius of four hundred yards, without combustibles to the south of the isolated house which I was to occupy, and as the wind was so strongly from the north, I simply left my two vehicles at the door of the house, without fear of any injury: nor did any occur. I then went up to the top of the tower, lit the candles, and ate voraciously of the dinner which I had left ready, for since the morning I had taken nothing; and then, with hands and heart that quivered, I arranged the clothes of the low spring-bed upon which to throw my frame in the morning hours. Opposite the wall, where lay the bed, was a Gothic window, pretty large, with low sill, hung with poppy-figured muslin, and looking directly south, so that I could recline at ease in the red-velvet easy-chair, and see. It had evidently been a young lady's room: for on the toilette were cut-glass bottles, a plait of brown hair, powders, *rouge-aux-lèvres*,* one little bronze slipper, and knick-knacks, and I loved her and hated her, though I did not see her anywhere. About half-past eight I sat at the window to watch, all being arranged and ready at my right hand, the candles extinguished in the red room: for the theatre was opened, was opened: and the atmosphere of this earth seemed turned into Hell, and Hell was in my soul.

Soon after midnight there was a sudden and very visible increase in the conflagration. On all hands I began to see blazing structures soar, with grand hurrahs, on high. In fives and tens, in twenties and thirties, all between me and the remote limit of my vision, they leapt, they lingered long, they fell. My spirit more and more felt, and danced – deeper mysteries of sensation, sweeter thrills. I sipped exquisitely, I drew out enjoyment leisurely. Anon, when some more expansive angel of flame would arise from the Pit with steady aspiration, and linger with outspread arms, and burst, I would lift a little from the chair, leaning forward to clap, as at some famous acting; or I would call to them in shouts of cheer, giving them the names of Woman. For now I seemed to see nothing but some bellowing pandemonic universe through crimson glasses, and the air was wildly hot, and my eye-balls like theirs that walk staring in the inner midst of burning fiery furnaces, and my skin itched with a fierce and prickly itch. Anon I touched the chords of the harp to the air of Wagner's 'Walküren-ritt'.

Near three in the morning, I reached the climax of my guilty sweets. My drunken eyelids closed in a luxury of pleasure, and my lips lay stretched in a smile that dribbled; a sensation of dear peace, of almighty power, consoled me: for now the whole area which through streaming tears I surveyed, mustering its ten thousand thunders, and brawling beyond the stars the voice of its southward-rushing torment, billowed to the horizon one grand Atlantic of smokeless and flushing flame; and in it sported and washed themselves all the fiends of Hell, with laughter, shouts, wild flights, and holiday; and I – first of my race – had flashed a signal to the nearer planets... *

Those words: 'signal to the nearer planets' I wrote nearly fourteen months ago, some days after the destruction of London, I being then on board the old *Boreal*, making for the coast of France: for the night was dark, though calm, and I was afraid of running into some ship, yet not sleepy, so I wrote to occupy my fingers, the ship lying still. The book in which I wrote has been near me: but no impulse to write anything has visited me, till now I continue; not, however, that I have very much to put down.

I had no intention of wearing out my life in lighting fires every morning to warm myself in the inhospitable island of Britain, and set out to France with the view of seeking some palace in the Riviera, Spain, or perhaps Algiers, there, for the present at least, to make my home.

I started from Calais toward the end of April, taking my things along, the first two days by train, and then determining that I was in no hurry, and a petrol motor easier, took one, and maintained a generally southern and somewhat eastern direction, ever-anew astonished at the wildness of the forest vegetation which, within so short a space since the disappearance of man, chokes this pleasant land, even before the definite advent of summer.

After three weeks of very slow travelling – for though I know several countries very well, France with her pavered villages, hilly character, vines, forests, and primeval country-manner, is always new and charming to me – after three weeks I came unexpectedly to a valley which had never entered my head; and the moment that I saw it, I said: 'Here I will live,' though I had no idea what it was, for the monastery which I saw did not look at all like a monastery, according to my ideas: but when I searched the map, I discovered that it must be La Chartreuse de Vauclaire in Périgord. *

It is my belief that this word 'Vauclaire' is nothing else than a corruption of the Latin *Vallis Clara*, or Bright Valley, for *l*'s and *u*'s did interchange about in this way, I remember: *cheval* becoming *chevau(x)* in the plural, like 'fool' and 'fou', and the rest: which proves the dear laziness of French people, for the 'l' was too much trouble for them to sing, and when they came to *two* 'l's' they quite succumbed, shying that vault, or vo*u*te, and calling it some *y*. But at any rate, this Vauclaire, or Valclear, was well named: for here, if anywhere, is Paradise, and if anyone knew how and where to build and brew liqueurs, it was those good old monks, who followed their Master with *entrain* in that Cana miracle, and in many other things, I fancy, but æsthetically shirked to say to any mountain: 'Be thou removed.'

The general hue of the vale is a deep cerulean, resembling that blue of the robes of Albertinelli's Madonnas;* so, at least, it strikes the eye on a clear forenoon of spring or summer. The monastery consists of an oblong space, or garth, around three sides of which stand sixteen small houses, with regular intervals between, all identical, the cells of the fathers; between the oblong space and the cells come the cloisters, with only one opening to the exterior; in the western part of the oblong is a little square of earth under a large cypress-shade, within which, as in a home of peace, it sleeps: and there, straight and slanting, stand little plain black crosses over graves...

To the west of the quadrangle is the church, with the hostelry, and an asphalted court with some trees and a fountain; and beyond, the entrance-gate.

All this stands on a hill of gentle slope, green as grass; and it is backed close against a steep mountain-side, of which the tree-trunks are conjectural, for I never saw any, the trees resembling rather one continuous leafy tree-top, run out high and far over the extent of the mountain.

I was there four months, till something drove me away. I do not know what had become of the fathers and brothers, for I only found five, four of whom I took in two journeys in the motor beyond the church of Saint Martial d'Artenset, and left them there; and the fifth remained three weeks with me, for I would not disturb him in his prayer. He was a bearded brother of forty years or thereabouts, who knelt in his cell robed and hooded in all his phantom white: for in no way different from whatever is most phantom, visionary and eerie must a procession of these people have seemed by gloaming, or dark night. This particular brother knelt, I say, in his small chaste room, glaring upward at his Christ, who hung long-armed in a little recess between the side of three narrow book-shelves and a projection of the wall; and under the Christ a gilt and blue Madonna; the books on the three shelves few, leaning different ways. His right elbow rested on a square plain table, at which was a wooden chair; behind him, in a corner, the bed: a bed all enclosed in dark boards, a broad perpendicular board along the foot, reaching the ceiling, a horizontal board at the side over which he got into bed, another narrower one like it at the ceiling for fringe and curtain, and another perpendicular one hiding the pillow, making the clean bed within a very shady and cosy little den, on the wall of this den being another smaller Christ, and a little picture. On the perpendicular board at the foot hung two white garments, and over a second chair at the bed-side another: all very neat and holy. He was a large stern man, blond as corn, but with some red, too, in his hairy beard; and appalling was the significance of those eyes that prayed, and the long-drawn cavity of those saffron cheeks. I cannot explain to myself my deep reverence for this man; but I had it, certainly. Many of the others, it is clear, had fled: but not he: and to the near-marching cloud he opposed the Cross, holding one real as the other – he alone among many. For Christianity was an *élite* religion, in

which all were called, but few chosen, differing from Moham-
medanism and Buddhism, which grasped and conquered all
within their reach: the effect of Christ rather resembling Plato's
and Dante's, it would seem: but Mahomet's more like Homer's
and Shakespeare's.

It was my way to plant at the portal the big, carved chair
from the chancel on the hot days, and rest my soul, refusing to
think of anything, drowsing and smoking for hours. All down
there in the plain waved gardens of delicious fruit about the
prolonged silver thread of the river Isle, whose course winds
loitering quite near the foot of the monastery-slope. This slope
dominates a tract of distance that is not only vast, but looks
immense, although the horizon is bounded by a semicircle of
low hills, rather too stiff and uniform for perfect beauty; the
interval of plain being occupied by yellow ploughed lands
which were never sown, weedy now, and crossed and recrossed
by vividly-green ribbons of vine, with stretches of pale-green
lucerne, orchards, and the white village of Monpont near the
railway, all embowered, the Isle drawing its mercurial streams
through the village-meadow, which is dark with shades of oaks:
and to have played there a boy, and used it familiarly from
birth as one's own hand or foot, must have been very sweet and
homely; after this, the river divides, and takes the shape of a
heart; and very far away are visible the grey banks of the
Gironde. On the semicircle of hills, when there was little
distance-mist, I saw the ruins of some seigneurial château, for
the seigneurs, too, knew where to build; and to my left, between
a clump of oaks and an avenue of poplars, the bell-tower of the
village-church of Saint Martial d'Artenset – a very ancient type
of tower, I believe, and common in France, rather ponderous,
consisting of a square mass with a smaller square mass stuck
on, the latter having large Gothic windows; and behind me the
west face of the monastery-church, over the door being the
statue of Saint Bruno.

Well, one morning after four months, I opened my eyes in
my cell to the piercing consciousness that I had burned Monpont over-night: and so overcome was I with regret for this
poor inoffensive little place, that for two days, hardly eating, I

paced between the oak and walnut pews of the nave, massive
stalls they are, separated by grooved Corinthian pilasters, wondering what was to become of me, and if I was not already
mad; and there are some little angels with extraordinarily
human Greuze-like faces,* supporting the nerves of the apse,
which, after a time, every time I passed them, seemed conscious
of me and my existence there; and the wood-work which ornaments the length of the nave, and of the choir also, elaborate
with carved marguerites and roses, here and there took in my
eyes significant forms from certain points of view; and there is
a partition – for the nave is divided into two chapels, one for
the brothers and one for the fathers, I conclude – and in this
partition a massive door, which yet looks quite light and
graceful, carved with oak and acanthus leaves, and every time
I passed through I had the impression that the door was a
sentient thing, subconscious of me; and the delicate Italian-
Renaissance brick vault which springs from the vast nave
seemed to look upon me with a gloomy knowledge of me, and
of the heart within me; and at about four in the afternoon of
the second day, after pacing the church for hours, I fell down at
one of the two altars near that carved door of the screen, praying God to have mercy upon my soul; and in the very midst of
my praying, I was up and away, the devil in me, and I got into
the motor, and did not come back to Vauclaire for another
month, and came leaving great tracts of burned desolation
behind me, towns and forests, Bordeaux burned, Lebourne
burned, Bergerac burned.

I returned to Vauclaire, for it seemed now my home; and there
I experienced a true, a deep repentance; and I humbled myself
before my Maker. And while in this state, sitting one bright day
in front of the monastery-gate, something said to me: 'You will
never be a good man, nor permanently escape Hell and Frenzy,
unless you have an aim in life, devoting yourself heart and soul
to some great work, which will exact all your science, your
thought, your ingenuity, your knowledge of modern things,
your strength of body and will, your skill of head and hand:
otherwise you are bound to succumb. Do this, therefore, begin-

ning, not to-morrow nor this afternoon, but now: for though no man will see your work, there is still the Almighty God, who is also something, in His way: and He will see how you strive, and try, and groan: and perhaps, seeing, He may have mercy upon you.'

In this way arose the idea of the Palace – an idea, indeed, which had entered my brain before, but merely as a bombastic and visionary outcome of my raving moods: now, however, in a very different way, soberly, and soon concerning itself with details, difficulties, means, limitations, and every kind of practical matter-of-fact; and every obstruction which, one by one, I foresaw was, one by one, as the days passed, over-borne by the vigour with which that thought, rapidly becoming a mania, possessed me. After a week of incessant meditation, I decided Yes: and I said: I will build a palace, which shall be both a palace and a temple: the first human temple worthy the King of Heaven, and the only human palace worthy the King of Earth.*

After this decision I remained at Vauclaire another week, a very different man to the lounger it had seen, strenuous, converted, humble, making plans of this and of that, of the detail, and of the whole, drawing, multiplying, dividing, adding, conic sections and the rule-of-three, totting up the period of building, which came out at a little over twelve years, estimating the quantities of material, weight and bulk, my nights full of nightmare as to the *sort*,* deciding as to the size and structure of the crane, forge and work-shop, and the necessarily-limited weights of their component parts, making a list of over 2,400 objects, and finally, up to the third week after my departure from Vauclaire, skimming through the topography of nearly the whole earth, before fixing upon the island of Imbros for my site.*

I returned to England, and, once more, to the hollow windows and strewn streets of black, burned-out and desolate London: for its bank-vaults, etc., contained the necessary complement of the gold brought from Paris, and then lying in the *Speranza* at Dover; nor had I sufficient familiarity with French industries

and methods to find, even with the aid of *Bottins*,* one half of
the 4,000 odd objects which I had now catalogued. My ship
was the *Speranza*, which brought me from Havre, for at Calais,
to which I first went, I could find nothing suitable for all purposes, the *Speranza** being an American yacht, very palatially
fitted, three-masted, air-driven, with a carrying capacity of 2,000
tons, Tobin-bronzed,* in good condition, containing sixteen
interacting tanks, with a five-block pulley-arrangement amid-
ships that enables me to lift very considerable weights without
the aid of the hoisting air-engine, high in the water, sharp, handsome, containing a few tons only of sand-ballast, and needing
when I found her only three days' work at the water-line and
engines to make her decent and fit. I threw out her dead, backed
her from the Outer to the Inner Basin to my train on the quai,
took in the twenty-three hundred-weight bags of gold, and the
half-ton of amber, and with this alone went to Dover, thence to
Canterbury by motor, and thence in a long train, with a store of
dynamite from the Castle for blasting possible obstructions, to
London: meaning to make Dover my *dépôt*, and the London
rails my thoroughfare from all parts of the country.

Instead of three months, as I had calculated, it took me
nine: a harrowing slavery. I had to blast no less than forty-
three trains from the path of my loaded wagons, several times
blasting away the metals as well, and then having to travel
hundreds of yards without metals: for the labour of kindling
the obstructing engines, to shunt them down sidings perhaps
distant, was a thing which I would not undertake. However,
all's well that ends well, though if I had it to go through again,
certainly I should not. The *Speranza* is now lying seven miles
off Cape Roca,* a heavy mist on the still water, this being the
19th of June at 10 in the night: no wind, no moon: cabin full
of mist: and I pretty listless and disappointed, wondering in
my heart why I was such a fool as to take all that trouble, nine
long servile months, my good God, and now seriously thinking of throwing the whole vile thing to the devil; she pretty
deep in the water, pregnant with the palace. When the thirty-
three...*

*

Those words: 'when the thirty-three' were written by me over seventeen years since – long years – seventeen in number, nor have I now any idea to what they refer. The book in which I wrote I had lost in the cabin of the *Speranza*, and yesterday, returning to Imbros from an hour's aimless cruise, discovered it there behind a chest.

I find now considerable difficulty in guiding the pencil, and these few lines now written have quite an odd look, like the handwriting of a man not very proficient in the art: it is seventeen years, seventeen, seventeen...ah! And the expression of my ideas is not fluent either: I have to think for the word a minute, and I should not be surprised if the spelling of some of them is queer. My brain has been thinking inarticulately perhaps, all these years: and the English words and letters, as they now stand written, have rather an improbable and foreign air to me, as a Greek or Russian book might look to a man who has not so long been learning those languages as to forget the impossibly foreign impression received from them on the first day of tackling them. Or perhaps it is only my fancy: for that I have fancies I know.

But what to write? The history of those seventeen years could not be put down, my good God: at least, it would take me seventeen more to do it. If I were to detail the building of the palace alone, and how it killed me nearly, and how I twice fled from it, and had to return, and became its bounden slave, and dreamed of it, and grovelled before it, and prayed, and raved, and rolled; and how I forgot to make provision on the west side for the contraction and expansion of the gold in the colder weather and the heats of summer, and had to break down nine months' work, and how I cursed Thee, how I cursed Thee; and how the lake of wine evaporated faster than the conduits replenished it, and the three journeys which I had to take to Constantinople for shiploads of wine, and my frothing despairs, till I had the thought of placing the reservoir in the platform; and how I had then to break down the south side of the platform to the very bottom, and of the month-long nightmare of terror that I had lest the south side of the palace would undergo subsidence; and how the petrol failed, and of the

three-weeks' search for petrol along the coast; and how, after
list-rubbing all the jet, I found that I had forgotten the necessary rouge for polishing; and how, in the third year, I found
the fluate,* which I had for water-proofing the pores of the
platform-stone, nearly all leaked away in the *Speranza's* hold,
and I had to get silicate of soda at Gallipoli; and how, after
two years' observation, I had to come to the conclusion that
the lake was leaking, and discovered that this Imbros sand
was not suitable for mixing with the skin of Portland cement
which covered the cement concrete, and had to substitute
sheet-bitumen in three places; and how I did all, all for the
sake of God, thinking: 'I will work, and be a good man, and
cast Hell from me: and when I see it stand finished, it will be
an Altar and a Testimony to me, and I shall find peace, and be
well': and how I have been cheated – seventeen years, long
years of my life – for there is no God; and how my plasterers'-
hair failed me, and I had to use flock, hessian, scrym, wadding,
wood-street paving-blocks, and whatever I could find, for filling the interspaces between the platform cross-walls; and of
the espagnolette bolts,* how a number of them mysteriously
disappeared, as if snatched to Hell by harpies, and I had to
make them; and how the crane-chain would not reach two of
the silver-panel castings when they were finished, and they
were too heavy for me to lift, and the wringing of the hands of
my despair, and my biting of the earth, and the transport of
my fury; and how, for a whole wild week, I searched in vain
for the text-book which describes the ambering process; and
how, when all was nearly over, in the blasting away of the
forge and crane with dynamite, a long crack appeared down
the gold of the east platform-steps, and how I would not be
consoled, but mourned and mourned; and how, in spite of all
my tribulations, it was sweetly interesting to watch my power
slowly grow from the first feeble beginnings of the landing of
materials and unloading them from the motor, a hundred-
weight at a time, till I could swing four tons – see the solid
metals flow – enjoy the gliding sounds of the handle, crank-
shaft, and system of levers, forcing inwards the mould-end,
and the upper and lower plungers, for pressing the material –

build at ease in a travelling-cage – and watch from my hut-door through sleepless hours, under the electric moon-light of this land, the three piles of gold stones, the silver panels, the two-foot squares of jet, and be comforted; and how the putty-wash – but it is past, it is past: and not to live over again that vulgar nightmare of means and ends have I taken to this writing again – but to put down something else, if I dare.

Seventeen years, my good God, of that delusion! I could write down no sort of explanation for all those groans and griefs, at which a reasoning being would not shriek with laughter. I should have lived at ease in some palace of the Middle-Orient, and burned my cities: but no, I must be 'a good man' – vain thought. The words of a wild madman, that preaching man in England who prophesied what happened, were with me, where he says: 'the defeat of Man is *His* defeat'; and I said to myself: 'Well, the last man shall not be quite a fiend, just to spite That Other.' And I worked and groaned, saying: 'I will be a good man, and burn nothing, nor utter aught unseemly, nor debauch myself, but choke back the blasphemies that Those Others shriek through my throat, and build and build, with moils and groans.' And it was Vanity: though I do love the house, too, I love it well, for it is my home on the waste earth.

I had calculated to finish it in twelve years, and I should undoubtedly have finished it in fourteen, instead of in sixteen and seven months, but one day, when the south, north, and east platform-steps were already finished – it was in the July of the third year, and near sunset – as I left off work, instead of going to the tent where my dinner lay ready, I walked down to the ship – most strangely – in a daft, mechanical sort of way, without saying a word to myself, an evil-meaning smile of malice on my lips; and at midnight I was lying off Mitylene, thirty miles to the south, having bid, as I thought, a last farewell to all those toils. I was going to burn Athens.

I did not, however: but kept on my way westward round Cape Matapan, intending to destroy the forests and towns of Sicily, if I found there a suitable motor for travelling, for I had not been at the pains to take the motor on board at Imbros; otherwise I would ravage parts of southern Italy. But when I came thereabouts, I was confronted with an awful horror: for no southern Italy was there, and no Sicily was there, unless a small new island, probably not five miles long, was Sicily; and nothing else I saw, save the still-smoking crater of Stromboli.* I cruised northward, searching for land, and for a long time would not believe the evidence of the instruments, thinking that they wilfully misled me, or I stark mad. But no: no Italy was there, till I came to the latitude of Naples, it, too, having disappeared, engulfed, engulfed, all that stretch. From this monstrous thing I received so solemn a shock and mood of awe, that the evil mind in me was quite chilled and quelled: for it was, and is, my belief that a widespread re-arrangement of the earth's surface is being purposed, and in all that drama, O my God, how shall *I* be found?

However, I went on my way, but more leisurely, not daring for a long time to do anything, lest I might offend anyone; and, in this foolish cowering mind, coasted all the western coast of Spain and France during five weeks, in that prolonged intensity of calm weather which now alternates with storms that transcend all thought, till I came again to Calais: and there, for the first time, landed.

Here I would no longer contain myself, but burned; and that magnificent stretch of forest that lay between Agincourt and Abbéville, covering five square miles, I burned; and Abbéville I burned; and Amiens I burned; and three forests between Amiens and Paris I burned; and Paris I burned; burning and burning during four months, leaving behind me smoking districts, a long tract of ravage, like some being of the Pit that blights where pass his flaming wings.

This city-burning has now become a habit with me more enchaining – and infinitely more debased – than ever was opium to the smoker, or alcohol to the drunkard. I count it among the prime necessaries of my life: it is my brandy, my bacchanal, my secret sin. I have burned Calcutta, Pekin and San Francisco.* In spite of the restraining influence of this palace, I have burned and burned. I have burned two hundred cities and countrysides. Like Leviathan disporting himself in the sea, so I have rioted in this earth.

*

After an absence of six months, I returned to Imbros: for I was for looking again upon the work which I had done, that I might mock myself for all that unkingly grovelling: and when I saw it, standing there as I had left it, frustrate and forlorn, and waiting its maker's hand, some pity and instinct to build took me – for something of God was in Man – and I fell upon my knees, and spread my arms to God, and was converted, promising to finish the palace, with prayers that as I built so He would build my soul, and save the last man from the enemy. And I set to work that day to list-rub the last few dalles of the jet.*

I did not leave Imbros after that during four years, except for occasional brief trips to the coast – to Kilid-Bahr, Gallipoli, Lapsaki, Gamos, Rodosto, Erdek, Erekli, or even once to Constantinople and Scutari – if I happened to want anything, or if I was tired of work: but without once doing the least harm to anything, but containing my humours, and fearing my Maker. And full of peaceful charm were those little cruises through this Levantic world, which, truly, is rather like a light sketch in water-colours done by an angel than like the dun real earth; and full of self-satisfaction and pious contentment would I return to Imbros, approved of my conscience, for that I had surmounted temptation, and lived tame and stainless.

I had set up the southern of the two closed-lotus pillars, and the platform-top was already looking as lovely as heaven, with its alternate two-foot squares of pellucid gold and pellucid jet, when I noticed one morning that the *Speranza*'s bottom was really now too foul, and the whim took me then and there to leave all, and clean her as far as I could. I at once went on board, descended to the hold, took off my sudeyrie, and began to shift the ballast over to starboard, so as to tilt up her port bottom to the scraper. This was wearying labour, and about noon I was sitting on a bag, resting in the almost darkness, when something seemed to whisper to me these words: '*You dreamed last night that there is an old Chinaman alive in Pekin.*' Horridly I started: I *had* dreamed something of the sort, but, from the moment of waking, till then, had forgotten it: and I leapt livid to my feet.

I cleaned no *Speranza* that day, nor for four days did I anything, but sat on the cabin-house and mused, my supporting palm among the hairy draperies of my chin: for the thought of such a thing, if it could by any possibility be true, was detestable as death to me, changing the colour of the sun, and the whole aspect of the world: and anon, at the outrage of that thing, my brow would flush with wrath, and my eyes blaze: till, on the fourth afternoon, I said to myself: 'That old Chinaman in Pekin is likely to get burned to death, I think, or blown to the clouds!'

So, a second time, on the 4th March, the poor palace was left to build itself. For, after a short trip to Gallipoli, where I got some young lime-twigs in boxes of earth, and some preserved limes and ginger, I set out for a long voyage to the East, passing through the Suez Canal, and visiting Bombay, where I was three weeks, and then destroyed it.

I had the thought of going across Hindostan by engine, but did not like to leave my ship, to which I was very attached, not sure of finding anything so suitable and good at Calcutta; and, moreover, I was afraid to abandon my petrol motor, which I had taken on board with the air-windlass, since I was going to uncivilised land. I therefore coasted down western Hindostan.

All that northern shore of the Arabian Sea has at the present time an odour which it wafts far over the water, resembling odours of happy vague dream-lands, sweet to smell in the early mornings as if the earth were nothing but a perfume, and life an inhalation.

On that voyage, however, I had, from beginning to end, twenty-seven fearful storms, or, if I count that one near the Carolines,* then twenty-eight. But I do not wish to write of these rages: they were too inhuman: and how I came alive through them against all my wildest hope, Someone, or Something, only knows.

I will write down here a thing: it is this, my God – something which I have observed: a definite obstreperousness in the mood of the elements now, when once roused, which grows, which grows continually. Tempests have become very very far more

wrathful, the sea more truculent and unbounded in its inso-
lence; when it thunders, it thunders with a venom new to me,
cracking as though it would split the firmament, and bawling
through the heaven of heavens, as if roaring to devour all
things; in Bombay once, and in China thrice, I was shaken by
earthquakes, the second and third marked by a certain extravagance of agitation, that might turn a man grey. Why should this
be, my God? I remember reading very long ago that on the
American prairies, which from time immemorial had been
swept by great storms, the storms gradually subsided when
man went to reside permanently there.* If this be true, it would
seem that the mere presence of man had a certain subduing or
mesmerising effect upon the native turbulence of Nature, and
his absence now may have removed the curb. It is my belief that
within fifty years from now the huge forces of the earth will be
let fully loose to tumble as they will; and this planet will become
one of the undisputed playgrounds of Hell, and the theatre of
commotions stupendous as those witnessed on the face of
Saturn.*

The Earth is all on my brain, on my brain, O dark-minded
Mother, with thy passionate cravings after the Infinite, thy
regrets, and mighty griefs, and comatose sleeps, and sinister
coming doom, O Earth: and I, poor man, though a king, sole
witness of thy bleak tremendous woes. Upon her I brood, and
do not cease, but brood and brood – the habit, if I remember
right, first becoming fixed and fated during that long voyage
eastward: for what is in store for her God only knows, and I
have seen in my broodings long visions of her future, which, if
a man should see with the eye of flesh, he would spread the
arms, and wheel and wheel through the mazes of a hiccuping
giggling frenzy, for the vision only is the very verge of madness.
If I might cease but for one hour that perpetual brooding upon
her! But I am her child, and my mind grows and grows to her
like the off-shoots of the banyan-tree, that take root downward, and she sucks and draws it, as she draws my feet by
gravitation, and I cannot take wing from her: for she is greater
than I, and there is no escaping her; and at the last, I know, my

soul will dash itself to ruin, like erring sea-fowl upon pharos-
lights, against her wild and mighty bosom. Often a whole night
through I lie open-eyed in the dark, with bursting brain, thinking of that hollow Gulf of Mexico, how identical in shape and
size with the protuberance of Africa just opposite, and how the
protuberance of the Venezuelan and Brazilian coast fits in with
the in-curve of Africa: so that it is obvious to me – it is quite
obvious – that they once were one; and one night rushed so far
apart; and the wild Atlantic knew that thing, and ran gladly,
hasting in between: and how if eye of flesh had been there to
see, and ear to hear that cruel thundering, my God, my God –
what horror! And if now they meet again, so long apart…but
that way fury lies. Yet one cannot help but think: I lie awake
and think, for she fills my soul, and absorbs it, with all her
moods and ways. She has meanings, secrets, plans. Strange,
strange, for instance, that similarity between the scheme of
Europe and the scheme of Asia: each with three southern peninsulas pointing south: Spain corresponding with Arabia, Italy
with India, the Morea and Greece, divided by the Gulf of Cor-
inth, corresponding with the Malay Peninsula and Annam,
divided by the Gulf of Siam; each with two northern peninsulas
pointing south, Sweden and Norway, and Korea and Kam-
schatka; each with two great islands similarly placed, Britain
and Ireland, and the Japanese Hondo and Yezo; the Old World
and the New has each a peninsula pointing north – Denmark
and Yucatan: a forefinger with long nail – and a thumb – pointing to the Pole. What does she mean? What can she mean, O Ye
that made her? Is she herself a living being, with a will and a
fate, as sailors said that ships were living entities? And that
thing that wheeled at the Pole, wheels it still yonder, yonder, in
its dark ecstasy? Strange that volcanoes are all near the sea: I
don't know why; I don't think that anyone ever knew. This fact,
in connection with submarine explosions, used to be cited in
support of the chemical theory of volcanoes, which supposed
the infiltration of the sea into ravines containing the materials
which form the fuel of eruptions: but God knows if that is true.
The lofty ones are intermittent – a century, two, ten, of silent
waiting, and then their talk silenced for ever some poor district;

the low ones are constant in action. Who could know the dark way of the world? Sometimes they form a linear system, consisting of several vents which extend in one direction, near together, like chimneys of some long foundry beneath. In mountains, a series of serrated peaks denotes the presence of dolomites; rounded heads mean calcareous rocks; and needles, crystalline schists. The preponderance of land in the northern hemisphere denotes the greater intensity there of the causes of elevation at a remote geologic epoch: that is all that one can say about it: but whence that greater intensity? I have some knowledge of the earth for only ten miles down: but she has eight thousand miles: and whether through all that depth she is flame or fluid, hard or soft, I do not know, I do not know. Her method of forming coal, geysers and hot sulphur-springs, and the jewels, and the atols and coral reefs; the metamorphic rocks of sedimentary origin, like gneiss, the plutonic and volcanic rocks, rocks of fusion, and the unstratified masses which constitute the basis of the crust; and harvests, the burning flame of flowers, and the passage from the vegetable to the animal: I do not know them, but they are of her, and they are like me, molten in the same furnace of her fiery heart. She is dark and moody, sudden and ill-fated, and rends her young like a cannibal lioness; and she is old and wise, and remembers Hur of the Chaldees which Uruk built, and that Temple of Bel which rose in seven pyramids to symbolise the planets, and Birs-i-Nimrud, and Haran, and she bears still, as a thing of yesterday, old Persepolis and the tomb of Cyrus,* and those cloister-like vihârah-temples of the ancient Buddhists, cut from the Himalayan rock; and returning from the Far East, I stopped at Ismailia, and so to Cairo, and saw where Memphis was, and stood one bright midnight before that great pyramid of Shafra, and that dumb Sphynx, and, seated at the well of one of the rock-tombs, looked till tears of pity streamed down my cheeks: for great is the earth, and her Ages, but man 'passeth away'. These tombs have pillars extremely like the two palace-pillars, only that these are round, and mine are square: for I chose it so: but the same band near the top, then over this the closed lotus-flower, then the small square plinth, which separates them from the architrave,

only mine have no architrave; the tombs consist of a little
outer temple or court, then comes a well, and inside another
chamber, where, I suppose, the dead were, a ribbon-like astragal
surrounding the walls, which are crowned with boldly-
projecting cornices, surmounted by an abacus. And here, till the
pressing want of food drove me back, I remained: for more and
more the earth over-grows me, wooes me, assimilates me; so that
I ask myself this question: 'Must I not, in time, cease to be a man,
and become a small earth, precisely her copy, extravagantly weird
and fierce, half-demoniac, half-ferine, wholly mystic – morose
and turbulent – fitful, and deranged, and sad – like her?'

A whole month of that voyage, from May the 15th to June the
13th, I wasted at the Andaman Islands near Malay: for that any
old Chinaman could be alive in Pekin began, after some time,
to seem the most quixotic notion that ever entered a human
brain; and these jungled islands, to which I came after a shocking vast orgy one night at Calcutta, when I fired not only the
city but the river, pleased my fancy to such an extent, that at
one time I intended to abide there. I was at the one called in the
chart 'Saddle Hill', the smallest of them, I think: and seldom
have I had such sensations of peace as I lay a whole burning
day in a rising vale, deeply-shaded in palm and tropical rank-
nesses, watching thence the *Speranza* at anchor: for there was a
little offing here at the shore whence the valley arose, and I
could see one of its long peaks lined with cocoanut-trees, and
all cloud burned out of the sky except the flimsiest lawn-
figments, and the sea as absolutely calm as a lake roughened
with breezes, yet making a considerable noise in its breaking on
the shore, as I have noticed in these sorts of places: I do not
know why. These poor Andaman people seem to have been
quite savage, for I met a number of them in roaming the island,
nearly skeletons, yet with limbs and vertebræ still, in general,
cohering, and in some cases dry-skinned and mummified relics
of flesh, and never anywhere a sign of clothes: a very singular
thing, considering their nearness to high old civilisations all
about them. They looked small and black, or almost; and I
never found a man without finding on or near him a spear and

other weapons: so that they were eager folk, and the wayward dark earth was in them, too, as she should be in her children. They had in many cases some reddish discoloration, which may have been the traces of betel-nut stains: for betel-nuts abound there. And I was so pleased with these people, that I took on board with the gig one of their little tree-canoes: which was my foolishness: for gig and canoe were only three nights later washed from the decks into the middle of the sea.

I passed down the Straits of Malacca, and in that short distance between the Andaman Islands, and the S.W. corner of Borneo I was thrice so mauled, that at times it seemed quite out of the question that anything built by man could escape such unfettered cataclysms, and I resigned myself, but with bitter reproaches, to perish darkly. The effect of the third upon me, when it was over, was the unloosening afresh of all my evil passion: for I said: 'Since they mean to slay me, death shall find me rebellious'; and for weeks I could not sight some specially happy village, or umbrageous spread of woodland, that I did not stop the ship, and land the materials for their destruction; so that nearly all those spicy lands about the north of Australia will bear the traces of my hand for many a year: for more and more my voyage became dawdling and zig-zaged, as the merest whim directed it, or the movement of the pointer on the chart; and I thought of eating the lotus of surcease and nepenthe in some enchanted nook of this bowering summer, where from my hut-door I could see through the pearl-hues of opium the sea-lagoon slaver lazily upon the old coral atol, and the cocoanut-tree would droop like slumber, and the bread-fruit tree would moan in sweet and weary dream, and I should watch the *Speranza* lie anchored in the pale atol-lake, year after year, and wonder what she was, and whence, and why she dozed so deep for ever, and after an age of melancholy peace and burdened bliss, I should note that sun and moon had ceased revolving, and hung inert, opening anon a heavy lid to doze and drowse again, and God would sigh 'Enough,' and nod, and Being would swoon to sleep: for that any old Chinaman should be alive in Pekin was a thing so fantastically maniac, as to draw from me at times sudden fits of wild red laughter that left me faint.

During a space of four months, from the 18th June to the 23rd October, I visited the Fijis, where I saw skulls still surrounded with remnants of extraordinary haloes of stiff hair, women clad in girdles made of thongs fixed in a belt, and, in Samoa near, bodies crowned with coronets of nautilus-shell, and traces of turmeric-paint and tattooing, and in one townlet a great assemblage of carcasses, suggesting by their look some festival, or dance: so that I believe that these people were overthrown without the least fore-knowledge of anything. The women of the Maoris wore an abundance of green-jade ornaments, and I found a peculiar kind of shell-trumpet, one of which I have now, also a tattooing chisel, and a nicely-carved wooden bowl. The people of New Caledonia, on the other hand, went, I should think, naked, confining their attention to the hair, and in this resembling the Fijians, for they seemed to wear an artificial hair made of the fur of some creature like a bat, and also they wore wooden masks, and great rings – for the ear, no doubt – which must have fallen to the shoulders: for the earth was in them all, and made them wild, perverse and various like herself. I went from one to the other without any system whatever, searching for the ideal resting-place, and often thinking that I had found it: but only wearying of it at the thought that there was a yet deeper and dreamier in the world. But in this search I received a check, my God, which chilled me to the marrow, and set me flying from these places.

One evening, the 29th November, I dined rather late – at eight – sitting, as was my custom in calm weather, cross-legged on the cabin-rug at the port aft corner, a small semicircle of *Speranza* gold-plate before me, and near above me the red-shaded lamp with green conical reservoir, whose creakings never cease in the stillest mid-sea, and beyond the plates the array of preserved soups, meat-extracts, meats, fruit, sweets, wines, nuts, liqueurs, coffee on the silver spirit-tripod, glasses, cruet, and so on, which it was always my first care to select from the storeroom, open, and lay out once for all in the morning on rising. I was late, seven being my hour: for on that day I had been engaged in the occasionally necessary, but always deferred, task of over-hauling the ship, brushing here a rope with tar, there a board with paint, there a crank with oil, rubbing a door-handle, a brass-fitting, filling the three cabin-lamps, dusting mirrors and furniture, dashing the great neat-joinered plains of deck with bucketfulls, or, high in air, chopping loose with its rigging the mizzen top-mast, which since a month was sprained at the clamps, all this in cotton drawers under loose *quamis*, bare-footed, my beard knotted up, the sun a-blaze, the sea smooth and pale with the smooth pallor of strong currents, the ship still enough, no land in sight, yet great tracts of sea-weed making eastward – I working from 11 A.M. till near 7, when sudden darkness interrupted; for I wished to have it all over in one obnoxious day. I was therefore very tired when I went down, lit the central chain-lever lamp* and my own two, washed and dressed in my bedroom, and sat to dinner in the dining-hall corner. I ate voraciously, with sweat, as usual, pouring down my eager brow, using knife or spoon in the right hand, but never the Western fork, licking the plates clean in the Moham-medan manner,* and drinking pretty freely. Still I was tired, and went upon deck, where I had the threadbare blue-velvet easy-chair with the broken left arm before the wheel, and in it sat smoking cigar after cigar from the Indian D box,* half-asleep, yet conscious. The moon came up into a pretty cloudless sky, and she was bright, but not bright enough to out-shine the enlightened flight of the ocean, which that night was one con-tinuous swamp of Jack-o'-lantern phosphorescence, a wild but faint luminosity mingled with stars and flashes of brilliance, the whole trooping unanimously eastward, as if in haste with elfin momentous purpose, a boundless congregation, in the sweep of a strong oceanic current. I could hear it, in my slumbrous lassi-tude, struggling and gurgling at the tied rudder, and making wet sloppy noises under the sheer of the poop; and I was aware that the *Speranza* was gliding along pretty fast, drawn into that pro-cession, probably at the rate of four to six knots: but I did not care, knowing very well that no land was within two hundred miles of my bows, for I was in longitude 173°, in the latitude of Fiji and the Society Islands, between those two: and after a time the cigar drooped and dropped from my mouth, and sleep overcame me, and I slept there, in the lap of the Infinite.

So that something preserves me, Something, Someone: *and for what?* ... If I had slept in the cabin, I must most certainly have perished: for lying there on the poop, I dreamed a dream which once I had dreamed on the ice, far, far yonder in the forgotten hyperborean North: that I was in an Arabian paradise, a Garden of Peaches; and I had a very long vision of it, for I walked among the trees, and picked the fruit, and pressed the blossoms to my nostrils with breathless inhalations of love: till a horrible sickness woke me: and when I opened my eyes, the night was black, the moon gone down, everything wet with dew, the sky arrayed with most glorious stars like a thronged bazaar of tiaraed rajahs and begums with spangled trains, and all the air fragrant with that mortal scent; and high and wide uplifted before me – stretching from the northern to the southern limit – a row of eight or nine inflamed smokes, as from the chimneys of some Cyclopean foundry a-work all night, most solemn, most great and dreadful in the solemn night: eight or nine, I should say, or it might be seven, or it might be ten, for I did not count them; and from those craters puffed up gusts of encrimsoned material, here a gust and there a gust, with tinselled fumes that convolved upon themselves, and sparks and flashes, all veiled in a garish haze of light; for the foundry worked, though languidly; and upon a rocky land four miles ahead, which no chart had ever marked, the *Speranza* drove straight with the current of the phosphorus sea.

As I rose, I fell flat: and what I did thereafter I did in a state of existence whose acts, to the waking mind, appear unreal as dream. I must at once, I think, have been conscious that here was the cause of the destruction of mankind; that it still surrounded its own neighbourhood with poisonous fumes; and that I was approaching it. I must have somehow crawled, or dragged myself forward. There is an impression on my mind that it was a purple land of pure porphyry; there is some faint memory, or dream, of hearing a long-drawn booming of waves upon its crags: I do not know whence I have them. I think that I remember retching with desperate jerks of the travailing intestines; also that I was on my face as I moved the regulator in the engine-room: but any recollection of going down the stairs, or of coming up again, I have not. Happily, the wheel was tied, the rudder hard to port, and as the ship moved, she must, therefore, have turned; and I must have been back to untie the wheel in good time, for when my senses came, I was lying there, my head against the under-gimbal, one foot on a spoke of the wheel, no land in sight, and morning breaking.

This made me so sick, that for either two or three days I lay without eating in the chair near the wheel, only rarely waking to sufficient sense to see to it that she was making westward from that place; and on the morning when I finally roused myself I did not know whether it was the second or the third morning: so that my calendar, so scrupulously kept, may be a day out, for to this day I have never been at the pains to ascertain whether I am here writing now on the 5th or the 6th of June.

Well, on the fourth, or the fifth, evening after this, just as the sun was sinking beyond the rim of the sea, I happened to look where he hung motionless on the starboard bow: and there I saw a clean-cut black-green spot against his red – a most unusual sight here and now – a ship: a poor thing, as it turned out when I got near her, without any sign of mast, heavily water-logged, some relics of old rigging hanging over, even her bowsprit apparently broken in the middle (though I could not see it), and she nothing more than a hirsute green mass of old weeds and sea-things from bowsprit-tip to poop, and from bulwarks to water-line, stout as a hedgehog, only awaiting there the next high sea to founder.

It being near my dinner-hour and night's rest, I stopped the *Speranza* some fifteen yards from her, and commenced to pace my spacious poop, as usual, before eating; and as I paced, I would glance at her, wondering at her destiny, and who were the human men that had lived on her, their Christian names,

and family names, their age, and thought, and way of life, and
beards; till the desire arose within me to go to her, and see; and
I threw off my outer garments, uncovered and unroped the
cedar cutter – the only boat, except the air-pinnace, left to me
intact – and got her down by the mizzen five-block pulley-
system. But it was a ridiculous nonsense, for having paddled to
her, I was thrown into paroxysms of rage by repeated failures
to scale her bulwarks, low as they were; my hands, indeed,
could reach, but I found no hold upon the slimy mass, and
three rope-ends which I caught were also untenably slippery: so
that I jerked always back into the boat, my clothes a mass of
filth, and the only thought in my blazing brain a twenty-pound
charge of guncotton, of which I had plenty, to blow her to
uttermost Hell. I had to return to the *Speranza*, get a half-inch
rope, then back to the other, for I would not be baulked in such
a way, though now the dark was come, only slightly tempered
by a half-moon, and I getting hungry, and from minute to
minute more fiendishly ferocious. Finally, by dint of throwing,
I got the rope-loop round a mast-stump, drew myself up, and
made fast the boat, my left hand cut by some cursed shell: and
all for what? the imperiousness of a whim. The faint moonlight
shewed an ample tract of deck, invisible in most parts under
rolled beds of putrid seaweed, and no bodies, and nothing
but a concave, large esplanade of seaweed. She was a ship of
probably 1,500 tons, three-masted, and a sailer. I got aft (for I
had on thick outer babooshes), and saw that only four of the
companion-steps remained; by a small leap, however, I could
descend into that desolation, where the stale sea-stench seemed
concentrated into a very essence of rankness. Here I experienced a singular ghostly awe and timorousness, lest she should
sink with me, or something: but striking matches, I saw an
ordinary cabin, with some fungoids, skulls, bones and rags, but
not one cohering skeleton. In the second starboard berth was a
small table, and on the floor a thick round ink-pot, whose continual rolling on its side made me look down; and there I saw a
flat square book with black covers, which curved half-open of
itself, for it had been wet and stained. This I took, and went
back to the *Speranza*: for that ship was nothing but an empti-

ness, and a stench of the crude elements of life, nearly assimilated now to the rank deep to which she was wedded, and soon to be absorbed into its nature and being, to become a sea in little, as I, in time, my God, shall be nothing but an earth in little.

During dinner, and after, I read the book, with some difficulty, for it was pen-written in French, and discoloured, and it turned out to be the journal of someone, a passenger and voyager, I imagine, who called himself Albert Tissu, and the ship the *Marie Meyer*. There was nothing remarkable in the narrative that I could see – commonplace descriptions of South Sea scenes, records of weather, cargoes, and the like – till I came to the last written page: and that was remarkable enough. It was dated the 13th of April – strange thing, my good God, incredibly strange – that same day, twenty long years ago, when I reached the Pole; and the writing on that page was quite different from the neat look of the rest, proving immoderate excitement, wildest haste; and he heads it '*Cinq Heures*', – I suppose, in the evening, for he does not say: and he writes: 'Monstrous event! phenomenon without likeness! the witnesses of which must for ever live immortalised in the annals of the universe, an event which will make even Mama, Henri and Juliette admit that I was justified in undertaking this most eventful voyage. Talking with Captain Tombarel on the poop, when a sudden exclamation from him – "*Mon Dieu!*" His visage whitens! I follow the direction of his gaze to eastward! I behold! eight *kilomètres* perhaps away – *ten monstrous waterspouts*, reaching up, up, high enough – all apparently in one straight line, with intervals of nine hundred *mètres*, very regularly placed. They do not wander, dance, nor waver, as waterspouts do; nor are they at all lily-shaped, like waterspouts: but ten hewn pillars of water, with uniform diameter from top to bottom, only a little twisted here and there, and, as I divine, fifty *mètres* in girth. Five, ten, stupendous minutes we look, Captain Tombarel mechanically repeating and repeating under his breath "*Mon Dieu!*" "*Mon Dieu!*" the whole crew now on the poop, I agitated, but collected, watch in hand. And suddenly, all is blotted out: the pillars of water, doubtless still there, can no more be seen: for the ocean all about them is steaming, hissing higher than the pillars a dense white vapour, vast in extent, whose venomous sibilation we at this distance can quite distinctly hear. It is affrighting, it is intolerable! the eyes can hardly bear to watch, the ears to hear! it seems unholy travail, monstrous birth! But it lasts not long: all at once the *Marie Meyer* commences to pitch and roll violently, and the sea, a moment since calm, is now rough! and at the same time, through the white vapour, we see a dark shadow slowly rising – the shadow of a mighty back, a new-born land, bearing upwards ten flames of fire, slowly, steadily, out of the sea, into the clouds. At the moment when that sublime emergence ceases, or seems to cease, the grand thought that smites me is this: "I, Albert Tissu, am immortalised: my name shall never perish from among men!" I rush down, I write it. The latitude is 16° 21′ 13″* South; the longitude 176° 58′ 19″ West.[1] There is a great deal of running about on the decks – they are descending. There is surely a strange odour of almonds – I only hope – it is so dark, *mon D—*'

So the Frenchman, Tissu.

With all that region I would have no more to do: for all here, it used to be said, lies a great sunken continent; and I thought it would be rising and shewing itself to my eyes, and driving me stark mad: for the earth is full of these contortions, sudden monstrous grimaces and apparitions, which are like the face of Medusa, affrighting a man into spinning stone; and nothing could be more appallingly insecure than living on a planet.

I did not stop till I had got so far northward as the Philippine Islands, where I was two weeks – exuberant, odorous places, but so hilly and rude, that at one place I abandoned all attempt at travelling in the motor, and left it in a valley by a broad, shallow, noisy river, full of mossy stones: for I said: 'Here I will live, and be at peace'; and then I had a fright, for during three days I could not re-discover the river and the motor, and I was in the greatest despair, thinking: 'When shall I find my way out of these jungles and vastnesses?' For I was where no paths were,

[1] This must be French reckoning, from meridian of Paris.

and had lost myself in deeps where the lure of the earth is too strong and rank for a single man, since in such places, I suppose, a man would rapidly be transformed into a tree, or a snake, or a tiger. At last, however, I found the place, to my great joy, but I would not shew that I was glad, and to hide it, fell upon a front wheel of the car with some kicks. I could not make out who the people were that lived here: for the relics of some seemed quite black, like New Zealand races, and I could still detect the traces of tattooing, while others suggested Mongolian types, and some looked like pigmies, and some like whites. But I cannot detail the two-years' incidents of that voyage: for it is past, and like a dream: and not to write of that – of all that – have I taken this pencil in hand after seventeen long, long years.

Singular my reluctance to put it on paper.

I will write rather of the voyage to China, and how I landed the motor on the wharf at Tientsin, and went up the river through a maize and rice-land most charming in spite of intense cold, I thick with clothes as an Arctic traveller; and of the three dreadful earthquakes within two weeks; and how the only map which I had of the city gave no indication of the whereabouts of its military depositories, and I had to seek for them; and of the three days' effort to enter them, for every gate was solid and closed; and how I burned it, but had to observe its flames, without deep pleasure, from beyond the walls to the south, the whole place being one cursed plain; yet how, at one moment, I cried aloud with wild banterings and glad laughters of Tophet to that old Chinaman still alive within it; and how I coasted, and saw the hairy Ainus,* man and woman hairy alike; and how, lying one midnight awake in my cabin, the *Speranza* being in a still glassy water under a cliff overhung by drooping trees – it was the harbour of Chemulpo* – to me lying awake came the thought: 'Suppose now you should hear a step walking to and fro, leisurely, on the poop above you – *just suppose*'; and the night of horrors which I had, for I could not help supposing, and at one time really thought that I heard it: and how the sweat rolled and poured from my brow; and how I went to

Nagasaki, and burned it; and how I crossed over the great
Pacific deep to San Francisco, for I knew that Chinamen had
been there, too, and one of them might be alive; and how, one
calm day, the 15th or the 16th April, I, sitting by the wheel in
the mid-Pacific, suddenly saw a great white hole that ran and
wheeled, and wheeled and ran, in the sea, coming toward me,
and I was aware of the hot breath of a reeling wind, and then
of the hot wind itself, which deep-groaned the sound of the
letter V, humming like a billion spinning-tops, and the *Speranza*
was on her side, sea pouring over her port-bulwarks, and myself
in the corner between deck and taffrail, drowning fast, but
unable to stir; but all was soon past and the white hole in the
sea, and the hot spinning-top of wind, ran wheeling beyond, to
the southern horizon, and the *Speranza* righted herself: so that
it was clear that someone wished to destroy me, for that a
typhoon of such vehemence ever blew before I cannot think;
and how I came to San Francisco, and how I burned it, and had
my sweets: for it was mine; and how I thought to pass over the
great trans-continental railway to New York, but would not,
fearing to leave the *Speranza*, lest all the ships in the harbour
there should be wrecked, or rusted, and buried under sea-weed,
and turned unto the sea; and how I went back, my mind all
given up now to musings upon the earth and her ways, and a
thought in my soul that I would return to those deep places of
the Filipinas, and become an autochthone* – a tree, or a snake,
or a man with snake-limbs, like the old autochthones: but I
would not: for Heaven was in man, too: Earth and Heaven;
and how as I steamed round west again, another winter come,
and I now in a mood of dismal despondencies, on the very
brink of the inane abyss and smiling idiotcy, I saw in the island
of Java the great temple of Boro Budor:* and like a tornado, or
volcanic event, my soul was changed: for my recent studies in
the architecture of the human race recurred to me with interest,
and three nights I slept in the temple, examining it by day. It is
vast, with that look of solid massiveness which above all char-
acterises the Japanese and Chinese building, my measurement
of its width being 529 feet, and it rises terrace-like in six stories
to a height of about 120 or 130 feet: here Buddhist and Brah-

min forms are combined into a most richly-developed whole, with a voluptuousness of tracery that is simply intoxicating, each of the five off-sets being divided up into an innumerable series of external niches, containing each a statue of the sitting Boodh, all surmounted by a number of cupolas, and the whole crowned by a magnificent dagop: and when I saw this, I had the impulse to return to my home after so long wandering, and to finish the temple of temples, and the palace of palaces; and I said: 'I will return, and build it as a testimony to God.'

Save for a time, near Cairo, I did not once stop on that home-ward voyage, but turned into the little harbour at Imbros at a tranquil sunset on the 7th of March (as I reckon), and I moored the *Speranza* to the ring in the little quay, and I raised the bat-tered motor from the hold with the middle air-engine (battered by the typhoon in the mid-Pacific, which had broken it from the rope-fastenings and tumbled it head-over-heels to port), and I went through the windowless village-street, and up through the plantains and cypresses which I knew, and the Nile mimosas, and mulberries, and Trebizond palms, and pines, and acacias, and fig-trees, till the thicket stopped me, and I had to alight: for in those two years the path had finally disappeared; and on, on foot, I made my way, till I came to the board-bridge, and leant there, and looked at the rill; and thence climbed the steep path in the sward toward that rolling table-land where I had built with many a groan; and halfway up, I saw the tip of the crane-arm, then the blazing top of the south pillar, then the shed-roof, then the platform, a blinking blotch of glory to the watery eyes under the setting sun. But the tent, and nearly all that it contained, was gone.

For four days I would do nothing, simply lying and watching, shirking a load so huge: but on the fifth morning I languidly began something: and I had not worked an hour, when a fever took me – to finish it, to finish it – and it lasted upon me, with only three brief intervals, nearly seven years; nor would the end have been so long in coming, but for the unexpected difficulty of getting the four flat roofs water-tight, for I had to take down half the east one. Finally, I made them of gold slabs one-and-a-quarter inch thick, smooth on both sides, on each beam double gutters being fixed along each side of the top flange to catch any leakage at the joints, which are filled with slaters'-cement. The slabs are clamped to the top flanges by steel clips, having bolts set with plaster-of-Paris in holes drilled in the slabs. These clips are 1½ in. by ³/₁₇ in., and are 17 in. apart. The roofs are slightly pitched to the front edges, where they drain into gold-plated copper-gutters on plated wrought-iron brackets, with one side flashed up over the blocks, which raise the slabs from the beam-tops, to clear the joint gutters... But now I babble again of that base servitude, which I would forget, but cannot: for every measurement, bolt, ring, is in my brain, like a burden; but it is past, it is past – and it was vanity.

Six months ago to-day it was finished: six months more protracted, desolate, burdened, than all those sixteen years in which I built.

I wonder what a man – another man – some Shah, or Tsar, of that far-off past, would say now of me, if eye could rest upon me! With what awe would he certainly shrink before the wild majesty of these eyes; and though I am not lunatic – for I am not, I am not – how would he fly me with the exclamation: 'There is the very lunacy of Pride!'

For there would seem to him – it must be so – in myself, in all about me, something extravagantly royal, touched with terror. My body has fattened, and my girth now fills out to a portly roundness its broad Babylonish girdle of crimson cloth, minutely gold-embroidered, and hung with silver, copper and gold coins of the Orient; my beard, still black, sweeps in two divergent sheaves to my hips, flustered by every wind; as I walk through this palace, the amber-and-silver floor reflects in its depths my low-necked, short-armed robe of purple, blue, and scarlet, a-glow with luminous stones. I am ten times crowned Lord and Emperor; I sit a hundred times enthroned in confirmed, obese old Majesty. Challenge me who will – challenge me who dare! Among those myriad worlds upon which I nightly pore, I may have my Peers and Compeers and Fellow-denizens...

but *here* I am Sole; Earth acknowledges my ancient sway and hereditary sceptre: for though she draws me, not yet, not yet, am I hers, but she is mine. It seems to me not less than a million million æons since other beings, more or less resembling me, walked impudently in the open sunlight on this planet, which is rightly mine – I can indeed no longer picture to myself, nor even credit, that such a state of things – so fantastic, so far-fetched, so infinitely droll – could have existed: though, at bottom, I suppose, I know that it must have been really so. Up to ten years ago, in fact, I used frequently to dream that there were others. I would see them walk in the streets like ghosts, and be troubled, and start awake: but never now could such a thing, I think, occur to me in sleep: for the wildness of the circumstance would certainly strike my consciousness, and immediately I should know that the dream was a dream. For now, at least, I am sole, I am lord. The golden walls of this palace which I have built look down, enamoured of their reflection, into a lake of the choicest, purplest wine.

Not that I made it of wine because wine is rare; nor the walls of gold because gold is rare: that would have been too childish: but because I would match for beauty a human work with the works of those Others: and because it happens, by some persistent freak of the earth, that precisely things most rare and costly are generally the most beautiful.

The vision of glorious loveliness which is this palace now risen before my eyes cannot be described by pen and paper, though there *may* be words in the lexicons of language which, if I sought for them with inspired wit for sixteen years, as I have built for sixteen years, might as vividly express my thought on paper, as the stones-of-gold, so grouped and built, express it to the eye: but, failing such labours and skill, I suppose I could not give, if there were another man, and I tried to give, the faintest conception of its celestial charm.

It is a structure positively as clear as the sun, and as fair as the moon – the sole great human work in the making of which no restraining thought of cost has played a part: one of its steps alone being of more cost than all the temples, mosques and

besestins, the palaces, pagodas and cathedrals, built between
the ages of the Nimrods and the Napoleons.

The house itself is very small – only 40 ft. long, by 35 broad,
by 27 high: yet the structure as a whole is sufficiently enormous, high uplifted: the rest of the bulk being occupied by the
platform, on which the house stands, each side of this measuring at its base 480 ft., its height from top to bottom 130 ft., and
its top 48 ft. square, the elevation of the steps being just nearly
30 degrees, and the top reached from each of the four points of
the compass by 183 low long steps, very massively overlaid
with smooth molten gold – not forming a continuous flight, but
broken into threes and fives, sixes and nines, with landings
between the series, these from the top looking like a great terraced parterre of gold. It is thus an Assyrian palace in scheme:
only that the platform has steps on all sides, instead of on one.
The platform-top, from its edge to the golden walls of the
house, is a mosaic consisting of squares of the glassiest clarified
gold, and squares of the glassiest jet, corner to corner, each
square 2 ft. wide. Around the edge of the platform on top run
48 square plain gold pilasters, 12 on each side, 2 ft. high, tapering upwards, and topped by a knob of solid gold, pierced with
a hole through which passes a lax inch-and-a-half silver chain,
hung with little silver balls which strike together in the breeze.
The mansion consists of an outer court, facing east toward the
sea, and the house proper, which encloses an inner court. The
outer court is a hollow oblong 32 ft. wide by 8 ft. long, the
summit of its three walls being battlemented; they are 18½ ft.
in height, or 8½ ft. lower than the house; around their gold
sides, on inside and outside, 3 ft. from the top, runs a plain flat
band of silver, 1 ft. wide, projecting ⅓ in., and at the gate,
which is a plain Egyptian entrance, facing eastwards, 2½ ft.
narrower at top than at bottom, stand the two great square pillars of massive plain gold, tapering upwards, 45 ft. high, with
their capital of band, closed lotus, and thin plinth; in the outer
court, immediately opposite the gate, is an oblong well, 12 ft.
by 3 ft., reproducing in little the shape of the court, its sides,
which are gold-lined, tapering downward to near the bottom of
the platform, where a conduit of ⅛ in. diameter automatically

replenishes the ascertained mean evaporation of the lake during the year, the well containing 105,360 litres when nearly full, and the lake occupying a circle round the platform of 980 ft. diameter, with a depth of 3½ ft. Round the well run pilasters connected by silver chains with little balls, and it communicates by a ⅛ in. conduit with a pool of wine let into the inner court, this being fed from eight tall and narrow golden tanks, tapering upwards, which surround it, each containing a different red wine, sufficient on the whole to last for all purposes during my lifetime. The ground of the outer court is also a mosaic of jet and gold: but thenceforth the jet-squares give place throughout to squares of silver, and the gold-squares to squares of clear amber, clear as solidified oil. The entrance is by an Egyptian doorway 7 ft. high, with folding-doors of gold-plated cedar, opening inwards, surrounded by a very large projecting coping of plain silver, 3½ ft. wide, severe simplicity of line throughout enormously multiplying the effect of richness of material. The interior resembles, I believe, rather a Homeric, than an Assyrian or Egyptian house – except for the 'galleries', which are purely Babylonish and Old Hebrew. The inner court, with its wine-pool and tanks, is a small oblong of 8 ft. by 9 ft., upon which open four silver-latticed window-oblongs in the same proportion, and two doors, before and behind, oblongs in the same proportion. Round this run the eight walls of the house proper, the inner 10 ft. from the outer, each parallel two forming a single long corridor-like chamber, except the front (east) two, which are divided into three apartments; in each side of the house are six panels of massive plain silver, half-an-inch thinner in their central space, where are affixed paintings, 22 or else 21 taken at the burning of Paris from a place called 'The Louvre', and 2 or else 3 from a place in England: so that the panels have the look of frames, and are surrounded by oval garlands of the palest amethyst, topaz, sapphire and turquoise which I could find, each garland being of only one kind of stone, a mere oval ring two feet wide at the sides and narrowing to an inch at the top and bottom, without designs. The galleries are five separate recesses in the outer walls under the roofs, two in the east façade, and one in the north, south, and west, hung with pavilions of purple, blue, rose and white silk on rings and rods of gold, with gold pilasters and banisters, each entered by four steps from the roof, to which lead, north and south, two spiral stairs of cedar. On the east roof stands the kiosk, under which is the little lunar telescope; and from that height, and from the galleries, I can watch under the bright moonlight of this climate, which is very like lime-light, the for-ever silent blue hills of Macedonia, and where the islands of Samothraki, Lemnos, Tenedos slumber like purplish fairies on the Ægean Sea: for, usually, I sleep during the day, and keep a night-long vigil, often at midnight descending to bathe my col-oured baths in the lake, and to disport myself in that strange intoxication of nostrils, eyes, and pores, dreaming long wide-eyed dreams at the bottom, to return dazed, and weak, and drunken. Or again – *twice* within these last void and idle six months – I have suddenly run, bawling out, from this temple of luxury, tearing off my gaudy rags, to hide in a hut by the shore, smitten for one intense moment with realisation of the past of this earth, and moaning: 'alone, alone...all alone, alone, alone...alone, alone...' For events precisely resembling erup-tions take place in my brain; and one spangled midnight – ah, how spangled! – I may kneel on the roof with streaming, up-lifted face, with outspread arms, and awe-struck heart, adoring the Eternal: the next, I may strut like a cock, wanton as sin, lusting to burn a city, to wallow in filth, and, like the Babylo-nian maniac, calling myself the equal of Heaven.

But it was not to write of this – of all this—!

Of the furnishing of the palace I have written nothing... But why I hesitate to admit to myself what I *know*, is not clear. If They speak to me, I may surely write of Them: for I do not fear Them, but am Their peer.

Of the island I have written nothing: its size, climate, form, vegetation... There are two winds: a north and a south wind; the north is cool, and the south is warm; and the south blows during the winter months, so that sometimes on Christmas-day it is quite hot; and the north, which is cool, blows from May to September, so that the summer is hardly ever oppressive, and the climate was made for a king. The mangal-stove* in the south hall I have never once lit.

The length, I should say, is 19 miles; the breadth 10, or there-abouts; and the highest mountains should reach a height of some 2,000 ft, though I have not been all over it. It is very densely wooded in most parts, and I have seen large growths of wheat and barley, obviously degenerate now, with currants, figs, valonia, tobacco, vines in rank abundance, and two marble quarries. From the palace, which lies on a sunny plateau of beautifully-sloping swards, dotted with the circular shadows thrown by fifteen huge cedars, and seven planes, I can see on all sides an edge of forest, with the gleam of a lake to the north, and in the hollow to the east the rivulet with its little bridge, and a few clumps and beds of flowers. I can also spy right through—

It shall be written now:

I have this day heard within me the contention of the Voices.

I thought that they were done with me! That all, all, all, was ended! I have not heard them for twenty years!

But to-day – distinctly – breaking in with brawling impas-sioned suddenness upon my consciousness… I heard.

This late *far niente* and vacuous inaction here have been undermining my spirit; this inert brooding upon the earth; this empty life, and bursting brain! Immediately after eating at noon to-day, I said to myself:

'I have been duped by the palace: for I have wasted myself in building, hoping for peace, and there is no peace. Therefore now I shall fly from it, to another, sweeter work – not of building, but of destroying – not of Heaven, but of Hell – not of self-denial, but of reddest orgy. Constantinople – beware!' I tossed the chair aside, and with a stamp was on my feet: and as I stood – again, again – I heard: the startlingly sudden wrangle, the fierce, vulgar outbreak and voluble controversy, till my consciousness could not hear its ears: and one urged: 'Go! go!' and the other: 'Not there!…where you like… but not there!…for your life!'

I did not – for I could not – go: I was so overcome. I fell upon the couch shivering.

These Voices, or impulses, plainly as I felt them of old, quarrel within me now with an openness new to them. Lately, influenced by my long scientific habit of thought, I have occasionally wondered whether what I used to call 'the two Voices' were not in reality two strong instinctive movements, such as most men may have felt, though with less force. But to-day doubt is past, doubt is past: nor, unless I be very mad, can I ever doubt again.

I have been thinking, thinking of my life: there is a something which I cannot understand.

There was a man whom I met once in that dark backward and abysm of time, when I must have been very young – I fancy at some college or school in England, and his name now is far enough beyond scope of my memory, lost in the vast limbo of past things. But he used to talk continually about certain 'Black' and 'White' Powers, and of their strife for this world. He was a short man with a Roman nose, and lived in fear of growing a paunch. His forehead a-top, in profile, was more prominent than the nose-end, he parted his hair in the middle, and had the theory that the male form was more beautiful than the female.*
I forget what his name was – the dim clear-obscure being. Very profound was the effect of his words upon me, though, I think, I used to make a point of slighting them. This man always declared that 'the Black' would carry off the victory in the end: and so he has, so he has.

But assuming the existence of this 'Black' and this 'White' being – and supposing it to be a fact that my reaching the Pole had any connection with the destruction of my race, according to the notions of that extraordinary Scotch parson – then it must have been the power of *'the Black'* which carried me, in spite of all obstacles, to the Pole. So far I can understand.

But *after* I had reached the Pole, what further use had either White or Black for me? Which was it – White or Black – that preserved my life through my long return on the ice – and *why*? It *could* not have been 'the Black'! For I readily divine that from the moment when I touched the Pole, the only desire of the Black, which had previously preserved, must have been to destroy me, with the rest. It must have been 'the White', then, that led me back, retarding me long, so that I should not enter the poison-cloud, and then openly presenting me the *Boreal* to bring me home to Europe. But his motive? And the significance of these recommencing wrangles, after such a silence? This I do not understand!

Curse Them, curse Them, with their mad tangles! I care nothing for Them! Are there any White Idiots and Black Idiots – *at all*? Or are these Voices that I hear nothing but the cries of my own strained nerves, and I all mad and morbid, morbid and mad, mad, my good God?

This inertia here is *not good* for me! This stalking about the palace! and long thinkings about Earth and Heaven, Black and White, White and Black, and things beyond the stars! My brain is like bursting through the walls of my poor head.

To-morrow, then, to Constantinople.

Descending to go to the ship, I had almost reached the middle of the east platform-steps, when my foot slipped on the smooth gold: and the fall, though I was not walking carelessly, had, I swear, all the violence of a fall caused by a push. I struck my head, and, as I rolled downward, swooned. When I came to myself, I was lying on the very bottom step, which is thinly washed by the wine-waves: another roll and I suppose I must have drowned. I sat there an hour, lost in amazement, then crossed the causeway, came down to the *Speranza* with the motor, went through her, spent the day in work, slept on her, worked again to-day, till four, at both ship and time-fuses (I with only 700 fuses left, and in Stamboul alone must be 8,000 houses, without counting Galata, Tophana, Kassim-pacha, Scutari, and the rest), started out at 5.30, and am now at 11 P.M. lying motionless two miles off the north coast of the island of Marmora, with moonlight gloating on the water, a faint north breeze, and the little pale land looking immensely stretched-out, solemn and great, as if that were the world, and there were nothing else; and the tiny island at its end immense, and the *Speranza* vast, and I only little. To-morrow at 11 A.M. I will moor the *Speranza* in the Golden Horn at the spot where there

is that low damp nook of the bagnio behind the naval magazines and that hill where the palace of the Capitan Pacha is.*

I found that great tangle of ships in the Golden Horn wonderfully preserved, many with hardly any moss-growths. This must
be due, I suppose, to the little Ali-Bey and Kezat-Hanah, which
flow into the Horn at the top, and made no doubt a constant
current.

Ah, I remember the place: long ago I lived here some months,
or, it may be, years. It is the fairest of cities – and the greatest. I
believe that London in England was larger: but no city, surely,
ever *seemed* so large. But it is flimsy, and will burn like tinder.
The houses are made of light timber, with interstices filled by
earth and bricks, and some of them look ruinous already, with
their lovely faded tints of green and gold and red and blue and
yellow, like the hues of withered flowers: for it is a city of paints
and trees, and all in the little winding streets, as I write, are
volatile almond-blossoms, mixed with maple-blossoms, white
with purple. Even the most splendid of the Sultan's palaces are
built in this combustible way: for I believe that they had a
notion that stone-building was presumptuous, though I have
seen some very thick stone-houses in Galata. This place, I
remember, lived in a constant state of sensation on account of
nightly flares-up; and I have come across several tracts already
devastated by fires. The ministers-of-state used to attend them,
and if the fire would not go out, the Sultan himself was obliged
to be there, in order to encourage the firemen. Now it will burn
still better.

But I have been here six weeks, and still no burning: for the
place seems to plead with me, it is so ravishing, so that I do not
know why I did not live here, and spare my toils during those
sixteen nightmare years; for two whole weeks the impulse to
burn was quieted; and since then there has been an irritating
whisper at my ear which said: 'It is not really like the great King
that you are, this burning, but like a foolish child, or a savage,
who liked to see fireworks: or at least, if you must burn, do not
burn poor Constantinople, which is so charming, and so very
old, with its balsamic perfumes, and the blossomy trees of white

and light-purple peeping over the walls of the cloistered painted
houses, and all those lichened tombs – those granite menhirs
and regions of ancient marble tombs between the quarters,
Greek tombs, Byzantine, Jew, Mussulman tombs, with their
strange and sacred inscriptions – overwaved by their cypresses
and vast plane-trees.' And for weeks I would do nothing: but
roamed about, with two minds in me, under the tropic brilliance of the sky by day, and the vast dreamy nights of this
place that are like nights seen through azure-tinted glasses, and
in each of them is not one night, but the thousand-and-one long
crowded nights of glamour and fancy: for I would sit on the
immense esplanade of the Seraskierat, or the mighty grey stones
of the porch of the mosque of Sultan Mehmed-fatih, dominat-
ing from its great steps all old Stamboul, and watch the moon
for hours and hours, so passionately bright she soared through
clear and cloud, till I would be smitten with doubt of my own
identity, for whether I were she, or the earth, or myself, or some
other thing or man, I did not know, all being so silent alike, and
all, except myself, so vast, the Seraskierat, and the Suleimanieh,
and Stamboul, and the Marmora Sea, and the earth, and those
argent fields of the moon, all large alike compared with me,
and measure and space were lost, and I with them.

These proud Turks died stolidly, many of them. In streets of
Kassim-pacha, in crowded Taxim on the heights of Pera, and
under the long Moorish arcades of Sultan-Selim, I have seen the
open-air barber's razor with his bones, and with him the half-
shaved skull of the faithful, and the long two-hours' narghile
with traces of burnt tembaki and haschish still in the bowl.
Ashes now are they all, and dry yellow bone; but in the houses
of Phanar and noisy old Galata, and in the Jew quarter of Pri-
pacha, the black shoe and head-dress of the Greek is still
distinguishable from the Hebrew blue. It was a mixed ritual of
colours here in boot and hat: yellow for Mussulman, red boots,
black calpac for Armenian, for the Effendi a white turban, for
the Greek a black. The Tartar skull shines from under a high
taper calpac, the Nizain-djid's from a melon-shaped head-piece;
the Imam's and Dervish's from a grey conical felt; and there is

here and there a Frank in European rags. I have seen the towering turban of the Bashi-bazouk,* and his long sword, and some
softas in the domes on the great wall of Stamboul, and the
beggar, and the street-merchant with large tray of water-melons,
sweetmeats, raisins, sherbet, and the bear-shewer, and the Bar-
bary organ, and the night-watchman who evermore cried 'Fire!'
with his long lantern, two pistols, dirk, and wooden javelin.
Strange how all that old life has come back to my fancy now,
pretty vividly, and for the first time, though I have been here
several times lately. I have gone out to those plains beyond the
walls with their view of rather barren mountain-peaks, the city
looking nothing but minarets shooting through black cypress-
tops, and I seemed to see the wild muezzin at some summit,
crying the midday prayer: '*Mohammed Resoul Allah!*' – the
wild man; and from that great avenue of cypresses which
traverses the cemetery of Scutari, the walled city of Stamboul
lay spread entire up to Phanar and Eyoub in their cypress-
woods before me, the whole embowered now in trees, all that
complexity of ways and dark alleys with overhanging balconies
of old Byzantine houses, beneath which a rider had to stoop the
head, where old Turks would lose their way in mazes of the
picturesque; and on the shaded Bosphorus coast, to Foundoucli
and beyond, some peeping yali, snow-white palace, or old
Armenian cot; and the Seraglio by the sea, a town within a
town; and southward the Sea of Marmora, blue-and-white,
and vast, and fresh as a sea just born, rejoicing at its birth and
at the jovial sun, all brisk, alert, to the shadowy islands afar:
and as I looked, I suddenly said aloud a wild, mad thing, my
God, a wild and maniac thing, a shrieking maniac thing for
Hell to laugh at: for something said with my tongue: '*This city
is not quite dead.*'

Three nights I slept in Stamboul itself at the palace of some
sanjak-bey or emir, or rather dozed, with one slumbrous eye
that would open to watch my visitors Sinbad, and Ali Baba,
and old Haroun,* to see how they slumbered and dozed: for it
was in the small luxurious chamber where the bey received
those speechless all-night visits of the Turks, long rosy hours of

perfumed romance, and drunkenness of the fancy, and visionary languor, sinking toward morning into the yet deeper peace
of dreamless sleep; and there, still, were the white *yatags** for
the guests to sit cross-legged on for the waking dream, and to
fall upon for the final swoon, and the copper brazier still scent-
ing of essence-of-rose, and the cushions, rugs, hangings, the
monsters on the wall, the haschish-chibouques, narghiles,
hookahs, and drugged pale cigarettes, and a secret-looking lattice beyond the door, painted with trees and birds; and the air
narcotic and grey with the pastilles which I had burned, and the
scented smokes which I had smoked; and I all drugged and
mumbling, my left eye suspicious of Ali there, and Sinbad, and
old Haroun, who dozed. And when I had slept, and rose to
wash in a room near the overhanging latticed balcony of the
façade, before me to the north lay old Galata in sunshine, and
that steep large street mounting to Pera, once full at every night-
fall of divans on which grave dervishes smoked narghiles, and
there was no space for passage, for all was divans, lounges,
almond-trees, heaven-high hum, chibouques in forests, the dervish, and the innumerable porter, the horse-hirer with his horse
from Tophana, and arsenal-men from Kassim, and traders from
Galata, and artillery-workmen from Tophana; and on the other
side of the house, the south end, a covered bridge led across a
street, which consisted mostly of two immense blind walls, into
a great tangled wilderness of flowers, which was the harem-
garden, where I passed some hours; and here I might have
remained many days, many weeks perhaps, but that, dozing one
foreday with those fancied others, it was as if there occurred a
laugh somewhere, and a thing said: 'But this city is not quite
dead!' waking me from deeps of peace to startled wakefulness.
And I thought to myself: 'If it be not quite dead, it *will* be soon
– and with some suddenness!' And the next morning I was at
the Arsenal.

It is long since I have so deeply enjoyed, even to the marrow. It
may be 'the White' who has the guardianship of my life: but
assuredly it is 'the Black' who reigns in my soul.

Grandly did old Stamboul, Galata, Tophana, Kassim, right

out beyond the walls to Phanar and Eyoub, blaze and burn.
The whole place, except one little region of Galata, was like so
much tinder, and in the five hours between 8 P.M. and 1 A.M. all
was over. I saw the tops of those vast masses of cemetery-
cypresses round the tombs of the Osmanlis outside the walls,
and those in the cemetery of Kassim, and those round the sacred
mosque of Eyoub, shrivel away instantaneously, like flimsy hair
caught by a flame; I saw the Genoese tower of Galata go heading obliquely on an upward curve, like Sir Roger de Coverley*
and wild rockets, and burst high, high, with a report; in pairs,
and threes, and fours, I saw the blue cupolas of the twelve or
fourteen great mosques give in and subside, or soar and rain,
and the great minarets nod the head, and topple; and I saw the
flames reach out and out across the empty breadth of the Etmei-
dan – three hundred yards – to the six minarets of the Mosque
of Achmet, wrapping the red Egyptian-granite obelisk in the
centre; and across the breadth of the Serai-Meidani it reached
to the buildings of the Seraglio and the Sublime Porte; and
across those vague barren stretches that lie between the houses
and the great wall; and across the seventy or eighty great
arcaded bazaars, all-enwrapping, it reached; and the spirit of
fire grew upon me: for the Golden Horn itself was a tongue of
fire, crowded, west of the galley-harbour, with exploding bat-
tleships, Turkish frigates, corvettes, brigs – and east, with tens
of thousands of feluccas, caiques, gondolas and merchantmen
aflame. On my left burned all Scutari; and between six and
eight in the evening I had sent out thirty-seven vessels under
low horse-powers of air, with trains and fuses laid for 11 P.M.,
to light with their wandering fires the Sea of Marmora. By midnight I was encompassed in one great furnace and fiery gulf, all
the sea and sky inflamed, and earth a-flare. Not far from me to
the left I saw the vast Tophana barracks of the Cannoniers, and
the Artillery-works, after long reluctance and delay, take wing
together; and three minutes later, down by the water, the bar-
rack of the Bombardiers and the Military School together,
grandly, grandly; and then, to the right, in the valley of Kassim,
the Arsenal: these occupying the sky like smoky suns, and shed-
ding a glaring day over many a mile of sea and land; I saw the

two lines of ruddier flaring where the barge-bridge and the raft-bridge over the Golden Horn made haste to burn; and all that vastness burned with haste, quicker and quicker – to fervour – to fury – to unanimous rabies: and when its red roaring stormed the infinite, and the might of its glowing heart was Gravitation, Being, Sensation, and I its compliant wife – then my head nodded, and with crooked lips I sighed as it were my last sigh, and tumbled, weak and drunken, upon my face.

O wild Providence! Unfathomable madness of Heaven! that ever I should write what now I write! I will not write it…

The hissing of it! It is only a crazy dream! a tearing-out of the hair by the roots to scatter upon the raving storms of Saturn! My hand will not write it!

In God's name—! During four nights after the burning I slept in a house – French as I saw by the books, &c., probably the Ambassador's, for it has very large gardens and a beautiful view over the sea, situated on the rapid east declivity of Pera; it is one of the few large houses which, for my safety, I had left standing round the minaret whence I had watched, this minaret being at the top of the old Mussulman quarter on the heights of Taxim, between Pera proper and Foundoucli. At the bottom, both at the quay of Foundoucli, and at that of Tophana, I had left under shelter two caiques for double safety, one a Sultan's gilt craft, with gold spur at the prow, and one a boat of those zaptias that used to patrol the Golden Horn as water-police: by one or other of these I meant to reach the *Speranza*, she being then safely anchored some distance up the Bosphorus coast. So, on the fifth morning I set out for the Tophana quay; but a light rain had fallen over-night, and this had re-excited the thin grey smoke resembling quenched steam, which, as from some reeking province of Abaddon, still trickled upward over many a square mile of blackened tract, though of flame I could see no sign. I had not accordingly advanced far over every sort of *débris*, when I found my eyes watering, my throat choked, and my way almost blocked by roughness: whereupon I said: 'I will turn back, cross the region of tombs and barren waste behind Pera, descend the hill, get the zaptia boat at the Foundoucli quay, and so reach the *Speranza*.'

Accordingly, I made my way out of the region of smoke, passed beyond the limits of smouldering ruin and tomb, and soon entered a rich woodland, somewhat scorched at first, but soon green and flourishing as the jungle. This cooled and soothed me, and being in no hurry to reach the ship, I was led on and on, in a somewhat north-western direction, I fancy. Somewhere hereabouts, I thought, was the place they called 'The Sweet Waters',* and I went on with the vague notion of coming upon them, thinking to pass the day, till afternoon, in the forest. Here nature, in only twenty years has returned to an exuberant savagery, and all was now the wildest vegetation, dark dells, rills wimpling through deep-brown shade of sensitive mimosa, large pendulous fuchsia, palm, cypress, mulberry, jonquil, narcissus, daffodil, rhododendron, acacia, fig. Once I stumbled upon a cemetery of old gilt tombs, absolutely overgrown and lost, and thrice caught glimpses of little trellised yalis* choked in boscage. With slow and listless foot I went, munching an almond or an olive, though I could swear that olives were not formerly indigenous to any soil so northern: yet here they are now, pretty plentiful, though elementary, so that modifications whose end I cannot see are certainly proceeding in everything, some of the cypresses which I met that day being immense beyond anything I ever heard of: and the thought, I remember, was in my head, that if a twig or leaf should change into a bird, or a fish with wings, and fly before my eyes, what then should I do? and I would eye a branch suspiciously anon. After a long time I penetrated into a very sombre grove. The day outside the wood was brilliant and hot, and very still, the leaves and flowers here all motionless. I seemed, as it were, to hear the vacant silence of the world, and my foot treading on a twig, produced the report of pistols. I presently reached a glade in a thicket, about eight yards across, that had a scent of lime and orange, where the just-sufficient twilight enabled me to see some old bones, three skulls, and the edge of a tam-tam peeping from a tuft of wild corn with corn-flowers, and here and there some golden champac,* and all about a profusion of musk-roses. I had stopped – *why* I do not recollect – perhaps thinking that if I was not getting to the Sweet Waters, I should seriously set about finding my way out. And as I stood looking about me, I remember that some cruising insect trawled near my ear its lonely drone.

Suddenly, God knows, I started, I started.

I imagined – I dreamed – that I saw a pressure in a bed of moss and violets, *recently made*! And while I stood gloating upon that impossible thing, I imagined – I dreamed – the lunacy of it! – that I heard a laugh!…the laugh, my good God, of a human soul.

Or it seemed half a laugh, and half a sob: and it passed from me in one fleeting instant.

Laughs, and sobs, and idiot hallucinations, I had often heard before, feet walking, sounds behind me: and even as I had heard them, I had known that they were nothing. But brief as was this impression, it was yet so thrillingly *real*, that my poor heart received, as it were, the very shock of death, and I fell backward into a mass of moss, supported on the right palm, while the left pressed my working bosom; and there, toiling to catch my breath, I lay still, all my soul focussed into my ears. But now I could hear no sound, save only the vast and audible hum of the silence of the universe.

There was, however, the foot-print. If my eye and ear should so conspire against me, that, I thought, was hard.

Still I lay, still, in that same pose, without a stir, sick and dry-mouthed, infirm and languishing, with dying breaths: but keen, keen – and malign.

I would wait, I said to myself, I would be artful as snakes, though so woefully sick and invalid: I would make no sound…

After some minutes I became conscious that my eyes were leering – leering in one fixed direction: and instantly, the mere fact that I had a sense of direction proved to me that I must, *in truth*, have heard something! I strove – I managed – to raise myself: and as I stood upright, feebly swaying there, not the terrors of death alone were in my breast, but the authority of the monarch was on my brow.

I moved: I found the strength.

Slow step by slow step, with daintiest noiselessness, I moved to a thread of moss that from the glade passed into the thicket, and along its winding way I stepped, in the direction of the sound. Now my ears caught the purling noise of a brooklet, and following the moss-path, I was led into a mass of bush only two or three feet higher than my head. Through this, prowling like a stealthy cat, I wheedled my painful way, emerged upon a strip of open long-grass, and now was faced, three yards before me, by a wall of acacia-trees, prickly-pear and pichulas,* between which and a forest beyond I spied a gleam of running water.

On hands and knees I crept toward the acacia-thicket, entered it a little, and leaning far forward, peered. And there – at once – ten yards to my right – I saw.

Singular to say, my agitation, instead of intensifying to the point of apoplexy and death, now, at the actual sight, subsided to something very like calmness. With malign and sullen eye askance I stood, and steadily I watched her there.

She was on her knees, her palms lightly touching the ground, supporting her. At the edge of the streamlet she knelt, and she was looking with a species of startled shy astonishment at the reflexion of her face in the limpid brown water.* And I, with sullen eye askance regarded her a good ten minutes' space.

I believe that her momentary laugh and sob, which I had heard, was the result of surprise at seeing her own image; and I firmly believe, from the expression of her face, that this was the first time that she had seen it.

Never, I thought, as I stood moodily gazing, had I seen on the earth a creature so fair (though, analysing now at leisure, I can quite conclude that there was nothing at all remarkable about her good looks). Her hair, somewhat lighter than auburn, and frizzy, was a real garment to her nakedness, covering her below the hips, some strings of it falling, too, into the water: her eyes, a dark blue, were wide in a most silly expression of bewilder-

ment. Even as I eyed and eyed her, she slowly rose: and at once
I saw in all her manner an air of unfamiliarity with the world,
as of one wholly at a loss what to do. Her pupils did not seem
accustomed to light; and I could swear that that was the first
day in which she had seen a tree or a stream.

Her age appeared eighteen or twenty. I guessed that she was
of Circassian blood, or, at least, origin. Her skin was whitey-
brown, or old ivory-white.

She stood up motionless, at a loss. She took a lock of her hair,
and drew it through her lips. There was some look in her eyes,
which I could plainly see now, somehow indicating wild hunger,
though the wood was full of food. After letting go her hair, she
stood again feckless and imbecile, with sideward-hung head,
very pitiable to see I think now, though no faintest pity touched
me then. It was clear that she did not at all know what to make
of the look of things. Finally, she sat on a moss-bank, reached
and took a musk-rose, laid it on her palm, and looked hopelessly at it.

One minute after my first actual sight of her my extravagance
of agitation, I say, died down to something like calm. The earth
was mine by old right: I felt that: and this creature a mere slave
upon whom, without heat or haste, I might perform my will:
and for some time I stood, coolly enough considering what that
will should be.

I had at my girdle the little cangiar,* with silver handle
encrusted with coral, and curved blade six inches long,
damascened in gold, and sharp as a razor; the blackest and the
basest of all the devils of the Pit was whispering in my breast
with calm persistence: 'Kill, kill – and eat.'

Why I should have killed her I do not know. That question I
now ask myself. It must be true, true that it is *'not good'* for
man to be alone. There was a religious sect in the Past which
called itself 'Socialist': and with these must have been the truth,
man being at his best and highest when most social, and at his
worst and lowest when isolated: for the Earth gets hold of all
isolation, and draws it, and makes it fierce, base, and materi-

alistic, like sultans, aristocracies, and the like: but Heaven is where two or three are gathered together. It may be so: I do not know, nor care. But I know that after twenty years of solitude on a planet the human soul is more enamoured of solitude than of life, shrinking like a tender nerve from the rough intrusion of Another into the secret realm of Self: and hence, perhaps, the bitterness with which solitary castes, Brahmins, patricians, aristocracies, always resisted any attempt to invade their slowly-acquired domain of privileges. Also, it may be true, it may, it may, that after twenty years of solitary selfishness, a man becomes, without suspecting it – not at all noticing the slow stages – a real and true beast, a horrible, hideous beast, mad, prowling, like that King of Babylon, his nails like birds' claws,* and his hair like eagles' feathers, with instincts all inflamed and fierce, delighting in darkness and crime for their own sake. I do not know, nor care: but I know that, as I drew the cangiar, the basest and the slyest of all the devils was whispering me, tongue in cheek: 'Kill, kill – and be merry.'*

With excruciating slowness, like a crawling glacier, tender as a nerve of the touching leaves, I moved, I stole, obliquely toward her through the wall of bush, the knife behind my back. Once only there was a restraint, a check: I felt myself held back: I had to stop: for one of the ends of my divided beard had caught in a limb of prickly-pear.

I set to disentangling it: and it was, I believe, at the moment of succeeding that I first noticed the state of the sky, a strip of which I could see across the rivulet: a minute or so before it had been pretty clear, but now was busy with hurrying clouds. It was a sinister muttering of thunder which had made me glance upward.

When my eyes returned to the sitting figure, she was looking foolishly about the sky with an expression which almost proved that she had never before heard that sound of thunder, or at least had no idea what it could bode. My fixed regard lost not one of her movements, while inch by inch, not breathing, careful as the poise of a balance, I crawled. And suddenly, with a rush, I was out in the open, running her down...

She leapt: perhaps two, perhaps three, paces she fled: then stock still she stood – within some four yards of me – with panting nostrils, with enquiring face.

I saw it all in one instant, and in one instant all was over. I had not checked the impetus of my run at her stoppage, and I was on the point of reaching her with uplifted knife, when I was suddenly checked and smitten by a stupendous violence: a flash of blinding light, attracted by the steel which I held, struck tingling through my frame, and at the same time the most passionate crash of thunder that ever shocked a poor human ear felled me to the ground. The cangiar, snatched from my hand, fell near the girl's foot.

I did not entirely lose consciousness, though, surely, the Powers no longer hide themselves from me, and their close contact is too intolerably rough and vigorous for a poor mortal man. During, I should think, three or four minutes, I lay so astounded under that bullying cry of wrath, that I could not move a finger. When at last I did sit up, the girl was standing near me, with a sort of smile, holding out to me the cangiar in a pouring rain.

I took it from her, and my doddering fingers dropped it into the stream.

Pour, pour came the rain, raining as it can in this place, not long, but a deluge while it lasts, dripping in thick liquidity, like a profuse sweat, through the forest, I seeking to get back by the way I had come, flying, but with difficulty and slowness, and a feeling in me that I was being tracked. And so it proved: for when I struck into more open space, nearly opposite the west walls, but now on the north side of the Golden Horn, where there is a flat grassy ground somewhere between the valley of Kassim and Charkoi, with horror I saw that *protégée* of Heaven, or of someone, not ten yards behind, following me like a mechanical figure, it being now near three in the afternoon, and the rain drenching me through, and I tired and hungry, and from all the ruins of Constantinople not one whiff of smoke ascending.

I trudged on wearily till I came to the quay of Foundoucli, and the zaptia boat; and there she was with me still, her hair nothing but a thin drowned string down her back.

*

Not only can she not speak to me in any language that I know: but she can speak in *no* language: it is my firm belief that she has *never* spoken.

She never saw a boat, or water, or the world, till now – I could swear it. She came into the boat with me, and sat astern, clinging for dear life to the gunwale by her finger-nails, and I paddled the eight hundred yards to the *Speranza*, and she came up to the deck after me. When she saw the open water, the boat, the yalis on the coast, and then the ship, astonishment was imprinted on her face. But she appears to know little fear. She smiled like a child, and on the ship touched this and that, as if each were a living thing.

It was only here and there that one could see the ivory-brown colour of her skin: the rest was covered with dirt, like old bottles long lying in cellars.

By the time we reached the *Speranza*, the rain suddenly stopped: I went down to my cabin to change my clothes, and had to shut the door in her face to keep her out. When I opened it, she was there, and she followed me to the windlass, when I went to set the anchor-engine going. I intended, I suppose, to take her to Imbros, where she might live in one of the broken-down houses of the village. But when the anchor was not yet half up, I stopped the engine, and let the chain run again. For I said, 'No, I will be alone, I am not a child.'

I knew that she was hungry by the look in her eyes: but I cared nothing for that. I was hungry, too: and that was all I cared about.

I would not let her be there with me another instant. I got down into the boat, and when she followed, I rowed her back all the way past Foundoucli and the Tophana quay to where one turns into the Golden Horn by St Sophia, around the mouth of the Horn being a vast semicircle of charred wreckage, carried out by the river-currents. I went up the steps on the Galata side before one comes to where the barge-bridge was. When she had followed me on to the embankment, I walked up one of those rising streets, very encumbered now with stone-*débris* and ashes, but still marked by some standing black wall-fragments, it being now not far from night, but the

air as clear and washed as the translucency of a great purple
diamond with the rain and the after-glow of the sun, and all
the west aflame.

When I was about a hundred yards up in this old mixed
quarter of Greeks, Turks, Jews, Italians, Albanians, and noise
and cafedjis and wine-bibbing,* having turned two corners, I
suddenly gathered my skirts, spun round, and, as fast as I could,
was off at a heavy trot back to the quay. She was after me, but
being taken by surprise, I suppose, was distanced a little at first.
However, by the time I could scurry myself down into the boat,
she was so near, that she only saved herself from the water by a
balancing stoppage at the brink, as I pushed off. I then set out
to get back to the ship, muttering: 'You can have Turkey, if you
like, and I will keep the rest of the world.'

I rowed sea-ward, my face toward her, but steadily averted,
for I would not look her way to see what she was doing. However, as I turned the point of the quay, where the open sea
washes quite rough and loud, to go northward and disappear
from her, I heard a babbling cry – the first sound which she had
uttered. I did look then: and she was still quite near me, for the
silly maniac had been running along the embankment, following me.

'Little fool!' I cried out across the water, 'what are you after
now?' And, oh my good God, shall I ever forget that strangeness,
that wild strangeness, of my own voice, addressing on this earth
another human soul?

There she stood, whimpering like an abandoned dog after
me. I turned the boat, rowed, came to the first steps, landed,
and struck her two stinging slaps, one on each cheek.

While she cowered, surprised no doubt, I took her by the
hand, led her back to the boat, landed on the Stamboul side,
and set off, still leading her, my object being to find some sort
of possible edifice near by, not hopelessly burned, in which to
leave her: for in all Galata there was plainly none, and Pera, I
thought, was too far to walk to. But it would have been better
if I had gone to Pera, for we had to walk quite three miles from
Seraglio Point all along the city battlements to the Seven-towers,
she picking her bare-footed way after me through the great

Sahara of charred stuff, and night now well arrived, and the moon a-drift in the heaven, making the desolate lonesomeness of the ruins tenfold desolate, so that my heart smote me then with bitterness and remorse, and I had a vision of myself that night which I will not put down on paper. At last, however, pretty late in the evening, I spied a large mansion with green lattice-work façade, and shaknisier, and terrace-roof, which had been hidden from me by the arcades of a bazaar, a vast open space at about the centre of Stamboul, one of the largest of the bazaars, I should think, in the middle of which stood the mansion, probably the home of pasha or vizier: for it had a very distinguished look in that place. It seemed very little hurt, though the vegetation that had apparently choked the great open space was singed to a black fluff, among which lay thousands of calcined bones of man, horse, ass, and camel, for all was distinct in the bright, yet so pensive and forlorn, moonlight, which was that Eastern moonlight of pure astral mystery which illumines Persepolis, and Babylon, and ruined cities of the old Anakim.

The house, I knew, would contain divans, *yatags*, cushions, foods, wines, sherbets, henna, saffron, mastic, raki, haschish, costumes, and a hundred luxuries still good. There was an outer wall, but the foliage over it had been singed away, and the gate all charred. It gave way at a push from my palm. The girl was close behind me. I next threw open a little green lattice-door in the façade under the shaknisier, and entered. Here it was dark, and the moment that she, too, was within, I slipped out quickly, slammed the door in her face, and hooked it upon her by a little hook over the latch.

I now walked some yards beyond the court, then stopped, listening for her expected cry: but all was still: five minutes – ten – I waited: but no sound. I then continued my morose and melancholy way, hollow with hunger, intending to start that night for Imbros.

But this time I had hardly advanced twenty steps, when I heard a frail and strangled cry, apparently in mid-air behind me, and glancing, saw the creature lying at the gateway, a white thing in black stubble-ashes. She had evidently jumped, well outward, from a small casement of lattice on a level with the little shaknisier grating, through which once peeped bright eyes, thirty feet aloft.

I hardly believe that she was conscious of any danger in jumping, for all the laws of life are new to her, and, having sought and found the opening, she may have merely come with blind instinctiveness after me, taking the first way open to her. I walked back, pulled at her arm, and found that she could not stand. Her face was screwed with silent pain – she did not moan. Her left foot, I could see, was bleeding: and by the wounded ankle I took her, and dragged her so through the ashes across the narrow court, and tossed her like a little dog with all my force within the door, cursing her.

Now I would not go back the long way to the ship, but struck a match, and went lighting up girandoles, cressets, candelabra, into a confusion of lights among great numbers of pale-tinted pillars, rose and azure, with verd-antique, olive, and Portoro marble, and serpentine. The mansion was large, I having to traverse quite a desert of embroidered brocade-hangings, slender columns, and Broussa silks, till I saw a stair-case doorway behind a Smyrna *portière*, went up, and wandered some time in a house of gilt-barred windows, with very little furniture, but palatial spaces, solitary huge pieces of *faïence* of inestimable age, and arms, my footfalls quite stifled in the Persian carpeting. I passed through a covered-in hanging-gallery, with one window-grating overlooking an inner court, and by this entered the harem, which declared itself by a greater luxury, bric-à-bracerie, and profusion of manner. Here, descending a short curved stair behind a *portière*, I came into a marble-paved sort of larder, in which was an old negress in blue dress, her hair still adhering, and an infinite supply of sweetmeats, French preserved foods, sherbets, wines, and so on. I put a number of things into a pannier, went up again, found some of those exquisite pale cigarettes which drunken in the hollow of an emerald, also a jewelled two-yard-long chibouque, and tembaki:* and with all descended by another stair, and laid them on the steps of a little raised kiosk of green marble in a corner of the court; went up again, and brought down a still-snowy *yatag* to sleep on; and there, by the kiosk-step, ate and passed the night, smoking for several hours in a state of languor. In the centre of the court is a square marble well, looking white through a rankness of wild vine, acacias in flower, weeds, jasmines, and roses, which overgrew it, as well as the kiosk and the whole court, climbing even the four-square arcade of Moorish arches round the open space, under one of which I had deposited a long lantern of crimson silk: for here no breath of the fire had come. About two in morning I fell to sleep, a deeper peace of shadow now reigning where so long the melancholy silver of the moon had lingered.

About eight in the morning I rose and made my way to the front, intending that that should be my last night in this ruined place: for all the night, sleeping and waking, the thing which had happened filled my brain, growing from one depth of incredibility to a deeper, so that at last I arrived at a sort of certainty that it could be nothing but a drunken dream: but as I opened my eyes afresh, the deep-cutting realisation of that impossibility smote like a pang of lightning-stroke through my being: and I said: 'I will go again to the far Orient, and forget': and I started out from the court, not knowing what had become of her during the night, till, having reached the outer chamber, with a wild start I saw her lying there at the door in the very spot where I had flung her, asleep sideways, head on arm. Softly, softly, I stept over her, got out, and went running at a cautious clandestine trot. The morning was in high *fête*, most fresh and pure, and to breathe was to be young, and to see such a sunlight lighten even upon ruin so vast was to be blithe. After running two hundred yards to one of the great broken bazaar-portals, I looked back to see if I was followed: but all that space was desolately empty. I then walked on past the arch, on which a green oblong, once inscribed, as usual, with some text in gilt hieroglyphs, is still discernible; and, emerging, saw the great panorama of destruction, a few vast standing walls, with hollow Oriental windows framing deep sky beyond, and here and there a pillar, or half-minaret, and down within the walls of the old Seraglio still some leafless, branchless trunks, and in Eyoub and Phanar leafless forests, and on the northern horizon Pera with the steep upper-half of the Iani-Chircha street still there, and on the height the European houses, and all between blackness, stones, a rolling landscape of ravine, like the hilly pack-ice of the North if its snow were ink, and to the right Scutari, black, laid low, with its vast region of tombs, and rare stumps of its forests, and the blithe blue sea, with the widening semicircle of floating *débris*, looking like brown foul scum at some points, congested before the bridge-less Golden Horn: for I stood pretty high in the centre of Stamboul somewhere in the region of the Suleimanieh, or of Sultan-Selim,* as I judged, with immense purviews into abstract distances and mirage. And to me it seemed too vast, too lonesome, and after advancing a few hundred yards beyond the bazaar, I turned again.

I found the girl still asleep at the house-door, and stirring her with my foot, woke her. She leapt up with a start of surprise, and a remarkable sinuous agility, and gazed an astounded moment at me, till, separating reality from dream and habit, she realised me: but immediately subsided to the floor again, being in evident pain. I pulled her up, and made her limp after me through several halls to the inner court, and the well, where I set her upon the weedy margin, took her foot in my lap, examined it, drew water, washed it, and bandaged it with a strip torn from my caftan-hem, now and again speaking gruffly to her, so that she might no more follow me.

After this, I had breakfast by the kiosk-steps, and when I was finished, put a mass of truffled *foie gras* on a plate, brushed through the thicket to the well, and gave it her. She took it, but looked foolish, not eating. I then, with my fore-finger, put a little into her mouth, whereupon she set hungrily to eat it all. I also gave her some ginger-bread, a handful of bon-bons, some Krishnu wine,* and some anisette.

I then started out afresh, gruffly bidding her stay there, and left her sitting on the well, her hair falling down the opening, she peering after me through the bushes. But I had not half reached the ogival bazaar-portal, when looking anxiously back,

I saw that she was limping after me. So that this creature tracks me in the manner of a nutshell following about in the wake of a ship.

I turned back with her to the house, for it was necessary that I should plan some further method of eluding her. That was five days ago, and here I have stayed: for the house and court are sufficiently agreeable, and form a museum of real *objets d'art*. It is settled, however, that to-morrow I return to Imbros.

It seems certain that she never wore, saw, nor knew of, clothes.

I have dressed her, first sousing her thoroughly with sponge and soap in luke-warm rose-water in the silver cistern of the harem-bath, which is a circular marbled apartment with a fountain and the complicated ceilings of these houses, and frescoes, and gilt texts of the Koran on the walls, and pale rose-silk hangings. On the divan I had heaped a number of selected garments, and having shewed her how to towel herself, I made her step into a pair of the trousers called *shintiyan* made of yellow-striped white-silk; this, by a running string, I tied loosely round the upper part of her hips; then, drawing up the bottoms to her knees, tied them there, so that their voluminous baggy folds, overhanging still to the ankles, have rather the look of a skirt; over this I put upon her a blue-striped chiffon chemise, or quamis, reaching a little below the hips; I then put on a short jacket or vest of scarlet satin, thickly embroidered in gold and precious stones, reaching somewhat below the waist, and pretty tight-fitting; and, making her lie on the couch, I put upon her little feet little yellow baboosh-slippers, then anklets, on her fingers rings, round her neck a necklace of sequins, finally dyeing her nails, which I cut, with henna. There remained her head, but with this I would have nothing to do, only pointing to the tarboosh which I had brought, to a square kerchief, to some corals, and to the fresco of a woman on the wall, which, if she chose, she might copy. Lastly, I pierced her ears with the silver needles which they used here: and after two hours of it left her.

About an hour afterwards I saw her in the arcade round the court, and, to my great surprise, she had a perfect plait down her back, and over her head and brows a green-silk feredjeh, or hood, precisely as in the picture.

Here is a question, the answer to which would be interesting to me: Whether or not for twenty years – or say rather twenty centuries, twenty eternal æons – I have been stark mad, a raving maniac; and whether or not I am now suddenly sane, sitting here writing in my right mind, my whole mood and tone changed, or rapidly changing? And whether such change can be due to the presence of only one other being in the world with me?

This singular being! Where she has lived – and how – is a problem to which not the faintest solution is conceivable. She had, I say, never seen clothes: for when I began to dress her, her perplexity was unbounded; also, during her twenty years, she has never seen almonds, figs, nuts, liqueurs, chocolate, conserves, vegetables, sugar, oil, honey, sweetmeats, orange-sherbet, mastic, salt, raki, tobacco, and many such things: for she showed perplexity at all these, hesitation to eat them: but she has known and tasted *white wine*: I could see that. Here, then, is a mystery.

I have not gone to Imbros, but remained here some days longer observing her.

I have allowed her to sit in a corner at meal-time, not far from where I eat, and I have given her food.

She is wonderfully clever! I continually find that, after an incredibly short time, she has most completely adapted herself to this or that. Already she wears her outfit as coquettishly as though born to clothes. Without at all seeming observant – for, on the contrary, she gives an impression of great flightiness – she watches me, I am convinced, with pretty exact observation. She knows precisely when I am speaking roughly, bidding her go, bidding her come, tired of her, tolerant of her, scorning her, cursing her. If I wish her to the devil, she quickly divines it by my face, and will disappear. Yesterday I noticed something queer about her, and soon discovered that she had been staining her lids with black kohol, like the *hanums*, so that, having found a box, she must have guessed its use from the pictures. Wonderfully clever! – imitative as a mirror. Two mornings ago I found an old mother-of-pearl kittur, and sitting under the arcade, touched the strings, playing a simple air; I could just see her behind one of the arch-pillars on the opposite side, and she was listening with apparent eagerness, and, I fancied, panting. Well, returning from a walk beyond the Phanar walls in the afternoon, I heard the same air coming out from the house, for she was repeating it pretty faultlessly by ear.

Also, during the forenoon of the previous day, I came upon her – for footsteps make no sound in this house – in the pacha's visitors'-hall: and what was she doing? – copying the poses of three dancing-girls frescoed there! So that she would seem to have a character as light as a butterfly's, and is afraid of nothing.

Now I know.

I had observed that at the beginning of every meal she seemed to have something on her mind, going toward the door, hesitating as if to see whether I would follow, and then returning. At length yesterday, after sitting to eat, she jumped up, and to my infinite surprise, said her first word: said it with a most quaint, experimental effort of the tongue, as a fledgling trying the air: the word '*Come.*'

That morning, meeting her in the court, I had told her to repeat some words after me: but she had made no attempt, as if shy to break the long silence of her life; and now I felt some sort of foolish pleasure in hearing her utter that word, often no doubt heard from me: and after hurriedly eating, I went with her, saying to myself: 'She must be about to shew me the food to which she is accustomed: and perhaps that will solve her origin.'

And so it has proved. I have now discovered that to the moment when she saw me, she had tasted only her mother's milk, dates, and that white wine of Ismidt which the Koran permits.*

As it was getting dark, I lit and took with me the big red-silk lantern, and we set out, she leading, and walking confoundedly fast, slackening when I swore at her, and getting fast again: and she walks with a certain levity, flightiness, and liberated *furore*, very hard to describe, as though space were a luxury to be revelled in. By what instinctive cleverness, or native vigour of memory, she found her way I cannot tell, but she led me such a walk that night, miles, miles, till I became furious, darkness having soon fallen with only a faint moon obscured by cloud, and a drizzle which haunted the air, she without light climbing and picking her thinly-slippered steps over mounds of *débris* and loosely-strewn masonry with unfailing agility, I occasionally splashing a foot with horror into one of those little ponds which always marked the Stamboul streets. When I was nearer her, I would see her peer across and upward toward Pera, as if that were a remembered land-mark, and would note the perpetual aspen oscillations of the long coral drops in her ears, and the nimble ply of her limbs, wondering with a groan if Pera was our goal.

Our goal was even beyond Pera. When we came to the Golden Horn, she pointed to my caique which lay at the Old Seraglio steps, and over the water we went, she lying quite at ease now, with her face at the level of the water in the centre of the crescent-shape, as familiarly as a *hanum* of old engaged in some escapade through the crowded Babel of Galata and that north side of the Horn.

Through Galata we passed, I already cursing the journey: and, following the line of the coast and the great steep thoroughfare of Pera, we came at last, almost in the country, to a great wall, and the entrance to an immense terraced garden, whose limits were invisible, many of the trees and avenues being still intact.

I knew it at once: I had lain a special fuse-train in the great palace at the top of the terraces: it was the royal palace, Yildiz.

Up and up we went through the grounds, a few unburned old bodies in rags of uniform still discernible here and there as the lantern swung past them, a musician in sky-blue, a fantassin and officer-of-the-guard in scarlet, forming a cross, with domestics of the palace in red-and-orange.

The palace itself was quite in ruins, together with all its surrounding barracks, mosque, and seraglio, and, as we reached the top of the grounds, presented a picture very like those which I have seen of the ruins of Persepolis, only that here the columns, both standing and fallen, were innumerable, and all more or less blackened; and through doorless doors we passed, down immensely-wide short flights of steps, and up them, and over strewed courtyards, by tottering fragments of arcades, all roofless, and tracts of charcoal between interrupted avenues of pillars, I following, expectant, and she very eager now. Finally, down a flight of twelve or fourteen rather steep and narrow steps, very dislocated, we went to a level which, I thought, must be the floor of the palace vaults: for at the bottom of the steps we stood on a large plain floor of plaster, which bore the marks of the flames; and over this the girl ran a few steps, pointed with excited recognition to a hole in it, ran further, and disappeared down the hole.

When I followed, and lowered the lantern a little, I saw that the drop down was about eight feet, made less than six feet by a heap of stone-rubbish below, the falling of which had caused the hole: and it was by standing on this rubbish-heap, I knew at once, that she must have been enabled to climb out into the world.

I dropped down, and found myself in a low flat-roofed cellar, with a floor of black earth, very fusty and damp, but so very vast in extent that even in the day-time, I suppose, I could not have discerned its boundaries; I fancy, indeed, that it extends beneath the whole palace and its environs – an enormous stretch of space: with the lantern I could only see a very limited portion of its area. She still led me eagerly on, and I presently came upon a whole region of flat boxes, each about two feet square, and nine inches high, made of very thin laths, packed to the roof; and about a-hundred-and-fifty feet from these I saw, where she pointed, another region of bottles, fat-bellied bottles in chemises of wicker-work, stretching away into gloom and total darkness. The boxes, of which a great number lay broken open, as they can be by merely pulling with the fingers at a pliant crack, contain dates; and the bottles, of which many thousands lay empty, contain, I saw, old Ismidt wine. Some fifty or sixty casks, covered with mildew, some old pieces of furniture, and a great cube of rotting, curling parchments, showed that this cellar had been more or less loosely used for the occasional storage of superfluous stores and knick-knacks.

It was also more or less loosely used as a domestic prison. For in the lane between the region of boxes and the region of bottles, near the former, there lay on the ground the skeleton of a woman, the details of whose costume were still appreciable, with thin brass gyves on her wrists: and when I had examined her well, I knew the whole history of the creature standing silent by my side.

She is the daughter of the Sultan, as I assumed when I had once determined that the skeleton is both the skeleton of her mother, and the skeleton of the Sultana.

That the skeleton was her mother is clear: for the cloud occurred just twenty-one years since, and the dead woman was, of course, at that moment in the prison, which must have been air-tight, and with her the girl: but since the girl is quite certainly not much more than twenty – she looks younger – she must at that time have been either unborn or a young babe: but a babe would hardly be imprisoned with another than its own mother. I am rather inclined to think that the girl was unborn at the moment of the cloud, and was born in the cellar.

That the mother was the Sultana is clear from her fragments of dress, and the symbolic character of her every ornament, crescent ear-rings, heron-feather, and the blue campaca enamelled in a bracelet. This poor woman, I have thought, may have been the victim of some unbounded fit of imperial passion, incurred by some domestic crime, real or imagined, which may have been pardoned in a day had not death overtaken her master and the world.

There are four steep stone steps at about the centre of the cellar, leading up to a locked iron trap-door, apparently the only opening into this great hole: and this trap-door must have been so nearly air-tight as to bar the intrusion of the poison in anything like deadly quantity.

But how rare – how strange – the coincidence of chances here. For, if the trapdoor was absolutely air-tight, I cannot think that the supply of oxygen in the cellar, large as it was, would have been sufficient to last the girl twenty years, to say nothing of what her mother used up before death: for I imagine that the woman must have continued to live some time in her dungeon, sufficiently long, at least, to teach her child to procure its food of dates and wine; so that the door must have been only just sufficiently hermetic to bar the poison, yet admit some oxygen; or else, the place may have been absolutely air-tight at the time of the cloud, and some crack, which I have not seen, opened to admit oxygen after the poison was dispersed: in any case – the all-but-infinite rarity of the chance!

Thinking these things I climbed out, and we walked to Pera, where I slept in a great white-stone house in five or six acres of garden overlooking the cemetery of Kassim, having pointed out to the girl another house in which to sleep.

This girl! what a history! After existing twenty years in a sunless world hardly three acres wide, she one day suddenly saw the only sky which she knew collapse at one point! a hole appeared into yet a world beyond! It was *I* who had come, and kindled Constantinople, and set her free.

Ah, I see something now! I see! it was for this that I was pre-served: I to be a sort of new-fangled Adam – and this little creature to be my Eve! That is it! *The White* does not admit defeat: he would recommence the Race again! At the last, the eleventh hour – in spite of all – he would turn defeat into victory, and outwit that Other.

However, if this be so – and I seem to see it quite clearly – then in that White scheme is a singular flaw: at *one* point, it is obvious, that elaborate Forethought fails: for I have a free will – and I refuse, I refuse.

Certainly, in this matter I am on the side of the Black: and since it depends absolutely upon me, this time Black wins.

No more men on the earth after me, ye Powers! To *you* the question may be nothing more than a gambling excitement as to the final outcome of your aërial squabble: but to the poor men who had to bear the wrongs, Inquisitions, rack-rents, Waterloos, unspeakable horrors, it was hard earnest, you know! Oh the wretchedness – the deep, deep pain – of that bungling ant-hill, happily wiped out, my God! My sweetheart Clodagh...she was not an ideal being! There was a man called Judas who betrayed the gentle Founder of the Christian Faith, and there was some Roman king named Galba, a horrid dog, and there was a French devil, Gilles de Raiz:* and the rest were all much the same, much the same. Oh no, it was not a good race, that small infantry which called itself Man: and here, falling on my knees before God and Satan as I write, I swear, I swear: Never through me shall it spring and fester again.

I cannot realise her! Not at all, at all, at all! If she is out of my sight and hearing ten minutes, I fall to doubting her reality. If I lose her for half a day, all the old feelings, resembling certainties, come back, that I have only been dreaming – that this appearance cannot be an actual objective fact of life, since the impossible is impossible.

Seventeen long years, seventeen long years, of madness...

To-morrow I start for Imbros:* and whether this girl chooses to follow me, or whether she stays behind, I will see her from the moment I land no more.*

She must rise very early.* I who am now regularly on the palace-roof at dawn, sometimes from between the pavilion-curtains of the galleries, or from the steps of the telescope-kiosk, may spy her far down below, a dainty microscopic figure, generally running about the sward, or gazing up in wonder at the palace from the lake-edge.

It is now three months since she came with me to Imbros.

I left her the first night in that pale-yellow house with the two green jalousies* facing the beach, where there was everything that she would need; but I knew that, like all the houses there now, it leaked profusely, and the next day I went down to the curving stair, cut through the rock at the back and south of the village, climbed, and half a mile beyond found that park and villa with gables, which I had noted from the sea. The villa is almost intact, very strongly built of purplish marble, though small, and very like a Western house, with shingles, and three gables, so that I think it must have been the yali of some Englishman, for it contains a number of English books, though the only body I saw there was what looked like an Aararat Kurd, with spiral string wound down his turban, yellow ankle-pantaloons, and flung red shoulder-cloak; and all in the heavily-wooded park, and all about the low rock-steps up the hill, profusions of man-dragora; and from the rock-steps to the house a narrow long avenue of acacias, mossy underfoot, that mingle overhead, the house standing about four yards from the edge of the perpendicular sea-cliff, whence one can see the *Speranza*'s main top-mast, and broken mizzen-mast-head, in her quiet haven. After examining the place I went down again to the village, and her house: but she was not there: and two hours long I paced about among the weeds of these amateur little alleys and flat-roofed windowless houses (though some have terrace-roofs, and a rare aperture), whose once-raw yellows, greens, and blues look now like sunset tints when the last flush is gone, and they fade dun. When at last she came running with open mouth, I took her up the rock-steps, and into the house, and there she has lived, one of the gable-tips, I now find (that overlooking the sea), being just visible from the north-east corner of the palace-roof, two miles from it.

That night again when I was leaving her, she made an attempt to follow me. But I was resolved to end it, then: and cutting a sassafras-whip I cut her deep, three times, till she ran, crying.

So, then, what is my fate henceforth? – to think always, from sun to moon, and from moon to sun, of one only thing – and that thing an object for the microscope? – to become a sneaking Paul Pry to spy upon the silly movements of one little sparrow, like some fatuous motiveless gossip of old, his occupation to peep, his one faculty to scent, his honey and his achievement to unearth the infinitely unimportant? I would kill her first!

*

I am convinced that she is no stay-at-home, but roams continually over the island: for thrice, wandering myself, I have come upon her.

The first time she was running with flushed face, intent upon striking down a butterfly with a twig held in the left hand (for both hands she uses with dexterity). It was at about nine in the morning, in her park, near the bottom where there are high grass-growths and ferny luxuriance between the close tree-trunks, and shadow, and the broken wall of an old funeral-kiosk sunk aslant under moss, creepers, and wild flowers, behind which I peeped hidden and wet with dew. She has had the assurance to modify the dress I put upon her, and was herself a butterfly, for instead of the shintiyan, she had on a zouave, hardly reaching to the waist, of saffron satin, no feredjé, but a scarlet fez with violet tassel, and baggy pantaloons of azure silk; down her back the long auburn plait, quite neat, but all her front hair loose and wanton, the fez cocked backward, while I caught glimpses of her fugitive heels lifting out of the dropping slipper-sole. She is pretty clever, but not clever enough, for that butterfly escaped, and in one instant I saw her change into weary and sad, for on this earth is nothing more fickle than that Proteus face, which resembles a landscape swept with cloud-shadows on a bright day. Fast beat my heart that morning, owing to the consciousness that, while I saw, I was unseen, yet might be seen.

Another noontide, three weeks afterwards, I came upon her a good way up yonder to the west of the palace, sleeping on her arm in an alley between overgrown old trellises, where rioting wild vine buried her in gloom: but I had not been peeping through the bushes a minute, when she started up and looked wildly about, her quick consciousness, I imagine, detecting a presence: though I think that I managed to get away unseen. She keeps her face very dirty: all about her mouth was dry-stained with a polychrome of grape, *mûrs*, and other coloured juices, like slobbering *gamins** of old. I could also see that her nose and cheeks are now sprinkled with little freckles.

Four days since I saw her a third time, and then found that the primitive instinct to represent the world in *pictures* has been working in her: for she was drawing. It was down in the middle one of the three east-and-west village streets, for thither I had strolled toward evening, and coming out upon the street from between an old wall and a house, saw her quite near. I pulled up short – and peered. She was lying on her face all among grasses, a piece of yellow board before her, and in her fingers a chalk-splinter: and very intently she drew, her tongue-tip travelling along her short upper-lip from side to side, regularly as a pendulum, her fez tipped far back, and the left foot swinging upward from the knee. She had drawn her yali at the top, and now, as I could see by peering well forward, was drawing underneath the palace – from memory, for where she lay it is all hidden: yet the palace it was, for there were the waving lines meant for the steps, the two slanting pillars, the slanting battlements of the outer court, and before the portal, with turban reaching above the roof, and my two whisks of beard sweeping below the knees – myself.

Something spurred me, and I could not resist shouting a sudden 'Hi!' whereupon she scrambled like a spring-bok to her feet, I pointing to the drawing, smiling.

This creature has a way of mincing her pressed lips, while she shakes the head, intensely cooing a fond laugh: and so she did then.

'You are a clever little wretch, you know,' said I, she cocking her eye, trying to divine my meaning with vague smile.

'Oh, yes, a clever little wretch,' I went on in a gruff voice, 'clever as a serpent, no doubt: for in the first case it was the Black who used the serpent, but now it is the White. But it will not do, you know. Do you know what you are to me, you? You are my Eve! – a little fool, a little piebald frog like you. But it will not do at all, at all! A nice race it would be with you for mother, and me for father, wouldn't it? – half-criminal like the father, half-idiot like the mother: just like the last, in short. They used to say, in fact, that the offspring of a brother and sister was always weak-headed: and from such a wedlock cer-tainly came the human race, so no wonder it was what it was: and so it would have to be again now. Well no – unless we have the children, and cut their throats at birth: and *you* would not like that at all, I know, and, on the whole, it would not work, for the White would be striking a poor man dead with His lightning, if I attempted that. No, then: the modern Adam is some eight to twenty thousand years wiser than the first* – you see? less instinctive, more rational. The first disobeyed by commission: I shall disobey by omission: only his disobedience was a sin, mine is a heroism. I have not been a particularly ideal sort of beast so far, you know: but in me, Adam Jeffson – I swear it – the human race shall at last attain a true nobility, the nobility of self-extinction. I shall turn out trumps: I shall prove myself stronger than Tendency, World-Genius, Providence, Currents of Fate, White Power, Black Power, or whatever is the name for it. No more Clodaghs, Lucrezia Borgias, Semiramises, Pompadours, Irish Landlords, Hundred-Years' Wars – you see?'*

She kept her left eye obliquely cocked like a little fool, wondering, no doubt, what I was saying.

'And talking of Clodagh,' I went on, 'I shall call you that henceforth, to keep me reminded. So that is your name – not Eve – but Clodagh, who was a Poisoner, you see? She poisoned a poor man who trusted her: and that is your name now – not Eve, but Clodagh – to remind me, you most dangerous little speckled viper! And in order that I may no more see your foolish little pretty face, I decree that, for the future, you wear a *yashmak* to cover up your lips, which, I can see, were meant to be seductive, though dirty; and you can leave the blue eyes, and the little white-skinned freckled nose uncovered, if you like, they being commonplace enough. Meantime, if you care to see how to draw a palace – I will show you.'

Before I stretched my hand, she was presenting the board – so that she had guessed something of my meaning! But some hard tone in my talk had wounded her, for she presented it looking very glum, her under-lip pushing a little obliquely out, very pathetically, I must say, as always when she is just ready to cry.

In a few strokes I drew the palace, and herself standing at the portal between the pillars: and now great was her satisfaction, for she pointed to the sketched figure, and to herself, interrogatively: and when I nodded 'yes yes', she went cooing her fond murmurous laugh, with pressed and mincing lips: and it is clear that, in spite of my beatings, she is in no way afraid of me.

Before I could move away, I felt some rain-drops, and down in some seconds rushed a shower. I looked, saw that the sky was rapidly darkening, and ran into the nearest of the little cubical houses, leaving her glancing sideways upward, with the quaintest artlessness of interest in the down-pour: for she is not yet quite familiarised with the operations of nature, and seems to regard them with a certain amiable inquisitive seriousness, as though they were living beings, comrades as good as herself. She presently joined me, but even then stretched her hand out to feel the drops.

Now there came a thunder-clap, the wind was rising, and rain spattering about me: for the panes of these houses, made, I believe, of paper saturated in almond-oil, have long disappeared, and rains, penetrating by roof and rare window, splash the bones of men. I gathered up my skirts to run toward other shelter, but she was before me, saying in her strange experimental voice that word of hers: '*Come*.'

She ran in advance, and I, with the outer robe over my head, followed, urging flinching way against the whipped rain-wash. She took the way by the stone horse-pond, through an alley to the left between two blind walls, then down a steep path through wood to the rock-steps, and up we ran, and along the hill, to her yali, which is a mile nearer the village than the palace, though by the time we pelted into its dry shelter we were wet to the skin.

Sudden darkness had come, but she quickly found some matches, lit one, looking at it with a certain meditative air, and applied it to a candle and to a bronze Western lamp on the table, which I had taught her to oil and light. Near a Western fire-place was a Turkish mangal, like one which she had seen me light to warm bath-waters in Constantinople, and when I pointed to it, she ran to the kitchen, returned with some chopped wood, and very cleverly lit it. And there for several hours I sat that night, reading (the first time for many years): it was a book by the poet Milton, found in a glazed book-case on the other side of the fire-place: and most strange, most novel, I found those august words about warring angels that night, while the storm raved: for this man had evidently taken no end of pains with his book, and done it gallantly well, too, making the thing hum: and I could not conceive why he should have been at that trouble – unless it were for the same reason that I built the palace, because some spark bites a man, and he would be like – but that is all vanity, and delusion.

Well, there is a rage in the storms of late years which really transcends bounds; I do not remember if I have noted it in these sheets before: but I never could have conceived a turbulence so huge. Hour after hour I sat there that night, smoking a chibouque, reading, and listening to the batteries and lamentations of that haunted air, shrinking from it, fearing even for the *Speranza* by her quay in the sequestered harbour, and for the palace-pillars. But what astonished me was that girl: for, after sitting on the ottoman to my left some time, she fell sideways asleep, not the least fear about her, though I should have thought that nervousness at such a turmoil would be so natural to her: and whence she has this light confidence in the world into which she has so abruptly come I do not know, for it is as though someone inspired her with the mood of nonchalance, saying: 'Be of good cheer, and care not a pin about anything: for God is God.'

I heard the ocean swing hoarse like heavy ordnance against the cliffs below, where they meet the outer surface of the southern of the two claws of land that form the harbour: and the thought came into my mind: 'If now I taught her to speak, to read, I could sometimes make her read a book to me.'

The winds seemed wilfully struggling for the house to snatch and wing it away into the drear Eternities of the night: and I could not but heave the sigh: 'Alas for us two poor waifs and castaways of our race, little bits of flotsam and seaweed-hair cast up here a moment, ah me, on this shore of the Ages, soon to be dragged back, O turgid Eternity, into thy abysmal gorge; and upon what strand – who shall say? – shall she next be flung, and I, divided then perhaps by all the stretch of the trillion-distanced astral gulf?' And such a pity, and a wringing of the heart, seemed in things, that a tear fell from my eyes that ominous midnight.

She started up at a gust of more appalling volume, rubbing her eyes, with dishevelled hair (it must have been about midnight), listening a minute, with that demure, droll interest of hers, to the noise of the elements, and then smiled to me; rose then, left the room, and presently returned with a pomegranate and some almonds on a plate, also some delicious old sweet wine in a Samian cruche, and an old silver cup, gilt inside, standing in a zarf.* These she placed on the table near me, I murmuring: 'Hospitality.'

She looked at the book, which I read as I ate, with lowered left eye-lid, seeking to guess its use, I suppose. Most things she understands at once, but this must have baffled her: for to see one looking fixedly at a thing, and not know what one is looking at it for, must be very disconcerting.

I held it up before her, saying:

'Shall I teach you to read it? If I did, how would you repay me, you Clodagh?'

She cocked her eyes, seeking to comprehend. God knows, at that moment I pitied the poor dumb waif, alone in all the whole round earth with me. The candle-flame, moved by the wind like a slow-painting brush, flickered upon her face, though every cranny was closed.

'Perhaps, then,' I said, 'I will teach you. You are a pitiable little derelict of your race, you know: and two hours every day I will let you come to the palace, and I will teach you. But be sure, be careful. If there be danger, I will kill you: assuredly – without fail. And let me begin with a lesson now: say after me: "White".'

I took her hand, and got her to understand that I wanted her to repeat after me.

'White,' said I.

'Hwhite,' said she.

'Power,' said I.

'Pow-wer,' said she.

'White Power,' said I.

'Hwhite Pow-wer,' said she.

'Shall not,' said I.

'Sall not,' said she.

'White Power shall not,' said I.

'Hwhite Pow-wer sall not,' said she.

'Prevail,' said I.

'Fffail,' said she, pronouncing the 'v' with a long fluttering 'f'-sound.

'Pre-vail,' said I.

'Pe-vvvail,' said she.

'White Power shall not prevail,' said I.

'Hwhite Pow-wer sall not – fffail,' said she.

A thunder which roared as she said it seemed to me to go laughing through the universe, and a minute I looked upon her face with positive shrinking fear; till, starting up, I thrust her with violence from my path, and dashed forth to re-seek the palace and my bed.

Such was the ingratitude and fatality which my first attempt, four nights since, to teach her met with. It remains to be seen whether my pity for her dumbness, or some servile tendency toward fellowship in myself, will result in any further lesson. Certainly, I think not: for though I have given my word, the most solemnly-pledged word may be broken.

Surely, surely, her presence in the world with me – for I suppose it is that – has wrought some profound changes in my mood: for gone now apparently are those turbulent hours when, stalking like a peacock, I flaunted my monarchy in the face of the Eternal Powers, with hissed blasphemies; or else dribbled, shaking my body in a lewd dance; or was off to fire some vast city and revel in redness and the chucklings of Hell; or rolled in the drunkenness of drugs. It was mere frenzy! – I see it now – it was 'not good', 'not good'. And it rather looks as if it were past – or almost. I have clipped my beard and hair, removed the ear-rings, and thought of modifying my attire. I will just watch to see whether she comes loitering down there about the gate of the lake.

Her progress is like...

It is nine months since I have written, on these sheets, those words, 'Her progress is like...' being the beginning of some narrative in which something interrupted me: and since then I have had no impulse to write.

But I was thinking just now of the curious tricks and uncertainties of my memory, and seeing the sheets, will record it here. I have lately been trying to recall the name of a sister of mine – some perfectly simple name, I know – and the name of my old home in England: and they have completely passed out of my cognizance, though she was my only sister, and we grew up closely together: some quite simple name, I forget it now. Yet I can't say that my memory is bad: there are things – quite unexpected, unimportant things – which come up in my mind with considerable clearness. For instance, I remember to have met in Paris (I think), long before the poison-cloud, a little Brazilian boy of the colour of weak coffee-and-milk, of whom she now constantly reminds me. He wore his hair short like a convict's, so that one could spy the fish-white flesh beneath, and delighted to play solitary about the stairs of the hotel, dressed up in the white balloon-dress of a Pierrot. I have the impression now that he must have had very large ears. Clever as a flea he was, knowing five or six languages, as it were by nature, without having any suspicion that that was at all extraordinary. She has that same light, unconscious, and nonchalant cleverness, and easy way of life. It is little more than a year since I began to teach her, and already she can speak English with a quite considerable vocabulary, and perfect correctness (except that she does not pronounce the letter 'r'); she has also read, or rather devoured, a good many books; and can write, draw, and play the harp. And all she does without effort: rather with the flighty naturalness with which a bird takes to the wing.

What made me teach her to read was this: One afternoon, fourteen months or so ago, I from the roof-kiosk saw her down at the lake-rim, a book in hand; and as she had seen me looking steadily at books, so she was looking steadily at it, with pathetic sideward head: so that I burst into laughter, for I saw her clearly through the glass, and whether she is the simplest little fool, or the craftiest serpent that ever breathed, I am not yet sure. If I thought that she has the least design upon my honour, it would be ill for her.

I went to Gallipoli for two days in the month of May, and brought back a very pretty little caique, a perfect slender crescent of the colour of the moon, though I had two days' labour in cutting through bush-thicket for the passage of the motor in bringing it up to the lake. It has pleased me to see her lie among the silk cushions of the middle, while I, paddling, taught her her first words and sentences between the hours of eight and ten in the evening, though later they became 10 A.M. to noon, when the reading began, we sitting on the palace-steps before the portal, her mouth invariably well covered with the yashmak, the lesson-book being a large-lettered old Bible found at her yali. *Why* she must needs wear the yashmak she has never once asked; and how much she divines, knows, or intends, I have no idea, continually questioning myself as to whether she is all simplicity, or all cunning.

That she is conscious of some profound difference in our organisation I cannot doubt: for that I have a long beard, and she none at all, is among the most patent of facts.

I have thought that a certain *Western-ness* – a growing modernity of tone – may be the result, as far as I am concerned, of her presence with me? I do not know…

There is the gleam of a lake-end just visible in the north forest from the palace-top, and in it a good number of fish like carp, tench, roach, &c., so in May I searched for a tackle-shop in the Gallipoli Fatmeh-bazaar, and got four 12-foot rods, with reels, silk-line, quill-floats, a few yards of silk-worm gut, with a packet of No. 7 and 8 hooks, and split-shot for sinkers; and since red-worms, maggots and gentles* are common on the island, I felt sure of a great many more fish than the number I wanted, which was none at all. However, for the mere amusement, I fished several times, lying at my length in a patch of long-grass over-waved by an enormous cedar, where the bank is steep, and the water deep. And one mid-afternoon she was suddenly there with me, questioned me with her eyes, and when I consented, stayed: and presently I said I would teach her bottom-angling, and sent her flying up to the palace for another rod and tackle.

That day she did nothing, for after teaching her to thread the worm, and put the gentles on the smaller hooks, I sent her to hunt for worms to chop up for ground-baiting the pitch for the next afternoon; and when this was done it was dinner-time, and I sent her home, for by then I was giving the reading-lessons in the morning.

The next day I found her at the bank, taught her to take the sounding for adjusting the float, and she lay down not far from me, holding the rod. So I said to her:

'Well, this is better than living in a dark cellar twenty years, with nothing to do but walk up and down, sleep, and consume dates and Ismidt wine.'

'Yes!' says she.

'Twenty years!' said I: 'how did you bear it?'

'I was not closs,' says she.

'Did you never suspect that there was a world outside that cellar?' said I.

'Never,' says she, 'or lather, yes: but I did not suppose that it was *this* world, but another where he lived.'

'He who?'

'He who spoke with me.'

'Who was that?'

'Oh! a bite!' she screamed gladly.

I saw her float bob under, and started up, rushed to her, and taught her how to strike and play it, though it turned out when landed to be nothing but a tiny barbel:* but she was in ecstasies, holding it on her palm, murmuring her fond coo.

She re-baited, and we lay again. I said:

'But what a life: no exit, no light, no prospect, no hope—'

'Plenty of *hope*!' says she.

'Good Heavens! hope of what?'

'I knew vely well that something was lipening over the cellar, or under, or alound it, and would come to pass at a certain fixed hour, and that I should see it, and feel it, and it would be vely nice.'

'Ah, well, you had to wait for it, at any rate. Didn't those twenty years seem *long*?'

'No – at least sometimes – not often. I was always so occupied.'

'Occupied in doing what?'

'In eating, or dlinking, or lunning, or talking.'

'Talking to your*self*?'

'Not myself.'

'To whom, then?'

'To the one who told me when I was hungly, and put the dates to satisfy my hunger.'

'I see. Don't wriggle about in that way, or you will never catch any fish. The maxim of angling is: "Study to be quiet"—'

'O! another bite!' she called, and this time, all alone, very agilely landed a good-sized bream.

'But do you mean that you were never sad?' said I when she was re-settled.

'Sometimes I would sit and cly,' says she – 'I did not know why. But if that was "sadness", I was never miserlable, never, never. And if I clied, it did not last long, and I would soon fall to sleep, for he would lock me in his lap, and kiss me, and wipe all my tears away.'

'He who?'

'Why, what a question! he who told me when I was hungly, and of the thing that was lipening outside the cellar, which would be so nice.'

'I see, I see. But in all that dingy place, and thick gloom, were you never at all afraid?'

'Aflaid! *I!* of what?'

'Of the unknown.'

'I do not understand you. How could I be *aflaid*? The known was the very opposite of tellible: it was merely hunger and dates, thirst and wine, the desire to lun and space to lun in, the desire to sleep and sleep: there was nothing tellible in that: and the unknown was even less tellible than the known: for it was the nice thing that was lipening outside the cellar. I do not understand—'

'Ah, yes,' said I, 'you are a clever little being: but your continual fluttering about is fatal to all angling. Isn't it in your nature to keep still a minute? And with regard now to your habits in the cellar—?'

'*Another!*' she cried with happy laugh, and landed a young chub. And that afternoon she caught seven, and I none.

Another day I took her from the pitch to one of the kitchens in the village with some of the fish, till then always thrown away, and taught her cooking: for the only cooking-implement in the palace is the silver alcohol-lamp for coffee and chocolate. We both scrubbed the utensils, and boil and fry I taught her, and the making of a sauce from vinegar, bottled olives, and the tinned American butter from the *Speranza*, and the boiling of rice mixed with flour for ground-baiting our pitch. And she, at first astonished, was soon all deft housewifeliness, breathless officiousness, and behind my back, of her own intuitiveness, grated some dry almonds found there, and with them sprinkled the fried tench. And we ate them, sitting on the floor together: the first new food, I suppose, tasted by me for twenty-one years: nor did I find it disagreeable.

The next day she came up to the palace reading a book, which turned out to be a cookery-book in English, found at her yali; and a week later, she appeared, out of hours, presenting me a yellow-earthenware dish containing a mess of gorgeous colours – a boiled fish under red peppers, bits of saffron, a greenish sauce, and almonds: but I turned her away, and would have none of her, or her dish.

About a mile up to the west of the palace is a very old ruin in the deepest forest, I think of a mosque, though only three truncated internal pillars under ivy, and the weedy floor, with the courtyard and portal-steps remain, before it being a long avenue of cedars, gently descending from the steps, the path between the trees choked with long-grass and wild rye reaching to my middle. Here I saw one day a large disc of old brass, bossed in the middle, which may have been either a shield or part of an ancient cymbal, with concentric rings graven round it, from centre to circumference. The next day I brought some nails, a hammer, a saw, and a box of paints from the *Speranza*; and I painted the rings in different colours, cut down a slim lime-trunk, nailed the thin disc along its top, and planted it well, before the steps: for I said I would make a bull's-eye, and do rifle and revolver practice before it, from the avenue. And this the next evening I was doing at four hundred feet, startling the island, it seemed, with that unusual noise, when up she came peering with enquiring face: at which I was very angry, because my arm, long unused, was firing wide: but I was too proud to say anything, and let her look, and soon she understood, laughing every time I made a considerable miss, till at last I turned upon her saying: 'If you think it so easy, you may try.'

She had been wanting to try, for she came eagerly to the offer, and after I had opened and showed her the mechanism, the cartridges, and how to shoot, I put into her hands one of the *Speranza* Colts. She took her bottom-lip between her teeth, shut her left eye, vaulted out the revolver like an old shot to the level of her intense right eye, and sent a ball through the geometrical centre of the boss.

However, it was a fluke-shot, for I had the satisfaction of seeing her miss every one of the other five, except the last, which hit the black. That, however, was three weeks since, and now my hitting record is forty per cent, and hers ninety-six – most extraordinary: so that it is clear that this creature is the *protégée* of someone, and favouritism is in the world.

Her book of books is the Old Testament.* Sometimes, at noon or afternoon, I may look abroad from the roof or galleries, and see a remote figure sitting on the sward under the shade of plane or black cypress: and I always know that the book she cons there is the Bible – like an old Rabbi. She has a passion for stories: and there finds a store.

Three nights since when it was pretty late, and the moon very splendid, I saw her passing homewards close to the lake, and shouted down to her, meaning to say 'Good-night'; but she thought that I had called her, and came: and sitting out on the top step we talked for hours, she without the yashmak.

We fell to talking about the Bible. And says she: 'What did Cain to Abel?'

'He knocked him over,' I replied, liking sometimes to use such idioms, with the double object of teaching and perplexing her.

'Over what?' says she.

'Over his heels,' said I.

'I do not complehend!'

'He killed him, then.'

'That I know. But how did Abel feel when he was killed? What is it to be *killed*?'

'Well,' said I, 'you have seen bones all around you, and the bones of your mother, and you can feel the bones in your fingers. Your fingers will become mere bone after you are dead, as die you must. Those bones which you see around you, are, of course, the bones of the men of whom we often speak: and the same thing happened to them which happens to a fish or a butterfly when you catch them, and they lie all still.'

'And the men and the butterfly feel the same after they are dead?'

'Precisely the same. They lie in a deep drowse, and dream a nonsense-dream.'

'That is not dleadful. I thought that it was much more dleadful. I should not mind dying.'

'Ah!...so much the better: for it is possible that you may have to die a great deal sooner than you think.'

'I should not mind. Why were men so vely aflaid to die?'

'Because they were all such shocking cowards.'

'Oh, not all! not all!'

(This girl, I know not with what motive, has now definitely set herself up against me as the defender of the dead race. With every chance she is at it.)

'Nearly all,' said I: 'tell me one who was not afraid—'

'There was Isaac,' says she: 'when Ablaham laid him on the wood to kill him, he did not jump up and lun to hide.'

'Isaac was a great exception,' said I: 'in the Bible and such books, you understand, you read of only the best sorts of people; but there were millions and millions of others – especially about the time of the poison-cloud – on a very much lower level – putrid wretches – covetous, false, murderous, mean, selfish, debased, hideous, diseased, making the earth a very charnel of festering vices and crimes.'

This, for several minutes, she did not answer, sitting with

her back half toward me, cracking almonds, continually
striking one step with the ball of her outstretched foot. In the
clarid gold of the platform I saw her fez and corals reflected
as an elongated blotch of florid red. She turned and drank
some wine from the great gold Jarvan goblet which I had
brought from the temple of Boro Budor,* her head quite
covered in by it. Then, the little hairs at her lip-corners still
wet, says she:

'Vices and climes, climes and vices. Always the same. What
were these climes and vices?'*

'Robberies of a hundred sorts, murders of ten hundred—'

'But what made them *do* them?'

'Their evil nature – their base souls.'

'But *you* are one of them, *I* am another, yet you and I live
here together, and we do no vices and climes.'

Her astounding shrewdness! Right into the inmost heart of a
matter does her simple wit seem to pierce!

'No,' I said, 'we do no vices and crimes because we lack
motive. There is no danger that we should hate each other, for
we have plenty to eat and drink, dates, wines, and thousands of
things. (Our danger is rather the other way.) But *they* hated and
schemed, because they were very numerous, and there arose a
question among them of dates and wine.'

'Was there not, then, enough land to grow dates and wine
for all?'

'There was – yes: much more than enough, I fancy. But some
got hold of a vast lot of it, and as the rest felt the pinch of scar-
city, there arose, naturally, a pretty state of things – including
the vices and crimes.'

'Ah, but then,' says she, 'it was not to their bad souls that the
vices and climes were due, but only to this question of land.* It
is certain that if there had been no such question, there would
have been no vices and climes, because you and I, who are just
like them, do no vices and climes here, where there is no such
question.'

The clear limelight of her intelligence! She wriggled on her
seat in her effort of argument.

'I am not going to argue the matter,' I said. 'There *was* that question of dates and wine, you see. And there always must be on an earth where millions of men, with varying degrees of cunning, reside.'

'Oh, not at all necessalily!' she cries with conviction: 'not at all, at all: since there are much more dates and wine than are enough for all. If there should spling up more men now, having the whole wisdom, science, and expelience of the past at their hand, and they made an allangement among themselves that the first man who tlied to take more than he could work for should be killed, and sent to dleam a nonsense-dleam, the question could never again alise!'

'It arose before – it would arise again.'

'But no! I can guess clearly how it alose before: it alose thlough the sheer carelessness of the first men. The land was at first so vely, vely much more than enough for all, that the men did not take the tlouble to make an allangement among themselves; and afterwards the habit of carelessness was confirmed; till at last the vely oliginal carelessness must have got to have the look of an allangement; and so the stleam which began in a little long ended in a big long, the long glowing more and more fixed and fatal as the stleam lolled further flom the source. I see it clearly, can't you? But now, if some more men would spling, they would be taught—'

'Ah, but no more men will *spling*, you see—!'

'There is no telling. I sometimes feel as if they must, and shall. The tlees blossom, the thunder lolls, the air makes me lun and leap, the glound is full of lichness, and I hear the voice of the Lord God walking all among the tlees of the folests.'

As she said this, I saw her under-lip push out and tremble, as when she is near to crying, and her eyes moisten: but a moment after she looked at me full, and smiled, so mobile is her face: and as she looked, it suddenly struck me what a noble temple of a brow the creature has, almost pointed at the uplifted summit, and widening down like a bell-curved Gothic arch, draped in strings of frizzy hair which anon she shakes backward with her head.

'Clodagh,' I said after some minutes – 'do you know why I called you Clodagh?'

'No? Tell me?'

'Because once, long ago before the poison-cloud, I had a lover called Clodagh: and she was...'

'But tell me first,' cries she: 'how did one know one's lover, or one's wife, flom all the others?'

'Well, by their faces...'

'But there must have been many faces – all alike—'

'Not all alike. Each was different from the rest.'

'Still, it must have been vely clever to tell. I can hardly conceive any face, except yours and mine.'

'Ah, because you are a little goose, you see.'

'What was a goose like?'

'It was a thing like a butterfly, only larger, and it kept its toes always spread out, with a skin stretched between.'

'Leally? How caplicious! And am I like that? – but what were you saying that your lover, Clodagh, was?'

'She was a Poisoner.'

'Then why call me Clodagh, since *I* am not a poisoner?'

'I call you so to remind me: lest you – lest you – should become my – lover, too.'

'I am your lover already: for I love you.'

'What, girl?'

'Do I not love you, who are mine?'

'Come, come, don't be a little maniac!' I went. 'Clodagh was a *poisoner*...'

'Why did she poison? Had she not enough dates and wine?'

'She had, yes: but she wanted more, more, more, the silly idiot.'

'So that the vices and climes were not confined to those that lacked things, but were done by the others, too?'

'By the others chiefly.'

'Then I see how it was!'

'How was it?'

'The others had got *spoiled*. The vices and climes must have begun with those who lacked things, and then the others, always seeing vices and climes alound them, began to do them, too – as when one lotten olive is in a bottle, the whole mass soon becomes collupted: but originally they were not lotten,

but only became so. And all thlough a little carelessness at the
first. I am sure that if more men could spling now—'

'But I *told* you, didn't I, that no more men will spring? You
understand, Clodagh, that originally the earth produced men by
a long process, beginning with a very low type of creature, and
continually developing it, until at last a man stood up. But that
can never happen again: for the earth is old, old, and has lost her
producing vigour now. So talk no more of men *splinging*, and of
things which you do not understand. Instead, go inside – stop, I
will tell you a secret: to-day in the wood I picked some musk-
roses and wound them into a wreath, meaning to give them you
for your head when you came to-morrow; and it is inside on the
pearl tripod in the second room to the left: go, therefore, and put
it on, and bring the harp, and play to me, my dear.'

She ran quick with a little cry, and coming again, sat crowned,
incarnadine in the blushing depths of the gold. Nor did I send
her home to her lonely yali, till the pale and languished moon,
weary of all-night beatitudes, sank down soft-couched in quilts
of curdling opals to the Hesperian realms of her rest.

So sometimes we speak together, she and I, she and I.

That ever I should write such a thing! I am driven out from
Imbros!

I was walking up in a wood yesterday to the west – it was a
calm clear evening about seven, the sun having just set. I had
the book in which I have written so far in my hand, for I had
thought of making a sketch of an old windmill to the north-
west to show her. Twenty minutes before she had been with me,
for I had chanced to meet her, and she had come, but kept dart-
ing on ahead after peeping fruit, gathering armfuls of amaranth,
nenuphar, and red-berried asphodel, till, weary of my life, I had
called to her: 'Go away! out of my sight' – and she, with suddenly pushed under-lip, had walked off.

Well, I was continuing my stroll, when I seemed to feel some
quaking of the ground, and before one could count twenty, it
was as if the island was bent upon wracking itself to pieces. My
first thought was of her, and in great scare I went running, calling in the direction which she had gone, staggering as on the

deck of some labouring ship, falling, picking myself up, running again. The air was quite full of uproar, and the land waving like the sea: and as I went plunging, not knowing whither, I saw to my right some three or four acres of forest droop and sink into a gulf which opened to receive them. Up I flung my arms, crying out: 'Good God! save the girl!' and a minute later rushed out, to my surprise, into open space on a hill-side. On the lower ground I could see the palace, and beyond it, a small space of white sea which had the awful appearance of being higher than the land. Down the hill-side I staggered, driven by the impulse to fly somewhither, but about half way down was startled afresh by a shrill pattering like musical hail, and the next moment saw the entire palace rush with the jangling clatter of a thousand bells into the heaving lake.

Some seconds after this, the earthquake, having lasted fully ten minutes, began to lull, and soon ceased. I found her an hour later standing among the ruins of her little yali.

Well, what a thing! Probably every building on the island has been destroyed; the palace-platform, all cracked, leans half-sunken askew into the lake, like a huge stranded ark, while of the palace itself no trace remains, except a mound of gold stones emerging above the lake to the south. Gone, gone – sixteen years of vanity and vexation. But from a practical point of view, what is a worst calamity of all is that the *Speranza* now lies high-and-dry in the village: for she was bodily picked up from the quay by the tidal wave, and driven bow-foremost into a street not half her width, and there now lies, looking huge enough in the little village, wedged for ever, smashed in at the nip like a frail match-box, a most astonishing spectacle: her bows forty feet up the street, ten feet above the ground at the stem, rudder resting on the inner edge of the quay, foremast tilted forward, the other two masts all right, and that bottom, which has passed through seas so far, buried in every sort of green and brown seaweed, the old *Speranza*. Her steps were there, and by a slight leap I could catch them underneath and go up hand-over-hand, till I got foothold; this I did at ten the same night when the sea-water had mostly drained back from

the land, leaving everything very swampy, however; she there
with me, and soon following me upon the ship. I found most
things cracked into tiny fragments, twisted, disfigured out of
likeness, the house-walls themselves displaced a little at the nip,
the bow of the cedar skiff smashed in to her middle against the
aft starboard corner of the galley; and were it not for the fact
that the air-pinnace had not broken from her heavy ropings,
and one of the compasses still whole, I do not know what I
should have done: for the four old water-logged boats in the
cove have utterly disappeared.

I made her sleep on the cabin-floor amid the *débris* of berth
and everything, and I myself slept high up in the wood to the
west. I am writing now lying in the long-grass the morning
after, the sun rising, though I cannot see him. My plan for to-
day is to cut three or four logs with the saw, lay them on the
ground by the ship, lower the pinnace upon them, so get her
gradually down into the water, and by evening bid a long farewell to Imbros, which drives me out in this way. Still, I look
forward with pleasure to our hour's run to the Mainland, when
I shall teach her to steer by the compass, and manipulate liquid-
air, as I have taught her to dress, to talk, to cook, to write, to
think, to live. For she is my creation, this creature: as it were, a
'rib from my side'.

But what is the design of this expulsion? And what was it
that she called it last night? – 'this new going out flom Halan'!
'Haran', I believe, being the place from which Abraham went
out, when 'called' by God.*

We apparently felt only the tail of the earthquake at Imbros:
for it has ravaged Turkey! And we two poor helpless creatures
put down here in the theatre of all these infinite violences: it is
too bad, too bad. For the rages of Nature at present are perfectly astonishing, and what it may come to I do not know.
When we came to the Macedonian coast in good moonlight,
we sailed along it, and up the Dardanelles, looking out for
village, yali, or any habitation where we might put up: but everything has apparently been wrecked. We saw Kilid-Bahr,
Chanak-Kaleh, Gallipoli, Lapsaki in ruins; at the last place I

landed, leaving her in the boat, and walked a little way, but soon went back with the news that there was not even a bazaar-arch left standing whole, in most parts even the line of the streets being obliterated, for the place had fallen like a house of dice, and had then been shaken up and jumbled. Finally we slept in a forest on the other side of the strait, beyond Gallipoli, taking our few provisions, and having to wade at some points through morass a foot deep before we reached dry woodland.

Here, the next morning, I sat alone – for we had slept separated by at least half a mile – thinking out the question of whither I should go: my choice would have been to remain either in the region where I was, or to go Eastward: but the region where I was offered no dwelling that I could see; and to go any distance Eastward, I needed a ship. Of ships I had seen during the night only wrecks, nor did I know where to find one in all these latitudes. I was thus, like her 'Ablaham', urged Westward.

In order, then, to go Westward, I first went a little further Eastward, once more entered the Golden Horn, and once more mounted the scorched Seraglio steps. Here what the wickedness of man had spared, the wickedness of Nature had destroyed, and the few houses which I had left standing round the upper part of Pera I now saw low as the rest; also the house near the Suleimanieh, where we had lived our first days, to which I went as to a home, I found without a pillar standing; and that night she slept under the half-roof of a little funeral-kiosk in the scorched cypress-wood of Eyoub, and I a mile away, at the edge of the forest where first I saw her.

The next morning, having met, as agreed, at the site of the Prophet's mosque, we traversed together the valley and cemetery of Kassim by the quagmires up to Pera, all the landscape having to me a rather twisted unfamiliar aspect. We had determined to spend the morning in searching for supplies among the earthquake-ruins of Pera; and as I had decided to collect sufficient in one day to save us further pains for some time, we passed a good many hours in this task, I confining myself to the great white house in the park overlooking Kassim, where I had once slept, losing myself in the huge obliquities of its floors, roofs and wall-fragments, she going to the old Mussulman quarter of Djianghir near, on the heights of Taxim, where were many shops, and thence round the brow of the hill to the great French Embassy-house, overlooking Foundoucli and the sea, both of us having large Persian carpet-bags, and all in the air of that wilderness of ruin that morning a sweet, strong, permanent odour of maple-blossom.

We met toward evening, she quivering under such a load, that I would not let her carry it, but abandoned my day's labour, which was lighter, and took hers, which was quite enough: we went back Westward, seeking all the while some shelter from the saturating night-dews of this place: and nothing could we find, till we came again, quite late, to her broken funeral-kiosk at the entrance to the immense cemetery-avenue of Eyoub. There without a word I left her among the shattered catafalques, for I was weary; but having gone some distance, turned back, thinking that I might take some more raisins from the bag; and after getting them, said to her, shaking her little hand where she sat under the roof-shadow on a stone:

'Good-night, Clodagh.'

She did not answer promptly: and her answer, to my surprise, was a protest against her name: for a rather sulky, yet gentle, voice came from the darkness, saying:

'I am *not* a Poisoner!'

'Well,' said I, 'all right: tell me whatever you like that I should call you, and henceforth I will call you that.'

'Call me Eve,' says she.

'Well, no,' said I, 'not Eve, anything but that: for *my* name is Adam, and if I called you Eve, that would be simply absurd, and we do not want to be ridiculous in each other's eyes. But I will call you anything else that you like.'

'Call me Leda,' says she.

'And why Leda?' said I.

'Because Leda sounds something like Clodagh,' says she, 'and you are al-leady in the habit of calling me Clodagh; and I saw the name Leda in a book, and liked it: but Clodagh is most hollible, most bitterly hollible!'

'Well, then,' said I, 'Leda it shall be, and I shan't forget, for I like it, too, and it suits you, and you ought to have a name beginning with an "L".* Good-night, my dear, sleep well, and dream, dream.'

'And to you, too, my God give dleams of peace and pleasant-ness,' says she; and I went.

And it was only when I had lain myself upon leaves for my bed, my head on my caftan, a rill for my lullaby, and two stars, which alone I could see out of the heavenful, for my watch-lights; and only when my eyes were already closed toward slumber, that a sudden strong thought pierced and woke me: for I remembered that Leda was the name of a Greek woman who had borne twins. In fact, I should not be surprised if this Greek word Leda is the same word etymologically as the Hebrew Eve, for I have heard of v's, and b's, and d's interchang-ing about in this way, and if Di, meaning God, or Light, and Bi, meaning Life, and Iove and Iho$v$ah and God, meaning much the same, are all one, that would be nothing astonishing to me, as wi$d$ow, and veu$v$e, are one: and where it says, 'truly the Light is Good (tob, $b$on)', this is as if it said, 'truly the Di is Di'. Such, at any rate, is the fatality that attends me, even in the smallest things: for this Western Eve, or Greek Leda, had twins.

Well, the next morning we crossed by the ruins of old Greek Phanar across the triple Stamboul-wall, which still showed its deep-ivied portal, and made our way, not without climbing, along the Golden Horn to the foot of the Old Seraglio, where I soon found signs of the railway. And that minute commenced our journey across Turkey, Bulgaria, Servia, Bosnia, Croatia, to Trieste, occupying no day or two as in old times, but four months, a long-drawn nightmare, though a nightmare of rich happiness, if one may say so, leaving on the memory a vague vast impression of monstrous ravines, ever-succeeding profun-dities, heights and greatnesses, jungles strange as some moon-struck poet's fantasy, everlasting glooms, and a sound of mighty unseen rivers, cataracts, and slow cumbered rills whose bulrushes never see the sun, with largesse everywhere, secrecies, profusions, the unimaginable, the unspeakable, a savagery most lush and fierce and gaudy, and vales of Arcadie, and remote mountain-peaks, and tarns shy as old-buried treasure, and glaciers, and we two human folk pretty small and drowned and lost in all that amplitude, yet moving always through it.

We followed the lines that first day till we came to a steam train, and I found the engine fairly good, and everything necessary to move it at my hand: but the metals in such a condition of twisted, broken, vaulted, and buried confusion, due to the earthquake, that, having run some hundreds of yards to examine them, I saw that nothing could be done in that way. At first this threw me into a condition like despair, for what we were to do I did not know: but after persevering on foot for four days along the deep-rusted track, which is of that large-gauge type peculiar to Eastern Europe, I began to see that there were considerable sound stretches, and took heart.

I had with me land-charts and compass, but nothing for taking altitude-observations: for the *Speranza* instruments, except one compass, had all been broken-up by her shock. However, on getting to the town of Silivri, about thirty miles from our start, I saw in the ruins of a half-standing bazaar-shop a number of brass objects, and there found several good sextants, quadrants, and theodolites. Two mornings later, we came upon an engine in mid-country, with coals in it, and a stream near; I had a goat-skin of almond-oil in the bag, and found the machinery serviceable after an hour's careful inspection, having examined the boiler with a candle through the manhole, and removed the autoclaves of the heaters. All was red with rust, and the shaft of the connecting-rod in particular seemed so frail, that at one moment I was very dubious: I decided, however, and, except for a slight leakage at the tubulure which led the steam to the valve-chest, all went very well; at a pressure never exceeding three-and-a-half atmospheres, we travelled nearly a hundred and twenty miles before being stopped by a head-to-head block on the line, when we had to abandon our engine; we then continued another seven miles a-foot, I all the time mourning my motor, which I had had to leave at Imbros, and hoping at every townlet to find a whole one, but in vain.

It was wonderful to see the villages and downs going back to the earth, already invaded by vegetation, and hardly any longer breaking the continuity of pure Nature, the town now as much the country as the country, and that which is not-Man becoming all in all with a certain *furore* of vigour. A whole day in the southern gorges of the Balkan Mountains the slow train went tearing its way through many a mile of bind-weed tendrils, a continuous curtain, flaming with large flowers, but sombre as the falling shades of night, rather resembling jungles of Ceylon and the Filipinas; and she, that day, lying in the single car behind, where I had made her a little yatag-bed from Tatar Bazardjik, continually played the kittur, barely touching the strings, and crooning low, low, in her rich contralto, eternally the same air, over and over again, crooning, crooning, some melancholy tune of her own dreaming, just audible to me through the slow-travailing monotony of the engine; till I was drunken with so sweet a woe, my God, a woe that was sweet as life, and a dolour that lulled like nepenthe, and a grief that soothed like kisses, so sweet, so sweet, that all that world of wood and gloom lost locality and realness for me, and became nothing but a charmed and pensive Heaven for her to moan and lullaby in; and from between my fingers streamed plenteous tears that day, and all that I could keep on mourning was 'O Leda, O Leda, O Leda,' till my heart was near to break.

The feed-pump eccentric-shaft of this engine, which was very poor and flaky, suddenly gave out about five in the afternoon, and I had to stop in a hurry, and that sweet invisible mechanism which had crooned and crooned about my ears in the air, and followed me whithersoever I went, stopped too. Down she jumped, calling out:

'Well, I had a plesentiment that something would happen, and I am so glad, for I was tired!'

Seeing that nothing could be done with the feed-water pump, I got down, took the bag, and parting before us the continuous screen, we went pioneering to the left between a rock-cleft, stepping over large stones that looked black with moss-growths, no sky, but hundreds of feet of impenetrable leafage over-head, and everywhere the dew-dabbled profusion of dim ferneries, dishevelled maidenhairs mixed with a large-leaved mimosa, wild vine, white briony, and a smell of cedar, and a soft rushing of perpetual waters that charmed the gloaming. The way led slightly upwards three hundred feet, and presently, after some windings, and the climbing of five huge steps almost regular, yet obviously natural, the gorge opened in a roundish space, fifty feet across, with far over-hanging edges seven hundred feet high; and there, behind a curtain which fell from above, its tendrils defined and straight like a Japanese bead-hanging, we spread the store of foods, I opening the wines, fruits, vegetables and meats, she arranging them in order with the gold plate, and lighting both the spirit-lamp and the lantern: for here it was quite dark. Near us behind the curtain of tendrils was a small green cave in the rock, and at its mouth a pool two yards wide, a black and limpid water that leisurely wheeled, discharging a little rivulet from the cave: and in it I saw three owl-eyed fish, a finger long, loiter, and spur themselves, and gaze. Leda, who cannot be still in tongue or limb, chattered in her glib baby manner as we ate, and then, after smoking a cigarette, said that she would go and 'lun', and went, and left me darkling, for she is the sun and the moon and the host of the stars, I occupying myself that night in making a calendar at the end of this book in which I have written, for my almanack and many things that I prized were lost with the palace – making a calendar, counting the days in my head – but counting them across my thoughts of her.

She came again to tell me good-night, and then went down to the train to sleep; and I put out the lantern, and stooped within the cave, and made my simple couch beside the little rivulet, and slept.

But a fitful sleep, and soon again I woke; and a long time I lay so, gradually becoming conscious of a slow dripping at one spot in the cave: for at a minute's interval it darkly splashed, regularly, very deliberately; and it seemed to grow always louder and sadder, and the splash at first was 'Leesha', but it became 'Leda' to my ears, and it sobbed her name, and I pitied myself, so sad was I. And when I could no longer bear the anguished melancholy of its spasm and its sobbing, I arose and went softly, softly, lest she should hear in that sounding silence of the hushed and darksome night, going more slow, more soft, as I went nearer, a sob in my throat, my feet leading me to her, till I touched the carriage. And against it a long time I leant my clammy brow, a sob aching in my poor throat, and she all mixed up in my head with the suspended hushed night, and with the elfin things in the air that made the silence so musically a-sound to the vacant ear-drum, and with the dripping splash in the cave. And softly I turned the door-handle, and heard her breathe in sleep, her head near me; and I touched her hair with my lips, and close to her ear I said – for I heard her breathe as if in sleep – 'Little Leda, I have come to you, for I could not help it, Leda: and oh, my heart is full of the love of you, for you are mine, and I am yours: and to live with you, till we die, and after we are dead to be near you still, Leda, with my broken heart near your heart, little Leda –'

I must have sobbed, I think: for as I spoke close at her ears, with passionately dying eyes of love, I was startled by an irregularity in her breathing: and with cautious hurry I shut the door, and quite back to the cave I stole in haste.

And the next morning when we met I thought – but am not now sure – that she smiled singularly: I thought so. She may, she *may*, have heard— But I cannot tell.

Twice I was obliged to abandon engines on account of forest-tree obstructions right across the line, which, do what I might, I could not move, and these were the two bitterest incidents of the pilgrimage; and at least thirty times I changed from engine to engine, when other trains blocked. As for the extent of the earthquake, it is pretty certain that it was universal over the Peninsula, and at many points exhibited extreme violence, for up to the time that we entered upon Servian territory, we occasionally came upon stretches of the lines so dislocated, that it was impossible to proceed upon them, and during the whole course I never saw one intact house or castle; four times, where the way was of a nature to permit of it, I left the imbedded metals and made the engine travel the ground till I came upon other metals, when I always succeeded in driving it upon them. It was all very leisurely, for not everywhere, nor every day, could I get a nautical observation, and having at all times to go at low pressures for fear of tube and boiler weakness, crawling through tunnels, and stopping when total darkness came on, we did not go fast, nor much cared to. Once, moreover, for three days, and once for four, we were overtaken by hurricanes of such vast inclemency, that no thought of travelling entered our heads, our only care being to hide our poor cowering bodies as deeply and darkly as possible. Once I passed through a city (Adrianople) doubly devastated, once by the hellish arson of my own hand, and once by the earthquake: and I made haste to leave that place behind me.

Finally, three months and twenty-seven days from the date of the earthquake, having traversed only 900 odd English miles, I let go in the Venice lagoon, in the early morning of the 10th September, the lateen sail and stone anchor of a Maltese *spero-nare*, which I had found, and partially cleaned, at Trieste; and thence I passed up the Canalazzo in a gondola. For I said to Leda: 'In Venice will I pitch my Patriarch tent.'

But to will and to do are not the same thing, and still further Westward was I driven. For the stagnant upper canals of this place are now mere miasmas of pestilence: and within two days I was rolling with fever in the Old Procurazie Palace, she standing in pale wonderment at my beside, sickness quite a novel thing to her: and, indeed, this was my first serious illness since my twentieth year or thereabouts, when I had over-worked my brain, and went a voyage to Constantinople. I could not move from bed for some weeks, but happily did not lose my senses, and she brought me the whole pharmacopæia from the shops, from which to choose my medicines. I guessed the cause of this illness, though not a sign of it came near *her*, and as soon as my trembling knees could bear me, I again set out – always West-ward – enjoying now a certain luxury in travelling compared with that Turkish difficulty, for here were no twisted metals, more and better engines, in the cities as many good petrol motors as I chose, and Nature markedly less savage.

I do not know why I did not stop at Verona or Brescia, or some other neighbourhood of the Italian lakes, since I was fond of water: but I had, I think, the thought in my head to return to Vauclaire in France, where I had once lived, and there live: for I thought that she might like those old monks. At all events, we

did not remain long in any place till we came to Turin, where
we spent nine days, she in the house opposite mine, and after
that, at her own suggestion, went on still, passing by train into
the valley of the Isère, and then into that of the Western Rhone,
till we came to the old town of Geneva among some very great
mountains peaked with snow, the town seated at the head of a
long lake which the earth has made in the shape of the crescent
moon, and like the moon it is a thing of much beauty and many
moods, suggesting a creature under the spell of charms and
magics. However, with this idea of Vauclaire still in my head,
we left Geneva in the motor which had brought us at four in
the afternoon of the 17th May, I intending to reach the town
called Bourg that night about eight, and there sleep, so to go on
to Lyons the next morning by train, and so, by the Bordeaux
route, make Vauclaire. But by some chance for which I cannot
to this hour account (unless the train was the cause), I missed
the chart-road, which should have been fairly level, and found
myself on mountain-tracks, unconscious of my whereabouts,
while darkness fell, and a windless down-pour that had a certain sullen venom in its superabundance drenched us. I stopped
several times, looking about for château, châlet, or village, but
none did I see, though I twice came upon railway-lines; and not
till midnight did we run down a rather steep pass upon the
shore of a lake, which, from its apparent vastness in the moonless obscurity, I could only suppose to be the Lake of Geneva
once again. About two hundred yards to the left we saw through
the rain a large pile, apparently risen straight out of the lake,
looking ghostly livid, for it was of white stone, not high, but an
old thing of complicated white little turrets roofed with dark-
red candle-extinguishers, and oddities of Gothic nooks,
window-slits, and outline, very like a fanciful picture. Round to
this we went, drowned as rats, Leda sighing and bedraggled,
and found a narrow spit of low land projecting into the lake,
where we left the car, walked forward with the bag, crossed a
small wooden drawbridge, and came upon a rocky island with
a number of thick-foliaged trees about the castle. We quickly
found a small open portal, and went throughout the place,
quite gay at the shelter, everywhere lighting candles which we

found in iron sconces in the rather queer apartments: so that, as the castle is far-seen from the shores of the lake, it would have appeared to one looking thence a place suddenly possessed and haunted. We found beds, and slept: and the next day it turned out to be the antique Castle of Chillon,* where we remained five long and happy months, till again, again, Fate overtook us.

The morning after our coming, we had breakfast – our last meal together – on the first floor in a pentagonal room approached from a lower level by three little steps. In it is a ponderous oak-table pierced with a multitude of worm-eaten tunnels, also three mighty high-backed chairs, an old oak-desk covered still with papers, arras on the walls, and three dark religious oil-paintings, and a grandfather's-clock: it is at about the middle of the château, and contains two small, but deep, three-faced oriels, in each face four compartments with white-stone shafts between, these looking south upon shrubs and the rocky edge of the island, then upon the deep-blue lake, then upon another tiny island containing four trees in a jungle of flowers, then upon the shore of the lake interrupted by the mouths of a river which turned out to be the Rhone, then upon a white town on the slopes which turned out to be Villeneuve, then upon the great mountains back of Bouveret and St Gingolph, all having the surprised air of a resurrection just completed, everything new-washed in dyes of azure, ultramarine, indigo, snow, emerald, that fresh morning: so that one had to call it the best and holiest place in the world. These five old room-walls, and oak floor, and two oriels, became specially mine, though it was really common-ground to us both, and there I would do many little things. The papers on the desk told that it had been the *bureau* of one R. E. Gaud, '*Grand Bailli*', whose residence the place no doubt had been.

She asked me while eating that morning to stay here, and I said that I would see, though with misgiving: so together we went all about the house, and finding it unexpectedly spacious, I consented to stop. At both ends are suites, mostly small rooms, infinitely quaint and cosy, furnished with heavy Henri Quatre furniture and bed-draperies; and there are separate, and as it were secret, spiral stairs for exit to each: so we decided that she should have the suite overlooking the length of the lake, the mouths of the Rhone, Bouveret and Villeneuve; and I should have that overlooking the spit of land behind and the little drawbridge, shore-cliffs, and elm-wood which comes down to the shore, giving at one point a glimpse of the diminutive hamlet of Chillon; and, that decided, I took her hand in mine, and I said:

'Well, then, here we stay, both under the same roof – for the first time. Leda, I will not explain why to you, but it is dangerous, so much so that it *may* mean the death of one or other of us: deadly, deadly dangerous, my poor girl. You do not understand, but that is the fact, believe me, for I know it very well, and I would not tell you false. Well, then, you will easily comprehend, that this being so, you must never on any account come near my part of the house, nor will I come near yours. Lately we have been very much together, but then we have been active, full of purpose and occupation: here we shall be nothing of the kind, I can see. You do not understand at all – but things are so. We must live perfectly separate lives, then. You are nothing to me, really, nor I to you, only we live on the same earth, which is nothing at all – a mere chance. Your own food, clothes, and everything that you want, you will procure for yourself: it is perfectly easy: the shores are crowded with mansions, castles, towns and villages; and I will do the same for myself. The motor down there I set apart for your private use: if I want another, I will get one; and to-day I will set about looking you up a boat and fishing-tackle, and cut a cross on the bow of yours, so that you may know yours, and never use mine. All this is very necessary: you cannot dream how much: but I know how much. Do not run any risks in climbing, now, or with the motor, or in the boat…little Leda…'

I saw her under-lip push, and I turned away in haste, for I did not care whether she cried or not. In that long voyage, and in my illness at Venice, she had become too near and dear to me, my tender love, my dear darling soul; and I said in my heart: 'I will be a decent being: I will turn out trumps.'

*

Under this castle is a sort of dungeon, not narrow, nor very
dark, in which are seven stout dark-grey pillars, and an eighth,
half-built into the wall; and one of them which has an iron ring,
as well as the ground around it, is all worn away by some prisoner or prisoners once chained there; and in the pillar the word
'Byron' engraved. This made me remember that a poet of that
name had written something about this place, and two days
afterwards I actually came upon three volumes of the poet in a
room containing a great number of books, many of them English, near the Grand Bailli's *bureau:* and in one I read the poem,
which is called 'The Prisoner of Chillon'. I found it very affect-
ing, and the description good, only I saw no seven rings, and
where he speaks of the 'pale and livid light',* he should speak
rather of the dun and brownish gloom, for the word 'light' dis-
concerts the fancy, and of either pallor or blue there is there no
sign. However, I was so struck by the horror of man's cruelty to
man, as depicted in this poem, that I determined that she should
see it: went up straight to her rooms with the book, and, she
being away, ferreted among her things to see what she was
doing, finding all very neat, except in one room where were a
number of prints called *La Mode*, and *débris* of snipped cloth,
and medley. When, after two hours, she came in, and I suddenly
presented myself, 'Oh!' she let slip, and then fell to cooing her
laugh; and I took her down through a big room stacked with
every kind of rifle, with revolvers, cartridges, powder, swords,
bayonets – evidently some official or cantonal magazine – and
then showed her the worn stone in the dungeon, the ring, the
narrow deep slits in the wall, and I told the tale of cruelty, while
the splashing of the lake upon the rock outside was heard with
a strange and tragic sound, and her mobile face was all one
sorrow.

'How cluel they must have been!' cries she with tremulous
lip, her face at the same time reddened with indignation.

'They were mere beastly monsters,' said I: 'it is nothing sur-
prising if monsters were cruel.'

And in the short time while I said that, she was looking up
with a new-born smile.

'Some others came and set the plisoner flee!' cries she.

'Yes,' said I, 'they did, but—'

'That was good of them,' says she.

'Yes,' said I, 'that was all right, so far as it went.'

'And it was a time when men had al-leady become cluel,' says she: 'if those who set him flee were so good when all the lest were cluel, what would they have been at a time when all the lest were kind? They would have been just like Angels... !'

At this place fishing, and long rambles, were the order of the day, both for her and for me, especially fishing, though a week rarely passed which did not find me at Bouveret, St Gingolph, Yvoire, Messery, Nyon, Ouchy, Vevay, Montreux, Geneva, or one of the two dozen villages, townlets, or towns, that crowd the shores, all very pretty places, each with its charm, and mostly I went on foot, though the railway runs right round the forty odd miles of the lake's length. One noon-day I was walking through the main-street of Vevay going on to the Cully-road when I had a fearful shock, for in a shop just in front of me to the right I heard a sound – an unmistakable indication of life – as of clattering metals shaken together. My heart leapt into my mouth, I was conscious of becoming bloodlessly pale, and on tip-toe of exquisite caution I stole up to the open door – peeped in – and it was she standing on the counter of a jeweller's shop, her back turned to me, with head bent low over a tray of jewels in her hands, which she was rummaging for something. I went '*Hoh!*' for I could not help it, and all that day, till sunset, we were very dear friends, for I could not part from her, we walking together by vor-alpen, wood, and shore all the way to Ouchy, she just like a creature crazy that day with the bliss of living, rolling in grasses and perilous flowery declines, stamping her foot defiantly at me, arrogant queen that she is, and then running like mad for me to catch her, with laughter, *abandon*, carolling railleries, and the levity of the wild ass's colt on the hills, entangling her loose-flung hair with Bacchic tendril and blossom, and drinking, in the passage through Cully, more wine, I thought, than was good: and the flaming darts of lightning that shot and shocked me that day, and the inner secret gleams and revelations of Beauty which I had, and the pangs of white-hot honey that tortured my soul and body, and were too much for me, and made me sick, oh Heaven, what tongue could express all that deep world of things? And at Ouchy with a backward wave of my arm I silently motioned her from me, for I was dumb, and weak, and I left her there: and all that long night her power was upon me, for she is stronger than gravitation, which may be evaded, and than all the forces of life combined, and the sun and the moon and the earth are nothing compared with her; and when she was gone from me I was like a fish in the air, or like a bird in the deep, for she is my element of life, made for me to breathe in, and I drown without her: so that for many hours I lay on that grassy hill leading to the burial-ground outside Ouchy that night, like a man sore wounded, biting the grass.

What made things worse for me was her adoption of European clothes since coming to this place: I believe that, in her adroit way, she herself made some of her dresses, for one day I saw in her apartments a number of coloured fashion-plates, with a confusion like dress-making; or she may have been only modifying finished things from the shops, for her Western dressing is not quite like what I remember of the modern female style, but is really, I should say, quite her own, rather resembling the Greek, or the eighteenth century. At any rate, the airs and graces are as natural to her as feathers to parrots; and she has changes like the moon; never twice the same, and always transcending her last phase and revelation: for I could not have conceived of anyone in whom *taste* was a faculty so separate as in her, so positive and salient, like smelling or sight – more like *smelling:* for it is the faculty, half Reason, half Imagination, by which she fore-scents precisely what will suit exquisitely with what; so that every time I saw her, I received the impression of a perfectly novel, completely bewitching, work of Art: the special quality of works of Art being to produce the momentary conviction that anything else whatever could not possibly be so good.

Occasionally, from my window I would see her in the wood beyond the drawbridge, cool and white in green shade, with her Bible probably, training her skirt like a court-lady, and looking much taller than before. I believe that this new dressing produced a separation between us more complete than it might have been; and especially after that day between Vevay and Ouchy I was very careful not to meet her. The more I saw that she bejewelled herself, powdered herself, embalmed herself like sachets of sweet scents, chapleted her Greek-dressed head with gold fillets, the more I shunned her. Myself, somehow, had now resumed European dress, and, ah me, I was greatly changed, greatly changed, God knows, from the portly inflated monarch-creature that strutted and groaned four years previously in the palace at Imbros: so that my manner of life and thought might once more now have been called modern and Western.

All the more was my sense of responsibility awful: and from day to day it seemed to intensify. An arguing Voice never ceased to remonstrate within me, nor left me peace, and the curse of unborn hosts appeared to menace me. To strengthen my fixity I would often overwhelm myself, and her, with muttered oppro-briums, calling myself 'convict', her 'lady-bird'; asking what manner of man was I that I should dare so great a thing; and as for her, what was she to be the Mother of a world? – a versatile butterfly with a woman's brow! And continually now in my fiercer moods I was meditating either my death – or hers.

Ah, but the butterfly did not let me forget her brow! To the south-west of Villeneuve, between the forest and the river is a well-grown gentian field, and returning from round St Gingolph to the Château one day in the third month after an absence of three days, I saw, as I turned a corner in the descent of the mountain, some object floating in the air above the field. Never was I more startled, and, above all, perplexed: for, beside the object soaring there like a great butterfly, I could see nothing to account for it. It was not long, however, before I came to the conclusion that she has re-invented *the kite* – for she had almost certainly never seen one – and I presently sighted her holding the string in the mid-field. Her invention resembles the kind called 'swallow-tail' of old.

But mostly it was on the lake that I saw her, for there we chiefly lived, and occasionally there were guilty approaches and *ren-*

contres, she in her boat, I in mine, both being slight clinker-built Montreux pleasure-boats, which I had spent some days in over-hauling and varnishing, mine with jib, fore-and-aft main-sail, and spanker, hers rather smaller, one-masted, with an easy-running lug-sail. It was no uncommon thing for me to sail quite to Geneva, and come back from a seven-days' cruise with my soul filled and consoled with the lake and all its many moods of bright and darksome, serene and pensive, dolorous and despairing and tragic, at morning, at noon, at sunset, at midnight, a panorama that never for an instant ceased to unroll its trans-formations, I sometimes climbing the mountains as high as the goat-herd region of hoch-alpen, once sleeping there. And once I was made very ill by a two-weeks' horror which I had: for she disappeared in her skiff, I being at the Château, and she did not come back; and while she was away there was a tempest that turned the lake into an angry ocean, and, ah my good God, she did not come. At last, half-crazy at the vacant days of misery which went by and by, and she did not come, I set out upon a wild-goose quest of her – of all the hopeless things the most hopeless, for the world is great – and I sought and did not find her; and after three days I turned back, recognising that I was mad to search the infinite, and coming near the Château, I saw her wave her handkerchief from the island-edge, for she divined that I had gone to seek her, and she was watching for me: and when I took her hand, what did she say to me, the Biblical simpleton? – 'Oh you of little Faith!' says she. And she had adventures to lisp, with all the *r*'s liquefied into *l*'s, and I was with her all that day again.

Once a month perhaps she would knock at my outermost door, which I mostly kept locked when at home, bringing me a sumptuously-dressed, highly-spiced red trout or grayling, which I had not the heart to refuse, and exquisitely she does them, all hot and spiced, applying apparently to their prepara-tion the taste which she applies to dress; and her extraordinary luck in angling did not fail to supply her with the finest speci-mens, though, for that matter, this lake, with its old fish-hatcheries and fish-ladders, is not miserly in that way, swarming now with the best lake trout, river trout, red trout,

and with salmon, of which last I have brought in one with the
landing-net of, I should say, thirty-five to forty pounds. As the
bottom goes off very rapidly from the two islands to a depth
of eight to nine hundred feet, we did not long confine ourselves
to bottom-fishing, but gradually advanced to every variety of
manœuvre, doing middle-water spinning with three-triangle
flights and sliding lip-hook for jack and trout, trailing with the
sail for salmon, live-baiting with the float for pike, daping with
blue-bottles, casting with artificial flies, and I could not say in
which she became the most carelessly adept, for all soon
seemed as old and natural to her as an occupation learned
from birth.

On the 21st October I attained my forty-sixth birthday in excellent health: a day destined to end for me in bloodshed and
tragedy, alas. I forget now what circumstance had caused me to
mention the date long beforehand in, I think, Venice, not
dreaming that she would keep any count of it, nor was I even
sure that my calendar was not faulty by a day. But at ten in
the morning of what I called the 21st, descending by my private spiral in flannels with some trout and par bait, and tackle
– I met her coming up, my God, though she had no earthly
right to be there. With her cooing murmur of a laugh, yet pale,
pale, and with a most guilty look, she presented me a large
bouquet of wild flowers.

I was at once thrown into a state of great agitation. She was
dressed in rather a frippery of *mousseline de soie*,* all cream-
laced, with wide-hanging short sleeves, a large diamond at the
low open neck, the ivory-brown skin there contrasting with the
powdered bluish-white of her face, where, however, the freckles
were not quite whited out; on her feet little pink satin slippers,
without any stockings – a divinely pale pink; and well back on
her hair a plain thin circlet of gold; and she smelled like heaven,
God knows.

I could not speak. She broke an awkward silence, saying,
very faint and pallid:

'It is the day!'

'I – perhaps –' I said, or some incoherency like that.

I saw the touch of enthusiasm which she had summoned up quenched by my manner.

'I have not done long again?' she asked, looking down, breaking another silence.

'No, no, oh no,' said I hurriedly: 'not done wrong again. Only, I could not suppose that you would count up the days. You are…considerate. Perhaps – but—'

'Tell Leda?'

'Perhaps…I was going to say…you might come fishing with me…'

'O luck!' she went softly.

I was pierced by a sense of my base cowardice, my incredible weakness: but I could not at all help it.

I took the flowers, and we went down to the south side, where my boat lay; I threw out some of the fish from the well; arranged the tackle, and then the stern cushions for her; got up the sails; and out we went, she steering, I in the bows, with every possible inch of space between us, receiving delicious intermittent whiffs from her of ambergris, frangipane, or some blending of perfumes, the morning being bright and hot, with very little breeze on the water, which looked mottled, like colourless water imperfectly mixed with indigo-wash, we making little headway; so it was some time before I moved nearer her to get the par for fixing on the three-triangle flight, for I was going to trail for salmon or large lake-trout; and during all that time we spoke not a word together.

Afterwards I said:

'Who told you that flowers are proper to birthdays? or that birthdays are of any importance?'

'I suppose that nothing can happen so important as birth,' says she: 'and perfumes must be ploper to birth, because the wise men blought spices to the young Jesus.'

This *naïveté* was the cause of my immediate recovery: for to laugh is to be saved: and I laughed right out, saying:

'But you read the Bible too much! all your notions are biblical. You should read the quite modern books.'

'I have tlied,' says she: 'but I cannot lead them long, nor

often. The whole world seems to have got so collupted. It makes me shudder.'

'Ah, well now, you see, you quite come round to my point of view,' said I.

'Yes, and no,' says she: 'they had got so *spoiled*, that is all. Everlybody seems to have become quite dull-witted – the plainest tluths they could not see. I can imagine that those faculties which aided them in their stlain to become lich themselves, and make the lest more poor, must have been gleatly sharpened, while all the other faculties withered: as I can imagine a person with one eye seeing double thlough it, and quite blind on the other side.'

'Ah,' said I, 'I do not think they even *wanted* to see on the other side. There were some few tolerably good and clear-sighted ones among them, you know: and these all agreed in pointing out how, by changing one or two of their old man-in-the-moon Bedlam arrangements, they could greatly better themselves: but they heard with listless ears: I don't know that they ever made any considerable effort. For they had become more or less unconscious of their misery, so miserable were they: like the man in Byron's "Prisoner of Chillon", who, when his deliverers came, was quiet indifferent, for he says:

> "It was at length the same to me
> Fettered or fetterless to be:
> I had learned to love Despair."'

'Oh my God,' she went, covering her face a moment, 'how dleadful! And it is tlue, it seems tlue: – they had learned to love Despair, to be even ploud of Despair. Yet all the time, I feel *sure* flom what I have lead, flom what I scent, that the individual man was stluggling to see, to live light, but without power, like one's leg when it is asleep: that is so pletty of them all! that they meant well – everly one. But they were too tloubled and sad, too awfully burdened: they had no chance at all. Such a queer, unnatulal feeling it gives me to lead of all that world: I can't desclibe it; all their motives seem so tainted, their life so lopsided. Tluely, the whole head was sick, and the whole heart faint.'

'Quite so,' said I: 'and observe that this was no new thing: in the very beginning of the Book we read how God saw that the wickedness of man was great on the earth, and every imagination of his heart evil...'*

'Yes,' she interrupted, 'that is tlue: but there must have been some *cause*! We can be quite *sure* that it was not natulal, because you and I are men, and our hearts are not evil.'

This was her great argument which she always trotted out, because she found that I had usually no answer to give to it. But this time I said:

'Our hearts not evil? Say yours: but as to mine you know nothing, Leda.'

The semicircles under her eyes had that morning, as often, a certain moist, heavy, pensive and weary something, as of one fresh from a revel, very sweet and tender: and, looking softly at me with it, she answered:

'I know my own heart, and it is not evil: not at all: not even in the very least: and I know yours, too.'

'You know *mine*!' cried I, with a half-laugh of surprise.

'Quite well,' says she.

I was so troubled by this cool assurance, that I said not a word, but going to her, handed her the baited flight, swivel-trace, and line, which she paid out; then I got back again almost into the bows.

After a ten-minutes I spoke again:

'So this is news to me: you know all about my heart. Well, come, tell me what is in it!'

Now she was silent, pretending to be busy with the trail, till she said, speaking with low-bent face, and a voice that I could only just hear:

'I will tell you what is in it: in it is a lebellion which you think good, but is not good. If a stleam will just flow, neither tlying to climb upward, nor over-flowing its banks, but lunning modestly in its fated channel just wherever it is led, then it will finally leach the sea – the mighty ocean – and lose itself in fulness.'

'Ah,' said I, 'but that counsel is not new. It is what the philosophers used to call "yielding to Destiny", and "following Nature". And Destiny and Nature, I give you my word, often led mankind quite wrong—'

'Or *seemed* to,' says she – 'for a time: as when a stleam flows north a little, and the sea is to the south: but it is bound for the sea all the time, and will turn again. Destiny never could, and cannot yet, be judged, for it is not finished: and our lace should follow blindly whither it points, sure that thlough many curves it leads the world to our God.'

'Our God indeed!' I cried, getting very excited: 'girl! you talk speciously, but falsely! whence have you these thoughts in that head of yours? Girl! you talk of "our race"! But there are only two of us left? Are you talking *at* me, Leda? Do not *I* follow Destiny?'

'You?' she sighed, with down-bent face: 'ah, poor me!'

'What should I do if I followed it?' said I, with a crazy curiosity.

Her face hung lower, paler, in trouble: and she said:

'You would come now and sit near me here. You would not be there where you are. You would be always and for ever near me...'

My good God! I felt my face redden.

'Oh, I could not *tell* you...!' I cried: 'you talk the most disastrous...! you lack all responsibility...! Never, never...!'

Her face now was covered with her left hand, her right on the tiller: and bitingly she said, with a touch of venom:

'I could *make* you come – *now*, if I chose: but I will not: I will wait upon my God...'

'*Make* me!' I cried: 'Leda! How make me?'

'I could cly before you, as I cly often and often...in seclet... for my childlen...'

'*You* cry in secret? This is news—'

'Yes, yes, I cly. Is not the burden of the world heavy upon me, too? and the work I have to do *vely*, *vely* gleat? And often and often I cly in seclet, thinking of it: and I could cly now if I chose, for you love your little girl so much, that you could not lesist me one minute...'

Now I saw the push and tortion and trembling of her poor

little under-lip, boding tears: and at once a flame was in me which was altogether beyond control; and crying out: 'why, my poor dear,' I found myself in the act of rushing through the staggering boat to take her to me.

Mid-way, however, I was saved: a whisper, intense as lightning, arrested me: 'Forward is no escape, nor backward, but *sideward* there may be a way!' And at a sudden impulse, before I knew what I was doing, I was in the water swimming.

The smaller of the islands was two hundred yards away, and thither I swam, rested some minutes, and thence to the Castle. I did not once look behind me.

Well, from 11 A.M. till five in the afternoon, I thought it all out, lying in the damp flannels on my face on the sofa in the recess beside my bed, where it was quite dark behind the tattered piece of arras: and what things I suffered that day, and what deeps I sounded, and what prayers I prayed, God knows. What infinitely complicated the awful problem was this thought in my head: that to kill her would be far more merciful to her than to leave her alone, having killed myself: and, Heaven knows, it was for her alone that I thought, not at all caring for myself. To kill her was better, but to kill her with my own hands – that was too hard to expect of a poor devil like me, a poor common son of Adam, after all, and never any sublime self-immolator, as two or three of them were. And hours I lay there with brows convulsed in an agony, groaning only those words: 'To kill her! to kill her!' thinking sometimes that I should be merciful to myself too, and die, and let her live, and not care, since, after my death, I would not see her suffer, for the dead know not anything: and to expect me to kill her with my own hand was a little too much. Yet that one or other of us must die was perfectly certain, for I knew that I was just on the brink of failing in my oath, and matters here had reached an obvious crisis: unless we could make up our minds to part...? putting the width of the earth between us? That conception occurred to me: and in the turmoil of my thoughts it seemed a possibility. Finally, about 5 P.M., I resolved upon something: and first I leapt up, went down and across the house into the arsenal, chose a small revolver, fitted it with cartridge, took it up-stairs, lubricated it with lamp-oil, went down and out across the drawbridge, walked two miles beyond the village, shot the revolver at a tree, found its action accurate, and started back. When I came to the Castle, I walked along the island to the outer end, and looked up: there were her pretty cream Valenciennes, put up by herself, waving inward before the light lake-breeze at one open oriel; and I knew that she was in the Castle, for I felt it: and always, always, when she was within, I knew, for I felt her with me; and always when she was away, I knew, I felt, for the air had a dreadful drought, and a barrenness, in it. And I looked up for a time to see if she would come to the window, and then I called, and she appeared. And I said to her: 'Come down here.'

Just here there is a little rock-path to the south, going down to the water between rocks mixed with shrub-like little trees, three yards long: a path, or a lane, one might call it, for at the lower end the rocks and trees reach well over a tall man's head. There she had tied my boat to a slender linden-trunk: and sadder now than Gethsemane that familiar boat seemed to my eyes, for I knew very well that I should never enter it more. I walked up and down the path, awaiting her: and from the jacket-pocket in which lay the revolver I drew a box of Swedish matches, from it took two matches, and broke off a bit from the plain end of one; and the two I held between my left thumb and forefinger joint, the phosphorus ends level and visible, the other ends invisible: and I awaited her, pacing fast, and my brow was as stern as Azrael and Rhadamanthus.

She came, very pale, poor thing, and flurried, breathing fast. And 'Leda,' I said, meeting her in the middle of the lane, and going straight to the point, 'we are to part, as you guess – for ever, as you guess – for I see very well by your face that you guess. I, too, am very sorry, my little child, and heavy is my heart. To leave you...alone...in the world...is – death for me. But it must, ah it must, be done.'

Her face suddenly turned as sallow as the dead were, when the shroud was already on, and the coffin had become a stale added piece of room-furniture by the bed-side; but in recording that fact, I record also this other: that, accompanying this mortal sallowness, which painfully shewed up her poor freckles, was a steady smile, a little turned-down: a smile of steady, of slightly disdainful – Confidence.

She did not say anything: so I went on.

'I have thought long,' said I, 'and I have made a plan – a plan which cannot be effective without *your* consent and co-operation: and the plan is this: we go from this place together – this same night – to some unknown spot, some town, say a hundred miles hence – by train. There I get two motors, and I in one, and you in the other, we separate, going different ways. We shall thus never be able, however much we may want to, to rediscover each other in all this wide world. That is my plan.'

She looked me in the face, smiling her smile: and the answer was not long in coming.

'I will go in the tlain with you,' says she with slow decisiveness: 'but where you leave me, there I will stay, till I die; and I will patiently wait till my God convert you, and send you back to me.'

'That means that you refuse to do what I say?'

'Yes,' said she, bowing the head with great dignity.

'Well, you speak, not like a girl, Leda,' said I, 'but like a full woman now. But still, reflect a minute…O reflect! If you stayed where I left you, I *should* go back to you, and pretty soon, too: I know that I should. Tell me, then – reflect well, and tell me – do you definitely refuse to part with me?'

The answer was pretty prompt, cool, and firm:

'Yes; I lefuse.'

I left her then, took a turn down the path, and came back.

'Then,' said I, 'here are two matches in my grasp: be good enough to draw one.'

Now she was hit to the heart: I saw her eyes widen to the width of horror, with a glassy stare: she had read of the drawing of lots in the Bible: she knew that it meant death for me, or for her.

But she obeyed without a word, after one backward start and then a brief hovering indecision of thumb and forefinger over my held-out hand. I had fixed it in my mind that if she drew the shorter of the matches, then she should die; if the longer, then I should die.

She drew the shorter...

This was only what I should have expected: for I knew that God loved her, and hated me.

But instantly upon the first shock of the enormity that I should be her executioner, I made my resolve: to drop shot, too, at the moment after she dropped shot, so disposing my body, that it would fall half upon her, and half by her, so that we might be close always: and that would not be so bad, after all.

With a sudden movement I snatched the revolver from my pocket: she did not move, except her white lips, which, I think, whispered:

'Not yet...'

I stood with hanging arm, forefinger on trigger, looking at her. I saw her glance once at the weapon, and then she fixed her eyes upwards upon my face: and now that same smile, which had disappeared, was on her lips again, meaning confidence, meaning disdain.

I waited for her to open her mouth to say something – to stop that smile – that I might shoot her quick and sudden: and she would not, knowing that I could not kill her while she was smiling; and suddenly, all my pity and love for her changed into a strange resentment and rage against her, for she was purposely making hard for me what I was doing for her sake: and the bitter thought was in my mind: 'You are nothing to me: if you want to die, you do your own killing; and I will do my own killing.' And without one word to her, I strode away, and left her there.

I see now that this whole drawing of lots was nothing more than a farce: I *never* could have killed her, smiling, or no smiling: for to each thing and man is given a certain strength: and a thing cannot be stronger than its strength, strive as it may: it is so strong, and no stronger, and there is an end of the matter.

I walked up to the Grand Bailli's *bureau*, a room about twenty-five feet from the ground. By this time it was getting pretty dark, but I could see, by peering, the face of a grand-father's-clock which I had long since set going, and kept wound. It is on the north side of the room, over the writing-desk opposite the oriels. It then pointed to half-past six, and in order to fix some definite moment for the bitter effort of the mortal act, I said: 'At Seven.' I then locked the door which opens upon three little steps near the desk, and also the stair-door; and I began to pace the chamber. There was not a breath of air here, and I was hot; I seemed to be stifling, tore open my shirt at the throat, and opened the lower half of the central mullion-space of one oriel. Some minutes later, at twenty-five to seven, I lit two candles on the desk, and sat to write to her, the pistol at my right hand; but I had hardly begun, when I thought that I heard a sound at the three-step door, which was only four feet to my left: a sound which resembled a scraping of her slipper; I stole to the door, and crouched, listening: but I could hear nothing further. I then returned to the desk, and set to writing, giving her some last directions for her life, telling her why I died, how I loved her, much better than my own soul, begging her to love me always, and to live on to please me, but if she *would* die, then to be sure to die near me. Tears were pouring down my face, when, turning, I saw her standing in a terrified pose hardly two feet behind me. The absolute stealth which had brought and put her there, unknown to me, was like miracle: for the ladder, whose top I saw intruding into the open oriel, I knew well, having often seen it in a room below, and its length was quite thirty feet, nor could its weight be trifling: yet I had heard not one hint of its impact upon the window. But there, at all events, she was, wan as a ghost.

Immediately, as my conciousness realised her, my hand instinctively went out to secure the weapon: but she darted upon it, and was an instant before me. I flew after her to wrench it away, but she flew, too: and before I caught her, had thrown it cleanly through two rungs of the ladder and the window. I dashed to the window, and after a hurried peer thought that I saw it below at the foot of a rock; away I flew to the stair-door, wrung open the lock, and down the stairs, three at a time, I ran to recover it. I remember being rather surprised that she did not follow, forgetting all about the ladder.

But with a horrid shock I was reminded of it the moment I reached the bottom, before ever I had passed from the house: for I heard the report of the weapon – that crack, my God! and crying out: 'Well, Lord, she has died for me, then!' I tottered forward, and tumbled upon her, where she lay under the incline of the ladder in her blood.

That night! what a night it was! of fingers shivering with haste, of harum-scarum quests and searches, of groans, and piteous appeals to God. For there were no surgical instruments, lint, anæsthetics, nor antiseptics that I knew of in the Château; and though I knew of a house in Montreux where I could find them, the distance was quite infinite, and the time an eternity in which to leave her all alone, bleeding to death; and, to my horror, I remembered that there was barely enough petrol in the motor, and the store usually kept in the house exhausted. However, I did it, leaving her there unconscious on her bed: but *how* I did it, and lived sane afterwards, that is another matter.

If I had not been a medical man, she must, I think, have died: for the bullet had broken the left fifth rib, had been deflected, and I found it buried in the upper part of the abdominal wall. I did not go from her bed-side: I did not sleep, though I nodded and staggered: for all things were nothing to me, but her: and for a frightfully long time she remained comatose. While she was still in this state I took her to a châlet beyond Villeneuve, three miles away on the mountain-side, a homely, but very salubrious place which I knew, imbedded in verdures, for I was desperate at her long collapse, and had hope in the higher air. And there after three more days, she opened her eyes, and smiled with me.

It was then that I said to myself: 'This is the noblest, sagest, and also the most loveable, of the creatures whom God has made in heaven or earth. She has won my life, and I will live... But at least, to save myself, I will put the broadest Ocean that there is between her and me: for I wish to be a decent being, for

the honour of my race, being the last, and to turn out trumps...
though I do love my dear, God knows...'

And thus, after only fifty-five days at the châlet, were we
forced still further Westward.

I wished her to remain at Chillon, intending, myself, to start for
the Americas, whence any sudden impulse to return to her could
not be easily accomplished: but she refused, saying that she would
come with me to the coast of France: and I could not say her no.

And at the coast, after thirteen days we arrived, three days
before the New Year, traversing France by steam, air, and petrol
traction.

We came to Havre – infirm, infirm of will that I was: for in
my deep heart was the secret, hidden away from my own upper
self, that, she being at Havre, and I at Portsmouth, we could
still speak together.

We came humming into the dark town of Havre in a four-
seat motor-car about ten in the evening of the 29th December:
a raw bleak night, she, it was clear, poor thing, bitterly cramped
with cold. I had some recollection of the place, for I had been
there, and drove to the quays, near which I stopped at the
Maire's large house, a palatial place overlooking the sea, in
which she slept, I occupying another near.

The next morning I was early astir, searched in the _mairie_ for a
map of the town, where I also found a _Bottin_: I could thus locate
the Telephone Exchange. In the _Maire_'s house, which I had fixed
upon to be her home, the telephone was set up in an alcove adjoining a very stately _salon_ Louis Quinze; and though I knew that
these little dry batteries would not be run down in twenty odd
years, yet, fearing any weakness, I broke open the box, and substituted a new one from the Company's stores two streets away, at
the same time noting the exchange-number of the instrument. This
done, I went down among the ships by the wharves, and fixed
upon the first old green air-boat that seemed fairly sound, broke
open a near shop, procured some buckets of oil, and by three
o'clock had tested and prepared my ship. It was a dull and mournful day, drizzling, chilly. I returned then to the _mairie_, where for the
first time I saw her, and she was heavy of heart that day: but when

I broke the news that she would be able to speak to me, every day, all day, first she was all incredulous astonishment, then, for a moment, her eyes turned white to Heaven, then she was skipping like a kid. We were together three precious hours, examining the place, and returning with stores of whatever she might require, till I saw darkness coming on, and we went down to the ship.

And when those long-dead screws awoke and moved, bearing me toward the Outer Basin, I saw her stand darkling, lonely, on the Quai through heart-rending murk and drizzly inclemency: and oh my God, the gloomy under-look of those red eyes, and the piteous out-push of that little lip, and the hurried burying of that face! My heart broke, for I had not given her even one little, last kiss, and she had been so good, quietly acquiescing, like a good wife, not attempting to force her presence upon me in the ship; and I left her there, all widowed, alone on the Continent of Europe, watching after me: and I went out to the bleak and dreary fields of the sea.

Arriving at Portsmouth the next morning, I made my residence in the first house in which I found an instrument, a spacious dwelling facing the Harbour Pier. I then hurried round to the Exchange, which is on the Hard near the Docks, a large red building with facings of Cornish moor-stone, a bank on the ground-floor, and the Exchange on the first. Here I plugged her number on to mine, ran back, rang – and, to my great thanksgiving, heard her speak. (This instrument, however, did not prove satisfactory: I broke the box, and put in another battery, and still the voice was muffled: finally, I furnished the middle room at the Exchange with a truckle-bed, stores, and a few things, and here have taken up residence.)

I believe that she lives and sleeps under the instrument, as I here live and sleep, sleep and live, under it. My instrument is quite near one of the harbour-windows, so that, hearing her, I can gaze out toward her over the expanse of waters, yet see her not; and she, too, looking over the sea toward me, can hear a voice from the azure depths of nowhere, yet see me not.

I this morning early to her:

'Good morning! Are you there?'

'Good morning! No: I am there,' says she.

'Well, that was what I asked – "are you there?"'

'But I not here, I am there,' says she.

'I know very well that you are not "here",' said I, 'for I do not see you: but I asked if you were there, and you say "No," and then "Yes."'

'It is the paladox of the heart,' says she.

'The what?'

'The paladox,' says she.

'But still I do not understand: how can you be both there and not there?'

'If my ear is here, and I elsewhere?' says she.

'An operation?'

'Yes!' says she.

'What doctor?'

'A specialist!' says she.

'An ear-specialist?'

'A heart!' says she.

'And you let a heart-specialist operate on your ear?'

'On myself he operlated, and left the ear behind!' says she.

'Well, and how are you after it?'

'Fairly well. Are you?' says she.

'Quite well. Did you sleep well?'

'Except when you lang me up at midnight. I have had such a dleam...'

'What?'

'I dleamed that I saw two little boys of the same age – only I could not see their faces, I never can see anybody's face, only yours and mine, mine and yours always – of the same age – playing in a wood...'

'Ah, I hope that one of them was not called Cain, my poor girl.'

'Not at all! neither of them! Suppose I tell a stoly, and say that one was called Caius and the other Tibelius, or one John and the other Jesus?'

'Ah. Well, tell me the *dleam*...'

'Now you do not deserve.'

'Well, what will you do to-day?'

'I? It is a lovely day…have you nice weather in England?'

'Very.'

'Well, between eleven and twelve I will go out and gather Spling-flowers in the park, and cover the *salon* deep, deep. Wouldn't you like to be here?'

'Not I.'

'You would!'

'Why should I? I prefer England.'

'But Flance is nice too: and Flance wants to be fliends with England, and is waiting, oh waiting, for England to come over, and be fliends. Couldn't some *lapplochement* be negotiated?'

'Good-bye. This talking spoils my morning smoke…'

So we speak together across the sea, my God.

On the morning of the 8th April, when I had been separated thirteen weeks from her, I boarded several ships in the Inner Port, a lunacy in my heart, and selected what looked like a very swift boat, one of the smaller Atlantic air-steamers called the *Stettin*, which seemed to require the least labour in oiling, &c., in order to fit her for the sea: for the boat in which I had come to England was a mere tub, though sound, and I pined for the wings of a dove, that I might fly away to her, and be at rest.

I toiled with fluttering hands that day, and I believe that I was of the colour of ashes to my very lips. By half-past two o'clock I was finished, and by three was coasting down Southampton Water by Netley Hospital* and the Hamble-mouth, having said not one word about anything at the telephone, or even to my own guilty heart not a word. But in the silent depths of my being I felt this fact: that this must be a 35-knot boat, and that, if driven hard, hard, in spite of the heavy garment of seaweed which she trailed, she would do 30; also that Havre was 120 miles away, and at 7 P.M. I should be on its quay.

And when I was away, and out on the bright and breezy sea, I called to her, crying out: '*I am coming!*' And I knew that she heard me, and that her heart leapt to meet me, for mine leapt, too, and felt her answering.

The sun went down: it set. I was tired of the day's work, and of standing at the high-set wheel; and I could not yet see the coast of France. And a thought smote me, and after another ten minutes I turned the ship's head back, my face screwed with pain, God knows, like a man whose thumbs are ground between the screws, and his body drawn out and out on the rack to tenuous length, and his flesh massacred with pincers: and I fell upon the floor of the bridge contorted with anguish: for I could not go to her. But after a time that paroxysm passed, and I rose up sullen and resentful, and resumed my place at the wheel, steering back for England: for a fixed resolve was in my breast, and I said: 'Oh no, no more. If I could bear it, I would, I would...but if it is impossible, how can I? To-morrow night as the sun sets – without fail – so help me God – I will kill myself.'

So it is finished, my good God.

On the early morning of the next day, the 9th, I having come back to Portsmouth about eleven the previous night, when I bid her 'Good morning' through the telephone, she said 'Good morning,' and not another word. I said:

'I got my hookah-bowl broken last night, and shall be trying to mend it to-day.'

No answer.

'Are you there?' said I.

'Yes,' says she.

'Then why don't you answer?' said I.

'Where were you all yesterday?' says she.

'I went for a little cruise in the basin,' said I.

Silence for three minutes: then she says:

'What is the matter?'

'Matter?' said I, 'nothing!'

'*Tell me!*' she says – with such an intensity and rage, as to make me shudder.

'There is nothing to tell, Leda!'

'Oh, but how can you be so *cluel* to me?' she cries, and ah, there was anguish in that voice! 'There *is* something to tell – there *is*! Don't I know it *vely* well by your voice?'

Ah, the thought took me then, how, on the morrow, she would ring, and have no answer; and she would ring again, and have no answer; and she would ring all day, and ring, and ring; and for ever she would ring, with white-flowing hair and the staring eye-balls of frenzy, battering reproaches at the doors of God, and the Universe would cry back to her howls and ravings only one eternal answer of Silence, of Silence. And as I thought of that – for very pity, for very pity, my God – I could not help sobbing aloud:

'May God pity you, woman!'

I do not know if she heard it: she *must*, I think, have heard: but no reply came; and there I, shivering like the sheeted dead, stood waiting for her next word, waiting long, dreading, hoping for, her voice, thinking that if she spoke and sobbed but once, I should drop dead, dead, where I stood, or bite my tongue through, or shriek the high laugh of distraction. But when at last, after quite thirty or forty minutes she spoke, her voice was perfectly firm and calm. She said:

'Are you there?'

'Yes,' said I, 'yes, Leda.'

'What was the colour,' says she, 'of the poison-cloud which destloyed the world?'

'Purple, Leda,' said I.

'And it had a smell like almonds or peach-blossoms, did it not?' says she.

'Yes,' said I, 'yes.'

'Then,' says she, 'there is *another* eluption. Everly now and again I seem to scent stlange whiffs like that...and there is a purple vapour in the East which glows and glows...just see if you can see it...'

I flew across the room to an east window, threw up the grimy sash, and looked: but the view was barred by the plain brick back of a tall warehouse: I rushed back, gasped to her to wait, rushed down the two stairs, and out upon the Hard. For a minute I ran dodging wildly about, seeking a purview to the East, and finally ran up the dock-yard, behind the storehouses to the Semaphore, and reached the top, panting for life. I looked abroad: the morning sky, but for a bank of cloud to the north-west, was cloudless, the sun blazing in a region of clear azure pallor. And back again I flew.

'I cannot see it...!' I cried.

'Then it has not tlavelled far enough to the north-west yet,' she said with decision.

'My wife!' I cried: 'you are my wife now!'

'Am I?' says she: 'at last? Are you glad?...But shall I not soon die?'

'No! You can escape! My home! My heart! If only for an hour or two, then death – just think, together – on the same couch, for ever, heart to heart – how sweet!'

'Yes! how sweet! But how escape?'

'It travelled slowly before. Get quick – will you? – into one of the smaller boats by the quay – there is one just under the crane that is an air-boat – you have seen me turn on the air, haven't you? – that handle on the right as you descend the steps under the dial-thing – get first a bucket of oil from the shop next to the clock-tower in the quay-street, and throw it over everything that you see rusted. Only, spend no time – for me, my heaven! You can steer by the tiller and compass: well, the wheel is quite the same, only just the opposite. First unmoor, then to the handle, then to the wheel. The course is directly North-East by North. I will meet you on the sea – go now –'

I was wild with bliss. I thought that I should take her between my arms, and have the little freckles against my face, and taste her short firm-fleshed upper-lip, and moan upon her, and whimper upon her, and mutter upon her, and say 'My wife.' And even when I knew that she was gone from the telephone, I still stood there, hoarsely calling after her: 'My wife! My wife!'

I flew down to where the steamer lay moored that had borne me the previous day. Her joint speed with the speed of Leda's boat would be forty knots: in three hours we must meet. I had not the least fear of her dying before I saw her: for, apart from the deliberate movement of the vapour that first time, I foretasted and trusted my love, that she would surely come, and not fail: as dying saints foretasted and trusted Eternal Life.

I was no sooner on board the *Stettin* than her engines were straining under what was equivalent to forced draught. On the previous day it would have little surprised me at any moment, while I drove her, to be carried to the clouds in an explosion from her deep-rusted steel tanks: but this day such a fear never crossed my mind: for I knew very well that I was immortal till I saw her.

The sea was not only perfectly smooth, but placid, as on the previous day: only it seemed far placider, and the sun brighter, and there was a levity in the breezes that frilled the sea in fugitive dark patches, like *frissons* of tickling; and I thought that the morning was a true marriage-morning, and remembered that it was a Sabbath; and sweet odours our wedding would not lack of peach and almond, though, looking eastward, I could see no faintest sign of any purple cloud, but only rags of chiffon under the sun; and it would be an eternal wedding, for one day in our sight would be as a thousand years, and our thousand years of bliss would be but one day, and in the evening of all that eternity death would come and sweetly lay its finger upon our languid lids, and we should die of weary bliss; and all manner of dancings and singings – fandango and light galliard, corantoes and the solemn gavotte – were a-tune in my heart that happy day; and running by the chart-house to the wheel, I saw under the table a great roll of old flags, and presently they were flying in a long curve of gala from the main; and the sea rumpled in a long tract of tumbling milk behind me; and I hasted homeward, to meet my heart.

No purple cloud could I see as, on and on, for two hours, I tore southward: but at hot noon, on the weather beam I spied through the glass across the water something else which moved, and it was you who came to me, Oh Leda, my spirit's breath!

I bore down upon her, waving: and soon I saw her stand like an ancient mariner, but in white muslins that fluttered, at her wheel on the bridge – it was one of those little old Havre-Antwerp craft very high in the bows – and she waved a little white thing. And we came nearer, till I could spy her face, her smile, and I shouted her to stop, and in a minute stopped myself, and by happy steering came with slowing head-way to a slight crash by her side, and ran down the trellised steps to her, and led her up; and on the deck, without saying a word, I fell to my knees before her, and I bowed my brow to the floor, with obeisance, and I worshipped her there as Heaven.

And we were wedded: for she, too, bowed the knee with me under the jovial blue sky; and under her eyes were the little moist semicircles of dreamy pensive fatigue, so dear and wifish: and God was there, and saw her kneel: for He loves the girl.

And I got the two ships apart, and they rested there some yards divided all the day, and we were in the main-deck cabin, where I had locked a door, so that no one might come in to be with my love and me.

I said to her:

'We will fly west to one of the Somersetshire coal-mines, or to one of the Cornwall tin-mines, and we will barricade ourselves against the cloud, and provision ourselves for six months – for it is perfectly feasible, and we have plenty of time, and no crowds to break down our barricades – and there in the deep earth we will live sweetly together, till the danger is overpast.'

And she smiled, and drew her hand across my face, and said:

'No, no: don't you tlust in my God? do you think He would leally let me die?'

For she has appropriated the Almighty God to herself, naming Him 'my God' – the impudence: though she generally knows what she is saying, too. And she would not fly the cloud.

And I am now writing three weeks later at a little place called Château-les-Roses, and no poison-cloud, and no sign of any poison-cloud, has come. And this I do not understand.

It may be that she divined that I was about to destroy myself…she may be quite capable … But no, I do not understand, and shall never ask her.

But *this* I understand: that it is *the White* who is Master here: that though he wins but by a hair, yet he wins, he wins: and since he wins, dance, dance, my heart.

I look for a race that shall resemble its Mother: nimble-witted, light-minded, pious – like her; all-human, ambidextrous, ambicephalous, two-eyed – like her; and if, like her, they talk the English language with all the *r*'s turned into *l*'s, I shall not care.

They will be vegetable-eaters, I suppose, when all the meat now extant is eaten up: but it is not certain that meat is good for men: and if it is really good, then they will *invent* a meat: for they will be *her* sons, and she, to the furthest cycle in which the female human mind is permitted to orbit, is, I swear, all-wise.

There was a preaching man – a Scotchman he was, named Macintosh, or something like that – who said that the last end of Man shall be well, and very well: and she says the same: and the agreement of these two makes a Truth. And to that I now say: Amen, Amen.

For I, Adam Jeffson, second Parent of the world, hereby lay down, ordain, and decree for all time, clearly perceiving it now: That the one Motto and Watch-word essentially proper to each human individual, and to the whole Race of Man, as distinct from other races in heaven or in earth, was always, and remains, even this: 'Though He slay me, yet will I trust in Him.'*

Notes

Shiel was addicted to encyclopaedias, manuals and glossaries of technical vocabulary. I have not annotated all the multifarious jargon he decanted into his text, as *The Purple Cloud*'s narrative is full of ornate catalogues in which terms, unfamiliar to the general reader, tumble over each other in rich profusion. This verbal décor has greater effect, perversely, if one does not know what every noun means, as in a passage such as that describing Jeffson's dilemma over which craft in which he might make his future voyages:

> [there were] trawlers in hosts, war-ships of every nation, used, it seemed, as passenger-boats, smacks, feluccas, liners, steam-barges, great four-masters with sails, Channel boats, luggers, a Venetian *burchiello*, colliers, yachts, *remorqueurs*, training ships, dredgers, two *dahabeeahs* with curving gaffs, Marseilles fishers, a Maltese *speronore*, American off-shore sail, Mississippi steam-boats, Sorrento lug-schooners, Rhine punts, yawls, old frigates and three-deckers, called to novel use, Stromboli caiques, Yarmouth tubs, xebecs, Rotterdam flat-bottoms, floats, mere gunwaled rafts. [p. 70–71]

I suspect not every reader knows a felucca from a verruca, but to interrupt Shiel's verbal cascade with owlish definitions is to injure a kind of *poésie trouvée*.

Where, however, the word is useful in helping picture Adam Jeffson or his situation, I have briefly annotated. I have also annotated in some detail parallels with Nansen's *Farthest North* and Gresley's mining dialect dictionary, because they show the light-fingered, but deft, way in which Shiel extracted material useful to him.

Significant variations between the serialized *Royal Magazine* text, the 1929 'revised' edition and the 1901 text (which is the one followed here) are noted.

Epigraph. The Greek transliterates as *estai kai Samos ammos, eseitai Dēlos adēlos*. The Sibylline Prophecy translates as:

> Samos shall be sand, and Delos no more.

(p. 3) *About three months ago [...] toward the end of May of this year of 1900:* The book edition of *The Purple Cloud* was published on 26 September 1901. We are to suppose that 'Shiel' is here writing in August 1900. This foreword was wholly absent in the abbreviated text of the novel serialized in *Royal Magazine* (January–June 1901). In the 1929 text the year date is removed, reading: 'In May this year [unidentified] the writer received [...]'. There are also other dropped paragraphs and abbreviations (Browne's practice is not identified as being in Norfolk, for instance).

(p. 3) *spending most of my time in France*: Shiel had indeed spent most of the period 1898–1900 in France, where his Spanish-born new wife had been brought up. London, after the Oscar Wilde trials and the moral backlash they generated, may not have been entirely congenial to a man of Shiel's moral adventurism.

(p. 3) *Pitman's shorthand*: Pitman's has been the standard form of secretarial shorthand in Britain since it was devised by Isaac Pitman in 1837. Shiel, who worked intermittently as a 'clerk' (it was under this profession he was prosecuted in 1914), would have been able to read and write it.

(p. 3) *crutched by my own guess-work*: Of the variant meanings recorded in the *OED*, the following seems relevant: 'Misprint or error for cratch, to scratch.' It is also recorded as 'obsolete' – never something to deter Shiel.

(p. 4) *before night I had dyspnoea and laryngeal stridor*: Better known as diphtheria. In the era before antibiotics, the infection could well have been as rapidly fatal as is described here.

(p. 4) *from tic douloureux of the fifth nerve*: i.e. the trigeminal nerve, responsible for facial sensation. The condition is still often intractable and the removal of Mary Wilson's teeth to relieve it would have been a desperate, but not necessarily barbarous, remedy. In the 1929 edition, Shiel added an updating reference to X-rays.

(p. 5) *the Psychical Research Society*: The Society for Psychical Research was founded by eminently respectable academics and thinkers in 1882. The SPR, as Browne makes clear, was as keenly interested in discovering as in disproving parapsychological phenomena. In the 1929 edition, Shiel removed the reference to the

Society for Psychical Research. It is unlikely they would have authenticated what is described here.

(p. 6) *a stream of sounds in the trance state*: A number of details suggest that Shiel based Mary Wilson's visions and communications on the 'Seeress of Prevorst' (i.e. Frederika Hauffe, 1801–29). When 'magnetized' (hypnotized), she was clairvoyant, audio-clairant and capable of 'mental travel' (geognosia), bringing back geometrical maps of a circular kind. She claimed to be in communication with the living dead and to have communicated with them in their 'universal language', which sounded, to the human ear, like grunts and moans embellished with numbers and ideograms. A faithful (and credulous) account of the Seeress was published in 1845 by Catherine Crowe (herself a writer of ghost stories), which Shiel draws on here. For an authoritative account of the whole rich field of hypnotism and spiritualism in the nineteenth century, see Alison Winter, *Mesmerized* (1998). As Winter records, the anaesthetic property of hypnotism was of great interest to the medical profession, which, one presumes, is how Browne, like other doctors of the period, came to be an adept.

(p. 6) *the veil was rent*: See Matthew 27:51.

> And, behold, the veil of the temple was rent in twain from the top to the bottom; and the earth did quake, and the rocks rent.

Ominous, in the light of subsequent events in the narrative.

(p. 6) *Gibbon's "Decline and Fall"*: Edward Gibbon's *The History of the Decline and Fall of the Roman Empire* (1776–89). Similarly ominous.

(p. 7) *eight hundred and eleven miles above*: Located, one deduces, in what the Seeress of Prevorst identified as the 'Sun Sphere'. In 1929 it is reduced to 'eight hundred miles'.

(p. 8) *footnote*: *The Last Miracle* was published in 1907, *The Lord of the Sea* in 1901. See the Introduction and Note on the Text for the failure of the trilogy arrangement which Shiel was toying with. The footnote and the references to the other two novels are removed in the 1929 edition, although the business about 'note-books' and the fact that *The Purple Cloud* originates in 'Note-book III' are retained.

(p. 9) *Well, the memory seems to be getting rather impaired now*: Instalment One of the *Royal Magazine* serialization begins here.

(p. 9) *the* Boreal: Boreas is the god of the north wind, in Greek mythology. The aptness of the name indicates the craft was specially built for the expedition, as was Fridtjof Nansen's *Fram* ('Forward' in Norwegian), from which Shiel took details of the ship's innovative ice-resistant hull construction.

(p. 9) *in the loggia of this Cornish villa*: As the later narrative indicates, this is the (imaginary) house of Shiel's friend, the author Arthur Machen. Machen was, actually, touring the country as an actor in 1901. Shiel's motive in introducing his friend here and later in the narrative is unclear.

(p. 10) *can only be described as* fevered: Michael F. Robinson, in *The Coldest Crucible* (2006), describes the 'Arctic fever' to conquer the North Pole in the last decades of the nineteenth century. It was particularly fevered in America, where, 'after the rapid settlement of the western territories, Americans invested the Arctic with a special status as a frontier' (p. 164).

(p. 10) *Mr Charles P. Stickney of Chicago*: A fictitious personage. Expeditions were hugely expensive and Nansen (Shiel's main source) drummed up donations from rich men, as well as scientific societies. The American most enthusiastic about supporting expeditions to the North Pole was (as Shiel surely knew) a newspaper tycoon: James Gordon Bennett, proprietor of the *New York Herald*. See *The Coldest Crucible*, pp. 85–7.

(p. 10) *would have title to the fortune*: Changed to 'would have title to the "swag"' in 1929. This one word change is typical of hundreds of others Shiel made, almost all of a similarly minor nature. Here it is a somewhat vain attempt to introduce a whiff of contemporary slang.

(p. 11) *One against four hundred millions*: The population of the earth in 1900 is estimated, in fact, to have been 1.6 billion and no reliable authority of the time put the number as low as this. Pressured as he was, Shiel often chanced his arm with big numbers (see his later estimate of the population of London as 40–60 million, note to p. 93).

(p. 11) *and those who came to scoff remained to wonder*: An echo of the power of the Parson's sermons in Goldsmith's poem *The Deserted Village*:

> Truth from his lips prevailed with double sway,
> And fools, who came to scoff, remained to pray.

(p. 12) *camel-skin and all*: See Matthew 3:4 for the prophet's unusual furry garb.

(p. 12) *at No. 11, Harley Street [...] under twenty-five*: Changed, for
inscrutable reasons, to 24 Harley Street and twenty-five years
old in 1929. Such changes, as is suggested in the Note on the
Text, may have been done simply to reassure Gollancz that the
author was revising scrupulously.

(p. 14) *as it says in the poem*: The poem is Tennyson's 'The Higher
Pantheism':

> Speak to Him thou for He hears, and Spirit with Spirit can meet –
> Closer is He than breathing, and nearer than hands and feet.
> God is law, say the wise; O Soul, and let us rejoice,
> For if He thunder by law the thunder is yet His voice.

The allusion is apt. But Shiel, in the clash between the voices
(and their attendant 'Light' and 'Dark' moralities), is drawing
more consistently on the Polarion beliefs of H. P. Blavatsky, as
expressed in *The Secret Doctrine* (II.400):

> The two poles are the right and left ends of our globe – the right
> being the North Pole – or the head and feet of the earth. Every
> beneficent (astral and cosmic) action comes from the North; every
> lethal influence from the South Pole.

Shiel was steeped in Theosophy, the spiritual philosophy developed by Blavatsky – to what extent he was a devout believer is
not clear, although his biographer, Billings, confirms the interest
in the 'Secret Doctrines' was lifelong.

(p. 14) *One night, soon after my eleventh birthday*: Changed to 'thir-
teenth' in 1929, for no obvious reason.

(p. 15) *Scotland [...] Sappho and the Anthology*: Shiel alludes to
Henry Sidgwick (1838–1900), the eminent authority on ethics
and, for most of his life, a fellow of Trinity College. His ethical
system enjoined kindness to animals. The 'Sappho and the
Anthology' references hint at his homosexuality, Sappho being
a famously lesbian poet and the 'Anthology' being the surviving body of ancient Greek texts. Later in the narrative (see
note to p. 176), Shiel repeats the hint about Sidgwick's sexual
tastes.

(p. 16) *her favourite character [...] Lucrezia Borgia*: Reputed to have
been the possessor of an ingenious ring, with which she poisoned
those whose obstructed her rise to power in Renaissance Italy,
Lucrezia Borgia (1480–1519) was probably innocent of the

crimes that writers, such as Victor Hugo and Alexandre Dumas, and Donizetti's opera popularized about her.

(p. 17) *Peter takes atropine*: The addiction is unusual, but not apparently unknown. Atropine is a drug harvested from the Belladonna plant, or Deadly Nightshade. It is used as a medicine to stimulate the heart and can be illicitly used as a 'deliriant'. Why, one wonders, did Shiel (who is recorded as having himself taken morphine) introduce atropine so prominently? Because, one assumes, of the associations with 'bella donna' (beautiful woman). It is the beautiful woman, not the drug, which will kill the luckless Peters.

(p. 20) *delicate drugs – like Helen [...] Medea, and Calypso [...] all excellent chymists*: Helen of Troy was supposed to have acquired her power over men from a perfume, whose secret formula was given her by Venus. Medea, a woman closer to Clodagh's heart, one suspects, used her chemical skills to poison her rival Glauce's wedding gown and coronet. Shiel (or possibly Clodagh) seems to be confusing Calypso (who entrances Odysseus with her beauty and the promise of eternal life) with Circe – a ruthless virtuoso with drugs. These allusions raise the strong suspicion that Clodagh has administered aphrodisiacs to Jeffson, or substances to make him more amenable to her will.

(p. 23) *a powerful dose of atropine*: In the 1929 text there is the added clause: 'in spite of the morphia, the antidote of atropine, that he had in him'. The addition stresses the fact that Jeffson did not himself kill Peters, although he could have prevented Clodagh from doing so. Morphine has a sedative effect which would counteract atropine's stimulus.

(p. 24) *And this second thing I remember*: In 1929 the following passage about the 'old Bible' is cut. The second thing Jeffson remembers is the 'telegram' (in 1929 'wire') from Clodagh.

(p. 24) *The woman gave me of the tree, and I did eat*: Genesis 3:12. Shiel consistently, but deliberately, misquotes this line. In the King James version it is:

> And the man said, The woman whom you gave to be with me, she gave me of the tree, and I did eat.

Shiel knew his Bible well (the novel ends with an apt quote from it). He removed this clause because Jeffson is not to be with Clodagh (or, at least, her living body) ever again. God takes her away.

(p. 24) *'Be first – for Me'*: The first instalment in *Royal Magazine* breaks off here.

(p. 24) *The* Boreal *left St Katherine's Docks [...] the 19th June [...] bound for the Pole*: The second instalment in *Royal Magazine* begins here. In his account of the expedition which occupies the next major phase of the story, Shiel closely adheres to Fridtjof Nansen's account of the 1896 *Fram* expedition, published (in two illustrated volumes, in English, by Macmillan) in 1897 as *Farthest North*.

The following facts are useful in following Shiel's narrative. After studying the problem, and the failures of his predecessors, Nansen chose a counter-intuitive approach. He would not take the shorter North West Passage, but instead a long looping route from the East, allowing the ocean current to 'drift' his ship to the Pole. The *Fram* (its hull strengthened for the purpose) would be packed in crushing ice for the critical last stage of the voyage. Having reached the Pole, the vessel would then drift on past the 90th latitude to clear, warmer water and be free to make way again under sail. Unlike the Antarctic, the Arctic has no landmass underneath its ice, which is in constant movement. The *Fram* set off, like the *Boreal*, in mid-June. Nansen's timetable thereafter is followed exactly by Shiel.

Nansen's plan proved sound but for one detail: the speed of the current. He realized, once he was jammed in it, that the ice pack was moving so slowly that it would take five years to reach the Pole. He decided, when close enough (around 400km, as he estimated), and having spent two winters in the ice, to make the final assault in spring (March) by two-man team, dog-drawn sled, kayak canoe, skis and snow shoes. His expertise in surviving the horrific cold was drawn from the Eskimo natives. The plan almost worked, but having reached 86°35′ N, or thereabouts, he and his companion, Hjalmar Johansen, found themselves confronted by impassably turbulent ice and turned back – having nonetheless reached farther north than any of their predecessors and shown how to do it. After spending another winter in the icy wastes, the two men reached an outpost on Franz Josef Land in June 1896, and returned to a hero's welcome in Norway some three years after leaving port. The *Fram* arrived some time after.

Shiel follows Nansen's 'drift and dash' account closely, with a few differences. He cut a whole year out of Nansen's chronology, so that the *Boreal*, unlike the *Fram*, spends only one winter, not two, in the pack ice. Shiel has a three-man, not a two-man team for the 'dash'. He had Jeffson reach the Pole, despite the obstacles which had turned back Nansen and Johansen. And, having hunkered down in his 'hut' for the winter, Shiel has Jeffson reunite with the drifting *Boreal* at exactly the same time of year, and in the same place, as Nansen and Johansen were rescued. Jeffson's coinciding with the drifting *Boreal* at Franz Josef Land was highly unlikely, but, given east–west ocean currents, feasible. Otherwise (on such things as picking up coal at Kabarova in August, anchoring to an ice-floe off Taimur Island, passing Cape Chelyuskin, and reaching the northern pack ice), Shiel follows Nansen's dates and events, sometimes to the day.

(p. 25) *the last expedition – that of the* Nix: This is a thinly veiled pseudonym for Nansen's *Fram*.

(p. 25) *liquid air being our proper motor*: This is commonly put forward as one of the few imaginative futuristic inventions in *The Purple Cloud*. It has been examined, authoritatively, by the Shiel scholar John D. Squires, in an article, 'Shiel's Liquid Air Engines in *The Purple Cloud*', published in *The New York Review of Science Fiction* (December 2009). As Squires points out, liquid air propulsion was not entirely innovative:

> Shiel [described] ships powered by liquid air engines, which could easily be handled by Adam Jeffson, the last man alive, on his travels around the empty planet [...] I always assumed Shiel had just made his liquid air engines up – created a black box – to solve the problem of how to get his character around the world unaided in the era of coal power. But, I was wrong. There were numerous popular science articles about this wondrous new technology in 1899, the liquid air engine, based on the claimed discovery of a new process for producing liquid air at minimal cost.

Squires convincingly cites a selection of these articles, at least one of which presumably came Shiel's way and put the idea into his mind. The technology, alas, did not materialize – other than in *The Purple Cloud*.

(p.27 *But the childish attempt, my God, to read the immense riddle of the world [...] The thing can't be so simple*: in 1929 Shiel rewrote this as:

> But the baby attempt, My God, to read ... [sic] I laugh at poor Black-and-White Scotland! The thing ain't so simple.

It is a typical example of his sporadic attempts to spice up his thirty-year-old book for the modern reader.

(p. 28) *the smeared palette of some turbulent painter of the skies*: The first volume of Nansen's *Farthest North* has a number of vivid descriptions of the aurora borealis, so brilliant that it was visible even by day. The following may well have been present in Shiel's mind here:

> Later in the evening Hansen came down to give notice of what really was a remarkable appearance of aurora borealis [...] No words can depict the glory that met our eyes. The glowing fire-masses had divided into glistening, many-coloured bands, which were writhing and twisting across the sky both in the south and north. The rays sparkled with the purest, most crystalline rainbow colours, chiefly violet-red or carmine and the clearest green [...] It was an endless phantasmagoria of sparkling colour, surpassing anything that one can dream. (1.315–6)

(p. 28) *a liquid, coloured like pomegranate-seeds*: Not the atropine, to which Peters is addicted, but, we are to assume, cyanide.

(p. 29) *spirits-of-wine*: i.e. alcohol, which has a lower freezing point (−114°C) than mercury (−39°C). The need for it in extremely cold temperatures is referred to in Nansen's account.

(p. 29) *It was five days before Christmas*: Changed in 1929 to 'four days' – presumably to tighten the action up a little.

(p. 30) *a moon surrounded by a ring, with two mock-moons*: Shiel picked this up from a reference in Nansen's journal for 27 November:

> These last days the moon has sometimes had rings round it, with mock-moons and axes, accompanied by rather strange phenomena. When the moon stands so low that the ring touches the horizon, a bright field of light is formed where the horizon cuts the ring [...]Sometimes there are two large rings, the one outside the other, and then there may be four mock-moons. (1.307–8)

(p. 30) *watch-gun*: As the OED defines it: 'a gun sometimes fired on shipboard at 8 p.m., when the night watch begins'. On a craft as lightly crewed as the *Boreal*, the gun would very seldom be necessary, except for emergencies. The above detail about a polar bear getting among the dogs actually happened on the *Fram* in its first November in the ice.

(p. 32) *Arctic petrels and snow-buntings*: Shiel mentions here and elsewhere a number of species of Arctic migratory birds which he lifted from Nansen's account. Keen country walker that he was, one assumes Shiel was also an amateur ornithologist. Nansen does not seem to have been as interested, but there were naturalists on board with him who filled him in as to the species.

(p. 35) *I fired perhaps ten seconds later than he*: Changed in 1929 to 'five seconds', rendering Adam marginally less cold-blooded a killer.

(p. 35) *An Arctic fire-ball had traversed the sky*: Shiel took this dramatic detail from Nansen's journal for 27 October:

> The boys have taken up the rudder again to-day. While they were working at this in the afternoon, it suddenly grew as bright as day. A strange fireball crossed the sky in the west – giving a bluish-white light, they said. [1.297]

(p. 35) *On the 13th March*: Nansen left on the 14th, at the same latitude, some 350 miles from the Pole. The inventory of supplies taken follows Nansen, with the difference that Jeffson's was a three-man team.

(p. 35) *aleuronate bread*: As Nansen explains: 'aleuronate bread, which I had caused to be made of wheat flour mixed with about 30 per cent. of aleuronate flour (vegetable albumen)' (2.126).

(p.36) *the furthest point yet reached by man [...] 86° 53′ [...] the* Nix *explorers four years previously*: The *Nix* is, of course, Nansen's *Fram*. The latitude reference is taken from Nansen's journal for 14 April:

> I have calculated our previous latitudes and longitudes over again to see if I can discover any mistake in them. I find that we should yesterday have come farther south than 86° 5.3′ N.; but, according to our reckoning, assuming that we covered 50 miles during the three days, we should have come down to 85 degrees and 50 odd minutes. [2.176]

By this point Nansen and Johansen had turned back. The 'four years' reference is important, locating as it does the voyage of the *Boreal* at around 1901.

(p. 36) *Arctic thirst*: Nansen writes about this at precisely the same point in his dash to the Pole:

Most Arctic travellers who have gone on sledge journeys have com-
plained of the so-called Arctic thirst, and it has been considered an
almost unavoidable evil in connection with a long journey across
wastes of snow. It is often increased, too, by the eating of snow.
[1.150]

(p. 36) *Böotes only, and that Great Bear*: Two northern constellations
of the stars. Shiel improved this passage in 1929, revising it to:

On we pressed, wending our petty way over the boundless [sic],
upon whose hoar muteness, from before the old Silurian till now,
only Böotes had pored and brooded.

(p. 38) *Mew picked up a diamond-crystal as large as a child's foot*:
Downsized in 1929 to the rather neater: 'Clark picked up a dia-
mond-splinter as large as a child's thumb'. Shiel also recalled that
Mew is snow blind and changed it to 'Clark'.

(p. 38) *meteor-stones [...] ferruginous substance [...] frigidity of the
air*: The American arctic explorer Robert Peary (who may have
been the first man actually to reach the North Pole in 1908)
brought back three huge iron meteorites from Cape York on his
third Greenland trip, in 1894. They were fragments of the largest meteor shower ever recorded. Shiel's putting two and two
together (magnetic pole + iron + carbon + diamond) is wildly
imaginative, but not wholly implausible. There were no diamonds found in the Cape York meteors. In 1929, after 'frigidity
of the air', Shiel added: 'but, as the Pole's H is not strong, my
own view is that they are due to the greater drag of gravity and
the much greater shallowness of the atmosphere there'. He was
evidently worried about these diamonds, which have rather too
much of Sinbad and the *Arabian Nights* about them.

(p. 39) *We were within ten miles of the Pole*: Changed in 1929 to
'nine miles', to match the reference on p. 40: 'the odometer measured nine miles'.

(p. 39) *Gadarean swine*: Usually 'Gadarene'. See Luke 8:26–39. One
of Jesus's miracles. He transplants the many 'devils' which afflict
a man of the country of the Gadarenes into a herd of swine. Possessed, 'the herd ran violently down a steep place into the lake,
and were choked'.

(p. 39) *daft eyes*: Shiel elsewhere uses the word 'daft' in this slightly
idiosyncratic way. Here it seems to mean something along the
lines of 'blurry'.

(p. 39) *like the Symplegades*: According to Greek mythology, rocks in the Bosphorus which came close to wrecking Jason and the Argonauts.

(p. 40) *a circular clean-cut lake*: Having left the reality of Nansen behind, Shiel is now deep in the unreality of Madame Blavatsky and her mythic geographies of the North Pole, as laid out in her *Secret Doctrine* (1888). For example:

> Even in our day, science suspects beyond the Polar seas, at the very circle of the Arctic Pole, the existence of a sea which never freezes and a continent which is ever green.

In point of fact, science was not at all convinced in 1888 about a tropical crest of the world. Nonetheless, that there was a warm sea at the North Pole was believed by Arctic explorers until well into the nineteenth century. Edgar Allan Poe's *The Narrative of Arthur Gordon Pym of Nantucket* (1838), a clear influence on Shiel, fantasizes about a similar warm-water feature at the Antarctic. For Blavatsky's influence on Shiel's depiction of the Arctic, see the Introduction, pp. xxiv–xxv. The fullest discussion of North Pole esotericism can be found in Joscelyn Godwin, *Arktos: The Polar Myth* (1996).

(p. 41) *which it was a most burning shame for a man to see*: Changed in 1929 to 'for a worm to see'. There are a number of other small tonings-down, which suggests a certain uneasiness in Shiel as to this wild section of his narrative.

(p. 42) *But what it could be I did not understand*: The second instalment of the *Royal Magazine* serialization finishes here. The description of the 'Sanctity of Sanctities' was cut back in the magazine version. One presumes the editors felt it was becoming altogether too mystical for their readers.

(p. 42) *Well, onward through the desert ice*: The third instalment in *Royal Magazine* begins here with the slightly altered: 'I continued my lonely way south through the desert ice [...]' In 1929 it is 'Well, onward through the desert I went my solitary way'.

(p. 43) *an actual aroma like peach-blossom [...] the algid air about me!*: 'algid' is a term used in medical description. See the *OED* definition: 'Cold, chill, chilly; especially pertaining to or designating the cold stage of an ague. *Spec.* in algid cholera, Asian cholera, which is marked by copious watery alvine discharges, etc.' Cyanide has a fragrant odour, more often likened to almonds (which contain tiny amounts of the poison) than peaches. The word cyanide is derived from the Greek 'kyanos' – deep blue, or purple.

(p. 44) *'Reinhardt,' [...] little pert up-sticking ears*: This follows Nansen's killing his last dog, Kaifas, of whom he was particularly fond, on 27 August 1895. A photograph (pert ears prominent) memorializes the hound. Nansen felt his four-legged friend merited the dignity of a bullet. The other dogs were strangled and fed to their mates when they could no longer pull the sled.

(p. 45) *basalt columns [...] shattered temple of Antediluvians*: Nansen devotes many paragraphs and photographs to the majestic black basalt cliffs of Franz Josef Land, often comparing them to castles, or cathedrals. Shiel is still closely following Nansen's account at this stage of his narrative.

(p. 46) *I built myself a semi-subterranean Eskimo den for the long Polar night*: As did Nansen and Johansen. Shiel's description is taken from the photographs of the hut in *Farthest North*. Although called a 'hut', with the implication of something wooden, it was made out of solid shards of basalt sealed with tent fabric and, when winter set in, ice. Blubber-oil, from shot walruses, was used to warm the refuge, for light, and to cook with.

(p. 48) *Up to the 29th June [...]* the masts of a ship: Shiel follows Nansen's timetable very closely. It was on 23 June that the two Norwegians, fortuitously, met a hiking Englishman, who was responsible for arranging their journey home. Jeffson's transport will be more exotic but similarly accidental.

(p. 49) *Something put it into my head that it was Sallitt*: 'Burns' in *Royal Magazine*. This episode, from Jeffson's taking winter refuge in his hut onward, was extensively cut and compressed in serial form. It was done not at all smoothly. Since the previous two instalments had not been substantially shortened, one concludes the editors had got wind that Shiel's story was not going down all that well with their readers. (See Note on the Text.)

(p. 51) *the larch-wood pram*: More commonly 'dinghy', or small boat. Shiel, it will be observed, was knowledgeable about ships and things maritime, having been brought up in a port with a merchant-trader father.

(p. 53) *two excellent Belleville boilers*: Topical. In 1900 the engineer Alexander Kennedy was commissioned by the Admiralty to advise on the installation of French-designed Belleville water-tube boilers into Royal Navy vessels.

(p. 54) *my eventful Argo*: Dropped in *Royal Magazine* and changed to the more familiar word, 'bark', in 1929. 'Argo' was the name of the ship in which Jason and the Argonauts sailed to get the Golden Fleece. In the serial text, the account of Jeffson on the *Boreal* is hacked down to less than half the length it here occupies. Virtually the whole account of his next encounter, with the unnamed whaler and the *Lazare Tréport*, were, for example, cut away. The *Yaroslav* episode was dropped wholly.

(p. 55) *the Ming Tombs*: Outside Beijing. Jeffson will go there in the narrative, but Shiel never did. He perhaps saw the magnificent monuments in the *Illustrated London News* or some other pictorial source.

(p. 57) *Well, I saw at last what whalers used to call 'the blink of the ice'*: Shiel evidently recalled this detail from Southey's *Life of Nelson*, standard reading for Victorian boys:

> The sailors always knew when they were approaching the ice long before they saw it, by a bright appearance near the horizon, which the Greenlandmen called the blink of the ice. The season was now so far advanced that nothing more could have been attempted, if indeed anything had been left untried; but the summer had been unusually favourable, and they had carefully surveyed the wall of ice, extending for more than twenty degrees between the latitudes of 80° and 81°, without the smallest appearance of any opening.

(p. 57) *Lafoden cod and herring fishers*: i.e. from the Lofoten islands, off Norway.

(p. 59) *Mount Hekla*: Ominous. Mount Hekla is an active Icelandic volcano.

(p. 60) *eight Shetland sixerns*: Vessels unique to Shetland, derived originally from Norwegian design, with a characteristically high stern. Shiel, one suspects, is using one of the handy nautical dictionaries in the British Museum reading room.

(p. 61) *the lighthouse light on Smoelen Island*: Changed in *Royal Magazine*'s savagely truncated account to 'Moskaenes Island'.

(p. 63) *her mænad way*: In Greek mythology, female followers of Bacchus, famous for their intoxicated violence – especially against men.

(p. 64) *the fjord-mouth where I knew that Aadheim was*: Whoever was editing Shiel's text (possibly him, but unlikely) for *Royal Magazine* created real confusion here. In that text, the course of events is backdated to read 'On the 10th of August I passed into Trondheim Fjord'. The vivid description of the city of the dead which follows in the magazine is (we are told again)

Trondheim – except that, towards the end, it suddenly becomes
Aadheim. This too creates a problem, since Aadheim, some 250
miles from Trondheim, is properly 'Aaheim' or 'Aheim'. It is
rationalized in the book versions to 'Aadheim'.

(p. 65) *one of those Norwegian sulkies that were called karjolers*: For
'sulky', see the OED: 'A light two-wheeled carriage or chaise
(sometimes without a body), seated for one person.' 'Karjol' is
most commonly translated from the Norwegian as 'buggy'.

(p. 66) *ten or twelve shallops*: See the OED: 'A large, heavy boat,
fitted with one or more masts and carrying fore-and-aft or lug
sails and sometimes furnished with guns; a sloop.'

(p. 68) *that monstrous, infuriate flood*: An echo of James Beattie's
poem, *The Minstrel*:

> Or hags, that suckle an infernal brood,
> And ply in caves the unutterable trade,
> 'Midst fiends and spectres, quench the moon in blood,
> Yell in the midnight storm, or ride the infuriate flood.

(p. 70) *Out to sea, then, I went again [...] I visited Bergen, and put
in at Stavanger [...] turned my bow toward my native land*: This
passage is significantly different in *Royal Magazine*:

> I stopped at Christianasund, and again at Bergen; and I saw that
> Christianasund and Bergen were dead. I turned my bows toward
> my native land.

Christianasund was where Nansen, on his return, was greeted by
his monarch and cheering crowds.

(p. 71) *the eruption of the volcano of Krakatoa*: Krakatoa, a volcanic
island off Indonesia, erupted cataclysmically in August 1883,
killing tens of thousands of people and rendering the island an
uninhabitable desert. Shiel locates his even more destructive
eruption in the same oceanic area.

(p. 72) *I had some knowledge of Morse telegraphy*: Samuel F. B.
Morse's communication system (basically dot-and-dash, or
on-off code sequences) was incorporated into the embryo telegraphic system in the 1840s. It was still operational in 1901.
Shiel did not modernize this antique communications apparatus
in 1929, by which time it was quaintly out of date.

(p. 73) *Nore Light, nor Girdler Light*: i.e. lighthouses.

(p. 73) *the great revolving-drum on Calais pier*: The imposing Calais lighthouse was built in 1874, at the end of the city pier. Fifty-one metres high, it required 274 steps to reach the revolving drum at its pinnacle. As someone moving regularly between England and France, Shiel would have known Dover and Calais well – as the narrative of *The Purple Cloud* proves.

(p. 74) *Thou hast destroyed the work of Thy hand*: Shiel recalls the terrible verses of Deuteronomy 7:

> And the Lord your God will put out those nations before you by little and little: you may not consume them at once, lest the beasts of the field increase on you. But the Lord your God shall deliver them to you, and shall *destroy* them with a mighty destruction, until they be *destroyed*. And he shall deliver their kings *into your hand*, and you shall destroy their name from under heaven: there shall no man be able to stand before you, until you have destroyed them. [my italics]

The third instalment of the *Royal Magazine* serial ends here.

(p. 75) *After a time I got up*: The fourth instalment of the *Royal Magazine* serial begins here, with 'In Dover there were wonderfully few dead', cutting the next twelve pages of the 1901 volume text. The cuts continue thereafter to slash savagely into Shiel's narrative and are not comprehensively noted from here onward.

(p. 75) *my disembodied spirit*: In 1929 this is 'my disembodied anima', which raises the interesting speculation that Shiel had been reading Carl Jung, for whom 'anima' is a key concept. He would have been a congenial investigator of the psyche to the author of *The Purple Cloud*.

(p. 75) *a portly Karaite priest*: see the OED:

> A member of a Jewish sect (founded in the eighth cent. AD), which rejects rabbinical tradition and bases its tenets on a literal interpretation of the scriptures. They are found chiefly in the Crimea, and the adjacent parts of Russia and Turkey.

There was, at this period in Britain, a moral panic about immigration – principally focused on Jews fleeing Eastern European pogroms. It led to the British Aliens Act of 1905. Shiel makes the current xenophobia (and attendant anti-Semitism) a central feature in *The Lord of the Sea* and touches on it here and elsewhere in *The Purple Cloud*.

(p. 76) *called, I believe, 'The Shaft'*: Like the above Strond Street and

Snargate Street, an actual Dover feature. Better known as 'the Grand Shaft', it is one of the town's Napoleonic War fortifications, with lengthy flights of steps rising to high ground and sinking deep into the earth. As noted earlier, Shiel frequently travelled via Dover, and must have spent idle hours wandering round the town waiting for his ferry.

(p. 76) *coronachs and drear funereal nenias*: Coronachs are Scottish musical laments: nenia is a lament named after the funeral deity of Rome.

(p. 78) *touching the transmitting key [...] the ABC dial*: In 1929 Shiel modernized this, to bring it up to date with contemporary telegrammatic technology in the GPO. He did some similar tinkering with the following description (p. 81) of taking over the steam-engined train which will carry him to London. In general, however, his updatings are sparse.

(p. 79) *Though He slay me [...] look down, and save!*: Job 13:15–17:

> Though he slay me, yet will I trust in him: but I will maintain mine own ways before him. He also *shall be* my salvation: for an hypocrite shall not come before him. Hear diligently my speech, and my declaration with your ears.

In 1901 the allusion was somewhat damaged by the misprint (or misremembering) of 'Here' for 'Hear'.

(p. 80) *Already 700 of the 1000 millions of our race*: In 1929 this is changed to '850 out of the 1500 millions of our race'. In 1930 the population of the earth is in fact estimated to have been 2.07 billion. Shiel rarely troubles to be accurate about such statistics.

(p. 81) *I saw [...] the manometer move*: See the *OED*:

> An instrument for measuring the pressure in a gas or liquid; esp. one consisting of a U-tube containing mercury or other liquid, a difference in the pressures acting on the two ends of the liquid column being indicated by a difference in the levels reached by the liquid in the two arms of the U-tube.

The word, unfamiliar to most readers, is dropped in 1929.

(p. 82) *men like trees walking*: See Mark 8:22. One of Christ's miracles:

> And he cometh to Bethsaida; and they bring a blind man unto him, and besought him to touch him. And he took the blind man by the

hand, and led him out of the town; and when he had spit on his
eyes, and put his hands upon him, he asked him if he saw ought.
And he looked up, and said, I see men as trees, walking.

This biblical allusion was dropped in the 1929 edition, whose
revisions elsewhere play down the religiosity of the 1901
text.

(p. 84) *By the Dane John and the Cathedral*: The Dane John is a mysterious mound, just outside Canterbury city walls. It is thought
to be the site of an early timber castle and the name may be a
corruption of 'Dungeon'.

(p. 85) *a pavered alley*: i.e. asphalted.

(p. 86) *red Ruabon tiles*: i.e. tiles from the Ruabon quarry in Wales.

(p. 86) *clary-water*: See the *OED*: 'a sweet cordial or medicinal drink
made from clary-flowers'.

(p. 87) *a certain hypertrophic tendency [...] and some creepers*: Shiel,
well up with chemistry, certainly knew (although Jeffson apparently doesn't) that cyanide is a fertilizer.

(p. 87) *tiny bleaks, or ablets*: Two regional terms for the same small
fish. Shiel rarely uses one word where two will do.

(p. 87) *the batrachians also*: i.e. of the frog or toad family. Shiel rarely
uses a short word where a long one is handy.

(p. 88) *fields of lucerne*: i.e. clover, to which word 'lucerne' is altered
in 1929.

(p. 89) *in low-necked dress*: the reference to this immodestly revealing
garment is cut in 1929.

(p. 90) veilleuse: Night light.

(p. 90) *a million fathoms deep*: Altered in 1929 to 'a trillion furlongs
down'.

(p. 91) *an ABC guide*: Unlike its main competitor, *Bradshaw*, the *ABC
Railway Guide* listed times and routes alphabetically by station,
here allowing Jeffson to plot his route across the thirty miles to
London. As he notes, Guildford was (in 1900) the junction of at
least four countrywide rail lines.

(p. 93) *this city of dreadful night [...] forty to sixty millions swarmed*:
An allusion to James Thomson's infernal vision of London in his
1874 poem, 'The City of Dreadful Night'. The number of London's inhabitants is altered to 'not less than twenty millions' in
1929. The actual population of the city is reckoned at 6.5 million
in 1901 and 8 million in 1929.

(p. 95) *vials of the wrath of God*: See Revelation 16:1:

And I heard a great voice out of the temple saying to the seven angels, Go your ways, and pour out the vials of the wrath of God upon the earth.

(p. 97) *What I read in* The Times *was not very definite*: *Royal Magazine* offered its readers something much more definite, sparing them Shiel's following chemistry lesson:

> What I read in *The Times* in the main confirmed the inferences which I had previously made. There had occurred a great volcanic event – another Krakatoa – in the South Seas. It occurred either on the 14th, 15th, or 16th of April – for no one was certain – one, two, or three days after the arrival of the *Boreal* party at the Pole; and it had poured forth scoria, which travelled westward at a rate varying from a hundred to a hundred and fifty miles a day, involving the whole world, with the exception of the region round the Poles, or, at last, the North Pole.

This does not have the ring of Shiel's prose (nor the indefiniteness of the 1901 volume version) and one assumes the magazine editors decided to boil down the explanation for the destruction of the whole human race to something more accessible for the general reader.

(p. 100) *I came to the British Museum, the cataloguing-system of which I knew well [...] a 'reader' to the last*: This macabre vignette helps to explain the erudition displayed so ostentatiously by Shiel. From reading the novel, one would think he possessed professional expertise in geology, mineralogy, chemistry, architecture, medicine, classics and astronomy – but, in fact, he had no education beyond that of a colonial boarding school. He was, however, an indefatigable autodidact with an extraordinarily absorptive mind, and it was principally from the wonderful collection of reference books on open shelves in the British Museum's Round Reading Room that he equipped himself to write *The Purple Cloud*. Indeed, the novel is as much a product of the great domed reading room (the 'brain pan of London', as Thackeray called it in one of his 'Roundabout Papers') as Marx's *Das Kapital*.

(p. 104) *so that I had to conclude [...] and then by death*: This passage was rewritten in 1929:

> I was compelled to conclude that they, too, had fled before the cloud from country to country, till conquered by weariness and

astonishment at Him who by sixty million years of persistence and achievement had completed them into the things they were.

The reference to Darwin is one of the few to be found in *The Purple Cloud*, although clearly Shiel accepted the truth of evolution.

(p. 104) *belemnites*: Fossils. See the *OED*: 'an extinct order of cephalopods which existed during the Mesozoic era'.

(p. 104) *a cave called the Hob-Hole*: In fact a village: Hob Holes, near Runswick Bay. The actual cave has, since Shiel's day, been destroyed by the jet-quarriers Shiel mentions. The prefix 'hob' indicates that it was occupied by a devil, or demon. Dracula, it will be recalled, came to England a few miles up the coast at Whitby.

(p. 106) *winzes*: For his description of mines and their operations, Shiel drew heavily on the OED:

> Winze. A vertical or inclined opening, or excavation, connecting two levels in a mine, differing from a raise only in construction. A winze is sunk underhand and a raise is put up overhand. When the connection is completed, and one is standing at the top, the opening is referred to as a winze, and when at the bottom, as a raise, or rise.

It is clear in the pages that follow that Shiel was also drawing on *Her Majesty's Inspectors of Mines Annual Report for 1896*, or some such review.

(p. 107) *a Davy-lamp*: See Gresley:

> A safety lamp, invented by the late Sir Humphrey Davy in 1815. It will indicate the presence of fire-damp in a mine, which, when mixed with certain proportions of atmospheric air, becomes ignited within the gauze cylinder forming the 'top', or upper part of the lamp. The flame, however, cannot pass through the wire gauze and set fire to the gas outside.

(p. 107) *everywhere, in English duckies and guggs*: See Gresley:

> Dukey (Som[erset].). 1. A large carriage or platform running upon wheels on rails working on a dip inclined plane underground, upon which a number of small trams of coal are raised by engine-power at one operation. So named after the double coach called the 'Duke of Beaufort'.

Gug (Som[erset].). A self-acting inclined plane underground; sometimes a dip incline.

The slight mistranscriptions arise, I suspect, from Shiel's working
from his own hastily taken notes.

(p. 107) *my sister Ada*: See also p. 108. Harold Billings notes that
Shiel had been devastated by the death of his favourite sister, Ada
Shiell, in 1886 and inserted this as a private memorial.

(p. 111) *Barrowdale in Cumberland*: Misprint for 'Borrowdale' in
both the 1901 and 1929 versions (the episode, along with most
of the mining business, was dropped in the serial version). The
ladder was a famous feature, but the graphite mines were abandoned in 1891 and would, at this point, have been disused and
dangerous.

(p. 111) *adit-levels*: See Gresley:

Adit. An underground level to the surface from the level of the mine
workings, or from part of the way down the shaft generally used
for drainage purposes.

(p. 111) *horse-whinn*: Evidently a mistranscription for 'horse-gin'.
See Gresley:

Gin or Horse Gin. A drum and framework carrying small pulleys,
&c., by which the minerals and dirt are raised from a shallow pit.

(p. 113) *cage-shoes*: Evidently 'cage shuts'. See Gresley:

Cage Shuts. Short props or catches upon which cages stand during
caging.

(p. 113) *dogs*: See Gresley:

Dog. An iron bar, spiked at the ends, with which timbers are held
together or steadied.

(p. 114) *punt-shaped putts*: See Gresley:

Puts. Great oars by which keels [of coal trolleys] are pulled and
steered about.

(p. 114) *dipples [...] twin-way*: see Gresley:

Dipple. A heading or other underground way driven to the deep.

Twin-Way. Two branch roads set away, one on either side, out of a main road to the face of the stalls, through which trams are pushed by twin boys.

(p. 114) *chogg-holes*: See Gresley:

Chogs. Blocks of wood for keeping pump-trees or other vertical pipes plumb.

(p. 115) *with guss and tugger at his feet*: See Gresley:

Guss (Bristol Coal-field) a short piece of rope by which a boy draws a tram or sled in a pit.

Tugger. A short chain by which boys draw tubs along.

(p. 116) *the house of the poet Machen [...] beautiful young girl of eighteen, obviously Spanish [...] a baby*: This is one of the odder episodes in *The Purple Cloud*. Shiel had come to know Arthur Machen (1863–1947) through his connection with the publisher John Lane. Like Shiel, Machen made his name as a writer of occult fiction. Machen helped Shiel professionally, although he always had some reservations about the other writer's character. They seem to have been particularly close at the time of Shiel's wedding to his eighteen-year-old Spanish bride, Carolina Garcia Gomez, in 1898 (the period when he began work on *The Purple Cloud*). Machen's wife, Amy, died of cancer in 1899. It devastated her husband, who is supposed to have wandered the London streets, day and night, in the depths of his inconsolable grief. He was not living in Cornwall, as Shiel records, nor did he remarry. What is strange here is that Shiel has bestowed on Machen his own wife, the Spanish eighteen-year-old 'Lina'. What Machen thought of this generous gesture is unrecorded.

(p. 117) *a tricycle-motor*: I am indebted to the 'wiki-enthusiast' who records that 'In 1896, John Henry Knight showed a tri-car, recognized as the first British-made motorcar, at the Great Exhibition'. Three-wheelers proved generally uncommercial and, in 1929, Shiel changed it to the (then) more plausible 'motor-bicycle'.

(p. 118) *carbonic anhydride*: better known as carbon dioxide.

(p. 120) *I returned to it – the Sultan*: In 1929, it was even grander: 'the Sultan's Sultan'.

(p. 120) *that great hotel in Bloomsbury*: The Imperial. Built in 1898, it was pulled down and rebuilt in the 1960s.

(p. 120) *the Turkish embassy in Bryanston Square*: Slightly anachronistic. In 1901, the Turkish embassy moved from 1 Bryanston Square to 69 Portland Place. Shiel did not correct the address in 1929.

(p. 121) *Redouza Pasha*: I think Shiel must be referring to the highly esteemed ambassador to London, from 1885 to 1895, Rustem pasha.

(p. 121) *Sennacherib [...] Sardanapalus*: Sennacherib was the Assyrian monarch who, in the eighth century BC, created a magnificent palace for himself in Ninevah. Sardanapalus was the last king of Ninevah, famous for his even more luxurious self-indulgence.

(p. 121) *the Arch-one*: i.e. the archangel Lucifer.

(p. 121) *Cyclades [...] scarlet luxurious Orients*: These, it may not be immediately clear, indicate not comestibles but luxurious regions in Greece and the Far East.

(p. 123) scóriæ: Volcanic dust. A dramatic feature, but it is somewhat unlikely that scoriae would have simultaneously stopped all the clocks in London, since the eruption took place near Indonesia and the dust, heavier than the clouds of cyanogen gas, would surely have dropped to the earth before reaching Big Ben.

(p. 124) *London views in heliograph*: A strangely anachronistic reference, unless Shiel is being sarcastic about the traditionally antique reading matter in doctors' waiting rooms. Heliography was the very earliest technique of photography in the first decades of the nineteenth century, using the light of the sun to project (necessarily static) images onto chemically coated glass. Shiel did not change the reference in 1929.

(p. 124) *a towering celebrity [...] a studio in St John's Wood*: Shiel indicates the famous artist and portraitist, Sir Lawrence Alma-Tadema (1836–1912), whose studio was at 17 Grove End Road, St John's Wood.

(p. 126) *and plunge into his heart?*: The murderous thought is removed in 1929.

(p. 130) *cylinders with records*: At the period Shiel is writing, wax-coated cylinders, which had been the main device since Bell invented acoustic recordings in the late 1870s, were being replaced by disc-shaped gramophone records. Slightly anachronistic in

1901, the references to cylinders were wholly so in 1929. Shiel did not update the technology for the revised edition.

(p. 131) *Chypre-wine*: i.e. from Cyprus.

(p. 131) *head of gold, breast brazen, feet of clay – head man-like, heart cannibal, feet bestial – like ægipeds, and mermaids, and puzzling undeveloped births*: 'feet of clay' refers to the symbolic dream of Nebuchadnezzar, frequently alluded to in *The Purple Cloud* (see Daniel 2:31–33). Aegipeds are humans born with limbs of animals, as mermaids have the tails of fish. The phrase 'undeveloped births' is made clearer in 1929 with 'absurd immature [i.e. premature] births'.

(pp. 131–2) *At any rate, their lyddites, melanites, cordites, dyna-mites, powders, jellies, oils, marls, and civilised barbarisms and obiahs, came in very well for their own destruction*: A typical Shiel catalogue. 'Lyddite' is high explosive, with principally mili-tary applications. 'Jelly' is the explosive gelignite, invented, for civil use, by Alfred Nobel in 1875. 'Marl' is the term for the 'clay' which Alfred Nobel had earlier mixed with TNT to render that explosive stable. The term 'obiah' or 'obeah' (i.e. a charm to ward off destruction) is a rare hint at Shiel's Caribbean origins. He dropped it in 1929.

(p. 132) *at midnight of the twelfth day*: In 1929 Shiel changed this to 'the seventh day'. As altered, it parallels, inversely, the creation of the world by God – a neat touch.

(p. 132) *Nero, and Nebuchadnezzar*: Two tyrants associated with fire, the element which dominates this section of the narrative. Nero burned Rome. In Daniel, Chapter 3, King Nebuchadnezzar orders a fire, seven times hotter than the ordinary fire, to destroy Shadrach, Meshach and Abednego. Protected by Jehovah, they miraculously survive the furnace.

(p. 133) *I have taken a dead girl [...] mad, mad*: This necrophile con-fession is the most controversial episode in *The Purple Cloud*. It was dropped in the 1929 edition. Even for Shiel, the 'snake-stamping zebra' is surreal.

(p. 133) *new power-station in St Pancras*: Shiel refers to one of the newest, most technologically advanced generating stations in London. It was opened in 1895 in what is now Royal College Street, Camden, half a mile from the St Pancras railway station. It closed operation in 1965.

(p. 134) *Drink Roboral!*: i.e. Bovril. A sardonic private joke. In 1870, Edward Bulwer Lytton published his science fiction novel, *The Coming Race*. The hero, an engineer, descends through a mine

shaft to the centre of the earth, where he finds an advanced
alien race (hollow-earthism, incidentally, was one of Blavatsky's
beliefs – access was commonly believed to be through a hole
at the North Pole). This underground super-race has developed
a new energy source, Vril, which has made them invincible. In
1870, a Scotsman, John Lawson Johnston, was commissioned
to create a compact energy food for the French Army, then fighting the Prussians. He came up with a 'fluid beef'. This was later
launched in Britain as 'Bovril' – from 'bos' (beef) and Lytton's
'Vril'. The name caught on. The sales slogan, on billboards all
over London in 1900, was 'Bovril Restores Health', alluded to
in Jeffson's dark comment: 'Roboral would not cure the least of
all my sores'.

(p. 136) *an Abyssinian Galla*: i.e. a member of the Ethiopian Oromo
tribe. The term is nowadays considered pejorative.

(p. 139) *'Vision of St Helena' [...] 'Christ at the Column'*: i.e.
Veronese's 'The Dream of St Helena' (two angels bearing away
the Cross – inspiring her to discover where the Cross was buried)
and Velázquez's painting depicting Christ being scourged.

(p. 140) *house at Hampstead [...] tower at the south-east angle*: i.e.
the Clock Tower, Heath Street, built in 1873. Ironically it housed
the local fire station until 1915.

(p. 140) *gold harp of the musician Krasinski*: The allusion to Nero
fiddling while Rome burns is obvious. Krasinski is fictitious, but
Shiel was evidently fond of the name and used it later in the
'medical mystery' *Dr Krasinski's Secret* (1929).

(p. 141) Rouge-aux-lèvres: Lipstick. It was still a novelty imported
from France (notably by the cosmeticist Guerlain) at this date.

(p. 142) *to the nearer planets*: The fourth instalment in *Royal Magazine* ends here. The last words are changed to 'the planet Mars'.
'Nearer planets' was retained in 1929. Presumably some sub-
editor in the magazine office had read H. G. Wells's *War of the
Worlds* (1898). The fifth instalment begins 'Those words: "A
signal to the planet Mars"'.

(p. 143) *La Chartreuse de Vauclaire in Périgord*: Shiel sets the following events in an actual Carthusian monastery, which he evidently
knew well. Virtually nothing is known of his frequent and sometimes lengthy residences in France, but, demonstrably, from this
section of *The Purple Cloud*, he must have spent at least one
summer in the Dordogne. The linguistic speculations which
follow are shortened in the 1929 text. *Royal Magazine* cuts out
the Vauclaire months altogether.

(p. 143) *Albertinelli's Madonnas*: An allusion to the vivid blue mantle worn by the Virgin in Mariotto Albertinelli's (1474–1515) many paintings of the Madonna. Shiel is probably thinking of 'The Virgin adoring the Child with Saint Joseph', which he would have seen in the National Gallery.

(p. 146) *Greuze-like faces*: Jean-Baptiste Greuze (1725–1805) was famous for his studies of cherubic children. There are several in the National Gallery. The current catalogue discreetly notes Greuze's 'covertly erotic representations of young girls', which may, conceivably, have caught Shiel's eye.

(p. 147) *only human palace worthy the King of Earth*: Toned down in the 1929 version to: 'the only human palace worthy the satrap of earth'. A satrap was, originally, the governor of a province in ancient Persia.

(p. 147) *sort*: Jeffson here lapses into French. The sense is: 'selection'.

(p. 147) *fixing upon the island of Imbros for my site*: One of the Aegean islands, at this point in history Greek, now Turkish.

(p. 147) Bottins: Regional business guides, precursors of the modern *Yellow Pages*.

(p. 148) Speranza: the word means 'hope' in Italian, and is found most commonly as a girl's name. It carries a faint echo of Joshua Slocum's *Spray*, in which the American circumnavigated the globe single-handed in 1898–9.

(p. 148) *Tobin-bronzed*: Also known as 'Admiralty Brass' – brass mixed with tin to make the hull resistant to sea-water.

(p. 148) *Cape Roca*: The westernmost point of Europe, in Portugal.

(p. 148) *When the thirty-three*: As the occultist Shiel would have known, a number packed with numerological symbolism. See e.g. http://www.ridingthebeast.com/numbers/nu33.php:

> The thirty-third year of a person is the perfect age, that of full development, according to Mary Agreda. It is at this age that Jesus Christ was crucified and that Krishna, the god with 16,000 wives and 180,000 sons, died to repurchase the Karma of humanity. Saint Joseph was also thirty-three years old when he took for his wife the Virgin Mary, according to the visions of Mary Agreda. And according to some authors, it will be the age of the Antichrist at the time of his advent.

Jeffson is, by rough calculation, thirty-three at this point in the narrative.

(p. 150) *list-rubbing all the jet [...] rouge [...] fluate*: 'Rouge', as used here, is a 'red amorphous powder consisting of ferric oxide used in polishing glass, metal, or gems'. 'List' is a strip of cloth. 'Fluate' is more commonly known as fluoride. The catalogue of builder's items suggests that Shiel may have had a manual to hand.

(p. 150) *espagnolette bolts*: Still in use for lever handles, mainly on windows.

(p. 152) *no southern Italy was there [...] still-smoking crater of Stromboli*: According to H. P. Blavatsky's 'secret doctrine', the next phase of the earth's evolution would be marked by cataclysm and the sinking of the continents. Shiel alludes to the prophecy in number of places in the later narrative. According to Blavatsky, the North Pole would rise, as the other continents sank. The volcano on Stromboli, one of the Aeolian Islands off Sicily, has been in continuous eruption for almost 2,000 years.

(p. 152) *I have burned Calcutta, Pekin and San Francisco*: It is easy to assume that *The Purple Cloud* is the work of a real-life Phileas Fogg. There is scarcely a corner of the globe – from the Arctic snows, to the scorched sands of Africa, to the tropical jungles of Burma – that Adam Jeffson is not made to visit. Yet Shiel travelled hardly at all: after coming to Britain from Montserrat, he never made another substantial ocean voyage in his life, and his excursions from home were confined to short hops across the Channel to France. 'Calcutta, Pekin and San Francisco' were as much *terrae incognitae* to him as was the North Pole, and his ostentatiously exotic descriptions of far-flung places were almost entirely the product of his reading in the British Museum.

(p. 153) *dalles of the jet*: 'dalles' are flagstones, or slabs.

(p. 154) *near the Carolines*: i.e. the small Caroline islands, in the West Pacific, near New Guinea.

(p. 155) *the American prairies [...] the storms gradually subsided when man went to reside permanently there*: Shiel alludes to the 'degeneration' thesis expounded by Georges Louis Leclerc, comte de Buffon (1707–88). In America, Buffon believed, nature – thanks to the incursion of large numbers of white men – was becoming ever tamer and less wild.

(p. 155) *the face of Saturn*: In 1929 'the face of Jupiter'. Both planets are storm-wracked.

(p. 157) *Hur of the Chaldees which Uruk built [...] that Temple of Bel [...] in seven pyramids to symbolise the planets, and Birs-i-Nimrud, and Haran [...] old Persepolis and the tomb of Cyrus*:

A typical Shielian verbal cascade, which it would be owlish to annotate. I suspect (from the spellings of the ancient places) that he was using George Rawlinson's (1812–1902) multi-volume *Seven Great Monarchies of the Ancient Eastern World*, conveniently accessible on the open shelves of the British Museum Reading Room (see the note on Shiel's working methods).

(p. 161) *chain-lever lamp*: i.e. a gas lamp with two chain pulls. One would turn on the gas (to be lit, carefully, with match or taper). The other chain, when pulled, would turn off the gas.

(p. 161) *licking the plates clean in the Mohammedan manner*: This, as manuals of Islamic etiquette indicate, is something permitted by the Prophet as a gesture of gratitude. I suspect Shiel picked it up from his reading of Richard Burton, the explorer and translator.

(p. 161) *cigar after cigar from the Indian D box*: This eludes me, but in some of the writing on cigars 'D' is used as an index of size and quality – as is implied here.

(p. 166) *16° 21′ 13″*. South: the latitude here is significantly close to that of Krakatoa, 16.7S.

(p. 167) *glad laughters of Tophet [...] hairy Ainus*: see Jeremiah 7:31:

> And they have built the high places of Tophet, which [is] in the valley of the son of Hinnom, to burn their sons and their daughters in the fire; which I commanded [them] not, neither came it into my heart.

Hairy ainus are aboriginal peoples, native to islands off Japan and Russia.

(p. 167) *the harbour of Chemulpo*: a port city in South Korea.

(p. 168) *become an autochthone*: i.e. native inhabitant of a place. More commonly used as a noun without the terminal 'e'.

(p. 168) *the great temple of Boro Budor*: Hindu temple in Java. It was abandoned and fell into ruin after the Islamic conquest in the fifteenth century. European interest was revived by the first photographs which were published in the 1870s and which, evidently, Shiel saw.

(p. 175) *The mangal-stove*: Turkish room heater. It burned charcoal in a brazier contained in decorated metal.

(p. 176) *his name [...] lost in the vast limbo of past things [...] the male form was more beautiful than the female*: i.e. the previously mentioned Scotland / Henry Sidgwick. The hint at homosexuality (see note to p. 15) is now broader. Why Shiel should have invoked this personage is mysterious.

(p. 178) *where the palace of the Capitan Pacha is*: Hayreddin Barbarossa (1478–1546), the notorious pirate chief and later
Ottoman admiral. An appropriate allusion here, given Jeffson's
propensities. Barbarossa retired to the palace in Constantinople,
alongside the Bosphorus, shortly before his death.

(p. 180) *the towering turban of the Bashi-bazouk*: Turkish irregular
soldiers, much feared for their savagery.

(p. 180) *Sinbad, and Ali Baba, and old Haroun*: Central characters in
the *Arabian Nights*, from which (in the later section of the narrative) much detail and colour is taken. Shiel presumably used
Richard Burton's translation.

(p. 181) *white* yatags: i.e. yataks – Turkish term for beds made of rugs
piled on one another.

(p. 182) *an upward curve, like Sir Roger de Coverley*: Obscure – unless
it refers to the elegant patterns described by dancers in the Roger
de Coverley dance.

(p. 184) *the place they called 'The Sweet Waters'*: A flat grass-and-
wooded delta, near Constantinople, where two streams join to
flow into the Bosphorus. In the scene-setting which follows Shiel
draws on a number of sources. Most directly evoked is William
Purser's famous, and much reproduced painting, 'The Meadow of
the Sweet Waters of Asia'. There were numerous other idyllic pictorial depictions, celebrating the serene natural beauty of the place.

(p. 184) *trellised yalis*: i.e. houses by the waterfront.

(p. 184) *of a tam-tam [...] golden champac*: Champac is an Asian
variant of magnolia. Tam-tam, better known as 'tom-tom' is a
drum. It was being played to the end, presumably by the now
skeletal corpse.

(p. 186) *prickly-pear and pichulas*: Pichulas are sparsely leafed trees,
better known by the term 'tamarisk'. The word is also Spanish
slang for penis which – given the currency of the language in the
Caribbean – Shiel may have known from growing up in a port
town.

(p. 186) *looking with [...] astonishment at the reflexion of her face
in the limpid brown water*: A deliberate evocation of new-born
Eve, in Book IV, 455–65 of *Paradise Lost*, regarding her image
for the first time in the 'smooth lake'. In the *Royal Magazine* version, the stress on Leda's nakedness is played down and Jeffson's
first inclination to 'eat' her (after killing her) is removed.

(p. 187) *the little cangiar*: A Turkish curved dagger.

(p. 188) *that King of Babylon, his nails like birds' claws*: Nebuchadnezzar, in his madness. See Daniel 4:33:

The same hour was the thing fulfilled upon Nebuchadnezzar: and
he was driven from men, and did eat grass as oxen, and his body
was wet with the dew of heaven, till his hairs were grown like
eagles' feathers, and his nails like birds' claws.

(p. 188) *Kill, kill – and be merry*: In 1929 'Kill, kill – and wallow'.

(p. 191) *cafedjis and wine-bibbing*: The word 'cafedji', more common
in French, means 'someone who owns a place where coffee is
served'. As such it seems slightly awkward here.

(p. 193) *a jewelled two-yard-long chibouque, and tembaki*: A chibouque is a Turkish tobacco pipe, with a long stem feeding off a
central clay bowl. Tembaki is tobacco. See p. 179, 'These proud
Turks died stolidly, many of them [...] I have seen the open-air
barber's razor with his bones, and with him the half-shaved skull
of the faithful, and the long two-hours' narghile with traces of
burnt tembaki and haschish still in the bowl.' The narghile is
better known as the hookah.

(p. 195) *the Suleimanieh, or of Sultan-Selim*: i.e. the Sulaimaniya
Mosque and the Mausoleum of Sultan Selim II.

(p. 195) *Krishnu wine*: i.e. wine from Sangli, the 'Turmeric city', on
the river Krishna, in India.

(p. 198) *that white wine of Ismidt which the Koran permits*: Wine is
forbidden by the Qu'ran, but crystal white fountains of wine are
forecast in Paradise. Izmit is a wine-producing region of Turkey,
within easy reach of Imbros.

(p. 203) *some Roman king named Galba, a horrid dog [...] a French
devil, Gilles de Raiz*: The emperor Galba came after Nero, a hard
act to follow for imperial vice. He was renowned mainly for his
meanness and was slain by his own Praetorian Guard, AD 69.
Gilles de Rais (1404–40) was legendary as a serial child killer. He
would abduct his young victims, sexually abuse them, and sacri-
fice them to obscure occult deities. He was hanged for his crimes.
S. R. Crockett published a novel in which he is the villain, *The
Black Douglas* (1899), as Shiel was writing *The Purple Cloud*.

(p. 203) *I cannot realise her [...] To-morrow I start for Imbros*: This
passage is substantially different in *Royal Magazine*:

> Ah! I see now! I see! It was for *this* that I was preserved. I am a sort
> of modern Adam – and this little creature is my Eve.

> Whilst I have a free will a woman shall not enter into my life. I
> am done with them. They are not ideal beings. There was Clodagh

– that poisoner – bah!

Well, tomorrow I set out for Imbros ...

It is very heavy handed and one has to suspect it was written by someone at the magazine.

(p. 203) *I will see her from the moment I land no more*: The fifth instalment of the *Royal Magazine* serialization ends here.

(p. 203) *She must rise very early*: The sixth and final instalment of the *Royal Magazine* serialization begins here.

(p. 203) *two green jalousies*: Jalousies are louvred windows – i.e., having built-in shutters.

(p. 205) *mûrs ... slobbering* gamins: More normally *mûres*, wild berries. 'Gamin', in this context, is a 'street arab', or 'urchin'.

(p. 207) *eight to twenty thousand years wiser than the first*: Wildly wrong for the author of a book on science, as Jeffson once professed himself to be. In 1900, estimates confidently put the age of the earth at between 12 and 20 million years. The current estimate is 4.5 billion earth years. Some Christian sects, to the present day, follow Bishop Ussher's estimate in the seventeenth century that the Creation took place four millennia before the birth of Christ. Jeffson's mis-estimate could be read as evidence of the increasingly religious cast of Jeffson's mind at this stage of the narrative. In 1929 the number is changed to 'some six hundred thousand years', which is similarly perplexing.

(p. 207) *No more Clodaghs, Lucrezia Borgias, Semiramises, Pompadours, Irish Landlords, Hundred-Years' Wars – you see?*: In 1929 this catalogue is changed, interestingly, to:

> No more Clodaghs, Borgias, 'lords', Napoleons, Peaces, Rockefellers, Hundred Years' Wars – you see?

Shiel drops the reference to Irish land reform (a burning topic in 1899, less so in 1929) and includes references to the American millionaire, John D. Rockefeller (1839–1937), and the notorious murderer, Charles Peace (1832–79).

(p. 210) *a Samian cruche [...] a zarf*: 'cruche' is French for pitcher. A zarf (Turkish) is a holder, usually for a coffee cup.

(p. 213) *gentles*: 'gentle' is a maggot, or grub, used as bait. It will be evident that Shiel was a keen angler. This is gear for coarse fishing in Britain.

(p. 214) *a tiny barbel*: a small carp.

(p. 217) *Her book of books is the Old Testament*: Changed in 1929 to 'Her book of books is the chemistry-book, and next the Old Testament.'

(p. 219) *the great gold Jarvan goblet [...] the temple of Boro Budor*: See above, note to p. 168.

(p. 219) *What were these climes and vices?*: In 1929 Leda answers her own rhetorical question:

> The point was their cleverness – to find out that the atmosphere of Mars has more oxygen than ours – to talk across the continents – how inspired! If they were clever enough for all that, in time they would have been clever enough to find out how to live together. What were these climes and vices?

It is an effective updating of a kind which is sadly infrequent in the revised 1929 text.

(p. 219) *this question of land*: As will be clear from what comes after, Shiel (like Leda) was a firm follower of Henry George (1839–97), whose 'Georgism' argued that there could be no ownership of land, which – like air – was a common good. Land should be owned by society, not individuals. Shiel introduces Georgism more prominently into *The Lord of the Sea*.

(p. 224) *Haran [...] the place from which Abraham went out, when 'called' by God*: In Genesis 11:12–24, Abraham, as part of God's plan and covenant, is called from Ur of the Chaldees (a pagan city) to Haran – now identified as Carrhae in south-eastern Turkey, close to where Jeffson and Leda now are.

(p. 227) *you ought to have a name beginning with an 'L'*: A private joke, as Shiel had nicknamed his newly married wife Carolina 'Lina'. Leda in mythology was beloved by Zeus, who made violent love to her in the form of a swan.

(p. 234) *the antique Castle of Chillon*: Immortalized by Byron, in the poem about the imprisonment of the monk François Bonivard there (1532–36), referred to a couple of pages on in the narrative.

(p. 236) *pale and livid light*: See *The Prisoner of Chillon*:

> They chain'd us each to a column stone,
> And we were three – yet, each alone;
> We could not move a single pace,
> We could not see each other's face,
> But with that pale and livid light

> That made us strangers in our sight:
> And thus together – yet apart.

There is indeed an inscribed memorial (with the single word 'Byron' on it) on a pillar at the castle, as Shiel describes. Byron's poem does not refer to 'seven rings', but 'seven pillars', one for each of the original seven prisoners, only one of whom, Bonivard, survives to be released.

(p. 242) mousseline de soie: Silk muslin.

(p. 244) *and every imagination of his heart evil [...]*: The 1929 text continues:

> 'Oh, but none of that is tlue', she interrupted with a pout – 'not tlue of the Polynesians, who, enjoying their land in common, lived in sinless gladness at this garden of God, till white slaves, debased by centulies of slavelly, went to pleach to their betters and steal flom them – not tlue of you and me, whose hearts are not evil.'

See Henry George, *Progress and Poverty*, Chapter 29:

> Wherever we can trace the early history of society – in Europe, Asia, Africa, America, and Polynesia – land was once considered common property. All members of the community had equal rights to the use and enjoyment of the land of the community.

(p. 255) *Netley Hospital*: The Royal Military Hospital, near Southampton, founded after the Crimean War, principally for those injured in the conflict. It was expanding rapidly at the time Shiel was writing.

(p. 261) *Though He slay me, yet will I trust in Him*: See above, note to p. 79, for the Biblical quotation from the Book of Job. Shiel rewrote this last paragraph rather carefully for the 1929 edition, where it reads:

> For I, Adam Jeffson, parent of a race, hereby lay down, ordain, and decree for all time, perceiving it now: That the one motto and watchword proper to the riot and odyssey of Life in general, and in especial to the race of men, ever was, and remains, even this: 'Though He slay me, yet will I trust in Him'.

PENGUIN CLASSICS

FRANKENSTEIN
MARY SHELLEY

> 'Now that I had finished, the beauty of my dream vanished,
> and breathless horror and disgust filled my heart ...'

Obsessed by creating life itself, Victor Frankenstein plunders graveyards for the material to fashion a new being, which he shocks into life by electricity. But his botched creature, rejected by Frankenstein and denied human companionship, sets out to destroy his maker and all that he holds dear. Mary Shelley's chilling gothic tale was conceived when she was only eighteen, living with her lover Percy Shelley near Byron's villa on Lake Geneva. It would become the world's most famous work of horror fiction, and remains a devastating exploration of the limits of human creativity.

Based on the third edition of 1831, this contains all the revisions Mary Shelley made to her story, as well as her 1831 introduction and Percy Bysshe Shelley's preface to the first edition. It also includes as appendices a select collation of the texts of 1818 and 1831 together with 'A Fragment' by Lord Byron and Dr John Polidori's 'The Vampyre: A Tale'.

Edited with an introduction by Maurice Hindle

PENGUIN CLASSICS

THE PICTURE OF DORIAN GRAY
OSCAR WILDE

'The horror, whatever it was, had not yet entirely spoiled that marvellous beauty'

Enthralled by his own exquisite portrait, Dorian Gray exchanges his soul for eternal youth and beauty. Influenced by his friend Lord Henry Wotton, he is drawn into a corrupt double life; indulging his desires in secret while remaining a gentleman in the eyes of polite society. Only his portrait bears the traces of his decadence. *The Picture of Dorian Gray* was a *succès de scandale*. Early readers were shocked by its hints at unspeakable sins, and the book was later used as evidence against Wilde at the Old Bailey in 1895.

This definitive edition includes a selection of contemporary reviews condemning the novel's immorality, and the introduction to the first Penguin Classics edition by Peter Ackroyd.

Edited with an introduction and notes by Robert Mighall

PENGUIN CLASSICS

THE WAR OF THE WORLDS H. G. WELLS

'For countless centuries Mars has been the star of war'

The night after a shooting star is seen streaking through the sky from Mars, a cylinder is discovered on Horsell Common in London. At first, naïve locals approach the cylinder armed just with a white flag – only to be quickly killed by an all-destroying heat-ray, as terrifying tentacled invaders emerge. Soon the whole of human civilisation is under threat, as powerful Martians build gigantic killing machines, destroy all in their path with black gas and burning rays, and feast on the warm blood of trapped, still-living human prey. The forces of the Earth, however, may prove harder to beat than they at first appear.

The first modern tale of alien invasion, *The War of the Worlds* remains one of the most influential of all science fiction works. Part of a brand new Penguin series of H. G. Wells's works, this edition includes a newly-established text, a full biographical essay on Wells, a further reading list and detailed notes. The introduction, by Brian Aldiss, considers the novel's view of religion and society.

Introduced by Brian Aldiss

Textual Editing by Patrick Parrinder

Notes by Andy Sawyer

PENGUIN CLASSICS

THE SHAPE OF THINGS TO COME
H. G. WELLS

'Everyone was to be exposed to the contagion of modernity'

When Dr Philip Raven, an intellectual working for the League of Nations, dies in 1930 he leaves behind a powerful legacy – an unpublished 'dream book'. Inspired by visions he has experienced for many years, it appears to be a book written far into the future: a history of humanity from the date of his death up to 2105. *The Shape of Things to Come* provides this 'history of the future', an account that was in some ways remarkably prescient – predicting climatic disaster and sweeping cultural changes, including a Second World War, the rise of chemical warfare and political instabilities in the Middle East.

Foretelling an era of war, plague and political chaos, this remains one of the greatest of all works of social prophecy. Part of a brand new Penguin series of H. G. Wells's works, this edition includes a newly established text, a full biographical essay on Wells, a further reading list and detailed notes. The introduction, by John Clute, explores the political message of the novel and considers the later Wells's growing sense of disillusionment.

With an introduction by John Clute

Textual Editing by Patrick Parrinder

With notes by John Partington

Penguin Classics

TONO-BUNGAY H. G. WELLS

'I never really determined whether my uncle regarded Tono-Bungay as a fraud'

Presented as a miraculous cure-all, Tono-Bungay is in fact nothing other than a pleasant-tasting liquid with no positive effects. Nonetheless, when the young George Ponderevo is employed by his Uncle Edward to help market this ineffective medicine, he finds his life overwhelmed by its sudden success. Soon, the worthless substance is turned into a formidable fortune, as society becomes convinced of the merits of Tono-Bungay through a combination of skilled advertising and public credulity. As the newly rich George discovers, however, there is far more to class in England than merely the possession of wealth.

An acerbic account of human gullibility and a damning indictment of the British class-system, *Tono-Bungay* remains one of the greatest of all satires on the power of advertising and the press. Part of a brand new Penguin series of H. G. Wells's works, this edition includes a newly established text, a full biographical reading list and detailed notes. The introduction, by Edward Mendelson, explores the many ways in which the work satirises the fictions and delusions that shape modern life.

Introduced by Edward Mendelson

Textual Editing by Edward Mendelson and Patrick Parrinder

Notes by Edward Mendelson

PENGUIN CLASSICS

THE INVISIBLE MAN
H. G. WELLS

' "It's very simple," said the voice. "I'm an invisible man." '

With his face swaddled in bandages, his eyes hidden behind dark glasses and his hands covered even indoors, Griffin – the new guest at *The Coach and Horses* – is at first assumed to be a shy accident-victim. But the true reason for his disguise is far more chilling: he has developed a process that has made him invisible, and is locked in a struggle to discover the antidote. Forced from the village, and driven to murder, he seeks the aid of an old friend, Kemp. The horror of his fate has affected his mind, however – and when Kemp refuse to help, he resolves to wreak his revenge.

Depicting one man's transformation and descent into brutality, *The Invisible Man* is a riveting exploration of science's power to corrupt. Part of a brand new Penguin series of H. G. Wells's works, this edition includes a newly-established text, a full biographical essay on Wells, a further reading list and detailed notes. Christopher Priest's introduction considers the novel's impact upon modern literature.

Introduced by Christopher Priest
Textual Editing by Patrick Parrinder
Notes by Andy Sawyer

PENGUIN CLASSICS

THE FIRST MEN IN THE MOON
H. G. WELLS

'I fell and fell and fell for evermore into the abyss of the sky'

When penniless businessman Mr Bedford retreats to the Kent coast to write a play, he meets by chance the brilliant Dr Cavor, an absent-minded scientist on the brink of developing a material that blocks gravity. Cavor soon succeeds in his experiments, only to tell a stunned Bedford the invention makes possible one of the oldest dreams of humanity: a journey to the moon. With Bedford motivated by money, and Cavor by the desire for knowledge, the two embark on the expedition. But neither are prepared for what they find – a world of freezing nights, boiling days and sinister alien life, on which they may be trapped forever.

The First Men in the Moon is one of the first and greatest science fiction novels. Part of a brand new Penguin series of H. G. Wells's works, this edition includes a newly-established text, a full biographical essay on Wells, a further reading list and detailed notes. China Mieville's introduction places the novel in literary context, and reveals it as a skilled critique of Imperialism.

Introduced by China Mieville

Textual Editing by Patrick Parrinder

Notes by Steve McLean

PENGUIN CLASSICS

LOVE AND MR LEWISHAM
H. G. WELLS

'He was no common Student, he was a man with a Secret Life'

Young, impoverished and ambitious, science student Mr Lewisham is locked in a struggle to further himself through academic achievement. But when his former sweetheart, Ethel Henderson, re-enters his life his strictly regimented existence is thrown into chaos by the resurgence of old passion. Driven by overwhelming desire, he pursues Ethel passionately, only to find that while she returns his love she also hides a dark secret. For she is involved in a plot of trickery that goes against his firmest beliefs, working as an assistant to her stepfather – a cynical charlatan 'mystic' who earns his living by deluding the weak-willed with sly trickery.

A biting critique on the spiritualist craze sweeping the nation, and a considered exploration of one man's conflict between love and ambition, *Love and Mr Lewisham* is the first of Wells's satires on social pretension in Edwardian England. Part of a brand new Penguin series of H. G. Wells's works, this edition includes a newly established text, a full biographical essay on Wells, a further reading list and detailed notes.

Introduction by Gillian Beer

Textual Editing by Simon J. James

Notes by Simon J. James

PENGUIN CLASSICS

A MODERN UTOPIA
H. G. WELLS

'There is no justice in Nature perhaps, but the idea of justice must be sacred'

While walking in the Swiss Alps, two English travellers fall into a space-warp, and suddenly find themselves in another world. In many ways the same as our own – even down to the characters that inhabit it – this new planet is still radically different, for the two walkers are now upon a Utopian Earth controlled by a single World Government. Here, as they soon learn, all share a common language, there is sexual, economic and racial equality, and society is ruled by socialist ideals enforced by an austere, voluntary elite: the 'Samurai'. But what will the Utopians make of these new visitors from a less perfect world?

A compelling blend of philosophical discussion and imaginative narrative, A Modern Utopia is one of Wells's most positive visions of a possible world. Part of a brand new Penguin series of H. G. Wells's works, this edition includes a newly established text, a full biographical reading list and detailed notes. The introduction, by Francis Wheen, considers the virtues and flaws of Wells's ideal society.

Introduced by Francis Wheen

Textual Editing by Gregory Claeys

Notes by Gregory Claeys